The Paradise Will

The Paradise Will

Elizabeth Hanbury

ROBERT HALE · LONDON

ISBN 978-0-7090-8549-2

Robert Hale Limited
Clerkenwell House
Clerkenwell Green
London EC1R 0HT

www.halebooks.com

2 4 6 8 10 9 7 5 3 1

Typeset in 10/13pt Dante
by Derek Doyle & Associates, Shaw Heath
Printed and bound in Great Britain
by Biddles Limited, King's Lynn

For my family

With love

ACKNOWLEDGEMENTS

Thanks to Julia and Gill for their unstinting support and to all my friends at C19 for their encouragement, especially Jo, Wendy, Glenda, Gilly, Mags, Christine, Sally and Eve.

CHAPTER ONE

London, February 1818

'There must be some mistake!'

'I assure you there is no mistake, Miss Paradise.'

'Are you certain?'

'Quite certain,' he replied. 'Everything is in order and providing you meet the conditions your uncle laid down in his will, Hawkscote Hall and the surrounding estate will be yours.'

Alyssa Paradise gazed in stunned silence at Mr Ezekiel Bartley, the only other occupant of the musty office and senior partner in the law firm Deathridge, Flyte and Bartley in Chancery Lane. She drew in a steadying breath and spoke again.

'Forgive my astonishment; when you asked me to visit your offices in London today, I certainly did not expect *this!*' She gave a sudden rueful smile. 'I am not a feather-headed creature generally, but it is bewildering to discover Uncle Tom has left Hawkscote to me when there is someone with a stronger claim.'

'Ah, I presume you mean Mr Piers Kilworth?'

'Yes, my cousin. Piers was expected to inherit Uncle Tom's estate.'

'Well, as to that, I cannot say *who* expected such a thing to happen – I was your uncle's lawyer for ten years and General Paradise never mentioned it during that time.' Mr Bartley gave a dry cough and looked over his spectacles. 'I would respectfully suggest the general regarded his nephew as a spendthrift; he confided to me occasionally his frustration at the haphazard way he conducts his life. Perhaps,' he concluded, raising his brows, 'it is Mr Kilworth himself who has these expectations?'

Alyssa, not in the least offended by this observation, acknowledged it by saying lightly, 'True! Piers has the highest opinion of his worth and considers anything other than pleasurable pursuits an inconvenience. Little wonder Uncle Tom thought him a wastrel, but Piers will be incensed when he hears of this – he is the nearest male relative after all.'

'I see,' said Mr Bartley, regarding her appreciatively and wondering why, at five and twenty, she was not married; the young men of her acquaintance must be either blind or fools!

With the prevailing fashion one for shy blonde ladies with soulful eyes, Miss Paradise could not be considered a diamond of the first water but that was not to do her justice. Luxuriant chestnut hair, a creamy complexion, almond-shaped azure eyes, captivating not only for their luminescence but for the candid way they looked out upon the world, and an enchanting mouth – all combined to present a delightful picture. Equally worthy of admiration were her trim figure and the elusive, dignified air which distinguished her. The affectations adopted by many fashionable young women were absent: she displayed no simpering artifice.

Mr Bartley, fleetingly wishing he were thirty years younger, recollected his duties. 'Your cousin should not have made that assumption,' he continued, removing his spectacles to place them on the desk. 'To your knowledge, did General Paradise ever hint to Mr Kilworth he would receive the bulk of his estate?'

Alyssa shook her head. 'Uncle Tom never mentioned his will. He expressed his opinion of Piers bluntly and often repudiated him but Piers took little notice. Is he to receive anything?'

'A reasonably handsome annuity but its value will not compare.'

'Oh dear!' She bit her lip, and exclaimed, 'How shocking! He will be furious! But I am not to blame – I had no notion of Uncle Tom's intentions!'

'I'm sure you didn't. As far as I am aware, your uncle only discussed this with me and even I was not privy to his reasoning.' Replacing his spectacles, he added, 'Now, let me explain the terms because you must understand exactly what is required.'

'Then I would be grateful if you could do so in plain language rather than abstruse legalities,' she pleaded, eyes twinkling.

Mr Bartley smiled, nodded and placed the stiff sheets of paper in order. 'Before I begin, you appreciate your uncle's estate was not entailed?'

'Yes. In essence, his property did not pass to his nearest male heir by default?'

'Quite so. Your uncle was knighted for his distinguished military service; his title was not hereditary, nor was his property entailed. As you know, his wife died some years ago and there were no children from the marriage. The general could therefore dispose of his land and property as he wished. This matter became more pressing in recent times and he desired to put his affairs in order. Could I ask when you last saw your uncle?'

'Two years ago. Until then, I spent most summers at Hawkscote. We contin-ued to correspond in the intervening period but I could not visit Dorset because my father's sight and health were failing. When he died last year, I planned to go but was obliged to sort through my father's papers first – he had not attended to such matters for months. When I was finally able to travel, it was too late: my uncle died in December after a short illness.' She sighed and sadness shadowed her features. 'I bitterly regret not seeing him one last time. I was extremely fond of Uncle Tom.'

'As he was of you: he spoke often of his pleasure in your company.'

'We shared the same mischievous sense of humour, you see,' she said, with a reflective smile. 'Indeed, my character more closely resembled my uncle's than my father's. My propensity to find amusement in almost every situation brought forth displeasure from my own sire but a wink of encouragement from Uncle Tom!'

'Perhaps the general's sense of mischief was one reason he decided on this unusual will,' he remarked. 'Of course, I merely speculate – he did not confide his motives to me – but it is fair to say no *logical* explanations are apparent from the text. I should add when land and property are being willed to a woman, it is usual for it to be left in trust and a trustee appointed. The general did not arrange his will in this way because you are already of age. Also, the trustee is commonly a family member and following the death of his brother and his sister, General Paradise felt there was no suitable person to appoint. Now, let me begin.' He cleared his throat ready for the task ahead. 'You must take up residence at Hawkscote for a period of six months from an agreed date.'

'Oh! But that will be extremely awkward because—'

'There will no doubt be difficulties involved,' interjected Mr Bartley, 'but I advise you to hear *all* the conditions first.' He paused briefly and then continued, 'You must dine alone once every week with Sir Giles Maxton.'

Alyssa gasped. 'W-Who is Sir Giles Maxton?' she asked, in a faint voice.

'The owner of the nearest estate to Hawkscote. He purchased the property that runs parallel eighteen months ago and became a trusted friend of General Paradise.'

'But what is that to *me* and why must I dine alone with him? Surely that cannot be proper?'

'It may be thought odd, but the general was insistent on that aspect,' he said. 'I will return later to how Sir Giles will benefit from agreeing.'

Alyssa shook her head in disbelief, a frown creasing her brow as she murmured, 'Good God – this is astonishing! Please tell me the rest.'

Mr Bartley squirmed in his leather chair. Discharging his duty was proving uncomfortable now the young woman most affected by this extraordinary will was before him. 'You may run the house as you wish, but you are required to seek advice and guidance from Sir Giles on any matters pertaining to the management of the estate, labourers and farmland.' He glanced down at the document again, acutely aware of her sharp intake of breath. 'If you can meet these terms, after six months you may either retain Hawkscote or choose to sell at full-market value, with first option to purchase offered to Sir Giles.'

'And if I cannot agree, or choose not to take up residence?' she asked.

'You may sell the property, but only at one third of market price. Again, first option to purchase must be offered to Sir Giles Maxton.'

'Infamous!' she exclaimed, her eyes glinting with indignation. 'Sir Giles Maxton must have helped my uncle write this will!'

'I can see why you might think so, but the document was drawn up by General Paradise. It was signed in my presence and independently witnessed, whereupon it passed immediately into my keeping. There was no involvement or coercion from Sir Giles. Indeed, I understand he twice offered to purchase Hawkscote from your uncle for a very generous sum, should he care to sell.'

'My apologies, Mr Bartley – I did not mean to question your integrity – I am simply astounded my uncle chose to place me *and* Sir Giles in this situation! My next question is no reflection upon your abilities but I have to ask it all the same: can the will be contested, either by myself or my cousin?'

'Yes, but it is unlikely you would succeed. The terms are whimsical, eccentric even, but it is valid.' He hesitated before adding, 'This news has come as a shock, but consider the implications carefully: Hawkscote is a valuable estate and if you can comply, you would benefit greatly.'

'You are right, of course,' she said, sighing. 'Piers may wish to contest but from what you say, there is little point.'

'Mr Kilworth will receive the same advice from any lawyer; the fees would be substantial with no guarantee of a positive outcome. Your uncle ensured every aspect was covered under the law.'

'Uncle Tom must have known how Piers would react! I wonder what possessed him to create this mischief after his death.'

'I have no idea. However, in addition to the will, I have in my possession two sealed letters – both are addressed to you. One is to be opened in the event that you are unable or unwilling to meet the conditions and the other when the terms have been fulfilled.'

'Two letters . . . how extraordinary!' she mused. 'Do you know what they say?'

Mr Bartley shook his head. 'General Paradise did not inform me of the contents, but perhaps they will answer some of your questions when the time arises.'

'Uncle Tom has placed me in an awkward situation with my cousin,' said

Alyssa. 'Naturally that concerns me but it is the notion of dining alone with Sir Giles Maxton I find particularly irksome. And I cannot believe Sir Giles will be happy about it either.'

'His feelings will shortly be revealed, Miss Paradise; I anticipate his arrival at any moment.'

'*What?*' cried Alyssa, stunned at the prospect of meeting him so soon.

'He is entitled to be present, being inextricably linked with the terms and a potential beneficiary,' replied the lawyer, 'but I set his appointment half an hour later than your own so you had time to adjust to the news. Mr Kilworth's presence was also requested, but he is out of town and cannot be reached. I will therefore write regarding his annuity.'

'It is fortunate Piers is away;' she said candidly, 'he would not have remained temperate. Your letter will strike him like a thunderbolt but at least we shall not be obliged to witness his reaction!' She glanced across the desk, colour rising to her cheeks. 'Mr Bartley, thank you for giving me this brief respite. Will Sir Giles keep the appointment, do you think?'

'He is usually punctual and businesslike, I believe.'

'I feel slightly nervous meeting him under these circumstances.'

Mr Bartley threw her a sympathetic look. 'I understand, my dear – but take comfort from the fact he will be as shocked as you have been.' The murmur of voices drifted in from the outer office and he rose to his feet. 'Ah, that will be Sir Giles now – please excuse me for a moment.'

Mr Bartley went out, leaving Alyssa alone. The clock on the wall behind the desk marked time in a loud unerring rhythm but she barely noticed. She felt staggered by what the lawyer had told her. With this unexpected bequest, she could soon own a valuable estate and be independently wealthy. The prospect was appealing, not least because of what she might achieve by using even a tiny proportion for the cause dearest to her heart. All that stood between her and the Hawkscote inheritance was meeting Uncle Tom's astonishing terms. *Why* had he done it? Alyssa knew he would have considered the matter carefully. Uncle Tom never acted on mere whim; he planned in depth and looked at a problem from every angle – a skill honed during his military service.

Even if she were willing to meet the arrangements, there was no guarantee Sir Giles would do the same. How would he react? By the sound of the approaching voices, she did not have to wait long to find out. Alyssa turned her chair slightly to face the door, thinking she might feel at less of a disadvantage if she saw him immediately he came in.

However, when Sir Giles entered her overriding emotion was one of incredulity. Expecting to see the rotund figure and ruddy jovial features of the elderly figure in her mind's eye, she was confronted instead by its antithesis in the form of a tall, unsmiling gentleman of thirty to thirty-five years. Nonplussed, Alyssa blinked in surprise, eventually remembering to rise to her feet to feel the cool hard brilliance of his gaze sweep over her as Mr Bartley made the obligatory introductions. Her cheeks grew warm under his critical, faintly sardonic scrutiny. Sir Giles seemed to be assessing her appearance and drawing conclusions from her neat but unfashionable gown.

Alyssa felt summarily dismissed as unworthy of consideration and indignation rose in her breast. She blushed and put up her chin in a gesture of contumacy. She might not be wealthy or move in London society but her family and background were impeccable – she had no need of his good opinion, notwithstanding Uncle Tom's Will!

Then, her indignation began to mingle slowly with amusement. She regarded his features, her lip quivering with the effort of suppressing the laughter that bubbled up in her throat. With black brows drawn together and a menacing glitter in his eyes, Sir Giles looked extremely forbidding. Well, she was no young miss to be easily cowed; his stern expression would not provoke a submissive response but one of amused defiance. Alyssa held out her hand and flashed a look of challenge into the grey-blue eyes which lay under those sweeping brows.

Sir Giles had already stripped off his driving coat and gloves and, as his fingers clung briefly to hers, Alyssa felt a shiver of intangible emotion. He was unarguably an imposing figure: his angular features were strongly drawn, if not conventionally handsome; his broad shoulders and deep chest were the result of excellent physique rather than strategically placed padding; his breeches could not hide the well-defined muscles of his thighs and his swarthy complexion was in marked contrast to the gelid coolness of his eyes. His physical presence was particularly daunting; Alyssa was of average height but she was forced to tilt her head to look into his face and the dusty office seemed half its previous size since he had entered.

When Mr Bartley indicated the second chair, Sir Giles abruptly wrenched his gaze from hers and sat down. Alyssa did likewise but continued to observe him surreptitiously, noting his dress was carelessly elegant with none of the extravagances of the dandy set. Modest shirt points, an impeccable neckcloth and only a single fob was worn at his waist but Alyssa recognized the subtle touches of sartorial excellence. His boots, too, were of fine quality, the gleaming sheen on his top boots visible as he stretched one long leg forward.

'I would be grateful if we can bring this matter to a conclusion quickly, Mr Bartley,' he began, in a rich deep voice, 'I have another appointment in an hour and Miss Paradise is no doubt as eager as I am to address the issues in the most efficient manner.'

'I will do my best, Sir Giles, but there are more than minor details to cover.'

'Very well. You will be succinct as you are able, I'm sure.'

'Quite,' he said, nodding. 'General Paradise has left Hawkscote to his niece if she fulfills conditions which require your involvement.'

Alyssa watched from under her lashes as Sir Giles gave an involuntary start of surprise. He quickly regained his composure, outwardly at least, only the rigid set of his shoulders indicating tension.

'So I am not to be offered the option to purchase?' he asked, after a long pause, a sliver of annoyance in his voice. 'That is disappointing – I tendered an extremely generous price.'

'You will be offered first option on its purchase under certain circumstances,' said Mr Bartley, and proceeded to explain.

Sir Giles did not speak but his countenance grew steadily more incredulous until details of the weekly dinners were reached and he broke his silence.

'By God, this passes the bounds of belief!' he exclaimed. 'What on earth was Tom – General Paradise thinking? It is nonsensical to expect us to agree!' He turned to Alyssa, his eyes cold and unfriendly. 'Surely you do not wish for this, Miss Paradise?'

'Of course not – it is abominable – but I cannot afford to be too proud to consider it!' she retorted.

'Can you contest? There must be grounds to overturn such a capricious document!' His glance flickered from Alyssa to the lawyer then back again; Mr Bartley shook his head and maintained a discouraging silence.

With a tiny shrug, Alyssa said, 'Mr Bartley informs me it will be a waste of money and effort and I have to take his advice. I cannot speak for my cousin Piers – he may choose to although I believe, after consideration, he too will decide not to outlay funds when there is little hope of success.'

There was another pause before Sir Giles said through gritted teeth, '*Intolerable!*' Suddenly, he thrust back his chair and strode to the window. After studying the scene outside for a few moments, he turned, scanning Alyssa's features as he said curtly, 'This places me in a deplorable position. If I do not agree, I shall be thought firstly a fool; secondly, ungentlemanly for refusing to assist you, and finally, when it is discovered Hawkscote has been offered to me at reduced value, I shall be considered a knave for taking advantage of your situation!'

'Why, I am sure you do not care for other people's opinions, Sir Giles,' she said, in a dry voice. 'Pray, do not let such considerations sway your decision.'

He regarded her steadily, eyes blazing but his temper well in check. 'You are partially correct; I would not care in the least if I am thought a fool, but I balk at being considered ungentlemanly, or guilty of taking pecuniary advantage of a young woman who is, moreover, the niece of a good friend. I have my family name and reputation to consider!' He stopped and gave her a quizzical look. 'It is obviously in your interests to meet the terms yet I am surprised *you* do not show more anger,' he said, his voice faintly mocking. 'Perhaps you had prior knowledge of your uncle's plans?'

She gasped. 'No, I did not! You suggest I persuaded my uncle to cut my cousin, and perhaps yourself, out of his will. How *dare* you! This has come as a great shock to me and any implication it is otherwise is offensive!'

Sir Giles looked discomfited at the bitter resentment in her voice. He flushed darkly, and executed a small bow. His reply, when it came, was rueful, his tone softer. 'Miss Paradise, accept my apologies – what I said a moment ago was unwarranted and maladroit.'

'Miss Paradise knew nothing of her uncle's will,' interjected Mr Bartley.

Returning to his seat, Giles nodded. 'I appreciate that now.'

Alyssa regarded him coolly. 'I had not seen my uncle for some time but you were his neighbour for eighteen months. You knew him well, so answer me this: have *you* any notion why he added these conditions?'

'None.' His lips compressed tightly before he added, 'And if you think I coerced the general, you are mistaken.'

'I merely wondered if my uncle mentioned anything.'

'Not regarding his will. We talked mostly of estate business and various local issues – he seemed to value my advice. On occasion, he spoke of his military career and his family – your father and yourself he described with affection, but he spoke less warmly of his nephew. He did not confide his reasons to me. However, we are now at this point. It is obvious why it is advantageous for you, but there is nothing to induce *me* to agree!' He shrugged. 'Why should I be part of this, other than to protect my reputation as an honourable man? The difficulties concomitant with meeting the terms might be worth some damage to my good name.'

Alyssa threw him a baleful glance but, before she could speak, he continued, 'It is true I wanted Hawkscote for a fair price, but not only for the property or the land – I have land enough of my own and other means of increasing my acreage if I choose. No, Hawkscote has another attribute that interests me and the general knew I was prepared to purchase the whole estate to acquire it.'

'Ah,' observed Mr Bartley, 'that must be the item in the additional clause – I have not yet had the opportunity to tell you of it, Sir Giles.' He shuffled the papers on his desk until he found what he was looking for then read from the document. 'If you meet the terms, General Paradise stipulated that even if his niece retains Hawkscote, you are to receive the deeds to the land between Winterborn Wood and the River Frome, thus giving you the associated water rights in perpetuity.'

'You old devil, Tom!' muttered Sir Giles, amusement flashing over his features.

'I presume this alters your view?' she asked, rather too sweetly.

He gave her a brooding look. 'Now I have reason to meet the terms, but it does not make the prospect more palatable.'

'I find it equally undesirable. Not only does this will place me in conflict with my cousin, my life will be ruled in a particular way for six months which is anathema to me.'

'That I can well believe,' he murmured, studying her with new respect.

Alyssa, mistaking Sir Giles's grudging compliment for sarcasm, avowed angrily, 'I want Hawkscote but not simply for wealth's sake! When he was alive, my uncle had my admiration and regard – I shall therefore do my best to adhere to his final wishes. However, I cannot force you to do the same. Perhaps spending time alone with me is too awful to countenance, even for the valuable water rights you seek?' She wondered in amazement why some inner demon was urging her to provoke him.

'Oh, I would find no fault with the *food*; General Paradise has an excellent cook,' he retorted, eyes hard as agate. 'As for the company, I have sufficient fortitude to survive the experience! And I can choose not to linger over dinner—'

Mr Bartley, who had thought it wiser to remain out of these exchanges until now, interjected quickly, 'Dinner must last at least one hour. A clerk from the solicitor's office in Dorchester will attend and act as an independent adjudicator. However, General Paradise was anxious you both understood this was not because he mistrusted you; it is simply a mechanism to meet the legal requirements. There is no stipulation as to where your meetings take place – the general left that to be decided between yourselves.'

Sir Giles was not mollified by this and snapped ironically, 'At least there is one thing I have control over.'

'I am sorry you find the notion of my company so *distasteful*, sir!' cried Alyssa.

An uncomfortable silence fell. The atmosphere was heavy with the antipathy that lay between the two protagonists. Sir Giles's expression was unreadable; Mr Bartley's apprehensive gaze flicked from one to the other; Alyssa flushed and bit her lip. She was annoyed at herself for provoking him and yet unreasonably angry and indignant he had replied in the same vein. Really, the man was too vexing! He was brusque, humourless and full of self-importance!

Mr Bartley coughed diplomatically. 'Dear me! Well, well – that is . . . this is not helpful. May I suggest we decide the fundamental issue? Miss Paradise, are you prepared to meet the conditions?'

'Yes.' Any doubts Alyssa previously entertained had been swept away. She wanted Hawkscote, but had now determined to be a thorn in Sir Giles's flesh too.

'Excellent,' said Mr Bartley, relieved to be making progress. 'Now, I ask the same question of you, Sir Giles: are you willing to meet these terms?'

'Yes,' he replied. 'In spite of what you may think, Miss Paradise, I liked and respected your uncle. He was a good friend and has been kind enough to offer me, albeit through strange means, access to the water rights and for that I am grateful. Let us hope we can rub along tolerably well until we both have what we desire. Of course, I state now for the record, if you decide to sell, I am willing to purchase the estate at full market price, notwithstanding my acquiring access to the water.'

Alyssa merely inclined her head to acknowledge his offer and his words regarding her uncle. 'Are there any other details I should be aware of, Mr Bartley?' she enquired.

'Only that General Paradise retained his staff in anticipation you would accept.' He tapped the documents with one finger. 'His long-serving staff and tenants have been left small gifts; I'll not trouble you with the details but will organize these, if you are in agreement?'

She nodded. 'I presume I may take my ward with me to Hawkscote?' Alyssa saw Sir Giles raise his brows, but he offered no comment.

'Of course – indeed, it would be best if you had company – but remember there must be no one else present when you dine with Sir Giles.'

'How could I forget?' she said, with heavy irony. 'Charles will find the situation difficult but that cannot be helped.'

'Charles?' queried Mr Bartley.

'Charles Brook, we are – er – betrothed,' This was not strictly correct: Charles was still waiting for her answer to his marriage proposal but Alyssa could hardly explain that now.

'Ah, I see,' he replied, pleased to have this detail clarified.

Sir Giles gave a short, humourless laugh. 'It will be equally difficult to reconcile Miss Caroline Nash to these arrangements,' he said. 'You have my word as a gentleman I will keep to the terms, Mr Bartley.'

'I do not doubt it,' replied the lawyer, with a warm smile. He then expatiated again on the main points until he concluded, 'I think I have covered everything. Have either of you further questions?'

'None,' said Alyssa.

'No, you have made everything perfectly clear.' Sir Giles rose to take his leave, bowing punctiliously before shaking the lawyer's hand and adding, 'I expect to hear from you again in due course.' Collecting his gloves, hat and driving coat, he glanced at Alyssa. 'Miss Paradise, I look forward to welcoming you to Dorset. When do you begin your tenancy?'

'Shortly after Easter, when I have made the necessary arrangements.'

'Then I will call after your arrival.' With that, he bowed once more and left.

Mr Bartley, observing Alyssa's expression and heightened colour, said, 'Do not think too badly of Sir Giles, my dear. He is considered a kind, if brusque, man, and the general's will shocked him also.'

'Sir Giles may possess admirable qualities but he is the rudest man I have ever met!' she replied. 'And now I am obliged to endure his company for six months.'

CHAPTER TWO

Three days later, in Dorset, Caroline Nash and her mother were taking tea with Sir Giles. Caroline regarded him with resentment over the rim of her teacup as they sat in the morning-room of Eastcombe House. Giles had been provokingly reticent since his return from London so she had travelled to his estate this morning to discover the details of the will for herself. Having heard them, Caroline expressed her contempt roundly.

'The most vexatious thing I ever heard! General Paradise must have been mad!' was her curt observation. 'Don't you agree, Mama?'

'Of course, my dear – quite mad,' said Mrs Nash, nodding; it was her invariable habit to agree with her daughter.

'What do you think, Giles?'

'Oh, Tom possessed all his wits,' he replied with a smile, 'but I admit his will *is* unusual and I cannot see why he chose this route.'

'But this passes what might be considered merely eccentric,' she complained. 'To every person of sense, it is a preposterous document.'

'Tom always was a mischievous rogue.'

'Yes, and I did not like him,' said Caroline, bluntly.

Gil's smile died away and his brows rose.

'Indeed?' he said, in a clipped voice. 'Have you grounds for this opinion? You never mentioned your dislike before.'

'One has to be polite to one's neighbours, naturally, but I thought he looked at me in a disparaging way. And he had too much levity.' She sniffed disapprovingly. 'A general should have had more decorum than to laugh when Mrs Cumbernatch lost her hat after Sunday service. The wind took it into a puddle and it was quite ruined, yet all General Paradise could do was snigger.'

'It was a large hat,' observed her mother, recalling the ornate confection that Mrs Cumbernatch had worn to impress her fellow churchgoers, 'and one I thought very handsome, but she should have used more hat pins.'

'She should have had more sense than wear that cornucopia of ribbon, fruit and flowers on a windy day,' retorted Gil in disgust. 'Mrs Cumbernatch was well-served for her vanity and I understand why Tom found the incident amusing,' he continued, adding defiantly, 'I did too.'

'But you did not demean yourself by laughing as the general did; it was most unseemly.'

'Most unseemly,' echoed Mrs Nash.

'Are you never tempted to behave in an *unseemly* manner, Caroline?' he asked, giving her an odd look.

She gave a trill of incredulous laughter. 'Never!'

'I thought not.'

'Caroline always behaves with propriety, Sir Giles,' commented Mrs Nash.

'I would not dine alone with a strange gentleman,' declared her daughter virtuously. 'Surely you will not accede to these ridiculous dinner engagements, Giles?'

He shrugged. 'I must. It was Tom's wish and I have given my word; this way, at least I obtain the water rights. And society would think me a poor sort of gentleman if I took pecuniary advantage of Miss Paradise.'

'But is there *no* way it can be avoided?'

'None. As you might expect, I explored the possibility with the lawyer as I considered the idea insupportable when I first heard it.'

'I'm sure you did. Miss Paradise, on the other hand, must be brazen to agree without demur.'

'The very same thing occurred to me, my dear,' agreed her mother, with relish.

'You are mistaken,' he said sharply, 'she found the clause equally provoking, and certainly is not brazen.'

'Then what sort of person is she?'

'I found her to be . . .' he hesitated and, after a thoughtful pause, added, 'not at all what I expected.'

'Pray, do not be obtuse,' urged Mrs Nash, putting her cup down on her saucer and leaning forward eagerly. 'What do you mean?'

A slight smile touched his lips. 'Oh, simply that I expected a shy miss but was confronted by a self-possessed young woman who did not mince her words. Of course, it was extremely awkward; I disliked being in a situation over which I had no control and Miss Paradise was similarly annoyed. I'm afraid I engaged in verbal sparring with the general's niece.' His smile widened as he recalled their exchanges. 'She has something of his lively nature, I believe.'

'She sounds unbecomingly forward,' protested Caroline. 'How impertinent to argue with a gentleman one has only just met.'

'Highly improper,' said Mrs Nash.

'Some of her comments were trenchant but I was guilty of provoking them,' acknowledged Gil, with a rueful shrug.

'But to agree to dine with you so readily, and after this . . . this verbal sparring too,' exclaimed Caroline. 'It shows a regrettable boldness.'

'She had no choice if she wishes to obtain Hawkscote,' he pointed out reasonably.

Fixing him with a basilisk glare, Caroline said witheringly, 'Really, Giles! Next you will say you admire her spirit!'

'Perhaps I do, in a way.'

'I find that hard to believe,' she said, with a tiny supercilious smile. 'You admire efficiency over spirit in a lady.'

'Is that your opinion of me?'

'Of course – otherwise you would not have made your preference for *my* company so clear,' she said.

In fact, the reverse was true; Caroline had determinedly insinuated herself into his attentions. She was not obliged to marry for money, but had every intention of doing so. Love was a vulgar, bourgeois expression in her estimation, but she admired Giles's sporting and business prowess, thought his lineage beyond reproach, and found his fortune most attractive of all. Despite his business success, in her opinion he exhibited a deplorable lack of ambition in other areas and, once they were married, she intended him to seek a position in government before progressing to a peerage.

This Giles had so far steadfastly refused to contemplate, citing no interest in politics. She was undeterred. Pressure would be brought to bear and he would be forced to reconsider. That they did not enjoy a close relationship troubled her not one iota – indeed, she considered him too well-bred for outpourings of emotion.

Silence had followed her last comment and Caroline willingly filled the breach.

'Naturally, one must disapprove of this eccentric behaviour,' she continued. 'I always suspected the tenor of his mind was unsteady and here we see my suspicions vindicated. My judgement is rarely inaccurate.' She pursed her lips, savouring this moment of self-righteous justification. 'From what you have said, Giles, Miss Paradise has inherited her uncle's unfortunate recklessness. Good God, one shudders to think of the damage this will do to her reputation! You may be certain gossip will be rife.' Replacing her cup, she added, 'When does she arrive?'

'After Easter.'

'Very well – if you are determined, I suppose I must offer my support.'

Gil raised his brows in surprise. Caroline's high-handed manner and animadversions on the general had irked him but she had ultimately given her approval. Contrite at misjudging her, he said quietly, 'Thank you. To hear I have your confidence means a great deal. It must be difficult for you to accept I am to dine with Miss Paradise.'

'It is not a question of having confidence in you, nor am I jealous,' she said, coldly. 'How could you think I might be? No, this must be viewed merely as a business proposition and you must obtain either the option to purchase or, at the very least, the water rights. Both would be important acquisitions for the expansion of our – that is, *your* estate.'

'Caroline is right, Sir Giles,' said Mrs Nash, 'you must do what is right financially.'

Her daughter gave a thin smile. 'Giles always does, Mama. He is not a man to be swayed by other issues.'

Gil listened with deepening anger. Caroline was not, as he had originally surmised, offering her support in difficult circumstances, nor had she admitted to jealousy; financial gain was her only concern. He recognized his anger was somewhat irrational – it was, after all, primarily for gain he had agreed – but part of his soul also wanted to comply with his friend's final wishes and for Caroline to be so coldly analytical was disconcerting. Surely moral support was worth more than a few pounds on a balance sheet? It appeared it was not and he wondered ironically at her reaction had he lost the opportunity of acquiring Hawkscote or the water rights. Regarding her self-satisfied expression, he knew the answer: she would have been furious. Suddenly, Gil felt deflated and irascible. His brows snapped together; impatience flickered in his gaze.

'I believe you mean that to be a compliment, Caroline,' he said, his voice laced with sarcasm.

'Of course. You are the most prominent businessman in the area; everyone expects you to be single-minded in pursuit of your interests.'

'Not at the expense of moral considerations, I hope?'

She did not respond directly; instead, observing, 'People look to you for guidance and you must act accordingly, even if the outcome is sometimes unpleasant.'

'But never sacrificing, for example, fairness, trust or loyalty? *Noblesse oblige* – surely that must be *your* view, knowing your sense of rectitude?' he pressed, still in an ironic tone.

'I suppose so, although one cannot expect uneducated people to have opinions on the matter,' she said, grudgingly.

Mrs Nash uttered an appreciative titter. 'Very true, my dear.'

Gil stared. There was a long silence before he said tersely, 'In my experience, ignorance through lack of education is no bar to understanding right from wrong. Even the simplest creature understands that principle.'

Caroline's reply was to smile sweetly and say she looked forward to him dining with them the following day. Gil, finding himself completely out of charity with her, was not sorry to see Caroline and her mother depart a short time later.

He studied the neat, rolling landscape through the window afterwards with an unseeing gaze and wondered what was wrong with him. He had come to believe Caroline was the sort of wife he needed: calm, ordered, and efficient. Gil was unsure exactly how or when he reached this decision. It had occurred by some sort of osmosis because Caroline was always *there* and, eventually, it seemed the inevitable outcome. He felt no deep passion or love, but whether this was Caroline's fault or his own, he did not know; she was not a woman to indulge in displays of affection and he . . . well, he wondered if he was capable of the passionate relationship enjoyed by others, including his own sister and her husband.

He had never fallen in love and believed, at two and thirty, he was past doing so. He had desired women in the past and experienced pleasant flirtations, but the deepest part of his being had never been engaged. Perhaps this was simply not a facet of his character and the thought he was not destined for a marriage with love, humour, and desire at its core saddened him.

So if such a marriage was unattainable, he should settle for what he *could* achieve. And yet, although he knew Caroline expected him to offer for her, thus far he could not bring himself to utter the words. He found her coldness annoying of late and since his trip to London, he felt even more dissatisfaction. Gil blamed the bizarre details of the will for this and hoped his discontent was temporary. It had to be. He must put his mind to business and, when things were more settled, offer Caroline marriage.

Meanwhile, he needed to prevent a pair of blue eyes, brimful of amusement and disdain, from continually intruding upon his thoughts.

Unlike his cousin, Piers Kilworth had eagerly anticipated the reading of the will. He waited to be summoned in the weeks following his uncle's death until one of his creditors – a fellow more pressing and unpleasant than the rest – forced him to decamp hurriedly from his lodgings in St James's. Thinking it wiser to leave no forwarding address, Piers took full advantage of his friends' hospitality and rusticated for a month.

When he returned to find the note from Deathridge, Flyte and Bartley, he cursed his luck at missing the appointment by a single day but was not unduly perturbed; he could wait a little longer for confirmation of his inheritance. The following morning, he shaved and dressed at an unusually early hour with the intention of going to Chancery Lane. However, when a letter was brought in by his servant, Piers smiled with satisfaction. It was obviously a legal missive containing the news he had been waiting for and, placing the unopened letter on the breakfast table, he indulged in some agreeable speculation as to its contents before breaking open the seal. As he read, his smile faded and his colour ebbed away. He scanned the contents again before screwing up the sheet and smashing a china dish into the fireplace with a strangled cry of fury.

His servant, who unwisely opened the door to investigate, encountered his master in a towering rage.

'Get out!' he screamed, 'Get out, damn you!'

The man hastily retreated to leave Piers striding back and forth, grinding his teeth and muttering King Lear-like threats of retribution.

When, eventually, his fury cooled and he had exhausted his vocabulary of curses and expletives, he retrieved the letter. Apart from requesting he call in Chancery Lane at his earliest convenience, the only other details were the amount of his annuity and that his cousin was to receive Hawkscote.

'Of all the scheming, manipulative, wicked *harpies!*' he cried.

In his way, he had always been fond of his cousin but now he was staggered by the depths of her deceit. Alyssa must have secretly encouraged Tom to leave Hawkscote to her! Piers tried to collect his thoughts. The letter was dated only yesterday so Alyssa was most likely still in town. He needed to speak to her; he would get more information from his cousin than from a crusty old attorney stuffed full of jurisprudence. Recalling where she stayed on her infrequent visits to London, he collected his hat and left his lodgings for Flemings Hotel in Half Moon Street.

A short time later, Alyssa, who was drawing on her gloves and about to venture forth to do some shopping, saw her cousin immediately he entered the hotel reception. Piers was dressed in his usual fashionable style, wearing an expertly cut blue superfine coat, striped waistcoat, buff-coloured pantaloons, Hessians, and a cravat tied in the most intricate arrangement she had ever seen. He noticed her and began to walk over, and Alyssa gave a little sigh of resignation. She was not surprised to see Piers; it was inevitable he would seek her out once he heard.

She held out her hand and greeted him, observing a sulky expression marred his handsome features. 'It is good to see you, Piers. You look well.'

'No thanks to you and Uncle Tom!'

'Whatever can you mean?' she said, her eyes twinkling. She was unable to resist briefly feigning ignorance, even in the face of his fury. Piers generally projected an air of boredom and Alyssa was amused to see this replaced for once by honest, simmering anger.

'Don't play the innocent, Alyssa! I suffered the shock of my life an hour ago.'

'Ah, you have received Mr Bartley's letter.'

'Yes, I've received the damned letter and I'm furious.'

'Naturally,' she replied, calmly. 'Pray, do not let us stand here arguing. If you must raise your voice, we should move somewhere a little less public.' She turned and led the way into the empty coffee-room which led off the hall.

When they were seated and Alyssa had ordered coffee, she began, 'I understand the news must have been a shock—'

'Do you?' he interposed, with a cynical sneer.

'Yes. Indeed, it came as a complete surprise to me too.'

'And you expect me to believe that?'

She said curtly, 'Let us have this out at the first, Piers. If you have accusations to make, do so openly! Having been subjected to Sir Giles Maxton's allegations, I have no wish to suffer yours.'

'Who in Hades is Sir Giles Maxton?' he cried.

Noting that Piers was trembling with fury and his face was as white as his shirt, Alyssa continued in a softer tone, 'We will come to that in a moment. What are you accusing me of?'

'If you must have it spelt out then I believe you influenced Uncle Tom to change his will! You – *you* are to receive Hawkscote instead of me! Damn it, how can that be equitable?' Piers then entered a long and disjointed invective, covering Alyssa's duplicity, the maliciousness of the general's actions, his misfortune and ill-treatment at the hands of his relatives, and concluded with, 'I think it monstrous! It has always been understood Hawkscote was *mine!*'

'I agree you had that understanding,' retorted Alyssa, who had listened to his diatribe in silence but with a gleam of anger in her eyes, 'but did Uncle Tom ever say as much?'

He shrugged and coloured. 'Well, no – but that is not the point. As his nearest male heir, it was his duty to leave it to me.'

'It was his duty to leave it to whomever he saw fit.'

'Then you deny you influenced him?'

'Of course I deny it!' she replied, with asperity. 'How could you believe me capable of such a thing?'

'It would not be your usual style, I grant you, but even someone of your high moral tone might be tempted by money!' he jeered.

'Well, I was not! I was blissfully ignorant of his intentions. Why, I have not seen Uncle these past two years and you must acknowledge it would be impossible to coerce Tom without *seeing* him!'

'But you were always his favourite—'

There was a knock at the door. Coffee was bought in by a porter and conversation halted until he left. Alyssa poured out two cups, handed one to her cousin and continued, 'It was your sybaritic lifestyle that irritated him, Piers. He could not understand why you did not make something of yourself by joining the military, or some other worthwhile occupation, instead of drifting between country house parties and London, amassing debts in the process.'

'Following the drum was never in my blood.'

She gave a little smile and eyed him mischievously. 'No, it wasn't, was it? The army would have mounted their next assault before you had risen from your slumbers.'

'I'm not in the mood for humour,' he said.

'Neither am I particularly. Let us call a temporary truce and be serious for a moment. You know I could not have influenced Tom but while it is true he has favoured me, only consider the terms I have to meet.'

'What are they?' Piers's interest was piqued; perhaps all was not yet lost.

'I am to live at Hawkscote for six months and dine once a week – *alone* – with Sir Giles Maxton, who owns the neighbouring estate, consulting him on all matters pertaining to the estate, farmland and staff. You may imagine how enamoured I was of *that* arrangement.'

Piers slammed his cup down upon its saucer. 'What?' he said, incredulous. 'Why would Tom want you to have dinner with some old fossil?'

'Well, I could not describe Sir Giles as an old fossil,' declared Alyssa, vividly recalling the dark, brooding man who had towered above her, 'but he is uncivil. Still, I am obliged to share his company and will no doubt suffer dyspepsia as a result.'

'Good God, the general must have lost his senses!'

'It seems not, but you know how mischievous he was, and his will is written in the same vein.'

Piers regarded her in moody silence. He clenched his right hand until the knuckles showed white beneath the skin and, in desperation, tried another avenue.

'Will Hawkscote revert to me if you don't meet the terms?'

'I'm afraid not.'

Piers's scowl grew deeper as she explained. Then, he rose to his feet, exclaiming fiercely, 'So – I am completely cut out; either you get the estate, or Maxton will purchase it.'

'You have your annuity. It is not what you wanted, I know, but—'

'Not what I wanted!' he repeated, scornful. 'You have no conception, dear cousin, how much expectation I had riding on this!'

'Piers, have you borrowed against the estate?'

He shrugged again, his mouth twisting in a grimace as he slumped back on to his chair. 'Not borrowed exactly, but I have run up debts on the understanding they would be paid when I received my inheritance.'

'But surely that is the same thing?'

'Not quite – it is easier to refuse to answer the door to my tailor than a money-lender.' Arms folded across his chest, his sullen gaze ran over her. 'Your naivety surprises me. You must have known I was living on the promise of money. God knows I have little enough else to survive on.'

'I-I suppose I did consider you might be but not to any great extent.'

'My tastes are expensive; let me assure you the extent is great,' he drawled.

'I will help you although I refuse to fund your gambling,' she said. 'It is high time you took control of your life and realized your actions have consequences.'

'Lord, don't moralize, Coz! Your efforts are wasted in my direction – I'm a lost cause.'

'Perhaps if you married—'

'Ha!' he interpolated, dismissively. 'And find myself tied to some lady who will increase my debts?' He gave a deep shudder. 'Thank you, but no. Unless an heiress or rich widow presents themselves, I'll avoid matrimony like the plague! Alyssa, I give you fair warning I intend to enquire about contesting the will.'

'You are at liberty to, of course, but I have already discussed it with Mr Bartley.'

'And?' he asked, watching keenly.

She threw out her hands in a hopeless gesture. 'You would need money to pay the costs and there is little hope of success.'

His eyes narrowed. 'So I am to live on my paltry annuity and go quietly like some whipped cur!' he said, vehemently. 'Damned if I will! There must be some-thing I can do.'

'There is nothing. I will try to repay your most pressing debts but I make no promises; the next six months will be difficult for me.'

'Not so difficult with the prize at the end! I suppose you plan to squander what is rightfully mine on your dirty brats!'

'Don't refer to the children as dirty brats!' she said belligerently. 'I should not warrant your contempt for helping to educate poor children in my village! Really,

Piers – you go too far! Continue and I shall not feel obliged to help at all.'

'Oh, it does not matter to me whether you teach one or twenty children their letters,' he observed, in a dry voice. 'If you wish to practise philanthropy, that is your business, but I find it galling that money that rightfully belongs to me is to be thrown their way.'

'I can think of no better way to spend it.'

'Well, I can! A new high perch phaeton, for a start.'

Her lips twitched. 'So that was what you intended to buy.'

'You approve?' he asked, raising his brows.

'No, but you always wanted to cut a figure in London so I see why it would appeal. Perhaps something might be arranged—'

'I won't need it yet,' he interjected, insouciantly. 'They are useless on country roads.'

'Oh? Where are you going?'

'To Dorset.'

She stared at him blankly for a moment and then protested, 'Why on earth do you want to come to Dorset? It would be a waste of time. Besides, you can't stay at Hawkscote – even though you are my cousin; it would not be proper for us to be under the same roof without a chaperon. It is ridiculous to need a duenna at my age, but we must abide by society's rules and enough gossip will be generated as it is from my dinners with Sir Giles.'

'Don't gammon me, Coz!' he said, with a short mirthless laugh, 'You're not in your dotage yet! Never fear, I won't put you to the blush – I'll stay with James Westwood at his estate outside Dorchester. I'm overdue a visit there anyhow, and I've a mind to see how this business progresses while I decide whether to contest. And if Maxton is as bad as you say, you might need support.'

'I can handle Sir Giles well enough in spite of his brusqueness.'

'You know, I rather pity him in a way,' he observed, 'I've been on the receiving end of your barbed set-downs.'

'Thank you for the compliment – I think,' replied Alyssa, tartly.

'I'm certain you can hold your own with him verbally, but how do you know he won't give poor advice?'

'Why should he?' she said, in bewilderment.

'To reduce the market value, of course! If you decide to sell, he could save himself a great deal of money. And, even if you retain it, he might have caused enough damage by then to oblige you to sell.'

'I had not considered that,' she admitted.

'Obviously! Don't be so damned independent for once, Alyssa; allow me to help.'

'Help?' she echoed, eyeing him suspiciously, 'This is a curious *volte-face*. First you protest, now you are magnanimous.'

'Oh, I'm still livid, but I protect my annuity a little this way. It is to be mostly drawn from investments and the remainder from either the sale or continued income from Hawkscote. So you see, maintaining the value is in my interest. How do you know Maxton didn't influence Tom?'

'The lawyer assured me he had no involvement and I trust his word. Also, I saw Sir Giles receive the news: he was as astonished as I was.'

'Hmm,' said Piers, unconvinced, 'He will bear watching.'

'Perhaps you are right. Piers, I can't stop you if you are set upon going to Dorset but please do not interfere.'

'Don't worry, Coz – I'll confine myself to watching and listening and let you know of anything suspicious. When do you go?'

'Letty and I will journey there after Easter.'

His brow furrowed. 'Now who the deuce is *Letty*? Your maid?'

'No. Oh, of course, you would not be aware. Letty is the daughter of the Ravenhills. Do you remember them? They were friends of Mother and Father but tragically, both died three years ago from scarlet fever. Letty was their only child. The nearest relative she had was an aunt in London with a young family and no easy means of supporting her, so Father and I offered for Letty to come and live with us. Of course, it's just Letty and me now – she is eighteen, nearly nineteen.'

'Why didn't I see her at your father's funeral?'

'She was ill at the time and the doctor advised her not to attend. The last time you would have seen her was at Mother's funeral, five years ago.'

'Letty . . . Letty Ravenhill,' he mused. 'Wait a moment – I think I do remember. She was a chit of about thirteen, if I recall, and bidding fair to become a beauty.'

'Well, she *is* quite lovely, as well as sweet-tempered and mature for her age.'

'Oh? Then I look forward to meeting her.'

'I'll not let you upset Letty.'

'Why do you think I would?' he countered, with an innocent look.

Alyssa merely regarded him quizzically from under her lashes. He lifted his brows and smiled but made no further comment. Then he rose to his feet.

'I'll see you in Dorset. In the meantime, I'll need all my skill to keep the wolves away when word gets out about my ill-fortune.' He turned away and muttered, 'What a damnable mess!'

'Piers, wait—' she began. He looked back and she hesitated before stammering, 'I-I am truly sorry matters have turned out this way.'

'So am I, Coz,' he said, with a reluctant laugh, 'but the wolves at my door need more than apologies to chew on.'

Piers left and Alyssa pondered her cousin's reaction. She understood his bitter disappointment, but she could not continue to apologize for her gain when she too had been living on little money. She and Letty received no payment for teaching at the school; that role, considered unsuitable by many amongst local genteel society, was undertaken out of choice and most of Alyssa's spare funds were sent there. She desired no thanks or praise for this, but had occasionally wished for greater financial comfort and now she had the chance of it. Charles had yet to hear of her good fortune or the extraordinary caveats attached to the will. Each attempt at writing him a letter had become lost in a morass of explanations and she eventually admitted defeat, deciding to tell him in person on her return to Oxfordshire.

In Alyssa's heart, there were unresolved issues concerning Charles and this news had only added to those uncertainties. She pulled on her gloves and gave a tiny shrug of resignation; Uncle Tom's singular will had already caused a good deal of turmoil and there would be more in the weeks to come.

CHAPTER THREE

As the lumbering vehicle travelled the last half-mile from Dorchester, Alyssa waited for her first sight of Hawkscote for two years. The fine architecture of the house suddenly came into view and while the warm grey stone and mullioned windows of the hall had always appealed, on a spring day, nestling against a blue sky and a swathe of daffodils, it looked spectacular and more welcoming than ever after the long journey.

The carriage began to meander up the beech-lined drive that led to the house and the thought struck her forcibly that Tom would not be waiting to greet her this time. A plethora of memories flooded back and her eyes filled with tears. Hurriedly, she blinked them away but not before someone else had noticed.

'Alyssa, what is wrong?' asked Charles.

'I was remembering Uncle Tom, but how stupid of me to cry now!' she said, with a wavering smile.

'Some distress is understandable when Hawkscote and your uncle are connected in your mind,' he acknowledged. 'However, I suspect you are emotional for another reason.'

Alyssa gave Charles a searching look. 'Oh?'

'You are suddenly apprehensive at what you have undertaken. I am not surprised you feel it keenly and if only you had listened to me. . . .' He paused, and added, 'Well, you know my opinion.'

Letty was sitting opposite and Alyssa caught her wry, faintly disparaging expression in response to his observation.

'You're wrong, Charles: my thoughts were only of Tom,' said Alyssa, firmly. 'Pray do not let us argue over the will again.'

'But I disapprove of it!'

'So you have told me – almost every day since I returned from London. I agree it is an awkward business, but I have to comply if I want Hawkscote.'

'I think it's a wonderful adventure!' said Letty, her eyes sparkling. 'I have never left Oxfordshire before and yet, in the last few days, I have visited London, travelled by the mail and now I am in Dorset.'

'I would hardly describe travelling in a malodorous mail coach, squeezed between a farmer's wife with a crying baby and a parson who described the minutiae of every sermon he had given in the last year, as an *adventure*,' said Charles, grimacing.

'The parson *was* a dead bore, but the farmer's wife and her baby were delightful,' said Letty.

Alyssa laughed. 'I thought they were, too. Mrs Farmer and I enjoyed a comfortable chat on the vagaries of cheese making. Apparently, it is common practice to bury the starter culture over winter. It is dug up the following spring and used again for making cheese—'

'I had no idea the process was so interesting,' interpolated Charles, peevishly. 'Why didn't you accept my offer to travel post, Alyssa? We would have been more comfortable.'

'Because of the expense.'

'I would have borne the cost.'

'It was kind of you but I had no objection to travelling by mail,' she replied, 'and if you recall, I did not desire you to accompany us – that was your decision.'

'A fine thing if I allowed you to travel on the London to Exeter Mail without my protection!' remarked Charles, affronted.

'Since there were no marauding highwaymen and we had only to contend with a garrulous farmer's wife and a tedious parson, I rather think you had better stayed in London and not put yourself to the discomfort,' said Alyssa, tartly. 'The journey has made you ill-tempered, but it is your own fault; I advised you not to come.'

Charles returned her gaze for a long moment and, acknowledging the truth of this *obiter dictum*, nodded and smiled faintly. 'I've been as moody as a bear, but it is only because I am anxious for you.'

'Why are you worried about Lyssa?' asked Letty, in surprise. 'She is very capable and all the arrangements are in place for our stay.'

'These dinner engagements concern me.'

'I can deal with Sir Giles.'

'My concern is not for your behaviour – it is for *his*!' protested Charles, a pugnacious set to his jaw. 'We know nothing about this man and yet you are to be alone with him. Good God, I cannot feel comfortable at the prospect!'

'Do you expect he will try to ravish her?' asked Letty, with feigned innocence.

'Letty!' admonished Alyssa, even though her eyes twinkled with laughter.

He shot Letty a reproving glance but admitted, 'I would not put it so bluntly, but she will be vulnerable, and for all we know, Maxton is a hardened rake.'

'That is nonsensical, Charles. His manner was brusque but his behaviour was that of a gentleman.'

'Easy enough to appear so in a lawyer's office,' he retorted, 'He may behave differently when you are alone with him.'

Letty, amused by Charles's heightened colour, cried, 'Oh, you are *jealous*! I declare it is famous – I always thought you too dul— I mean, reserved, for jealousy.'

'My dear girl, you are being impudent—' began Charles, indignantly.

Alyssa intervened. 'Letty, do stop being a tease. Charles – your concern for my welfare is gratifying but misplaced; I can't imagine Sir Giles will assault my virtue over the *soufflé au citron*. Ah, look – we have arrived and the servants are waiting.'

The carriage halted outside the main entrance. Alyssa was greeted warmly by Rowberry, the butler, and the housekeeper, Mrs Farnell, whom she knew well from her previous visits. After Alyssa had introduced Letty and Charles, they all moved into the house.

'Very imposing,' murmured Charles, looking with at his surroundings with interest.

The great hall was a testament to Hawkscote's medieval origins. A huge fireplace dominated the room and a tapestry depicting Samson slaying the lion hung above it. Portraits and landscape scenes adorned the other walls, a fine oak staircase rose to the galleried landing and, to the right of the entrance door, the afternoon sun filtered through a stained glass oriel window.

'It is a pleasure to see you again, miss,' declared the housekeeper.

'Thank you. Indeed, I am glad to be here at last. Is everything prepared?'

'Exactly as your instructions,' said Mrs Farnell, nodding, 'you have your usual room and Miss Ravenhill is in the blue bedroom.'

'Then could you see that our portmanteaux are carried up?' said Alyssa, smiling as she unbuttoned her pelisse. 'Mr Brook is staying at The Antelope in Dorchester for a few days while we settle in. He'll return to London afterwards.'

'Very good, miss. I'll bring some tea and cake.'

Mrs Farnell hurried away and Letty said, 'Would you mind if I went up to my room first?'

'Not at all. Charles and I will be downstairs when you are ready to join us.'

As Letty followed Rowberry up the sweeping staircase, Charles accompanied Alyssa into the drawing-room where a low fire burned in the hearth; even though it was April, there was a chill in the south-easterly blowing inland from the coast.

Alyssa warmed her hands and, looking around the room, immediately felt at home. The room was decorated in an attractive pale green with heavy brocade curtains of a darker shade. An ornate plaster ceiling, a carved fire surround, a number of silk-covered chairs, two *chaises*, a large mahogany cabinet, a writing bureau and several occasional tables completed the décor and the windows looked south on to a terrace, then to the formal gardens beyond.

Charles strode to one window to admire the view. 'I am impressed with what I have seen so far,' he said. 'What is the total acreage?'

'Roughly five hundred.'

'Excellent!' he observed. 'And no expense has been spared on furnishings – your uncle did not have to practise too many economies, it seems.'

'No, I don't believe he did,' she said. 'I'm glad you approve, Charles. I spent many happy hours here and, as you will see when I show you the rest of the house and gardens, the general ensured any improvements blended sympathetically with the original design.'

Charles picked up a bronze figure of a naked Hercules and studied it. 'This is an inappropriate item to have on display,' he remarked. 'Decidedly crude and unsophisticated.'

She laughed. 'Oh, do look around! Uncle Tom became an avid collector during his travels. The paintings, tapestries and *objets d'art* you see here and throughout the rest of the house speak of his eclectic tastes.'

Charles, inspecting an Egyptian scarab with disdain, said, 'Wildly eccentric would be a more accurate description.'

'Each item held an intrinsic charm for Uncle Tom, even if it was not valuable or fashionable,' she said, taking a chair near the fire and trying to suppress her annoyance at his derisive tone.

'Hmm . . . well, no doubt among these unappealing trifles there will be a few valuable pieces. I will engage to have it catalogued – then, you may keep anything of worth and dispose of the rest.'

Alyssa frowned. 'But I do not wish to, Charles,' she said, her voice losing some of its deliberate calm. 'I have not yet fully acquired Hawkscote and have no intention of selling Uncle Tom's collection for some time – if ever.'

'Foolish sentiment,' he said, drily. 'Many items will be worthless and you would be well rid of them.'

'All the same, I prefer to keep them for now. They remind me of my uncle and if that is being overly sentimental, then *mea culpa.*'

'As you wish. I was merely trying to be helpful,' he said, with a wounded expression.

'Come, Charles,' she replied lightly, 'we should not be arguing over trinkets.'

'Then tell me more about the house,' he said, sitting on one of the *chaises.*

'There is mention in the Domesday Book of a manor on the site but the current estate dates from the late fourteenth century when the Great Hall was built. There are three more reception rooms downstairs, as well as the King's chamber and the dining-room. Upstairs there is a large library, two bedrooms referred to as state rooms, although,' she commented, with a little laugh, 'I don't think royalty ever visited, and several other bedrooms. The servants' quarters are in the east wing. Oh, and I almost forgot – there is a secret passage, too!'

'Where?'

'Behind that panelling,' she said, indicating the far wall. 'When you open it, there is a spiral staircase which leads either to the library or to the cellars. I was fascinated by it as a child.'

'I'm sure you were,' he said, with a clipped smile. 'Most houses of the time had a secret passage or priest's hole added. Hawkscote is obviously well appointed. A pity, then, your uncle left this labyrinthine will as an obstacle to you acquiring it.'

'What would you have me do, Charles?' she said, raising her brows. 'Sell it for a fraction of its real value?'

Colour tinged his cheeks as he replied, 'No, not exactly.' Charles was willing to air objections, but had no alternative to offer; he did not want Hawkscote to escape Alyssa's grasp and soon, by virtue of their marriage, his own. He shrugged and protested, 'But a young woman needs protection and guidance. If you agree to marry before embarking on this . . . this farrago of nonsense, you would at least enjoy the security inherent in being betrothed to me.'

She looked up in surprise. 'You deserve an answer as soon as I can give it, but please do not press me now.'

He availed himself of her hand, saying earnestly, 'You have kept me waiting for some time, Alyssa. You *know* I care for you. Say you will be my wife and then I can go back to London with a lighter heart.'

He looked down appealingly and rubbed his thumb across the tender skin on the inside of her wrist, but what Alyssa should have found a sensual action, she found only irritating. Sighing inwardly, she acknowledged the fault lay with her feelings rather than his.

He was a respectable man, with reasonable fortune and of good manners and understanding. He was also handsome enough in a subtle way, being of average height with brown hair, dark eyes and a thick-set figure. His tendency to be pompous and superior was annoying, but she knew he would make a kind husband.

Alyssa had received two marriage proposals in the past but they were from unsuitable men for whom she did not care. However, Charles's qualities were laudable and there were sensible reasons why she should accept. Why then was she not more appreciative of his offer? Perhaps it was because there was no spark of excitement surrounding Charles. With the exception of egotism, moderation was his motto – Alyssa, on the other hand, wanted more than a moderate marriage.

He deserved an answer, even if it was the one he would not like, but Uncle Tom's will had thrown everything into turmoil and like a pebble thrown into a pool, the ripples of its effect moved ever outwards.

When Charles had learned of the terms, he lapsed into sulky petulance, but recently his behaviour had become proprietorial. He delivered pessimistic lectures on the dangers awaiting her in Dorset and gave instructions on what she should, and should not, do. Not only was he dull, thought Alyssa, he wanted to order her every movement.

Unsurprisingly, Alyssa's independent spirit railed against these dictates. Having witnessed his querulous, domineering behaviour, she was inclined to refuse immediately, but she felt it only right to let matters settle before giving her reply.

So, with this in mind, she replied, 'No, I'm sorry, Charles, There is much to think of now and I need more time.'

He released her wrist and turned away. 'I don't understand. I offer you the protection of my name yet still you will not answer,' he said, in a hollow voice.

'If you find my position difficult to comprehend, shall we decide at once to be nothing more than friends?'

He looked back, consternation flickering across his features, 'No! That is – perhaps I am rushing you – the last few weeks have been distracting.' He made the effort to smile. 'I can wait a little longer.'

'As you wish but I make no promises.'

They were interrupted by Mrs Farnell bringing in the tea. 'What time would you like to dine, miss?' she asked, placing the tray on a small table.

'Six o'clock will be suitable, I think.'

She nodded. 'There's pheasant pie, and a roast of lamb with potatoes and green beans.'

The housekeeper left, and Charles, his temper improved considerably by the promise of a good dinner, turned the conversation to less controversial matters so when Letty joined them shortly afterwards, the atmosphere was reasonably harmonious.

It remained so for the rest of the evening and throughout dinner, and Alyssa was grateful Charles did not mention the will again before leaving for Dorchester. After his departure, Alyssa and Letty sat in the drawing-room, conversing on general subjects for a while before Letty ventured, 'Tell me to mind my own affairs if you like, but are you really intending to marry Charles?'

'Why do you ask?' Alyssa countered, with a quizzical smile.

'Firstly, I need to consider my future; Charles will not want me in the way after you are married.'

'I see. And secondly?'

'To own the truth, I do not think him worthy of you. You are lively, clever and very witty, and he is—' Her colour rose and she hesitated, unsure whether to go on.

'Pray continue, Letty,' said Alyssa, amused, 'Don't worry about hurting my feelings – I fear I am shockingly insensitive where Charles is concerned.'

'Well, he is as dull as ditchwater! Oh, he's kind and I expect he has good intentions, but he continually throws a pall over everything with his gloomy cynicism and I couldn't bear it if he made you unhappy. And apart from being miserable, you would be bored within a month. There! Now I have said it and you can scold me,' she replied, blushing deeply.

'I won't do that,' Alyssa assured her. 'Having given the matter a great deal of thought recently, I've reached the same conclusion: we aren't suited. It's not Charles's fault – he is a good man and I know I could do worse – but I cannot reconcile to myself that is a strong enough foundation for marriage.' She smiled, and added a little wistfully, 'Perhaps I am being a romantic idiot now – there is much to be said for having a comfortable husband, after all – but I wanted something more.'

'You deserve more,' said Letty, resolutely. 'You looked after your mother during her illness, gave me a home when I had nowhere else to go, and nursed your father through failing eyesight and ill health. It is high time you paid attention to yourself and married someone who will care for you.'

'You make me sound like a martyr,' Alyssa said, with a little laugh.

'I don't mean to but you've never complained about your circumstances and always found opportunity to indulge what interests you, particularly in teaching the children. Charles would stifle your spirit – you would have to dance to his tune because he'd have a miserable face if you did not. And he is odiously priggish when you are never so. Why, even if I do something wrong, you have a clever way of acknowledging it: you don't ring a peal over me, or make me feel childish, whereas Charles . . .' Letty's voice trailed away, but she rolled her eyes, allowing her expression of dismay to say more than words.

'He can be sanctimonious, but we all have our faults. Perhaps it is unfair to dwell on Charles's when he has many good points as well.'

'But if you *loved* him, you wouldn't need to talk of his good or bad points; you would just accept they were all part of the man you loved and desired.'

'Just so, Letty,' agreed Alyssa softly, 'I could never love someone blindly, ignoring their flaws, but I shouldn't have to remind myself of his qualities.'

'Do you miss him when he is not with you?'

Alyssa, looking slightly guilty, said, 'No, I don't. If I am honest, I am flattered by his interest but don't return his regard in the same degree.'

'And how often do you laugh with him?'

'Hardly ever: a sense of humour is not one of his virtues.'

Letty leaned forward to murmur, 'And does your heart leap every time you look at him?'

Alyssa smiled. 'You are incorrigible, child!' she said, without malice.

'I know,' agreed Letty, her face glowing with mischief, 'but answer my question, if you please.'

'Oh, very well. No, it does not.'

Letty sat back, satisfied. 'Then it is settled: you do not love Charles; you are merely fond of him.'

'But perhaps that is because I cannot love anyone.'

'Bah!' said Letty, dismissively. 'Your nature lends itself to loving deeply – and that does not mean you will think him faultless – but rather you will feel he is the other half of you; someone you can laugh and cry with; someone to share your deepest fears, your hopes, your plans – a soul mate, if you will.'

'You astonish me sometimes,' said Alyssa, staring in admiration. 'For a young girl, you show a remarkable perspicacity of human nature and quite put me to shame.'

Letty considered this. 'Well, I don't know how I understand about love exactly since I have never felt more than the sad crush I had last summer on William Armstrong. It is just what I imagine, and have read, and gleaned from watching others who are in love. As for the rest of human nature, you and I have examples to observe at close quarters,' she said, with a grin.

'What can you mean—?' began Alyssa, puzzled until understanding suddenly dawned. 'Ah, of course – the children! How true. All of human nature is there, only in a more concentrated and uninhibited form.' She laughed and added, 'If I can deal with twenty little ones, I can surely manage one Sir Giles Maxton!'

'What sort of man is he?' asked her companion.

'The most condescending, self-important person I ever met.'

'So you have said. However, I actually meant what does he look like?'

'I suppose he is not handsome in the conventional sense, but he is imposing: tall, with a powerful physique, dark hair and eyes which emit a fierce stare.'

'You managed to take in some details of his appearance then?' said Letty, giving Alyssa a curious look from under her lashes.

'A few – I was too annoyed to notice everything.' This was not quite true; in the intervening weeks, Alyssa had realized she could vividly recall every detail of Sir Giles's face, figure and the sheer force of his presence. She murmured, 'I expect he will call soon. You can judge for yourself then.'

'I'll look forward it,' she replied, with a cryptic little smile.

In fact, Sir Giles arrived the next morning. Alyssa was in the drawing-room with Charles and, when Rowberry announced her visitor, she felt a tingling anticipation mingled with apprehension. She would have preferred Charles not to be present and stole a glance at him. He looked angry, but quickly schooled his features into indifference and stood with his back to the window.

When Sir Giles strode in, Alyssa found his presence as equally compelling as it had been in London. He was dressed in buckskin breeches and top boots, his dark-green double-breasted coat cut to fit closely across his broad shoulders. His cravat was tied in a waterfall knot but his hair was not lovingly teased into the longer, fashionably dishevelled style; it was cut slightly shorter and the breeze outside had done the rest. It seemed Sir Giles was no pink of the *ton*, inclined to spend time and effort on achieving a supposedly natural hairstyle. As he approached, his cool gaze met Alyssa's as he took her hand.

'Welcome to Dorset, Miss Paradise. I trust you had a good journey?'

'Yes – we arrived yesterday.' Her small fingers felt lost in his large, shapely hand and she removed them quickly.

'News travels quickly in this small community. Word of your arrival reached me and I decided to drive over this morning.' He glanced at Charles. 'I trust this is not an inconvenient time?'

'Oh, forgive me!' she exclaimed. 'May I introduce Charles Brook, my. . . .' Alyssa hesitated; she had been about to say he was her good friend.

'Your betrothed?' prompted Gil.

'Well, he – that is to say—' stammered Alyssa. Fortunately for her conscience, Charles chose that moment to intervene.

'Our betrothal is not yet official but soon will be,' he said, eyeing the other man with suspicion but extending his hand in response to Gil's outstretched one. 'I have heard of you from Alyssa, Sir Giles – along with details of your meeting in London.' His tone indicated he had heard nothing to the good.

'Indeed?' said Gil, raising his brows at this shrouded hostility. 'It was a most unusual first meeting. Miss Paradise and I were both hasty in our responses that day, I fear,' He turned to Alyssa and smiled, 'May I offer my congratulations on your forthcoming betrothal?'

'Oh! Y-yes, of course!' she murmured, feeling trapped. 'Th-Thank you.'

Charles, throwing Alyssa a puzzled look, asked bluntly, 'What say you to these ridiculous terms, Maxton?'

'What am I supposed to say?' replied Gil, equally candid. 'We must comply to obtain what we want. The general was a friend of mine so I also feel under some obligation to follow his wishes.'

'Have you no thought for Alyssa's reputation?'

'Charles, please!' she said, annoyed.

Again, Gil raised his brows. 'The scandalmongers will find our situation news-worthy for a time, but the novelty will die away. Most people will understand Miss Paradise is simply carrying out her uncle's request,' he observed in a cold voice. 'However, I can see why you are not happy with the arrangements—'

'Charles knows I'm determined,' interjected Alyssa.

'I didn't imagine you would change your mind,' said Gil, amusement hover-ing on his lips. 'I shall endeavour to remain compliant throughout dinner if you will do the same, Miss Paradise?'

'I will try, but the provocation might prove too great on occasion.'

His smile grew. 'Then shall we be content to see where our conversation leads?'

'A gentleman keeps a civil tongue in his head when in the presence of a lady!' said Charles.

Gil's brows snapped together as he queried in a suddenly arctic tone, 'True, but should I infer from your comment you do not consider me a gentleman?'

'I was not suggesting anything of the sort,' replied Charles mendaciously. 'I am merely concerned Alyssa's time here should be as pleasant as possible.'

'I also wish the least difficulty and disruption for both of us,' said Sir Giles in a curt voice.

Alyssa, feeling sidelined in this undeclared yet simmering confrontation, said quickly, 'Sir Giles, may I suggest seven o'clock on Saturday for our first meeting, here at Hawkscote? I will then have had time to settle in and meet my land agent.'

'That will be convenient. Ennis is your agent – he was your uncle's for some years. He is very capable but if there are particular matters you wish to discuss or require advice on, we may speak about them on Saturday.'

'Be aware, Sir Giles,' said Charles, through gritted teeth, 'Alyssa has friends who can offer advice.'

'I expect she has,' he replied, smoothly. 'Remember Miss Paradise has only to seek my advice – she is not obliged to take it, although I would strongly recom-mend she does, or at the very least listens to Ennis. My local knowledge and experience in estate management might prove useful.'

'I have estate management experience,' said Charles.

'Ah, I see.' Gil paused infinitesimally. 'May I enquire how many acres on your property?'

'Almost two hundred.'

'Eastcombe, my own estate, has one thousand acres. Perhaps we should leave Miss Paradise to decide who can offer the best advice?'

Charles, looking furious, made no further comment. It was clear he could not compete with Sir Giles on estate management or acreage.

Gil offered his hand and said, 'I'll take my leave now. We will surely meet again, Mr Brook.'

Charles murmured an indistinct response and could hardly bring himself to return the salutation. Afterwards, he turned away and Alyssa watched Sir Giles give a brief shrug in response. Feeling compelled to atone for Charles's childish behaviour, she smiled brilliantly at her guest and put out her hand.

'Thank you for driving over,' she said, warmly. 'I appreciate it and look forward to welcoming you again.'

His strong fingers closed over hers and he studied her smile with an expression that was hard to read. 'I will be here promptly at seven,' he replied. With that, he relinquished her hand and left.

Silence followed his departure until Charles snapped, 'Like you, I find I do not like Sir Giles Maxton in the least, Alyssa!'

She did not reply immediately but a martial light glinted in her eyes.

CHAPTER FOUR

'What possessed you to be so rude?' she demanded.

Charles stared and exclaimed, 'You said Maxton was overbearing in London and when I answer him in the same coin, you find fault with *me*!'

'The circumstances were different today; he was a visitor and deserved to be treated with civility unless he behaved to the contrary. He seemed determined to be cordial until piqued by your offensive tone.'

'I might ask why you find him acceptable now,' said Charles, nettled.

'I do not necessarily. I still believe him to be brusque and opinionated in general, but that does not mean you should be discourteous when given no provocation.'

'I was protecting you!'

'By being impolite?' she asked, her cheeks flushed with anger. 'You only made yourself look churlish! You do not hold sway over my actions, Charles, and I don't need your interference – please, respect my wishes on this.'

'Maxton is somehow aware we are betrothed in all but name – I had no need to tell him.'

'I mentioned it when we met in London,' admitted Alyssa, biting her lip, 'I did not intend to.'

'You speak as if it were something to be ashamed of.'

'No, I was pointing out I should not have said anything as I have not yet given you my answer.'

'Well, I'm glad you told him,' he said, giving a thin smile and puffing out his chest. 'If he thinks you are spoken for, he may curtail his behaviour. There is no guarantee – as I have said, many who appear gentleman later prove loose in the haft – but to know you are not without protection may deter him. You're a gently bred girl, by God, not one of the muslin company!'

'I'm sure he can see as much,' she murmured, ironically.

'Hmph! He realizes now I will stand no nonsense. Why, I would happily pelt him in the smeller if he lays one finger on you!'

Laughter rose to Alyssa's throat at his use of boxing cant, but she quickly stifled it, seeing he was in earnest. 'Ch-Charles, all this is fustian!'

'Fustian? I think not. And another thing – if he is a loose fish, he could make himself agreeable to get Hawkscote!'

'So now he will succumb to the allure of my money rather than my beauty?'

Charles merely scowled; he could not articulate the territorial instincts Giles Maxton had stirred in him on sight.

'It is lowering to think my attractions come a poor second,' she continued, amused. 'Perhaps he will ravish me first, *before* making himself agreeable. I shall bear it in mind and be on guard for my neighbour's iniquitous behaviour. However, if he owns a thousand-acre estate, he is already wealthy and has no need to ply me with soft words.'

'But foremost, he has an eye to business,' protested Charles. 'If Hawkscote could be obtained without payment, or at a reduced value, so much the better for him.'

'Can we leave the subject now, Charles?' she said drily. 'No purpose will be served by continuing.'

During the remainder of Charles's stay, the matter was not raised again although Alyssa knew this was only by considerable effort on his part. Two days later, she was truly thankful he was leaving. Relations between them had deteriorated further. Alyssa was at a loss to understand his surly attitude; Charles, on the other hand, saw it as a reasonable response to Alyssa's lack of empathy with his view. As he stood by the waiting carriage, he kissed her hand, saying gravely he would return soon and expect an answer. In the meantime, he would write. He climbed in, the equipage rumbled slowly away and Alyssa returned to the house.

Letty was reading, but looked up to see her companion's despondent expression. 'I'm glad Charles has gone,' she said, 'He has made you unhappy.'

'His behaviour only arouses my irritation,' observed Alyssa, rubbing her forehead wearily.

Letty closed her book. 'Now he has left, what shall we do for the rest of the day?'

'Ennis is due at eleven o'clock. I'll suggest he stays for lunch and shows me the estate afterwards. Would you care to join us?'

'I'd like to meet the farm workers, and their families.'

Alyssa agreed. 'Yes – it is time I introduced myself.'

The day passed quickly. Unhampered by Charles's presence, Alyssa enjoyed her new role. She discussed the running of the house with Mrs Farnell, listening to her ideas for improvements and cost savings and suggesting some of her own.

She met Ennis, a mild-mannered, middle-aged gentleman who had no qualms explaining business details to a woman, and he was neither patronizing nor sycophantic as they studied the accounts.

'I will not trouble you with too much detail at this stage, Miss Paradise,' he said, with a smile, 'it is better to learn a little as we go along. Of course, problems can be discussed as and when they arise. Does that meet with your approval?'

'Oh, yes! I have a great deal to learn, but I'm willing to apply myself. As you may know, my uncle requested I seek additional advice from Sir Giles Maxton.'

'Then you will receive help from an experienced source.'

'Do you regard him well?' she queried.

He nodded approvingly. 'He is a respected figure for many miles, both for his business expertise and his stewardship of his own estate. In my dealings with Sir Giles, he is always plainly spoken but eminently reliable. Your uncle, I believe, consulted him regularly.'

'So I understand.' Alyssa smiled, and added, 'Thank you for your help this morning. Would you stay for luncheon if you have the time?'

He agreed and, at Alyssa's request, gave her and Letty a partial tour of Hawkscote afterwards. They met most of the labourers and their families apart from Jonas Draper, who was out working in the fields. Alyssa discovered through careful questioning that the labourers did not own any land or property and, secretly shocked at the ragged, poorly nourished children and adults she had met, she was quiet on the return journey. As they walked back from the carriage to the house, Ennis was a little way behind when Letty asked softly, 'Are you feeling quite well? You have spoken little since we left the cottages.'

'I am troubled by the poverty I have seen,' she whispered. 'Having witnessed the privation striking farm workers in Oxfordshire, I did not expect much, but the harsh realities of country living are even more pronounced here.'

'The children were very thin,' agreed Letty.

Mr Ennis took his leave shortly afterwards, advising he would return on Monday. This was payment of wages day and, he said, smiling genially, Alyssa would be most welcome to attend.

Friday was spent showing Letty the rest of the house, including the secret passage which made her giggle delightedly, and looking over the account ledgers provided by Ennis. As seven o'clock on Saturday approached, Alyssa felt she could meet Sir Giles with a modicum of knowledge.

She checked her appearance with a critical eye; she had chosen her best evening gown, a dark-blue three-quarter crepe over a pale satin slip, for the occasion. The neckline was fashionably low and revealed enough of the smooth white skin of her shoulders without being *de trop*. A pearl necklace and earrings completed her toilette.

She looked stylish yet respectable, but when Sir Giles walked into the drawing-room, she felt a shiver of apprehension and wondered how the evening would progress. Alyssa's nature was not vindictive; she voiced her opinions too readily but was as happy to laugh at her own foibles as those of others. She might tease but she would never prolong disagreements unnecessarily. However, she could not remain silent on issues which troubled her deeply and there were questions she needed to ask when a suitable moment arose.

Alyssa, watching him approach, gave no outward hint of her unease. She greeted him politely and added, 'This is Miss Letty Ravenhill.'

'I have been eager to meet you,' said Letty, smiling. 'I did not have the opportunity when you first called. Alyssa has described you, of course.'

'I dare say Miss Paradise's description would be intriguing,' he said, with an amused glance at Alyssa, 'and Mr Brook's. Does he stay long?'

'Charles has business which has taken him back to London: he will not return for some time,' explained Alyssa.

'I see,' he murmured.

With a studied lack of tact, Letty said, 'Thank goodness he has gone; Charles was utterly miserable and making Lyssa the same!'

'Indeed? I gathered Mr Brook's mood was not a convivial one,' he said, smiling wryly.

Alyssa eyed him uncertainly. 'He was concerned for my welfare.'

'I have no quarrel with that, but why he must be in such high dudgeon, I can't imagine.' He raised his brows. 'Perhaps he ate something which disagreed with him?' he said solemnly.

'No, he did not,' replied Alyssa, biting her lip.

'So Friday-faced is his normal appearance then?' asked Gil, in an artless tone.

'N-No,' she faltered.

'Yes!' said Letty, simultaneously.

He executed a small bow and said, his smile lurking, 'I defer to your greater knowledge and trust it was not the Dorset air which affected his constitution, or his temper.'

'I-I believe something *in particular* annoyed him!' declared Alyssa with twinkling eyes.

He grinned. 'Ah, now I understand! Then perhaps a spell in London will restore his good humour.'

'Oh, I wouldn't depend upon it,' said Letty, cheerfully, 'Charles enjoys being gloomy.'

Any further observations were cut short by the news the clerk had arrived and Alyssa went out to find the dapper, smartly dressed Mr Forde already seated in an alcove outside the dining-room. She begged he make himself comfortable and enjoy the refreshments provided, to which Mr Forde, who silently considered this the easiest commission he had ever been asked to undertake, readily agreed.

The dining-room had been laid out in accordance with Alyssa's instructions: places had been set opposite each other at the oak table and candles placed along its length; the magnificent silver epergne decorated with fruit was at the centre; a fire crackled in the hearth, and spring blooms, their distinctive scent filling the air, had been situated about the room.

Alyssa sat across the table from Sir Giles and, as she waited for Rowberry to serve the soup, she glanced at the portrait of Uncle Tom above the fireplace. It had always been her favourite, the artist having captured the essence of his character as well as his physical likeness. Dressed in scarlet regimentals, General Paradise gazed down from his lofty position with the hint of devilment in his eyes she knew so well. She suddenly felt his presence keenly and looked again at the portrait; she was ready to swear his mouth was turned up in amusement!

For Alyssa, the scene was almost dreamlike. She was dining alone with a man who was practically a stranger and yet the setting felt curiously intimate, cocooned away from the world. She looked away from her uncle's image only to find Sir Giles regarding her steadily, and she could not suppress a shiver at his searching gaze.

'How strange,' she observed, 'when I looked a moment ago, I could have sworn Uncle Tom was watching us. He would be pleased we have met his wishes – thus far at least.'

'Amused too, I'd venture,' he said. 'I admired his sense of humour as well as his spirit.' He glanced at the portrait and then back to her face. 'I detect aspects of his features in you, Miss Paradise.'

'Not his side whiskers and grey flowing locks, I hope!'

'No,' he replied, smiling, 'perhaps a certain sweep to your cheekbones. More particularly, you have the same glint of amusement in your eyes that Tom possessed – there the resemblance is uncanny.'

'Our personalities are also similar.'

'So I am discovering. When we first met, however, you were not at all what I expected.'

Alyssa watched his long fingers curl around the stem of his glass, noting the soft, dark hair dusted across the back of his hand and wrist. 'Oh?' she said, quickly. 'Well, *you* were not what *I* anticipated so there we are equal. What did you expect to find?'

'A demure miss, and instead, there was a self-possessed young woman who gave her opinion decidedly. You reminded me of someone but the answer did not occur for several days.'

'May I ask who?'

'My sister, Marianne – she states her views candidly.'

'Do you dislike your sister?' asked Alyssa, arching her brows.

He stared, puzzled. 'Why do you ask that?'

'Because I sensed your antipathy to me that morning, Sir Giles.'

He smiled and shook his head. 'On the contrary, Marianne is a much loved sibling. My hostility was because I had no control over the situation.' He hesitated, then added ruefully, 'To feel powerless is not an everyday occurrence for me, I confess. However, I am prepared to make the best of things now and should apologize – it was wrong to suggest you knew about Tom's will. My manner is sometimes blunt, Miss Paradise. I cannot change it but hope you find me open and straightforward, nonetheless.'

'I admit I thought you brusque, and self-important.'

'Do you still think so?'

'I don't have enough evidence to make a further judgement.'

He laughed. 'At least you are honest!'

'I cannot help it. And if this is the time for confessions, I should say I deliberately provoked you.'

'Why?'

'I don't know,' she answered, incurably truthful. 'I'm not proud of it, but the opportunity was too irresistible to ignore.'

There was a gleam of appreciative humour in his eyes. 'Your uncle would have approved.'

'I expect he would,' she admitted. 'I am not a naive girl, easily browbeaten by a fierce look.'

'Mr Brook is concerned for you,' observed Sir Giles gently.

'He shouldn't be: I am quite capable of looking after my interests.'

'Surely it is natural for him to be unhappy about the arrangements?'

'Perhaps, but he should know if he tries to dictate terms, I'll go my own way.'

'It seems Mr Brook does not know the best way of dealing with his future wife,' he murmured, half under his breath.

'Indeed? And what would you suggest, Sir Giles?' This was an entirely improper question and by voicing it, Alyssa knew she was straying into dangerous territory, but once again, some spark prompted her.

He did not answer immediately, giving her a lingering, contemplative look. He leaned back in his chair and, with quick dexterity, broke the bread on his side

plate into small pieces with one hand. Eventually, his response came. 'A hypo-
thetical situation of course but, if we were betrothed, I would know how to deal
with you.'

'Oh? I am interested to hear your view – hypothetically speaking, of course.'

'Very well . . . since you ask, I would employ a simple but effective punishment – one that ensured you lost interest in obstinacy.'

'Now I *am* intrigued!' she said, laughing. 'What method you would use?'

'Ah, I shall not be specific, but it would be pleasant enough to take your breath
away.'

She stared, but his bland expression gave no clue to his meaning. Alyssa
suspected he meant kissing her thoroughly and her skin started to burn at the
surprisingly pleasant thought. He deserved a set-down, but then Alyssa remembered she was to blame for asking the question in the first place. Unbidden, her
gaze slowly traced the line of his jaw and firm mouth. Warmth coursed through
her veins and, for a moment, the breath seemed to be driven from her body. As
his eyes met hers, a deep blush rose to her cheeks.

He returned her scrutiny without a word until he said softly, 'But . . . we are
only speaking hypothetically.'

'Of course,' she whispered, hypnotized by those low tones and his eyes corus-
cating in the candlelight.

The spell was broken by Rowberry arriving with the roast capons and, during
these moments, Alyssa managed to regain a little composure. Sir Giles was
apparently not a rake – there had been no leering glances or lecherous behaviour
– but he might be a practised flirt and she would do well to remember it.
Rowberry departed and once more, they were alone.

'May I enquire how your cousin received the news?' he said.

'He was very angry. You see, for years he expected to receive Hawkscote.'

'Tom never spoke of him with manifest affection.'

'My uncle was fond of Piers but found the way he ran his life frustrating.'

'So why did your cousin still think he would receive the estate?'

'Oh, Piers can be remarkably thick-skinned when he chooses,' she replied. 'He
didn't believe Tom's frustration would result in Hawkscote being willed to me.'

'He does not sound a particularly perceptive youth.'

Alyssa looked at him quizzically. 'Piers is the same age as I am, Sir Giles; he is
hardly a youth.'

'In my eyes, he is,' he said, with a faint smile.

'You are not Methuselah.'

His smile deepened as he observed, 'Not yet, thank God! Do *you* hold your
cousin in affection?'

'Yes and no—'

'An ambivalent answer, if I may say so, Miss Paradise.'

She laughed and his lazy gaze studied the dimple which appeared in her cheek. 'Yes, but accurate! I like Piers when he abandons all pretension and reverts to his childhood character – fun-loving, adventurous, if sometimes exasperating. But since becoming an adult he has changed, and I am not enamoured of the altered Piers. He did not have a good role model in his father and was indulged by his mother; consequently, his general mien is one of bored selfishness. The will has only added to his cynicism, I'm afraid.'

'Did he fly into a fury?' he asked.

'Yes, but I would have none of it – the situation is hardly my fault.'

'Do you think he will contest, even at this late stage?'

'He might, but he can't really afford the legal fees. However, he's not convinced all is lost and is coming to Dorset soon.'

Sir Giles raised his brows. 'To what purpose?'

'I don't think even Piers knows that,' she said, giving a little shrug. 'Perhaps it will convince him there is nothing further he *can* do.'

'I hope he will not make things more difficult for you.'

'So do I, but I'm not sanguine – trouble seems to follow Piers!' she said, lightly. 'We have spoken of my circumstances; now can I ask you a question?'

'Should I be on my guard?' he queried, smiling. 'You are so direct I wonder what you will say next!'

'Oh, nothing too controversial! I simply want to know who Miss Caroline Nash is. You mentioned in London she would not approve of us dining together.'

Gil did not hurry to respond. He slowly sipped his wine, considering his reply. 'Miss Nash is a close friend,' he said, finally.

'You mean there is an understanding between you?'

'I suppose it could be described that way.'

'That explains her opposition to us being alone.'

'Yes.' For some reason, Gil had never felt more uncomfortable in his life.

'How awkward for you.'

'Caroline accepts the reasons behind it,' he said, choosing his words carefully.

'Then I hope for your sake she proves more accepting than Charles. The repercussions from Uncle Tom's will seem never ending,' said Alyssa, with a sigh.

Sir Giles gave her another searching look. 'Miss Ravenhill seems charming. She must have been surprised to learn she was moving to Dorset?'

'Yes, although she thinks it an adventure. Letty *is* delightful, and for one so young, she also gives her opinion unequivocally!' She laughed. 'However, I am hardly in a position to criticize her.'

'It would not be wise,' he observed, with smiling eyes.

The desserts arrived then, allowing Alyssa to glance surreptitiously at the ormolu clock on the shelf, and she was surprised to see that only ten minutes of the hour remained. She had not expected the time to pass so quickly.

His rich, smooth tones cut across her thoughts. 'Have you met Ennis yet?'

'Yes, I spent an interesting few hours studying the accounts – I did not realize there was so much involved in running Hawkscote.'

'It is a responsibility as well as a challenge, but I have no doubt you will be equal to the task.'

'You think a woman can run a large estate as well as a man?' she asked, incredulous.

'Why not? I am not so narrow-minded in my views on this subject as others. A woman can be successful with good advice.'

Alyssa was astonished, having anticipated he would have an intolerant view of women in business. 'Ennis was helpful and not in the least patronizing – for which, I was grateful.'

'Had he tried, I'm sure he would quickly have become aware of your displeasure!' he said, flashing a grin.

'Politely but firmly,' she acknowledged, as she smiled and held his gaze. 'We have arranged regular weekly meetings.'

'A sensible way to progress. Please do not be afraid to ask questions, either of Ennis or of me. Have you met your tenant labourers yet?'

'Yes, several. I admit I was shocked. They were all obviously undernourished, and they do not even own the land surrounding their house; it belongs to the estate.'

'That is the usual way of things now, Miss Paradise. During the war, corn prices soared and farming expanded to cope with the demand. Large farms engulfed smaller ones and small tenant farmers suffered the most, I'm afraid. Enclosure of land was needed for progress.'

'Couldn't the smaller farmers apply for enclosure?'

'No, because the high costs involved favoured larger landowners. Many small farmers were driven out and are now only labourers on land they once rented.'

'But if profits are high, why don't landowners provide better wages for these poor people driven from their livliehood?' she cried. 'It cannot be right to treat them so badly!'

'Farming is much less profitable than during the war. The Corn Laws have helped a little but even with this protection, profits are down and there must be further progress if even large estates like Hawkscote and my own are to survive.'

'Progress at what cost?' she protested. 'A cost to the labourers, no doubt.'

'Whatever is necessary, otherwise there will be no jobs at all. Mechanization is the future and everyone will have to accept it eventually,' he said, dismissively.

Irritated by the way he brushed aside the potential human suffering, she retorted, 'I witnessed the poverty creeping through Oxfordshire, but here I am encountering it at close quarters. While I am custodian of this estate, I'll do everything in my power to help those who work for me, and the local community.'

'A philanthropic but unprofitable stance – Hawkscote will soon be bankrupt if you try to deal with social problems,' he said, shrugging his broad shoulders.

'Surely profit can be balanced against workers' welfare?'

He eyed Alyssa across the table and said sternly, 'Take my advice, Miss Paradise, don't try any such thing.'

'Oh, I would not be foolish enough to jeopardize Hawkscote's profitability, but I can't stand by and watch the children of those who work for me starve!' she declared, her expression mutinous. 'And if that means ignoring your advice, so be it.'

'Your uncle advised you listen to me on business matters.'

'I'm aware of that, but this is a moral issue.'

'Dear God, are you always so stubborn?' he exclaimed frankly.

'Yes!'

After studying the flushed curve of her cheek and expressive eyes for a long moment, he drained his wine glass and murmured, 'I thought you might be – that does not augur well for my future equanimity.'

Following this candid exchange, conversation during the remainder of the meal was meagre. After the desserts and sweetmeats, he stayed to take a glass of port while she retired to the drawing-room. When he came in a short time later, Alyssa watched as he conversed easily with Letty and admitted to confusion. It seemed Sir Giles possessed a sense of humour; he had apologized for his curtness in London; he had even expressed surprisingly liberal views on women in business, but he had also acknowledged he could be blunt, and his views on the plight of the labourers were heartless. And what was she to glean, if anything, from those curiously hypnotic moments during dinner?

After over an hour in his company, when Alyssa had expected her first unfavourable impressions to be confirmed, she had instead discovered Sir Giles Maxton to be an enigma.

CHAPTER FIVE

The following afternoon, Alyssa was checking the linen cupboard with Letty and the housekeeper, when Rowberry announced they had visitors.

'We are not expecting anyone,' said Alyssa. 'Who is it?'

'Mrs Nash and Miss Caroline Nash, miss. I asked them to wait in the drawing-room.'

Letty grimaced. 'Can we say we are not at home? We are not dressed to receive visitors.'

'I suggested neither you nor Miss Paradise would be able to see them, but Miss Nash would not hear of it.' Rowberry sniffed, his tone obviously disapproving of Miss Nash's dictatorial manner.

'Very well, Miss Nash must take us as we are if she arrives at short notice,' said Alyssa, with a wry glance at her old gown. 'Come, Letty, our visitors await.'

'But I have a tear in my dress and we look positively shabby!' she exclaimed.

'What we are wearing cannot signify much – they would surely prefer not to be kept waiting. However, if you prefer, go and change and come when you are ready.'

'No, I think I'll accompany you after all. I want to see their reaction when we appear in these clothes,' said Letty, chuckling.

They followed Rowberry down the stairs and Alyssa, recalling the scrutiny she had been subjected to earlier in the day, was not completely surprised Miss Nash had called.

Seated in church for morning service, Alyssa had presumed that the young woman near Sir Giles and watching her and Letty intently was the close friend he had spoken of. Caroline Nash was of medium height with a neat, elegant figure and dark hair; her features were attractive, but spoilt by an expression of such haughty severity that Alyssa could well believe Letty's observation that Miss Nash's glance could curdle milk. Determined to be friendly, Alyssa acknowledged her with a smile, only to receive another superior glare in response.

She was prepared for some scrutiny following the strange terms of Uncle Tom's will, but many of the parishioners knew her from past visits, and those who did not were polite enough to study her from the shelter of convenient hymn books.

But Miss Nash made no attempt to disguise her critical appraisal. Alyssa endured it with composure, breathing a sigh of relief when she turned to murmur into the ear of the older lady next to her, presumably her mother. Had the inspection continued, Alyssa might have been tempted to react.

However, when *Mrs* Nash turned to stare and Alyssa was certain she had been the subject of their whispered conversation, it was too much. She repaid Mrs Nash for her blatant scrutiny with a beatific, simpering smile and fluttered her eyelashes. Unfortunately, Sir Giles chose that moment to glance over his shoulder and caught sight of her exaggerated expression. He raised his brows quizzically and a crimson blush stole into Alyssa's cheeks; she fervently hoped he did not think she was smiling like a mutton-headed idiot at him! To her relief, she saw his gaze flick to the still-staring Mrs Nash and his lips give an infinitesimal twitch.

Alyssa would have stayed to speak to him at the end of morning service – he was watching from across the churchyard as the congregation dispersed – but Miss Nash and her mother were already heading her way, and unwilling to undergo an inquisition there and then, Alyssa urged Letty *sotto voce* to make haste to the waiting carriage.

Unfortunately, notwithstanding this hurried exit, it seemed she could not escape an interview with Miss Nash and her mother now. Alyssa opened the door of the drawing-room to hear Caroline announce in cool voice, 'Ah, Miss Paradise! I am Caroline Nash – Sir Giles mentioned me, no doubt. I decided to call at the earliest opportunity.' She waved a hand in the direction of the lady on her right, upon whose grey crimped curls sat a flamboyant bonnet with purple trimmings. 'My mother, Mrs Eugenie Nash.' Mrs Nash smiled fatuously as her daughter continued, 'We live at Frampton Manor, five miles from here, and my father is Squire Nash – an important local dignitary.'

'Sir Giles did mention you,' said Alyssa smoothly, wondering if she had come on his bidding. 'You are his close friend, I understand.'

'Is that how he referred to me?' declared Caroline, visibly annoyed. 'We are more than friends – I expect an announcement regarding our betrothal to appear in the *Morning Post* very soon!' She gave a clipped smile. 'I was certain you would not mind us calling.'

'Not at all,' replied Alyssa, determined to be civil. 'This is Miss Letty Ravenhill, my ward.'

Caroline inclined her head graciously. Mrs Nash remarked, 'A pleasure, I'm sure.'

Sitting down on one of the *chaises* next to her mother, Caroline observed, 'We knew you would be anxious to see us.'

'Anxious?' repeated Alyssa, puzzled.

'Why, yes, because of our connections! My mother and I are at the pinnacle of local society and, since you need our patronage to enter it, we decided to call immediately.'

Mrs Nash nodded. 'There are people you need to be aware of. The Baileys from Dorchester – extremely well connected, you know – Mrs Bailey is a friend of Lady Jersey,' she cooed. 'Then there are the Barringtons, of course . . . oh, and the Westwoods! Indeed, we must not forget the Westwoods – such a venerable family!'

'Thank you, Mama,' interpolated Caroline firmly, with a speaking look. 'There is no need to give a complete list of our acquaintances.' She turned her hard gaze back to Alyssa. 'After seeing you in church, I told Sir Giles I would call as soon as possible.'

'That was kind,' murmured Alyssa, sitting opposite and making a mental note that he had not instigated this visit after all.

'Yes, we are well known—' began Caroline. She stopped suddenly and stared with distaste at her host's faded, worn dress. 'Miss Paradise – your gown! It is so—'

'Shabby?' suggested Alyssa, with a rueful smile. 'I apologize for our appearance but we were helping the housekeeper complete an inventory of the linen cupboard when you arrived. There was no time to change as I did not wish to keep you waiting.'

There was silence until Mrs Nash said in a shocked voice, 'Surely there was no need to assist your servant? Organizing the linen cupboard is not something you should be concerned with.'

'Mrs Farnell was grateful and it allowed me to say which linen I wanted replaced,' said Alyssa quietly. 'Don't you and your daughter undertake such tasks?'

'Certainly not!' declared Caroline. 'I would oversee the work but nothing more.'

'Then we differ, Miss Nash. I have never before in my life had so many servants. At home, we often assisted our maid with chores and it will be difficult to break the habit.'

Caroline laughed incredulously. 'I suppose you will help the kitchen maid with the summer preserving!'

'Perhaps – I have done so before.'

'A quaint idea,' said Mrs Nash, with a titter, 'but quite unsuitable for a lady in your position, or indeed Miss Ravenhill's. You must defer to Caroline's judgement on these matters; she knows *exactly* how a lady of fashion and breeding behaves.'

From under her lashes, Alyssa saw Letty struggling to contain her amusement and scrupulously avoided meeting her eye in case doing so caused her own mirth to bubble over.

'Thank you,' said Alyssa, gravely. 'I fear I have lacked guidance in recent times. You see, I am often tempted to behave unconventionally.'

'I am not surprised,' said Caroline. 'Giles has told me of your uncle's will – dining alone with a stranger should disconcert any respectable young woman's sensibilities and you must be unconventional to agree.'

'Indeed you must,' agreed Mrs Nash, nodding. 'Caroline would not contemplate it! However, if the arrangements cannot be altered, they must be endured, and you must therefore align yourself with Caroline from the start, Miss Paradise. That way no harm will come to your reputation.'

There was a moment's pause before Alyssa said, in a dangerously quiet voice, 'I have no idea what you mean.'

'Mama means you should cultivate my acquaintance as well as follow my advice. Then, by virtue of association, you will take credit from my good name,' explained Caroline, without a hint of irony. 'I carry sufficient authority and influence to limit gossip while you meet these ridiculous terms.'

Alyssa stared. Suddenly, a gleam of devilry appeared in her eyes. 'Oh, dining alone with a man is of little consequence to me,' she began, insouciantly. 'Compared to other situations I have been involved in, it is extremely tame.'

'What situations?' said Mrs Nash, who was a woman of insatiable curiosity.

'Alyssa, do you think you should speak of this?' said Letty. She had no idea what Alyssa was planning but wanted to join in any raillery of these visitors. 'Miss Nash and her mother might find it shocking.'

'I am a woman of the world: I doubt I could be surprised,' retorted Caroline.

'Ah! Then I shall be blunt,' said Alyssa. 'My past conduct has been deplorable. I had such a wild youth my parents despaired of me. I took to gambling—'

'Gambling!'

'Indeed, Mrs Nash. Not by design; I simply found I had passion and a skill for games of chance, and was drawn to them like a moth to a candle.' Alyssa clasped her hands together and sighed. 'I indulged in raucous card parties, playing for such high stakes I blush to recall them now. My mother wept and my father berated me, but all to no avail – I won, and then lost, a fortune.'

'Good gracious!' exclaimed Mrs Nash, her eyes wide with astonishment.

'That is indeed an unfortunate story,' said Caroline in a curt voice, 'but—'

'Oh, my dear Miss Nash, there is more,' cried Alyssa, hurrying on. 'Now you have allowed me association with your impeccable character, I must tell you the whole! My story did not end there, for I was not sated – my passion became an all-consuming craze and when I travelled to London to stay with a distant relative, there was worse to come.'

'Worse . . .' murmured Mrs Nash, faintly.

'*Much* worse!' said Alyssa, with dramatic emphasis and casting her eyes upwards momentarily.

'What happened?'

'When I was no longer satisfied with the stakes and company open to a woman, I disguised myself as man and visited the gaming hells of St James's!'

Mrs Nash's mouth fell open. '*Disguised yourself as a man*! Extraordinary! And gaming hells – how awful!'

Alyssa shook her head. 'On the contrary, I enjoyed the excitement; there was no end to my yearning for adventure. With my adopted disguise of a rich novice from the country, Mr Jack Esidarap' – she giggled like a schoolgirl, adding confidingly – 'that is Paradise backwards, Mrs Nash, and I thought it exceedingly clever of me to think of it – I continued on my path to perfidy. Disguised as Mr Esidarap, I attended prize fights, all-night Faro and Hazard games and even walked down St James's past the bow window of White's Club.'

'Good God!' cried Caroline, spurred into speech.

'Oh, no one saw through my disguise,' said Alyssa, with an elegant shrug. 'I knew what it would mean for a woman to walk in view of the gentlemen's clubs – she would be ostracized forever – but dressed as a *man*, I was nothing out of the ordinary. Of course, I only did it for a bet!'

Mrs Nash made a curious strangled sound and dropped her reticule.

'Oh dear,' said Alyssa, in a concerned tone. 'Do let me retrieve your reticule, Mrs Nash. You are not finding my revelations too shocking, I hope? I warned you my past is colourful.'

The elder woman's complexion had turned puce. She took her reticule from Alyssa, shook her head and valiantly managed to stammer in a choked voice, 'Oh n-no! Indeed, it is m-most illuminating!'

'Well, to return to my story's conclusion, I realized it was time to stop when I unintentionally found myself in – er – perilous circumstances.'

'Not a – not a *duel*, surely?' squeaked her main inquisitor, leaning forwards.

'Please, Mother,' exclaimed Caroline, revolted.

'Bah! Nothing so tedious!' said Alyssa, with a nonchalant wave of her hand. She lowered her voice to murmur conspiratorially, 'No, Mr Esidarap found himself at a most unsuitable revelry at a private club and was forced to leave immediately.'

'Oh! Gracious! Can you mean . . . surely you cannot mean an – an *orgy*!' said Mrs Nash in awed whisper, pressing her handkerchief to her mouth in a vain attempt to smother a gasp.

Alyssa nodded slowly. 'I see I need say no more – you are obviously a woman of great understanding, Mrs Nash,' she declared, with a guileless look. 'I leave the details to your imagination. The experience brought me to my senses, and I left London. Fortunately, my parents welcomed my return and even were willing to forgive my sins. Mr Esidarap was no more from that day onwards. He disap-peared, vanishing forever into the folklore of notorious London gamesters. My parents and I – we never spoke of it again.' She shook her head sadly, 'I settled down to the quiet life I now enjoy although occasionally some remnants of that unconventional character come to the fore and will not be gainsaid.'

'I won't hear a word against you,' said Letty, with a grin. Turning to their visi-tors, she added sweetly, 'Alyssa is the dearest, kindest creature.'

'You are very good, Letty,' replied Alyssa, with a heavy sigh, 'but perhaps Miss Nash, having heard my story, does not think even her reputation can save my tarnished character.'

'I have never heard such a tale,' said Caroline. She was more sceptical than her mother but it was too much, even for her, to accuse Alyssa of telling a Banbury story.

'Nor I – the most extraordinary thing,' agreed Mrs Nash. 'How fortunate you came to your senses in time.'

'Indeed it was, but I must ask you never to mention this to anyone. It pains me to remember, and I only recounted it because of your generous offer to protect me from gossip.'

'Oh, I will not breathe a word,' declared Mrs Nash.

Caroline protested. 'But Giles will want to hear this!'

'You may, of course, tell Sir Giles – I would not ask you to keep it from him.'

'Naturally, I shall tell him. I expect he will have much to say to you on the subject.'

'Oh dear, do you suppose so?' asked Alyssa, with another innocent look.

'He will deliver some words of wisdom on your behaviour!'

'I hope most sincerely that he does,' said Alyssa solemnly. 'Now, may I offer you refreshments?'

'Thank you, no – we have another call to make and must not detain you any longer.'

'That is a pity! Now I have secured your confidence, I hoped to give further details of Mr Esidarap's adventures; I declare there is enough to write a novel. Are you certain you will not stay a little longer and take a glass of ratafia?'

'Well, I would like to hear—' began Mrs Nash.

'No, Mother!' snapped Caroline, glaring. 'Have you forgotten the other engagement we have planned?'

'I must have because I cannot recall anything.' She suddenly caught sight of her daughter's face and blustered, 'Oh! Now I remember. Yes! Yes, we should be going at once, my dear!'

'Making your acquaintance has been enlightening, Miss Paradise,' said Caroline drily, rising to leave.

'For me also. Should I look forward to further guidance soon?'

'I shall offer advice whenever I think it necessary.'

'Then I must learn from you, Miss Nash.' Alyssa turned to Letty, saying, 'We may rest easy, Letty. Thanks to Miss Nash and her mother, we have every hope of being accepted into society.'

'How reassuring,' said Letty, smiling benignly at their visitors and then murmuring, 'So pleased to meet you.'

'Good day,' said Caroline, turning on her heel and urging her mother to hurry.

Not until Alyssa heard their guests depart did she allow herself to dissolve into laughter and tears were soon streaming down her face.

Letty, too, was helpless and when she could speak, said, 'Oh, Lyssa! You should not have done it, but it was extremely funny, all the same! How on earth did you invent Mr Esidarap? I thought Mrs Nash was going to choke on her astonishment.'

'I c-could not endure such appalling conceit any l-longer without exacting a little revenge,' said Alyssa, wiping her eyes as her laughter finally began to subside. 'But, in spite of finding it amusing, I am also angry. How *dare* they suggest we need their patronage? Such pompous nonsense! And I was determined to be civil at the outset too.'

'What will Sir Giles say? Will he guess it is all a fabrication?' asked Letty.

'If not, then he doesn't possess the intelligence I credit him with. How unfortunate he has chosen such a disagreeable, arrogant woman to be his partner. I suppose I shall have to apologize at some point – I would not like him to think I make a habit of inventing stories – but he shall also hear of the behaviour that provoked me.'

'Should you explain to Mrs Nash and her daughter?'

'No. If Miss Nash decides to apologize for her arrogance then I will do likewise, but since I don't anticipate an apology, I shan't enlighten them. Caroline Nash is no fool; she may have guessed but was unwilling to question me.'

'But won't her redoubtable mother tell half the county?' said Letty, still chuck-ling.

'No, poor Mrs Nash will have to keep quiet when she would rather tell the world! They are too nosy and meddlesome to stay away, Letty, and if the story became known, they could no longer associate with us.' Alyssa laughed. 'Let us see how Sir Giles reacts; it will not be long before he hears.'

Sir Giles heard that afternoon. He had called at Frampton Manor and was discussing farming business with Squire Nash in his study. The squire was jovial of countenance, ample of girth and renowned for his easy good humour. He loved his wine, billiards and even the occasional card party, but irritated the distaff side of his household with his blithe refusal to appreciate the importance of social nuances, saying while he did not enjoy tinkling teacups and gossip, he had no objection to his wife and daughter indulging as much as they wished.

He breezed in to the social gatherings held in his drawing-room, smiled, murmured a vague greeting at the ladies gathered there and ambled out again, happy to leave the wagging tongues wholly to his wife and daughter. Living in a female-dominated family, he was always pleased to snatch any opportunity for male conversation.

So, that afternoon, when there was an imperative knock at the door to inter-rupt his conversation with Sir Giles, he said 'Come in,' but his face evinced annoyance at finding no refuge, even in the sanctum of his study.

Mrs Nash, agog with excitement, rushed in, exclaiming, 'My dear, you cannot conceive what we have just heard! Indeed, it is too shocking and never was I in greater need of my smelling salts!' She hesitated, having suddenly noticed the visitor sitting in the winged chair opposite her husband's desk. 'Oh, Sir Giles. I-I am sorry, I did not realize . . . I came straight in without speaking to the servants. So foolish of me.'

'Don't trouble yourself, Mrs Nash. It is a brief visit only and I shall be leaving directly,' said Gil.

'No you won't, by God!' cried the squire, good-naturedly. 'Take another glass of Madeira, Giles. I'm outnumbered by females in this household so sensible conversation from you is always welcome. Help yourself.' He pushed the decanter towards his guest and said, 'Now Eugenie, why are you in such a taking? What gossip have you heard which warrants smelling salts?'

Mrs Nash flashed an uneasy glance at Sir Giles. 'I cannot remember, Henry. It has quite gone out of my mind.'

'Gone out of your mind?' repeated the squire, in amazement. 'Deuce take it, you only mentioned it a moment ago and it was important enough to send you rushing in here. Nothing wrong with your memory usually: you remind me of things often enough.' He shook his head and winked at Sir Giles before speaking again to his wife in a genial tone, 'Come, come – you must recall it. Giles will not mind hearing, I'm sure.'

'Oh dear!' she said, wringing her hands, 'I don't know if—'

Caroline, entering with a satisfied smile on her lips, said, 'I am pleased Giles is here, Mother. We have permission to tell him after all and I know Father will not breathe a word.'

Alyssa's story was retold, with Caroline remembering to intersperse it with asides on the perpetrator's moral corruption and Mrs Nash helpfully providing a running commentary on how her daughter would never be tempted into gambling or, heaven forbid, walking down St James's dressed as a man. 'It made my blood run cold to hear of it!' she declared in conclusion, gripping her hand-kerchief melodramatically.

However, the news was not received in the manner they expected. Sir Giles remained silent, while the squire roared with laughter and slapped his hand on the desk in delight. 'By God, Miss Paradise sounds resourceful! Those young bucks would have been astounded to know they had a woman in their midst!'

'Henry, I am surprised at your attitude!' declared his spouse, 'I thought you would be appalled!'

'Not in the least,' he said, chuckling. 'It's a mild tale compared to some from my youth and there's no damage done at the end of it. What do you think, Giles? Do you appreciate Miss Paradise's sense of adventure, or are you shocked?'

Gil had said nothing, his expression remaining inscrutable, but he had cleared his throat and taken a long draught of Madeira when it was revealed Mr Esidarap had attended an orgy.

At the squire's question, he raised his brows quizzically and said, 'No, not shocked, but Miss Paradise continues to surprise me. She appears a spirited young woman and I find that refreshing.' He turned to Caroline and declared softly, 'So, you have already visited Hawkscote. How odd Miss Paradise confided this at your first meeting – what prompted her to do so?'

'I cannot imagine. We conversed amicably for several minutes before she spoke of it,' said Caroline, displeased to hear Alyssa described as refreshing.

'Oh yes, everything was friendly between us,' agreed her mother. 'Caroline commented on their gowns at first – they were very shabby – then Miss Paradise told us that they had been *helping their servant!* As you may imagine, we gave some morsels of advice.'

Anger was visible on Giles's features but quickly masked, and he remarked sardonically, 'I expect that was well received.'

'She recounted this extraordinary tale afterwards,' said Caroline. 'Of course, I do not believe it.'

'So it's not true?' asked the squire, disappointment in his voice.

Caroline sniffed. 'I don't think so, but it would hardly have been proper to question her further.'

'But she was most persuasive, Caroline!' protested Mrs Nash. 'Indeed, she said expressly it was your offer to protect her from gossip that encouraged her to tell us!'

'Ah, I begin to understand,' said Gil, drily. He leaned back in his chair and stretched both legs out in front of him, crossing one exquisitely booted ankle over the other and pushing his hands into the pockets of his breeches before continuing, 'Why would you think Miss Paradise needs your assistance, Caroline? Surely that was high-handed?'

Caroline detected the hard edge in his voice and grew indignant. However, she fought against showing her irritation, clasping her hands together instead and remarking calmly, 'I offered association with my good name to benefit her; you may call that high-handed, I say it is generous. Do you condone her past then?'

'It is not for me to condone or condemn it. I know nothing of her past, only what I learnt from Tom.'

'Surely every fibre of your being is revolted by this amoral tale?'

'Good God, Caroline – stop being so prudish!' exclaimed her father in exasperation, 'You make too much of the matter!'

Gil looked anything but revolted. He smiled enigmatically, the laughter lines at the corners of his eyes creasing as he did so. 'But you have just told me it is not true. I cannot feel revulsion for something that did not happen.'

'Oh! But you intend to question her?' cried Caroline, frustrated.

'You can be certain I will.'

'That is something at least. I said you would enquire about her past iniquities.'

His smile grew. 'Did she respond?'

'She said she hoped you would try,' said Mrs Nash.

He grinned, murmuring cryptically under his breath, '*Touché*, Alyssa.'

'I beg your pardon, I did not hear what you said,' protested Caroline.

'No matter; rest assured I shall quiz Miss Paradise severely at our next meeting.'

'Good,' said Caroline, mollified by the thought of Alyssa receiving a cutting invective.

Squire Nash drained the remnants of his glass and said convivially, 'Now, Gil, don't be too hard on the girl! Whether this tale is true or false, she sounds a lively miss and I'd like to meet her. Far too many young women these days with not an ounce of spirit and Miss Paradise appears a mite different.'

Giles smiled at the squire. 'She is.'

When Gil drove away, he struggled with a desire to turn his carriage towards Hawkscote, but decided against it: the evening was growing late.

Miss Paradise had occupied his thoughts a great deal since they had dined together, although he preferred not to dwell on why he had spoken of his remedy for her obstinacy. Her defence of the workers' situation had led him to question his own conscience. When had he last visited his labourers? Not for many months, and he felt a pang of guilt at the realization he no longer knew how his employees lived, or how much they were paid individually; he was only aware of wage outgoings as a whole. Alyssa's comments had made him determined to rectify this. Of course, Caroline would not approve of illiterate labourers receiving any consideration.

Caroline. His dark brows drew together in a frown as he recalled her sadistic pleasure in retelling the story. He knew why – she wanted him to echo her outrage and utterly condemn Alyssa. Well, she had been disappointed; he found the episode highly amusing and succeeded only through iron resolve and a gulp of wine in containing his laughter. He could not recall when he had last felt so animated and entertained, and in that respect, Alyssa was unique. Propriety dictated she should not have invented the anecdote, but he had no doubt it had resulted from provocation. Caroline's conceit was becoming insufferable.

He grinned as he savoured again the image of Alyssa telling Caroline and her mother Mr Esidarap's story, and considered his next dinner appointment with Miss Paradise could not come soon enough.

CHAPTER SIX

Piers surveyed the south lawns of Hawkscote and moodily reflected again on his misfortune. He'd had a damnable time of it in London. Once his creditors discovered he was not to receive his uncle's estate, they had beaten an insistent path to his door and Piers was only too pleased to leave for the country. He was accustomed to being short of ready money, but it was a new and unpleasant experience to be dunned so assiduously by tradesmen, acquaintances and even friends.

The clock chimed four and he wondered where Alyssa was. Rowberry had asked him to wait in the drawing-room while she completed business with her agent, but that was half an hour ago, and, having arranged to meet James Westwood for dinner, he could not stay long. Still, he wanted to announce his arrival and cast his eye over Hawkscote. It was over a year since he had visited Tom and even then, he had only stayed a week. By the end of that time, his uncle's comments about his lifestyle had hit their mark and Piers was anxious to leave. At least he and Tom had separated on good terms, for which Piers was grateful – Tom had died before he could see him again.

Piers thought he knew the house and gardens well, but in truth he had never paid attention to the fine detail of either, partly because of his youth and, more recently, believing with nonchalant arrogance they would belong to him one day and he could inspect both at his leisure then. Now the prize had been taken away, he perversely found himself studying the room and its contents with an avaricious gaze. He strolled over to inspect a painting, leaning one hand on the mantelpiece as he did so, and noting with satisfaction it was by Gainsborough.

Piers hoped some plan to win the estate would present itself while he was in Dorset. He had the glimmer of an idea which seemed impetuous even to him but he had not yet discounted it. His musings were brought back to the present abruptly by a slight noise behind him. He jumped and his hand gripped the carved wooden fire surround – someone else was in the room. Impossible! He was alone, no one had entered from the hall, yet the sound had emanated from the other side of the room. Slowly, he looked over his shoulder.

'Hello.'

Before him, in the middle of the room and having materialized seemingly out of thin air, stood a slim, young woman in a grey silk gown; it was she who had apparently uttered the single word. He blinked, thinking his brain was deceiving him, and her large eyes, a peculiarly beautiful shade of greenish-grey, regarded him steadily as he stood in mute astonishment. Fair hair, dark brows and lashes and a dainty mouth upturned in a smile completed the vision. Piers rubbed his eyes and looked again, half expecting the image to have disappeared. However, still the girl gazed back, her figure infused with an almost ethereal calmness.

Finally, he struggled into speech, and whispered, 'W-where have you come from?'

'Did I startle you?'

'Are you *real*, or some kind of apparition?'

'Oh, I'm real enough!' said Letty, with a laugh.

'Then how the deuce did you get in here?' said Piers, exhaling slowly as he began to recover.

Letty indicated the panelling. 'There's a secret passage behind there. I was exploring it, came into this room and found you here.'

'Of course! Devil take it, I thought I was going mad!' He raked his fingers through his hair. 'I'd forgotten about that dam— I mean, deuced passageway! Lord, haven't been through there since I was a boy.'

'You know of its existence then,' said Letty, surprised. 'I suppose I should ask what you are doing here.'

'Waiting to see Miss Paradise.'

'Oh, I see. Do you live locally?'

'No.'

She sat down, looking at him quizzically. 'I didn't think I had seen you before.'

'I have seen *you*,' replied Piers, his eyes roaming over her face and recognition dawning.

'You have? When?'

Placing his hands on the chair in front of him, Piers said, 'Unless I am very much mistaken, you are Miss Letitia Ravenhill.'

'You have the advantage of me then, sir, for I cannot guess your identity. Indeed, you might be an escaped convict or some other nefarious creature, here to steal bounty. But, no – you cannot be. You are too well dressed and your expression is too benign for that, although it is sullen. Why do you scowl so?'

'I am not scowling!' cried Piers, affronted.

'Yes, you are. It does not suit you,' remarked Letty cordially. 'Why, if only you would remove those furrows from your brow, you could be described as pleasant-looking.'

He gasped. 'Well, of all the—'

'You are about to say that my manner is unbecoming, but I still don't know your name.'

'I'm Piers Kilworth. I saw you at my aunt's – that is to say, Alyssa's mother's – funeral a few years ago.'

She studied him with interest. 'So *you* are Lyssa's cousin. I don't remember, but I have heard about you recently.'

'Nothing good, I'll warrant,' he said, his mouth twisting into a sardonic smile as he walked over to sit near Letty. 'I'm the black sheep of the Paradise family, you know – totally irredeemable.'

'I've heard nothing *very* bad, Mr Kilworth.'

'Surely you can call me Piers, in view of our connection through Alyssa?'

She shook her head. 'That would not be right – I do not know you. Indeed, we should not be alone, but I suppose it must be considered unexceptional as you are Alyssa's cousin.'

'But you just said you had heard about me.'

'From Alyssa, yes, but I will judge you myself now.'

'What has she told you?' asked Piers, curious to hear what this forthright girl knew.

'Do you want the truth?'

'Of course. After receiving one jolt with your unexpected appearance, I believe I can withstand another,' he said, ironically.

'That you were a charming boy, who has grown into a self-indulgent man, wasting his talents on a sybaritic lifestyle.'

Piers gave a chuckle and folded his arms across his chest. He said, mockingly, 'A sad but correct indictment! I cannot fault Alyssa except in one thing: I have no talents to waste. My only aptitude is for spending money, at which I am exceedingly good.'

'Have I offended you?'

'No,' he said, shrugging.

She looked at him from under her lashes. 'I-I do not believe you should speak in that way,' she faltered, 'saying you have no talent – everyone has, you know.'

He shook his head. 'Not I. At least, none I have yet discovered – apart from the one I mentioned.'

'Bah! That is not a talent; any fool can squander money.'

'So I am a fool then?'

She blushed but tilted her chin defiantly. 'For getting into debt – yes.'

Regarding her with a fascinated eye, he asked, 'Are you appointing yourself my moral guardian, Miss Ravenhill?'

'No. If you are stupid enough to gamble and while away your life to no purpose that is your business.'

Piers stirred uneasily in his chair. With very few words, this doe-eyed slip of a girl had succeeded in making him feel ashamed. He pushed away the thought and said in a cutting voice, 'Don't flatter yourself you would have success lecturing me – my uncle and Alyssa chastized me for years, and to no end.'

Letty did not answer but studied his expression and, with a devastating smile, said eventually, 'Oh dear, it is too bad!'

'What is?' he replied, blankly.

'You are scowling again, Mr Kilworth,' she declared, shaking her head. 'An unfortunate habit, far worse than wasting money.'

He fell silent for a long moment, watching her. 'You're a curious young woman. You appear from nowhere to speak of morality, and then admonish me for scowling! What am I to make of you?'

'Whatever you like – I am not your conscience, or your keeper.' Looking hurriedly away, she smoothed her hand over the skirt of her gown. 'I-I'm sure Alyssa will be here any moment,' she said, adding, 'where are you staying?'

'With James Westwood and his family, outside Dorchester.'

'We have heard of the Westwoods; Mrs Nash told us of them.'

'Mrs Nash? I haven't had the pleasure of meeting that lady – a gap in my knowledge, for which I apologize.'

'She is the mother of Caroline Nash, Sir Giles Maxton's friend, and a *grande dame* of local society,' said Letty, with a shudder.

'Ah! I take it she does not meet with your approval?'

'She's an interfering sort, as is her daughter.'

He grinned. 'I'm sure my cousin dealt with them accordingly.'

'She did,' said Letty, with an answering smile.

'Has Alyssa met Sir Giles yet?'

'She dined with him last Saturday.'

'Hmm. And have you seen any of the estate?' asked Piers.

'Only a fraction, but Ennis, the land agent, introduced us to the labourers,' said Letty. 'Alyssa is with Ennis now – he invited her to attend when the wages are paid. She takes her new responsibilities seriously.'

'Why must she be so tediously righteous?' protested Piers with a sigh.

Letty chuckled and said, 'She wants to learn more about the property she has acquired.'

'How obliging of you to remind me of my disappointment,' he muttered.

'Oh, pray do not take refuge in sulking,' pleaded Letty, reproachfully. 'I find it dreadfully lowering to be with a person who is miserable for no good reason. Charles has the same effect on me.'

At this comparison, Piers leapt to his feet and paced about the room, expostulating, 'Charles! Good God, don't, I beg of you, draw parallels between me and that prosy bore! We are not at all alike.'

'Well, you don't appear to be a prosy bore—'

'Thank you!' he threw over his shoulder.

'—but before he went back to London, Charles cast a damper over everything with his sulks. I would not like to see Alyssa made unhappy again by unwarranted petulance on your part, Mr Kilworth.'

He stopped his pacing and stared. 'My dear girl, I've had every expectation removed by a single sweep of my uncle's pen – under the circumstances, I hardly think my resentment is unwarranted.'

'Some initial anger was understandable but you should not still be wallowing in self-pity. Why do you behave like a spoilt child?'

'*No one* has spoken to me in this manner before – not even Alyssa!' he exclaimed, a fierce rasp in his voice.

'Perhaps if they had, you would not act as you do,' observed Letty, offering a serene but knowing smile.

He glared and a deep frown gathered on his brow. He was about to voice a biting riposte but, observing Letty's smile and charming features, Piers suddenly seemed unable to sustain his rancour. His sneer died away, his bellicose manner softened and his mouth began to curve in genuine amusement. Taking a step towards her, Piers laughed and said in a low, husky voice, 'Why, Miss Ravenhill, you are the most—'

His reply was cut short by the door opening to admit Alyssa. She halted on the threshold, her surprised glance flicking between the two occupants. 'Piers! I did not expect you so soon.'

Swiftly, he moved away from Letty and drawled, 'Hello, Coz.'

'When did you arrive?'

'A short time ago. Didn't Rowberry inform you?'

'I asked not to be disturbed and came straight here from meeting Ennis,' she explained.

'I left London sooner than anticipated and wanted you to know I am in the area. Once it became known I could not settle my most pressing debts, it became a little uncomfortable there.'

'No doubt an unpleasant experience,' said Alyssa. She sat at the bureau and looked through the letters which had arrived earlier, adding, 'You have clearly introduced yourselves. Has he made himself agreeable, Letty? Piers can be irascible or engaging, depending upon his mood.'

'He has been tolerable, I suppose.'

'My behaviour has been exemplary under the circumstances, Coz – Miss Ravenhill gave me the most appalling shock earlier and my heart almost required a surgeon's ministrations.'

'Oh, what fustian!' cried Letty, laughing, 'Sir, you are untruthful – your heart was never in danger when I appeared from the passageway!'

He shook his head. 'I defy any gentleman not to be overset when confronted by such a charming spectre!'

'I wish I had seen your face at that moment, Piers,' said Alyssa, smiling. She put the letters on the desk, and looked into her cousin's face. 'Let me be frank – what do you hope to achieve by coming here?'

'I've no clear notion, Coz. Before I left town, that dusty old scribe Bartley confirmed there are no substantive grounds to contest but, as I told you, I've a mind to cast an eye over things. However, I have recently discovered my visit may hold unexpected compensations,' said Piers, his gaze resting momentarily on Letty.

'But you may not meet Sir Giles for some time,' said Alyssa, who thought it wiser to ignore this last, veiled comment.

'I intend to call and introduce myself. Have you any objection?'

'Several, but none you will regard. Please don't engage in impolitic conversation with Sir Giles, Piers.'

'Whatever my faults, you can't accuse me of bad manners,' he drawled. 'I would never display such a lamentable lack of subtlety.'

'Unlike Charles,' murmured Letty.

Piers laughed. 'Lord, yes!' He raised his brows quizzically and added, 'O-ho, has Charles been endearing himself to the locals already? Ah! No need to offer any confirmation – I see by Miss Ravenhill's expression I am correct. Really, he employs the most cow-handed methods! What do you see in The Brook Bore, Alyssa? You, my favourite cousin, are above him in so many ways; consider carefully before throwing yourself into Charles's dreary embrace.'

'I am your *only* cousin, and I don't think I should discuss my feelings for Charles with you,' said Alyssa, colouring. 'He has gone to London.'

'Thank God!' he said, with pithy disregard for circumspection. 'At least I shan't have to endure his company.' He yawned theatrically. 'You see, I find even discussing him soporific. Tell me, is the estate still lucrative?'

'Well enough, it seems, but farming in general is not as profitable since the war. The countryside is in the midst of change and Hawkscote needs to adapt.'

'What sort of change?' asked Piers.

'Mechanization is looming; more reliable machines are being developed which will alter the way estates like this are run,' she explained. 'The labourers are poorly paid and, when you add the fear of losing their jobs to machinery, their simmering anger is understandable. I have spoken to the labourers and they do not earn enough to feed and clothe themselves, let alone their families. I have promised to see if I can increase their pay.'

'You'll bankrupt the estate if you're too generous,' observed her cousin, who had been listening intently.

'There is room, I think, for a small increment, but before I take any action, I'll give it further consideration. Draper, who is one of the labourers and seemingly their spokesperson, was forceful in his pleadings today, until Ennis told him to watch his tongue.'

'Was he aggressive?' enquired Letty.

'No – not exactly aggressive, but he said he and his family would be better fed in the workhouse.'

'He sounds an ungrateful sort! Constrain your good deeds to educating your deserving brats, Coz, and leave Ennis to manage the labourers.'

'I intend to establish a school in Dorchester eventually, but I cannot ignore my workers' plight.' Alyssa sighed. 'It would be sensible to ask Sir Giles for his advice, I suppose.'

'I'll be interested to hear his suggestions,' he replied, with a sceptical look.

Later, Piers left for his dinner engagement after eliciting an invitation, against Alyssa's better judgement, to call at Hawkscote whenever he liked.

The rest of the week passed quickly. Alyssa and Letty received several cards to attend summer events and, to Alyssa's amazement, they were also invited, by virtue of a gilt-edged card grand enough to request an appearance at Court, to attend the Nashes' annual evening party. As Saturday approached once more, Alyssa became preoccupied with meeting Sir Giles again. Even upon reflection, she did not regret telling Mr Esidarap's story, but admitted to feeling nervous, and to offset this, allowed Letty to dress her hair in the newest fashion: swept into a careful disorder of curls, with several burnished ringlets allowed to fall loose. The knowledge she looked her best gave her extra courage.

On his arrival, she felt a shiver of feminine satisfaction at the frank admiration in his eyes, and, when they were once again plunged into the secluded aura of the dining-room, she blushed under his more obvious scrutiny.

Alyssa would have been gratified to know she presented an utterly delightful picture to her companion. His breath had caught in his throat the moment he saw her and now, seated opposite, her effect upon him was profound. The candlelight highlighted the copper and bronze hues in her hair, while dark expressive eyes gazed back with their usual hint of challenge mingled with humour. From under half-closed lids, he admired the alabaster skin of her neck and shoulders and the smooth swell of her breasts, tantalizingly just visible above the lace of her dress. Damnation! He felt as helpless as a callow youth, unable to contain his urges. Never before, he acknowledged somewhat bitterly, had he felt as attracted to any woman as he did to Alyssa Paradise, in spite of their fiery exchanges to date. But she was promised to someone else while he had Caroline to consider. However, try as he might to hold these dicta in his head, the feelings could not be annihilated. Struggling with his conscience and his desires, he curled his hand, which rested on the table, into a fist to control the gnawing compulsion to reach out and touch the slender fingers lying inches from his own.

Watching carefully from across the table, Alyssa discerned none of this from his urbane expression. While a coat of blue kerseymere showed his physique to advantage, he also wore a fine linen shirt and his neckcloth was tied with simple but exquisite style, the white fabric in potent contrast to the faint, dark shadow covering his jawline. Alyssa swallowed; Sir Giles exuded a heady mixture of masculine power, style and sharp intellect.

How long it would be before he broached the subject of Mr Esidarap? Alyssa observed his hand curling into a fist and wondered if it was an indication of his inner fury. Whatever his opinions, she would prefer to discuss the issue immediately rather than have it hang over them.

She was to have her wish. As soon as the servants withdrew, he began. 'Miss Paradise, I have to take you severely to task. You have, I understand, enjoyed an – er – unusual past, and stand in need of censure.'

Alyssa raised her brows. 'Oh? By all means try, but I cannot promise to take note,' said she, still trying to ascertain his underlying mood. Dear God, this man could be maddeningly inscrutable when he chose!

'Let us be clear: you told Caroline and Mrs Nash how you took up the disguise of a man – a certain Mr Jack *Esidarap* – and travelled about town for some weeks under this guise, taking part in most unsuitable activities?'

She nodded.

He touched his napkin to his lips. 'Caroline was greatly shocked – indeed, she told me so that same afternoon.'

'I thought it would not be long before you heard,' she said drily.

'Indeed.'

'Miss Nash and her mother were no doubt at pains to give you the sensational details,' murmured Alyssa, blushing but defiant.

'Every one,' he acknowledged.

'And doing so gave Miss Nash great satisfaction?'

'Without question; her gratification was marked,' he confirmed tonelessly.

There was a long silence. Alyssa felt obliged to apologize, even though she had felt no similar compunction towards Caroline Nash.

With the colour heightened in her cheeks, she said in a determined voice, 'I will apologize – but to you alone, Sir Giles. It was wrong of me, but I assure you it was not done without severe provocation. Some devil prompted me to speak of Mr Esidarap in response to their atrocious arrogance and condescension. I am forced to speak plainly, but you should know the reasons for my behaviour and, indeed, I am only sorry I didn't act in an even more outrageous manner. They might have been better served if I had.'

Alyssa concluded a little breathlessly and bit her lip, ready for his verbal onslaught and the ensuing argument; she would not give ground if he defended Miss Nash.

But Gil uttered no angry rejoinder. Instead, a smile played on his mouth at the sparkling fury in her eyes. 'So, it isn't true then?' he said, quietly.

She looked up at the amusement in his voice and relief flooded through her. He had not taken offence and she was pleased. For some reason, she did not wish to lose any of his good opinion so far gained.

'No, of course not! You are teasing me – you knew all along it was not, indeed you *must* have . . . didn't you?' she asked, with a chuckle.

'I guessed almost immediately. There is no need to apologize because I can imagine the provocation offered – suffice to say I am aware of Miss Nash and her mother's conduct on occasion.'

'Then you don't blame me?'

'No,' he said, a grin spreading across his face. He leant forward and said in a soft, accusing voice, 'You are a mischievous imp, Miss Paradise! I had a devilish game to contain my amusement when Caroline and her mother recounted your story. Thank God I had a glass of wine to hand when they mentioned the orgy!' He laughed. 'Caroline is sceptical, but I doubt Mrs Nash will recover from the excitement for some time!'

'Oh, I'm *desolated* to have caused you discomfort, Sir Giles,' she said, her eyes dancing. 'I don't make a habit of inventing stories, you know.'

'Next time, oblige me with prior notice: I would have given a great deal to be present during the first telling. You may be surprised to know I have a sense of humour.'

'So I am discovering. It *was* amusing. Mrs Nash hardly knew whether to be appalled, or laugh hysterically, and she had difficulty smothering her gasps with her handkerchief,' said Alyssa, a delicious dimple appearing.

'Perhaps I shall have the honour of meeting Mr Esidarap one day,' replied Sir Giles, giving a deep chuckle. 'He sounds an intriguing character!'

'There is one facet of my outrageous tale that is true: I am excellent at cards. I always won against Piers when we were younger, although we only bet half-penny points!' she said, laughing.

'Then I must be on my guard when we play.'

'I promise not to take too many vowels and relieve you of your fortune!'

'Precocious wretch,' he said, affably. 'I am no sluggish player – we should pitch our skills against each other at the first opportunity; I've a mind to teach *Mr Esidarap* a lesson!'

She pursed her lips and rolled her eyes in mock horror. 'Gracious, I am all of a quiver!'

He laughed and his eyes met hers. Suddenly, his laughter died away even as their gazes remained locked together. Tension crackled and arced between them. Alyssa could feel it . . . touch it almost. Her skin grew warm under his study, and she regarded him in some confusion, unable to comprehend the morass of feel-ings now unleashed within her. A spark of emotion – regret, resignation or perhaps even sadness – was briefly visible in his eyes until it was quickly hidden under lowered lids. Then, he gave a wry smile and reached forward. Alyssa consciously held her breath, thinking he was about to brush his fingertips across the bare skin of her arm, but he only took hold of the wine decanter.

'I-I am in need of some advice, Sir Giles,' she said, hurriedly. 'Since we discussed it last week, I have looked more closely at the wages and the amounts do not even cover essentials. I spoke with some of the workers on Monday, and Jonas Draper urged me to increase the wages—'

'I trust Draper was not offensive?'

'He was forceful but still polite. Do you know him?'

'Only by reputation. He is a good worker but renowned as a firebrand, and something of a troublemaker. He is relatively new to the area. From what I hear, I do not trust him; neither, I believe, did your uncle. General Paradise planned to dismiss him but was taken ill before he could do so. I strongly advise you not to be dragged into discussions about wages with a malcontent.'

'But I—'

'Do as I ask, on this one matter at least,' he interjected. 'Let Ennis handle it.'

'He works for me, Sir Giles – I cannot avoid him altogether.'

'You are the stubbornest woman I have ever met!'

'I can't help it,' protested Alyssa. 'I'm sorry if I displease you.'

'You do not displease me; on the contrary—' He hesitated, sighed heavily and rubbed his palm along his jaw before adding quietly, '*Please*, Miss Paradise, promise you will avoid Draper wherever possible?'

'Very well,' she agreed, seeing he was in earnest. 'I give you my word not to seek him out. Is that sufficient?'

'I suppose it must be.'

'I have made notes on the wages and the expenses of one labourer and his family – would you be kind enough to look at them?'

'You are still set on this?'

'Yes, perhaps even more so having spoken to the labourers.'

He nodded and said, 'Very well. Do you have your notes to hand?'

'It will take me but a moment to fetch them.' Alyssa was gone from the dining-room only a short while and returned in a rustle of silk, a single sheet of folded notepaper in her hand. She passed it to Sir Giles who skimmed his gaze over the page.

'I will study your figures, but it would help if I came to Hawkscote and looked through the accounts before giving my final opinion,' he said. 'Would that be acceptable?'

'Perfectly.'

He raised his brows. 'No disagreement this time?'

'No.'

'Miss Paradise – you surprise me!' he observed, with a grin.

Later, as Alyssa sat at her dressing-table unpinning her hair, she mused over the evening and saw her smile reflected in the mirror. Sir Giles was an engaging dinner companion and, despite their clashes, she found his company exhilarating. Too much perhaps, for when he suggested looking at the accounts, she had readily agreed.

Sir Giles seemed genuinely concerned about Draper. Surely there could be no other reason than wishing her not to become embroiled in discussions? And yet, for a moment, she believed Sir Giles was anxious for her personally. No, she must have imagined it. Draper's discontent was unlikely to extend beyond grumbling, but she resolved to keep to her promise and not ask his opinion again when there were other, less combative labourers she could speak to.

There was a tap at the door and Alyssa murmured, 'Come in,' to which request Letty entered, carrying a candle.

She sat down on the edge of the bed. 'I saw your light was still burning and wondered how your dinner had progressed. Was Sir Giles angry about Mr Esidarap?'

'Quite the opposite, love: he found it amusing.'

'Famous! I *knew* he wouldn't ring a peal over you – he has a healthy appreciation of the ridiculous, I think.'

'It seems so. He even understood the provocation I received.'

'Did he?' said Letty, astonished. 'If he realizes how odious Miss Nash can be, why is he going to marry her?'

'I-I don't know – that is not my concern,' faltered Alyssa, closing her jewel box and placing it in a drawer. 'He will be condemned to a miserable marriage, to be sure.' Alyssa finished unpinning her hair, and turned around to continue, 'I must tell you I have received two letters from Charles. His business in London is going well and it seems he has met, quite by chance, some old friends of his parents. They have a son and a daughter of whom Charles speaks highly and they have attended several functions together now the Season is underway.'

'At least his megrims have ceased and he is willing to wait.'

She nodded. 'I will give him my answer when he returns.' Smiling, she asked, 'Now, what do you think of Piers?'

Even in the subdued light, Alyssa could see the faint blush that rose to Letty's cheeks. 'I-I thought he was diverting and handsome, if a little moody.'

Alyssa looked at the glow in her companion's eyes and thought *Oh, no! Poor Letty!*

Piers, who had reasons of his own for encouraging discontent, wasted little time in seeking out Jonas Draper. As they stepped outside the labourer's cottage to converse in private a few days later, Draper's sullen gaze ran over his visitor with thinly veiled contempt but, using easy charm and sympathy, Piers gradually drew him into his confidence until Draper began to talk more freely.

'It be a disgrace, I tell you!' he muttered curtly. 'The wages we get ain't enough to feed one man, let alone a family! Lord knows something will come of it soon – there's unrest brewing in the countryside right enough and if the gentry don't take note of our complaints, I'm afeared bad things will 'appen. Food prices are risin' and them damn newfangled threshing machines are takin' men's work away as well. How us workers are treated be a scandal.'

'It seems a most unsatisfactory situation,' agreed Piers in a smooth voice. 'If I were running Hawkscote, I would make it my business to meet the labourers' demands.'

Draper looked at him with suspicion. 'Ye would?'

'Of course,' said Piers, nodding. 'After all, it is only a few miserly shillings a week to make the difference between a starving family and a well-fed one. No considerate employer should do less. Nor would I entertain purchasing one of those ridiculous machines when men can carry out the work more efficiently.' He gave a nonchalant shrug and added, 'However, I cannot speak for my cousin

– Alyssa might already be contemplating it.'

Draper's expression turned even sourer. 'Miss Paradise be storing up a bundle o' trouble if she be considerin' that!' he spat angrily.

'I will try to plead your case with my cousin. In my opinion, anything less than three shillings a week increase would be a nip-farthing gesture but' – Piers threw out his hands in a gesture of helplessness – 'it is not my decision.'

Draper's lip curled derisively. 'If she be thinkin' we'll settle quietly, she'll be mistaken. I like a mug of ale now and then and I can't be buying that with nothing.'

'I see. Well, if that is your view, perhaps you might consider carrying out certain – er – tasks on my behalf,' said Piers with a smile. 'Naturally, you would be paid for your efforts.'

After a pause, Draper fixed his eyes on Piers's face and gave him a penetrating look. 'Go on – I'm listenin'.'

CHAPTER SEVEN

May gave way to a warm, sunny June and Alyssa, who was in her room one morning preparing for a shopping expedition, was uneasy.

One reason for her current disquiet was Letty. Alyssa sensed her growing attraction to Piers and while she did not want to interfere, she did not wish to see her hurt. At present, her cousin's gallantry was marked; he was attentive, courteous and less petulant than Alyssa had ever known, but despite these promising signs, she was not sanguine. Even if Piers's congeniality was due to Letty's influence, he might still view her as a passing fancy, someone to be forgotten immediately he left Dorset. None of his previous *amours* had lasted long and she could not discern if his affections were engaged this time. However, Alyssa believed Letty's attachment was already sincere.

And Letty was not her only concern. Two more dinners with Sir Giles had taken place and during the intervening days, he had visited Hawkscote several times to look at the accounts. Alyssa expected these afternoon meetings to be easier, with the secluded atmosphere of dinner being absent, but they were proving equally disturbing. Having him close by as they pored over figures together was a peculiarly gratifying kind of torture. More often than not, he rejected sitting on the opposite side of the desk, preferring to stand at her shoulder. His closeness and the thrill engendered by his arm brushing accidentally against her could not be ignored when the resulting sensation, which began in the pit of her stomach and rushed through her body, was new and astonishingly agreeable.

Just as intoxicating was his warm breath on her cheek when he leant forward to indicate something of interest, mingled with the scent of fresh linen and soap. Every nerve ending tingled in response, her breathing came fast and shallow and her heart hammered against her ribs. Alyssa stubbornly refused to scrutinize why her traitorous body reacted this way and concentrated instead on preventing a tremor entering her voice when she answered his queries.

Alyssa quickly saw how Sir Giles's reputation for business acumen had been gained. Nothing escaped him; every item of expenditure was noted, his manner was direct but not offensive; his reasoning eminently logical; any suggestions practical and explained in terms with which Alyssa could find no fault. Her respect for his understanding of estate management grew, as did her appreciation of his general knowledge as their topics of debate extended wider. Sir Giles possessed a rapier-like intelligence combined with dry wit and Alyssa enjoyed the parry and thrust of their discussions. He also had a keen sense of humour and whenever they disagreed and a compromise was reached, it was accompanied by the deep chuckle Alyssa found attractive; she liked the way his smile reached his eyes.

And those thrilling oases, when the simmering connection between them flared into life, continued. Alyssa felt adrift during these moments for it was then that control over her unbidden responses slipped away.

She got up and pulling on her gloves impatiently, gave herself a mental shake: she spent too much time considering her neighbour. Hurrying downstairs, she found Letty in the hall and said, 'I'm sorry! Are you ready to leave?'

'Yes. I'm looking forward to seeing Dorchester – we only caught a glimpse when we first came.'

'So am I. I wish to visit Hanging Judge Jeffries's lodgings. Did you know he held the Bloody Assizes here, in 1685 and tried three hundred and twelve insurgents in only *five* days?'

'Did he?' replied Letty, shocked. 'Gracious! His blood-thirsty reputation is well deserved then. Ah, here is the carriage.'

They set off into the fine summer morning, the air heavy with the scent of May blossom.

After her eyes had scanned the passing countryside appreciatively, Alyssa turned to Letty and asked, 'What do you wish to purchase?'

'Ribbon to trim my straw bonnet, and new accessories for my evening gown – that is, if we are to attend the Nashes' party?'

'I had to accept, although I do not look forward to it with enthusiasm.'

'Then I cannot make do with my old evening slippers and gloves.'

'Because they are too shabby?'

'Exactly!' said Letty, laughing. 'I won't give Miss Nash and her mother any excuse to be condescending, although Lord knows they don't seem to need one.'

'That is why I intend for us to have new gowns.'

Letty's eyes glowed with delight. 'But how can we? Surely there is no time to order them now?'

'No, but there is an excellent cloth warehouse in Dorchester. We shall purchase whatever is necessary there and, since we are both adept with the needle, make up our own. I procured some ball gown patterns in London and there is no reason why we cannot appear perfectly well attired through our own endeavours. What do you think?'

'Oh, yes! I would enjoy making my gown – after all, we have made morning dresses before – but what of the cost?'

'Mr Bartley confirmed I may draw upon the Hawkscote account for any immediate needs.'

'Famous!' cried Letty. 'Then we shall put the local ladies to shame, including Miss Nash!'

Alyssa chuckled. 'I shall not complain if we do. And as Piers is a guest of the Westwoods, he will receive an invitation too.' Throwing Letty an assessing glance, she added, 'He has visited Hawkscote often, and seems to find as much pleasure in your company as in mine.'

'Do you think so?' pondered her companion. 'I hardly know. Sometimes he is attentive and yet I'm not certain what he thinks of me on other occasions.'

'Letty, I have no doubt Piers is fond of you, but be aware he can present a charming face whenever he wishes.'

She blushed. 'I'm not foolish enough to be entirely taken in by Mr Kilworth. I see his failings as clearly as his qualities.'

'I'm glad, for I would not wish you to be. . . .' Alyssa hesitated, before continuing, 'Well, I trust Piers continues to mind his manners, that is all.'

'At the moment he does. He can be sullen but I have detected no real malice in his character.'

'Piers has been allowed his own way for far too long and is selfish as a result. He could, if he chose, forgo his self-indulgence and become the man he promises to be. However, he could decide to plunge deeper into debt and selfishness. I hope something will be the catalyst for him to take the former path but Piers is an unknown quantity. I'm afraid the general's will angered him greatly.'

'He *is* still annoyed, but I told him to stop behaving like a spoilt child.'

Alyssa laughed. 'Oh, Lord! I'm sure he didn't appreciate that observation!'

'No,' admitted Letty, with a rueful smile, 'but he seemed to find it amusing afterwards. And in spite of his flippant comments, he must be as concerned about the labourers as you are: he told me he had visited the workers to see their living conditions.'

'No one has mentioned this to me,' exclaimed Alyssa, astonished. 'I saw the Fletchers twice last week, and again only yesterday – their young son Samuel is ill.'

'Maybe he did not visit that particular family. What is wrong with the child?'

'He has a fever. I took fruit and a few provisions and have asked Dr Plant from

Frampton to call; the poor boy is very thin and weak to fight illness.' Alyssa furrowed her brow. 'Why would Piers take an interest?'

'Couldn't he simply be worried for their welfare?'

'Perhaps, but I find it strange all the same. Do you know who he spoke to?'

'Draper was one name mentioned during our conversation. Are you going to increase the wages?' asked Letty.

'Sir Giles promised me his opinion on Saturday and I shall make my final decision then. Whatever amount I give, it will not cover all their needs but it will at least be some improvement.'

'How are your dinners with Sir Giles progressing, Lyssa? You seem more kindly disposed towards him recently.'

'He is blunt but not in an uncivil way. Indeed, I think I prefer his candour to pointless chatter – oh, and he has a droll sense of humour.' A tinge of pink rose to her cheeks and she added insouciantly, 'I suppose I like him more now than when we met.'

'Your dinners extend beyond the requisite hour.'

'We find many subjects to discuss, Letty. However, we often disagree.'

'How boring if you did not! Sir Giles must admire your enquiring mind and you no doubt provide welcome relief from his travails with Caroline Nash.' Alyssa grimaced at mention of Miss Nash but offered no comment. 'Have you heard from Charles?' ventured Letty.

'Another letter arrived yesterday. He has been to Almack's with the Crawford-Clarkes – that is the family who are old acquaintances of his parents. He described the people of note he saw, as well as the dancing and refreshments. Charles, it seems, was enamoured of the place although I hear it is considered poor in many respects.'

'I would like to visit London.'

'Would you, love?' answered Alyssa, smiling quizzically. 'Then I think it is time to write to your aunt – after all, she did offer to present you when it was time for your official come-out and wherever possible, every young girl should have a Season in London.'

Letty looked out of the carriage window and said imperatively, 'Yes, please write to Aunt Sophia. Hawkscote will be yours by the autumn, and matters here may make a sojourn in London even more desirable.'

'Why?'

'Because you may be married.'

'*Married*! To whom?'

'Oh, to . . . Charles, perhaps?' murmured Letty, with a queer smile.

'No! I am quite decided upon that issue: I will not be marrying Charles and shall tell him so when he returns.'

'I'm glad,' said her companion, with a little nod of agreement. 'He was not for you, although if you *had* chosen him, I would have tried to like him more. Even so, I still think it best for me to go to London then.'

'Of course. I should have considered it before. You will have a wonderful time and are pretty enough to become all the rage. Now, I see we have arrived on the outskirts of town so where would you like to go first?'

'The warehouse, I think.'

Two hours later, laden with packages and parcels, Alyssa was glad she had reserved luncheon at The Antelope. They had enjoyed a delightful morning browsing over ribbons, muslins, spider gauze, crepe and sarsnet and purchasing new gloves, evening slippers and reticules from the shops in Dorchester. Having arranged for the larger items to be sent on to Hawkscote, they arrived at the inn and were ushered into a private parlour by the landlord. Alyssa sank gratefully on to a chair, removed her bonnet and gloves, declaring, 'I had forgotten how tiring a morning spent shopping can be!'

'So had I,' admitted Letty, with a sigh. 'I'm pleased with all my purchases but particularly the ivory sarsnet and tiny pearl buttons which are an excellent match. Your new swansdown muff and parasol are enchanting too.'

'Shockingly expensive but irresistible,' Alyssa replied, 'How pleasant it is not to consider the expense too closely.'

'No, although I noticed you still haggled with the manager for a reduction!'

'Well, we did spend a significant amount there,' replied Alyssa, smiling, 'and old habits are hard to break.'

The landlord returned bearing the luncheon Alyssa had ordered: a ham, some cold chicken, cheese, bread and fruit. He placed them on the table and then said, 'Begging your pardon, but there is a gentleman outside who wishes you to be informed of his presence. It is Mr Kilworth, miss.'

'Oh, *Piers*! Ask him to come in, if you please.'

A moment later, Piers entered and greeted her as he stripped off his gloves, 'Hello, Alyssa.' Bowing in Letty's direction, he added with a smile, ' 'Servant, Miss Ravenhill.'

'How did you know we were here?' asked Alyssa.

'I was driving past when I saw you disappear inside, and I thought I'd see what had brought you into town.' He threw his coat across a chair, straightened his cravat and sat down, flicking a speck of dust from the sleeve of his jacket. 'Ah, but now I see the reason,' he said, eyeing the pile of packages on the chair. 'Good God, have you spent *all* the Hawkscote inheritance, Coz?'

'No, Letty and I have purchased a few essentials,' she replied, eyes twinkling.

'Deuce take it, you're plump in the pocket and I haven't a sixpence to scratch with,' he said, with a rueful smile. 'Essentials, eh? By gad, I'd hate to see the result of shopping for *luxuries*! Can't see the need myself; both of you look quite lovely today and don't require embellishment.'

'Piers, you are the most obvious toad-eater!' said Alyssa, laughing.

'You wound me, Coz!' said Piers, feigning a hurt expression. 'Miss Ravenhill, I appeal to you: would I utter a falsehood?'

Letty gave a chuckle, 'Yes, if you wanted to be offered lunch.'

'How well you understand my motives,' he said, grinning. 'May I join you? This looks acceptable fare and if you are standing huff, Alyssa, it looks even more enticing.'

They made a good lunch. Piers was at his most charming and erudite and, for the moment at least, seemed to know where the boundaries lay with regard to Letty. To Alyssa's relief, she took his flattery in good part and did not seem to place too much store by it.

Afterwards, as they sipped their coffee, Alyssa said, 'Letty tells me you visited the labourers.'

'I hope you don't mind,' said Piers, looking up quickly. 'I spoke mainly to Draper.'

'I don't mind, but I'm surprised you felt the need to. Did you glean anything?'

He shrugged. 'Just a better idea of their circumstances. He tells me there is an undercurrent of discontent amongst agricultural labourers in the area generally, and it is spreading.'

'I know,' replied Alyssa, 'it is one reason I am reviewing wages. Sir Giles has looked over the accounts and I am waiting for his opinion.'

'Why didn't you ask me? I would have assisted you!'

'If I were buying horses or a carriage, Piers, I would have asked your advice – your knowledge on those subjects is second to none – but you know less than me about farming.'

'You always had an independent streak, but you might welcome my help one day – Hawkscote is too much for you to manage alone.'

'Your confidence is overwhelming,' said Alyssa, drily. 'I believe I am managing perfectly well thus far – and Uncle Tom did request I listen to Sir Giles's advice, not yours.'

'But managing the estate is difficult in these changing times—' he began, aggrieved.

'Perhaps you could help me?' interpolated Letty. 'Alyssa said I might have a horse for riding out and I wonder if you have heard of anything suitable.'

He nodded, and smiled warmly. 'I would be honoured, Miss Ravenhill.

Indeed, there is a fellow locally with a sweet-going little mare for sale which is just the thing for you.' Turning to Alyssa, he asked, 'Are you willing to put up the necessary, Coz? Prime horseflesh doesn't come cheap.'

'As long as the price is not outlandish. There is a thoroughbred in the stables I can use, but Letty needs a suitable mount too, and I would not see her use jobbing horses.'

'Lord, no! I'm sure Letty has light hands, and she needs a beautiful stepper with fine manners.'

'I'm obliged to you for the compliment,' remarked Letty, smiling.

'Offering *you* a panegyric is no hardship, Miss Ravenhill,' he said, with a grin and a wink.

'We should go before you turn Letty's head with your nonsense,' said Alyssa, collecting her shawl. 'We plan to visit Judge Jeffries's lodgings before returning home.'

'What the deuce are you going to some stuffy old building for?' asked Piers.

'Out of interest, and to gain a flavour of local history. Will you accompany us, Cousin? Your education might be improved.'

'Not this time – I can spare myself the tedium of hearing how many of Monmouth's supporters the judge sent to the gallows. I'll accompany you as far as the lodgings then take my leave.'

They made their way down the High Street to the timber-framed frontage where the infamous judge had stayed and were about to enter when a shrill, unmistakable voice from behind Alyssa cried, 'Miss Paradise! Miss Ravenhill! How fortunate – we were on our way to call upon you.'

Alyssa turned to see Mrs Nash and her daughter; Mrs Nash was all flustered excitement while Caroline evinced her usual haughty demeanour.

Alyssa smiled sweetly. 'Oh, we would have been sorry to miss you. Have you been introduced to my cousin?'

The introductions were made with Piers regarding the twittering matron and her daughter with a diffident eye.

'Delighted!' said Mrs Nash, impressed by this pink of the *ton*. She hurried on in a bright voice, 'You are staying with the Westwoods, I believe? Indeed, we had already heard. Such a noble family! There have been Westwoods in the area since the Conquest, and any friend of *theirs* is welcome in our select circle. One cannot be too careful – so many people these days have the whiff of *trade* – and certain standards must be maintained, even in the country. Caroline is most particular about these things, aren't you, my dear?'

'There can be no excuse for lowering one's principles,' agreed her daughter.

Piers's exclamation of disgust, whispered under his breath, was loud enough only for Alyssa to hear. 'Good God!' he muttered, 'Far too high in the instep for my liking!'

'Mr Kilworth, did you receive your invitation to our little summer gathering?' asked Mrs Nash.

'Lord, I wouldn't know if I have,' replied Piers, affecting a bored nonchalance that once again impressed his audience. 'All the cards I receive look the same.'

She stared. 'But you must recall ours. It is distinctive and bears the address of Frampton Manor in large gold lettering.'

'Ah, yes. Now I remember.' He exchanged meaningful glances with Alyssa and Letty before raising his quizzing glass to observe Mrs Nash. 'My dear lady,' he drawled, 'was that *your* card? I am surprised!'

'Surprised? Is there a problem with the invitation?' snapped Caroline, looking down her patrician nose.

'Not with the invitation itself, but the card . . . . oh dear!' Piers sighed. 'Such cards are no longer the fashion – they are quite *out*. I thought ladies of your obvious good taste would know this.'

'No longer fashionable,' exclaimed Mrs Nash, horrified. 'Why not, pray?'

'Too ostentatious; the *haut ton* prefers a less showy affair. No self-respecting hostess in Town would be seen with such an' – he made a moue of distaste – 'extravagant card on her mantelpiece. Unassuming and tasteful is the aim if you want your invitations considered all the crack.'

'This is Louisa Bailey's fault!' protested Mrs Nash to her daughter. 'It was she who told me that style was favoured in London. I *knew* I should not have listened to her.'

'You have been grievously misled,' said Piers, shaking his head sadly. 'It pains me to disagree with your friend, but, having left town recently, I assure you Lady Jersey's invitations are beautifully discreet.'

Mrs Nash drew in a breath. 'You *know* Lady Jersey?'

'I count myself among her acquaintances,' he said, giving a slight bow.

'Then you move in exalted circles, Mr Kilworth!' trilled Mrs Nash. 'Oh, please never mention my little *faux pas* with the invitations to Lady Jersey! I would be *mortified* if she heard of it.'

'My lips are sealed, dear lady,' said Piers, the corner of his mouth quivering as he suppressed a smile.

'Thank you! You are too good.'

Piers bowed again with flawless grace, 'Merely happy to be of service.'

'Will you be attending our party, sir?' said Caroline.

'E'gad, having met you two delightful ladies, I would not miss it,' drawled Piers. 'I shall clear my diary of every other engagement and send off my acceptance as soon as I return to the Westwoods.'

'A distinguished London gentleman will be an asset to our little gathering,' said Mrs Nash.

Caroline, turning to address Alyssa, said in a biting tone, 'Of course, we maintain standards of evening dress.'

'I expected nothing less, Miss Nash. Letty and I are therefore obtaining our gowns from the finest *modiste*.'

'Oh? Madame Fauchon of Bruton Street, perhaps?'

Letty gave a short laugh. 'Madam Fauchon! Gracious, no! We have not patronized her for some time. We use an exclusive mantua maker now – expensive but original designs.'

'*Very* original!' agreed Alyssa.

'Your dresses are being sent down from London, I suppose,' said Mrs Nash, gloomily. 'Did I not distinctly say you should order a new gown from there, Caroline? Why does no one ever pay the least regard to my opinion? For shame if you are outdone by Miss Paradise and Miss Ravenhill at *our* evening party! What will Sir Giles think? Well, we shall have to make the best of it and prevail upon your father to supply funds for those new evening slippers. Ah, perhaps a quantity of lace to trim your jonquil. Yes, that will be just the thing.'

Piers squeezed Letty's elbow in an unseen signal and exchanged another amused glance with his cousin. 'I expect, my dear ma'am, *you* will wear ostrich feathers,' he said.

'Feathers!' shrieked Mrs Nash in astonishment. 'Fie! Whatever do you mean, sir? Feathers are worn at Court on debutantes' headdresses – not by a matron of my age!'

He shook his head. 'If you wish to be bang up to the knocker, there is only one thing to wear – ostrich plumes. Seen it m'self in London only last month when the most dashing dowager of my acquaintance was wearing them. Absolutely *the* latest thing! Three is acceptable – no less, mind you – but no more than eight large ostrich feathers, mounted upright on a tiara, jewelled aigrette or even on a silk turban. You will look magnificent.'

'B-but the inconvenience of wearing them,' wailed Mrs Nash.

'What, pray, is minor inconvenience when set against being a leader of fashion?' he observed, airily. 'Upon my word, you will create a stir among the Frampton ladies, ma'am.'

'Do you think so? I should like that very much,' said she, eagerly. 'I will endeavour to obtain some ostrich plumes although where they are to be found at short notice, I have no notion—'

'Mama, we can discuss this at home,' interjected Caroline. 'I understand Sir

Giles has visited Hawkscote regularly, Miss Paradise?'

'Yes – he agreed to look over the accounts.'

'In great detail, obviously: we have hardly seen him these past three weeks. Is his frequent assistance necessary?'

'He kindly offered his opinion on a matter regarding the labourers,' said Alyssa, bristling. 'I would not waste his time with an idle task.'

'I understand why a person of your inexperience might avail themselves of his knowledge. However, he can be generous to a fault. Sir Giles's own estate is extremely profitable and cannot be allowed to suffer as a consequence of him offering you advice – advice which, it seems to me, falls outside the remit of your uncle's will.'

Alyssa stifled her growing anger with difficulty. 'Surely what help he gives is his decision? In any event, I would not dream of abusing his generosity.'

In the distance, the church clock chimed three. 'It is getting late,' declared Letty, hurriedly. 'We should go inside if we hope to return in good time for dinner.'

'Yes, of course,' said Alyssa, relieved to bring the conversation to a close. 'Good day to you, ladies.'

'Miss Nash, I count myself fortunate to have met you,' murmured Piers. '*Adieu*, or rather *au revoir*, my dear Mrs Nash – and do not forget about the plumes.'

'I shall do my best, Mr Kilworth,' she vowed.

They walked away and Piers, still staring at their retreating figures, uttered a long, low groan. 'Dear God! Why didn't you warn me they were vulgar, pretentious tabbies!'

Alyssa looked at her cousin's profile. 'Piers – you – you *devil*!' she faltered, in a choked voice. '*Ostrich plumes*! Now Mrs Nash will be scouring Dorset for ostrich feathers, and it was all nonsense! I never realized until this moment how alike we are.'

'Have you pitched the gammon to them before then, Coz?' he asked, raising his brows. 'I don't blame you if you have. They deserve it: the mother is a bird-witted snob, and the daughter is a vixen. I don't feel contrite! If Mrs Nash were not so busy cultivating her superior manner, she might be less gullible. Perhaps I should have suggested panniers or an enormous hoop to accompany the plumes.'

'I'm glad you didn't,' admitted Letty, chuckling. 'I found it hard enough to hide my smiles.'

'What on earth is Maxton doing, making an offer for that hard-faced creature?' queried Piers. 'From what I understand of it, he's no need of money. Lord, he'd better cry off before it's too late.'

Neither Alyssa nor Letty could think of a suitable reply to this and, with a smile and a brief bow, Piers left them.

During the remainder of the week, Alyssa and Letty began to work on their gowns, altering the designs to suit their particular tastes. Saturday brought the now familiar sense of anticipation for Alyssa in spite of the headache and sore throat which had troubled her since waking that morning. Ensconced once more in the candlelit dining-room, Alyssa engaged in conversation with Sir Giles but ate very little; she did not feel hungry.

And not only had she lost her appetite; by the time the covers were removed, her headache had worsened considerably. Still, she wanted his thoughts on the labourers, so she asked, 'Have you reached any conclusions about the wages yet?'

He nodded. 'I have, and would like to you study some figures I prepared.' Sir Giles cleared away the wine glasses and laid out two sheets of paper, which he turned slightly to allow Alyssa to view them more easily. 'These,' he said, tapping the first sheet, 'are the calculations you made on the current expenses and wages – nine shillings per week expenses for a family against the seven shillings they receive in wages – and these,' he indicated the second, 'are my costing of what the estate can afford to offer as an increase. As you will see, I have underlined my recommendation at the bottom of the page.'

Alyssa quickly scanned the sheet covered with his bold, even handwriting. The writing blurred in and out of focus as a sudden wave of nausea assailed her. She frowned, trying to ignore it and focus on the page. 'I see. So, one shilling and sixpence is your recommendation. I had hoped to give more.'

'That is not possible unless you want to put the estate into considerable difficulty. You need to set aside capital to purchase some of the new machinery. If the harvest is good, a little further upward movement may be possible but only a few pennies at most.'

'Your calculations are extremely detailed and I can find no fault with them,' said Alyssa, studying the figures. She had no inclination to cavil on any point this evening and felt a curious detachment because of the pain now pulsating in her temples. With a heavy sigh, she said, 'I suppose I must take your advice.'

He smiled. 'Difficult as that may be, it would be the sensible course.'

'But to offer so little!' she cried. 'I feel their plight deeply; how awful it must be to struggle to feed your family.'

'Your conscience does you credit, but do not let it blind you to the wider view – your responsibility is to the estate as a whole. Costs are rising and wages must stay in proportion. The gap between prices and the wages the workers receive has grown too large, and you do right to address it – but only so far. Difficult times are ahead in farming and more uncomfortable decisions may follow, but these problems must be faced if Hawkscote is to survive.'

'If I cannot offer more in wages perhaps I can arrange some basic education for the children. To grow up in ignorance is very sad, and offers no future.'

He looked at her in admiration. 'You intend to act as a benefactor in that way too?'

'Yes, I hope to set up a school in Frampton or Dorchester using estate funds. I helped with a similar institution in Oxfordshire and Letty and I taught the children sometimes.'

'I see. You continue to surprise me, Miss Paradise.'

She blushed under his warm gaze and busied herself collecting the papers to cover her confusion. 'Th-Thank you for all your work – I'll give instructions to Ennis. I-I'm sorry to have taken up your time with this.'

'Not at all – in fact, I am reviewing my own workers' wages as a result. I would be happy to continue with our afternoon meetings and believe I can offer further advice, if you will allow me.

'I have no objection, but Miss Nash might.'

He frowned. 'Caroline? What has she to say in the matter?'

'She thinks you are spending too much time at Hawkscote and neglecting your own affairs,' said Alyssa, rubbing her forehead with a hand that trembled slightly; the intense pain was making her light-headed.

Alyssa was a little frightened. She had never experienced feeling unwell like this before. She studied Gil through clouded, misty vision: his firm jawline and bone structure, his hands, his muscular shoulders and chest – physical attributes which spoke of innate strength, as did his energy, efficacy, and resolution . . . every aspect distilled into the essence of controlled power. In her weakened state, this somehow gave her comfort. He was a man you could rely on, a man whose mere presence engendered confidence and Alyssa sighed faintly, thinking it would be very pleasant to be loved and protected from every care by Sir Giles. His voice recalled her wandering thoughts.

'How do you know this?' he asked, angrily.

'We met Miss Nash in Dorchester and she mentioned it then. I would not have told you, except you offered to continue our meetings and I thought you should be aware of her comments.'

'She's no business to interfere.'

'If you are to be betrothed, Sir Giles, perhaps she can express an opinion,' said Alyssa, wearily. She felt inordinately tired, and another wave of nausea swept through her.

'Betrothed?' He looked at Alyssa in surprise. 'Damnation! I've no inclination to—' He stopped, recollecting his fierce tone, and continued in more moderate voice, 'I will speak to Caroline. If you are agreeable, our afternoon meetings will continue.' Looking into her face, he frowned. 'Are you feeling well? Your cheeks look very heated.'

'I-I do not feel quite the thing, to be honest.'

'You are ill? You should have told me earlier!'

'I had hoped to feel better, but now my head aches abominably. Perhaps I have a caught a chill. I-I think I must retire, if you will excuse me.'

Alyssa's head swam alarmingly as she rose to her feet. She heard his deep voice which suddenly sounded a long way off. When her legs began to shake, she rested her hands against the table to steady herself and tried to speak again, but her lips would not obey her brain. Neither would her limbs. She stumbled slightly and there was ringing in her ears as the cloak of unconsciousness began to envelop her.

Floating on the precipice of oblivion, her last hazy memories were of the walls of the dining-room becoming strangely distorted and Sir Giles uttering a low, urgent expletive before rushing to grasp her upper arm. Turning her head towards him, his dark features wavered before her clouded vision. More words – murmured, indistinct but imperative – reached through the fog before fading away into the distance, 'Miss Paradise! Alyssa, my darling girl! What is wrong. . . ?'

But Alyssa could offer no reply: the dark void overwhelmed her.

CHAPTER EIGHT

Gil caught Alyssa as she swayed, feeling her body slump against his. Her head lay against his shoulder and her eyes were closed, the dark lashes sweeping down towards reddened cheeks. Fear, illogical, but stark and chilling all the same, clutched at his heart and drawing in a ragged breath, he felt down the exposed curve of her neck, exhaling in relief when he detected the rapid erratic beat. Her skin, however, felt unusually hot under his touch: it was the dry heat of fever. Dear God, for a moment he had thought the worst! Pulling her languid, unresponsive body closer, he touched his lips briefly to her brow before spurring himself to action.

'Rowberry, Miss Ravenhill! Hurry!' he cried and, lifting Alyssa into his arms, he carried her to the small *chaise* in the corner of the room.

Rowberry entered and when he saw Alyssa's inert form, his imperturbable manner was replaced by agitation and he wrung his hands.

'Your mistress has been taken ill. Fetch Miss Ravenhill, at once! And bring some water or cordial.'

'Very good, sir!'

Rowberry bustled out as Letty came in.

She glanced at Sir Giles, who knelt at Alyssa's side, holding her fingers in one hand with his dark brows knitted together in consternation, and cried, 'What is wrong?'

'She has a fever. The doctor must be brought to her immediately.'

Letty placed a hand on Alyssa's forehead. 'Oh, she is on fire! She commented on the headache which had troubled her all day but thought it might improve.'

'Perhaps she is worse for sitting through dinner,' he said, bitterly, his eyes fixed on Alyssa's flushed features. 'Dear God, if only I had known.'

Letty laid a reassuring hand on his sleeve. 'You had no way of knowing. She must have deteriorated quickly otherwise she would have told you. But whom should we send for the doctor? Only the stable lad, the elderly footman and

Rowberry are here this evening. The solicitor's clerk has already left.'

'None of them: *I* shall go.'

'You?'

'Of course,' he said, staring as if astonished Letty should query his decision. 'There must be no delay. I came in my carriage so I will collect the doctor.'

'It would be the quickest solution,' she admitted, 'but first, we must get Alyssa to her room. Sir Giles, do you think—?'

She had not finishing speaking before he lifted Alyssa once more and headed for the door, walking past the butler who was returning with a glass of cordial.

'Order my carriage, Rowberry,' he said.

'Second room on the right at the top of the stairs,' called Letty, hurrying across the hall in Gil's wake. 'You may give that to me, Rowberry, and when you have ordered the carriage, ask Mrs Farnell to come to Alyssa's room.'

Gil climbed the stairs with careful haste. As he did so, Alyssa began to murmur the incomprehensible disjointed phrases of delirium into his chest. He glanced down in concern but continued on until he reached the room, pushed the door open with one shoulder and laid his burden gently on the bed.

'Thank you, Sir Giles. I don't know how we would have got Alyssa upstairs so quickly without your help,' said Letty.

'Will you take good care of her?' His gaze did not leave Alyssa, who was still murmuring incoherently.

'I love her as a sister; you need have no anxiety on that point. But please hurry!'

He nodded. 'Doctor Plant is an excellent physician,' he said and, with a final glance towards the bed, he left.

Letty had already partially undressed Alyssa when Mrs Farnell arrived and together they removed the rest of her clothes, dressed her in a cotton nightgown and unpinned her hair. Letty bathed Alyssa's face with water which seemed to calm her a little, but made no impact on the heat emanating from her body. She thrashed to and fro, murmuring about her headache and crying out for a drink, her comments jumbled with other unintelligible phrases.

'Her fever is worsening and her cheeks are very flushed. I hope Sir Giles hurries back,' remarked Letty anxiously.

'So do I, miss,' said the housekeeper, shaking her head. 'The mistress is in a bad taking, for all she's young and strong.'

It was another half an hour before Sir Giles returned, and Letty met them in the hallway, 'I am relieved to see you, Doctor – the fever has taken firm hold and she is delirious.'

'Hmm . . . Sir Giles explained the symptoms on the way, Miss Ravenhill,' said the doctor, removing his coat. 'I fear I know what ails Miss Paradise, but I need to examine her to make certain.'

'You know? But how can you?'

Doctor Plant collected his bag. 'I will explain later, if I may. Where is the patient?'

'In her room. Follow me, if you please.'

Gil stood nearby, a frown carved on his forehead, and he called out to Letty as she began to climb the stairs. 'Miss Ravenhill, it is late, but would you mind if I stay to hear the doctor's opinion? I would appreciate it.'

'Not at all,' she replied, over her shoulder. 'Ask Rowberry to provide you with some refreshment.'

During his anxious wait, Sir Giles alternately paced the drawing-room floor or stared out at the sky, turned blood red by the approaching sunset. But he had no eyes for the beauty in this display. He was a rational man, but from the moment he realized Alyssa was ill, reasoned thought had deserted him. He had somehow managed to discuss her symptoms with Dr Plant dispassionately, all the while yearning for her condition to have improved on his return. However, judging by Letty's expression, her condition had worsened and the longer the doctor stayed with her, the more serious the illness was likely to be. By the time the doctor returned, anxiety had clawed savagely at Gil until he dreaded the news he must hear. Pale and drawn, he passed the doctor a glass of wine and asked, 'Do you know what Miss Paradise is suffering from?'

'It is as I suspected, Sir Giles: scarlet fever.'

Gil stared. 'Scarlet fever! Is that possible? I have heard of no cases in the area.'

'Nor had I, until yesterday,' said the doctor, sitting down. 'Miss Paradise asked me to visit a young child on the estate, Samuel Fletcher. He has been unwell for several days and I believe Miss Paradise visited the family during that time.'

Overhearing this as she came in, Letty observed, 'Yes, she was worried about the boy and took provisions to help his recovery.'

'In doing so, she unwittingly exposed herself to scarlet fever,' said the doctor. 'When I examined the child yesterday, the fever was well advanced and the rash which accompanies the disease already developing. I planned to send word and recommend precautions be put in place, but the damage was done as far as Miss Paradise was concerned: the child had already passed the disease on to her.'

'But there are no marks on Alyssa. You may yet be mistaken.'

Doctor Plant shook his head. 'I am not mistaken, Miss Ravenhill – the onset of the illness is very rapid, with the rash appearing within a day or so of the fever and sore throat. By morning, I fully expect Miss Paradise to be exhibiting that symptom also.'

'Her cheeks were very flushed.'

'Another classic manifestation of the illness, Sir Giles. The patient's cheeks become reddened, hence the name. Her headache and nausea are also evidence that scarlet fever is present.'

Gil asked urgently, 'And what is the prognosis for Miss Paradise? And the child, of course.'

'Not unfavourable but there is always a danger of complications. Young, healthy patients usually survive the illness, unpleasant though it is, but they can develop a weakness of the heart which leads to many months of convalescence and sometimes, no complete recovery. As for the child, thanks to Miss Paradise's prompt intervention, he is already showing signs of improvement, but it is too early to say whether he will recover fully – scarlet fever is the most severe and fatal of all the exanthematous fevers.'

Gil's face drained of its remaining colour and he raked his fingers through his hair in agitation. For a few moments, he struggled to reply, but finally managed to say with passable composure, 'She must receive the best possible care. Send all your expenses to Eastcombe, and engage a second opinion if necessary – from Matthew Baillie in London, if you think it appropriate.'

'It will not, I hope, be necessary to consult Dr Baillie. Surely Miss Paradise will deal with payment when she is well again?'

'I will attend to it. I do not want her troubled with the matter while she recuperates.'

'If that is what you wish,' he replied, throwing Gil a curious look. 'Scarlet fever, however, presents specific issues which need to be addressed.'

'Precautions must be taken to prevent the disease spreading,' said Letty.

'Quite so, my dear,' replied the doctor. 'The patient must be kept as quiet and isolated as possible. Have you some experience of the illness?'

'Unfortunately, yes. I know what must be done, and will care for Alyssa myself.'

'I am sure you are an excellent nurse Miss Ravenhill, but I will only allow it if you have help and take plenty of rest and fresh air.'

Letty nodded. 'I will do as you ask. The housekeeper will assist me.'

'And *you* must stay away until any danger is passed, Sir Giles,' declared the doctor.

'Stay away?' Gil repeated, incredulous. 'Impossible! I cannot – I need to enquire after Miss Paradise.' He sprang to his feet and began pacing about the room.

'Then you put your own health at risk.'

'It is of no matter! I dined with Miss Paradise this evening and will continue to visit to see how she goes on. I shall find no peace otherwise.' This last sentence was spoken too quietly for either the doctor or Letty to hear.

'That is your decision, of course. Her cousin must be informed, as should the gentleman to whom she is about to become betrothed who, Sir Giles informs me, is in London,' He looked at the clock and rose to his feet. 'There is nothing more I can do this evening. May I trouble you to take me back to Frampton, Sir Giles?'

'Yes, of course. I will contact Mr Kilworth if Miss Ravenhill can find a spare moment to write to Mr Brook?'

Letty agreed and Dr. Plant nodded, satisfied. 'I will return first thing in the morning. You have my instructions, Miss Ravenhill. With the aid of the laudanum, the patient should sleep, if only fitfully, and I shall decide tomorrow if a bleeding would be beneficial.'

As the doctor collected his coat, Gil said in a low earnest voice, 'Do not hesitate to send word during the night, no matter how slight your concern, Letty. Promise me you will do so if Aly – Miss Paradise's condition should deteriorate.' He added gruffly, 'I will drag the doctor back here at any hour if you think it necessary.'

'I promise I will.'

'Thank you. I, too, intend to return early tomorrow,' he said.

Gil and the doctor left, and Letty returned to Alyssa's room. After arranging for the housekeeper to relieve her, she remained to care for her charge.

Alyssa's fever and delirium continued, not helped by the sultry heat of a clear summer's night. She muttered constantly and cited Sir Giles, Piers, Letty, the Nashes and Charles in her ramblings. Most of it was confused although occasionally a few phrases were clear enough to be understood and caused Letty to raise her brows in surprise. The laudanum quietened Alyssa but did not lessen the fever or ease the sore throat which made her cry plaintively in her lucid moments.

Eventually, she fell into fitful sleep, exhausted from vomiting and the effects of the opiate. When Mrs Farnell came, Letty was reluctant to leave, but the housekeeper insisted.

'And what good will it do if you are taken ill as well, miss?' she asked, bluntly. 'The doctor included your well-being in his instructions.'

'Very well. I shall lie down, but call me at once if there is any change.'

Letty snatched two hours' sleep and awoke with a start to find dawn approaching. Hurriedly, she washed, dressed and returned to Alyssa's room to find her condition unaltered: she remained in a high fever.

Dr Plant confirmed this when he returned. 'There is no change but I expect none for a few hours.' He indicated the fine, raised rash that had begun to emerge on Alyssa's shoulders and neck. 'You see the evidence, Miss Ravenhill. There is no doubt it is scarlet fever and you and the housekeeper must take every precaution. No more than two hours in the sick-room before changing over, and as much rest and good food as you can reasonably manage in between.'

Letty looked down at Alyssa's sleeping figure and whispered, 'When she wakes, she is greatly troubled by her throat – can anything else be done to alleviate the pain?'

'Very little, apart from laudanum. I have heard cloths soaked in vinegar and hot water applied to the throat ease the symptoms a little. I have no objection to you trying this remedy, but please remember to offer water as often as possible and, when she will take it, some nourishing food – I have no time for these fashionable reducing diets. I will bleed Miss Paradise to lessen her fever.' Rolling up his shirt sleeves, Dr Plant looked quizzically at Letty. 'Are you squeamish at the sight of blood?' he asked. 'I require your assistance if you will stay.'

'Yes, I'll help you.' Letty did not relish Alyssa being subjected to a bleeding but she held the small bowl and could not help but admire the doctor's skill as he completed the task with the least amount of distress to his patient. He stayed for a short while, checking Alyssa's pulse and throat until he nodded with satisfaction. Reminding Letty of the precautions for her own care, he then collected his bag and said he would return later in the day.

Afterwards, Letty descended the stairs wearily. Worry had added to her tiredness and although she did not feel hungry, she was mindful of the doctor's words and thought a little breakfast might refresh her for the difficult day ahead.

She was in the breakfast parlour when Rowberry announced Sir Giles was waiting.

'Ask him to come in. I'm sure he will not mind a lack of formality this morning.'

Gil entered, his features etched with lack of sleep and concern. 'My apologies for the early hour, but I must know how Miss Paradise is.'

'I'm afraid she remains the same.'

'No improvement?'

Letty shook her head. 'None, but she is no worse either. The doctor thinks the fever will last until later today.'

'I see. I had hoped for better news.' he said, with a heavy sigh. 'I have sent word to Mr Kilworth.'

'Thank you, although I don't suppose he will come until Alyssa improves.'

As if to directly repudiate this, Piers strode in. 'Good God, Miss Ravenhill – I came as soon as I heard! How is she?' He suddenly spied the other figure in the room. 'Who the devil—? Ah, you must be Sir Giles. I have been intending to call upon you, sir; now this damnable business has done the work and allows me to introduce myself,' said Piers, extending his hand in greeting. 'Thank you for sending word so promptly.'

'It was the least I could do, Mr Kilworth.'

'Deuced good of you, all the same. Please also accept my thanks for bringing the doctor without delay.' He turned to Letty. 'So, Alyssa has caught scarlet fever from some urchin on the estate? Damn it, she is too well-meaning for her own good. Look where her kindness has left her.'

'I hardly think this is the time for recriminations,' observed Gil. 'Although I wish current circumstances were different, Miss Paradise should be admired for showing concern for the child and she could not have known the danger.'

Piers gave a short laugh. 'If she had, she would still have gone. Alyssa is the most headstrong girl I know.'

'I cannot disagree,' admitted Gil, ruefully.

'Oh, but that is part of her charm! It is awful to see her laid so low and I long to hear her to argue over her recuperation,' said Letty. 'Mr Kilworth, I am glad you are here, in spite of the possible risk to yourself.'

'Bah!' He shrugged, dismissing the notion. 'I would be a poor sort of fellow to stay away just because Alyssa's ill. I'm more at risk from riding neck-or-nothing across the countryside. Sir Giles obviously feels the same.'

Gil nodded. 'I prefer to be here also, for news of her condition and to offer assistance. Miss Ravenhill, would it help if I liaised with Ennis? There is much work to be done at this time of year, and Miss Paradise decided upon the wage rise last night. She wanted it put in place as soon as possible. I am happy to do so if you will give your approval.'

'Knowing everything is being dealt with would aid her recovery,' replied Letty.

'But I can assist Ennis!' said Piers, a mulish look about his mouth.

'Very true,' agreed Sir Giles, smoothly. 'Have you experience in managing a property like Hawkscote?'

'No, but I am Alyssa's nearest relative.'

Gil executed a small bow. 'Then perhaps you are better suited to the role for that reason alone. Forgive my presumption – I meant no offence.'

In response to this reply, deliberately designed as an emollient, Piers smiled. 'By Jove, you're a capital fellow! You are forthright and, much against my will, I approve of you! Let us not argue over a trivial matter when Alyssa must be our main concern. Perhaps we can share the task? If you work with Ennis, I will continue to smooth the workers' ruffled sensibilities.'

'You know of the unrest?' said Sir Giles with a hard, questioning look.

'Alyssa told me, and I have undertaken investigations of my own.'

He gave Piers another measured glance. 'Very well, I will liaise with Ennis.'

'Please keep me informed. Between us, Hawkscote will be in good hands.'

'I will do whatever is necessary to protect Miss Paradise's interests,' murmured Gil, with a hint of steel.

'Alyssa will appreciate both your efforts on her behalf,' said Letty.

'Will you convey my best wishes for her speedy recovery, Miss Ravenhill?'

'I will be happy to, Sir Giles, although it may be sometime before the effects of the fever and laudanum dissipate.'

Gil ventured, 'Might I be allowed to see her as soon as she is feeling a little better?'

Letty, detecting a note of desperation in his voice, said reassuringly, 'Of course! Alyssa will need company while she recovers.'

He gave a wry grin. 'Then I shall be happy to provide as much of my company as she can tolerate in her weakened state.'

'So shall I,' declared Piers.

Letty regarded Piers steadily and with a faltering smile, she remarked, 'Alyssa will be overwhelmed by this promised attention, but her recovery must come first.'

'Exactly so – I'll return this evening to see how she progresses,' replied Gil.

He took his leave, leaving Letty and Piers alone.

'Dash it, I was inclined to dislike that fellow but having met him, I can't,' said Piers, staring at the door that had closed behind Sir Giles. 'He is astute and does not dissemble. And I'll bet he's an excellent sportsman too, with that physique. Seems bang up to the mark all round which makes his offering for the abominable Miss Nash incomprehensible.' He shook his head in disbelief, and turned back to Letty. 'Now, I'm in dire need of coffee, but first tell me more about Alyssa's condition—'

He stopped abruptly. Large tears were brimming in Letty's eyes and more overflowed her lashes to course down her cheeks. She was still seated at the breakfast table and no sound emerged to accompany the tears, but when she realized Piers was looking at her, she hurriedly cast her eyes downwards.

'*Letty!*' he cried, starting forward in alarm, 'What is wrong?'

'N-nothing! Nothing in particular, that is . . . I-I must be tired to indulge in tears, a practice I do not normally succumb to,' she replied, sniffing prosaically as she wiped away the tears with her handkerchief. 'And I'm worried about Alyssa,' she continued, looking up at him once more. 'You must know there is a possibility, albeit slight, that she might not recover.'

'Not recover? But she *must*! Healthy adults do not die from scarlet fever. At least, I don't think they do – do they?'

'My parents did,' said Letty, quietly. Her bottom lip trembled and she gripped it between her teeth.

The effect upon Piers of this small, almost childlike gesture was profound. He had been subjected to lachrymose young women in the past, usually when they attempted to gain their way by insincere weeping, but without effect. However, the sight of Letty's silent tears, that prosaic little sniff and the way her lip quivered as she made the admission about her parents, pierced his soul and he cursed himself bitterly.

'Good God, forgive me Miss Ravenhill. You must think me an unfeeling brute. But I-I did not know about your parents, or if I did, I have forgotten, which is inexcusable.' He crouched beside her chair, taking her hands between his and saying firmly, 'Your parents were older than Alyssa. She *will* recover, I'm certain of it – especially with such an agreeable nurse. Indeed, if I were ill I should happily keep to my bed for months just for the pleasure of looking up into your face!'

She gave a watery chuckle, amusement shimmering through her remaining tears. 'You are the most complete flatterer!'

'Certainly!' he said affably, with a grin. 'Now, that is better – you are smiling. When do you have to return to Alyssa?'

'Not for another hour.'

'Then stroll with me in the garden; it is a beautiful morning and you need the fresh air. You may tell me while we walk how my cousin does.' Raising her hand to his lips, he pulled her gently to her feet and drew her arm within his.

'Yes, Mr Kilworth,' she replied, demurely.

He peered at her with a wry, quizzical look. 'Deuce take it, I'm wary when you are compliant,' he said, laughing. 'You must be severe again.'

'Very well, I suppose it will not do to be *too* conciliatory.' Letty's eyes twinkled at him as they walked outside.

On his return home, Gil organized fruit from his succession houses and personally selected items from the garden that Alyssa might find pleasing when her fever abated.

This completed, he went to his study and wrote to his sister. After sealing the note with a wafer, he began to look over some business papers, staying valiantly at his task until he realized he was achieving little, then thrust the papers impatiently to one side. Looking out over the lawns to the gardens beyond, Gil fell into a brown study, staring into middle distance. The turmoil in his mind was nothing to the turmoil in his heart, but there was nothing he could do until

Alyssa was well again. And she must get well – he could not consider any other outcome.

He dare not broach the subject of his feelings with Caroline until he could give the conversation his full attention and that was impossible with Alyssa gravely ill. Caroline needed to hear his decision in unequivocal terms, as did his friend the squire. But while Gil's torment at delaying his discussion with Caroline was acute, his anguish over the future was greater and his heart seemed to turn over painfully in his chest at the thought of Alyssa marrying Charles Brook. There was, however, one issue which could be dealt with now. In Caroline's opinion, he spent too much time at Hawkscote. Well, his patience with her incessant meddling was exhausted. Caroline's true character had been revealed: she was unfeeling, arrogant, and presumed too much – it was time he put an end to her interference.

He journeyed to Frampton Manor that afternoon, his mood bullish.

The squire received him warmly. 'Giles, always a pleasure to see you! We can escape the attentions of ladies for a while if you will take a glass of my new claret,' he said, conspiratorially.

'Thank you, but no, Henry. I am here only to impart news and to speak briefly with Caroline.'

'Oh? You seem sombre today. What's to do?' said the squire, squinting intently at Gil's set features.

'Miss Paradise is very ill. She has scarlet fever.'

'Scarlet fever, you say? Poor child! Has the doctor been summoned?'

'He has attended her several times but she continues in a high fever. I came to advise Caroline, and you and Mrs Nash.'

'Very proper of you. Well, I'm sorry to hear of the young lady being laid low. I hope she recovers quickly as Miss Paradise and her ward are invited to our summer party.' He shook his head and grimaced. 'That event – and the damned bill for it – grows bigger by the day. Eugenie is scouring the county for ostrich plumes. Ostrich plumes, I ask you!' He made a sound of disgust. 'But you are not interested in such flummery now. Let us hope Miss Paradise is well enough to attend – I was looking forward to meeting her.'

'I think you will approve, Henry.'

'Ah!' exclaimed Mrs Nash, entering the drawing-room like a ship under full sail. 'I declare it is an age since you came to Frampton, Sir Giles. Who should Henry approve of?'

'I was referring to Miss Paradise.'

'Oh. Yes, well,' she said, pursing her lips. 'She is a provokingly pert young woman to my mind, although one cannot argue her manners and style are acceptable. Why were you speaking of her?'

'I came to inform you she is ill. The doctor has diagnosed scarlet fever.'

The effect of this statement on Mrs Nash was alarming. She stood completely still, but her eyes widened until they threatened to pop out of her head, her jaw dropped slightly and the lace cap set upon her neat, grey curls began to bobble in an agitated fashion. 'Gracious! We must act at once! Caroline,' she cried, '*Caroline!*'

The squire raised his eyes briefly to the ceiling. 'Must you shriek, my love?' he asked. 'It offends my ears.'

'Indeed I must, Henry. This is shocking news. Caroline!'

'What is it, Mother?' Caroline entered holding an open book, which she snapped shut when she saw their visitor. 'So you have decided to visit at last, Giles. I thought you had forgotten us here at Frampton.'

'I could not forget you, Caroline,' he replied, a queer smile hovering around his mouth.

'Caroline, Miss Paradise has scarlet fever. Oh, I feel my palpitations coming on apace!' said Mrs Nash, shuddering. She took her hartshorn from the drawer in the nearby bureau and inhaled deeply before adding, 'We must advise our acquaintances not to go near until the danger is passed. And you, Sir Giles – you must stay away.'

'I was there this morning,' he said, in a dry voice.

'*This morning!*'

'Indeed. And last evening. Miss Paradise fainted away at the end of our dinner and I was obliged to help tend to her.'

'Then you most certainly should not be here! Come along, Henry,' she said peremptorily. 'Simmons will see you out, Sir Giles; I'm sure you understand. Thank you for advising us, but you would have done better to send a note.'

'Don't be ridiculous, Eugenie, there is nothing wrong with Giles. Why, he looks as fit as a flea,' protested the squire.

But Mrs Nash placed a hand on her husband's back and thrust him firmly towards the hallway. 'Please do not argue, Henry,' she said, in a low imperative voice, 'you will be better for a glass of claret this instant. Goodbye, Sir Giles.'

Obliged to retreat, the squire called out as he was propelled inexorably towards the door. 'Give my regards to the patient, Giles.'

'You were foolish to come here,' said Caroline severely.

Gil raised his brows. 'I do not have the illness.'

'It is impossible to be too careful,' she argued. 'I have heard of no cases in the area so how has she been exposed to it?'

'A labourer's child was ill and Miss Paradise visited the family.'

'Then she is well served for rubbing shoulders with illiterate workers,' she said, her tone biting. 'They are most unsuitable company for a lady even when one is carrying out charitable deeds.'

'I expect you would not visit a sick child?' he retorted.

'Not when there is any danger of illness. And certainly not a labourer's child: it is beneath me to do so, you must agree.'

'I do not.'

'So, once again you prefer Miss Paradise's view; an unfortunate habit you must dispense with.' She gave a trill of laughter. 'Goodbye, Giles. You will be welcomed back once the danger has passed. Miss Paradise will receive some of my embroidery silks along with my wishes for her recovery.'

She turned to leave but he said darkly, 'Stay a moment, Caroline. There is something I must discuss with you.'

'Very well, but be quick. I have letters to write.'

'I will not detain you long,' he replied, curtly. 'You think my additional visits to Hawkscote unnecessary, I understand.'

'What of it? You should not be embroiling yourself unduly in Hawkscote business.'

'Stay out of my dealings with Miss Paradise.'

'I beg your pardon?'

His mouth grim, he snapped, 'I believe you heard what I said. I can offer help in whatever fashion I choose and it is no business of yours.'

'Your affairs are mine also when we are practically betrothed.'

'I shall speak further on that subject very soon – now is not the time because of my uncertain temper and circumstances – but I reiterate what I said a moment ago: cease your interminable interference! I won't tolerate it.'

Caroline winced at the anger in his voice. However, his first words indicated he intended to set a wedding date soon so she replied by smiling thinly and saying, 'You seem a little overwrought, Giles; perhaps you are concerned about developing scarlet fever, given the situation you found yourself in.'

He threw her a fulminating look. 'Good day to you, Caroline,' he muttered through gritted teeth, before striding to the door and slamming it shut behind him.

CHAPTER NINE

The incomparable perfume reached Alyssa as she awoke. She blinked, trying to focus on her surroundings and recognized the familiar décor of her bedroom but there was something delightfully different: the musky scent of roses filled the air.

She breathed deeply in appreciation and swallowed, waiting for the searing agony to follow but to her relief the pain was muted. Recalling the dreadful choking sensation she had endured, Alyssa offered up a silent prayer of thanks but still hesitated until she had tentatively swallowed again and found the discomfort had indeed abated. Turning her head to search for the source of the scent, she was rewarded by a view of sunlight streaming on to a blue and white earthenware jug containing damask, gallica and moss roses, their glorious fragrance released by the warmth.

She smiled and murmured, 'Beautiful!' Her voice, husky and strained, sounded strange to her ears.

Letty, who had been dozing in the chair on the other side of the bed, whispered apprehensively, 'How are you feeling?'

'Never better,' replied Alyssa, with a valiant attempt at a chuckle, 'except my throat feels like someone has tried to strangle me.'

'Oh, thank God your fever has gone!'

'H-How long have I been feverish?'

'Almost three days.'

'Three days!'

Letty nodded. 'It's Tuesday afternoon and you've been very ill.'

'I remember little, except that you were an attentive nurse, Letty.' Her brow furrowed. 'I have never felt so ill in all my life – it was terrifying. My last coherent memory is suffering from a headache and feeling faint. What was wrong with me?'

'Scarlet fever, which you almost certainly caught from young Samuel Fletcher.'

Alyssa's eyes widened. 'Then I've been fortunate.' Looking at Letty, she added, 'It must have been difficult to nurse me, knowing what happened to your parents.'

'The thought did prey on my mind, but you were under the care of an excellent physician.'

'But what of Samuel?' asked Alyssa, struggling to raise her head. 'Is he – has he recovered?'

'Samuel is doing well.'

'Thank goodness!' She sank back on to the bed, exhausted. 'The fever might have gone, but I'm as weak and helpless as a new born kitten.'

'Tiredness and a poor appetite are to be expected, according to the doctor. You will need to follow his advice carefully.'

'And my nurse will not countenance any argument either,' said Alyssa with a weak smile.

'None,' said Letty gaily, moving to shake out Alyssa's pillow. 'For once, you must do exactly as you are told and I shall accept nothing less. Neither will Sir Giles.'

'Has he visited while I have been ill?'

'Visited?' echoed Letty, amused. 'Why, he has been here constantly, enquiring after your progress and bringing flowers or fruit from his succession houses. I swear he has not slept in three days. He fetched the doctor, wrote to Piers to advise him about your condition and has dealt with Ennis.' Smoothing out the bed covers, she continued, 'I cannot speak highly enough of how he dealt with the crisis. He is a man to be relied on and one who commands confidence, but although he tries not to show it, I believe he is almost demented with worry.'

'Oh?' Alyssa, vaguely recalling Sir Giles's words before she fainted, immediately decided she must be mistaken: he could not have referred to her as his 'darling girl'. More likely she had misheard in her growing delirium and when her memories of the dinner were so hazy, it was useless speculate on what might have been said, and inconceivable to bring up the subject with Sir Giles.

Letty interrupted her thoughts. 'He brought the flowers from his rose garden at Eastcombe.'

'They are exquisite,' said Alyssa, running her gaze once more over the bouquet. Sir Giles, it seemed, could be a man of considerate gestures and she was grateful for the concern he had shown as a neighbour. Why, then, did she feel irritable and wanting more? A sudden wave of despondency threatened to swamp her and she turned away, anxious Letty should not see the tears which had unaccountably sprung to her eyes. She said quietly, 'May I have a drink?'

'Of course! How stupid of me not to think of it sooner.'

'You mentioned Piers. Has he been to Hawkscote?' asked Alyssa.

'Yes. He offered to speak with the labourers while Sir Giles dealt with Ennis. I thought it kind of Piers. I wondered if he would come here at all because of the potential danger,' said Letty, pouring out a glass of cordial.

'Piers continues to confound me although he never worried much about illness. I'm grateful for his help, but I'll be well enough to run the estate again soon.' Alyssa took the glass from Letty's outstretched hand and exclaimed, 'Oh, I have just thought – do I fail to meet the terms if I cannot attend dinner with Sir Giles?'

'As to that, I have spoken to Mr Forde. It is his opinion that if the will does not stipulate what should happen in the event of illness on either side, the dinner engagements can be waived until you've recovered. He expects Mr Bartley to confirm this so you may rest easy. Besides,' said Letty, with an affectionate grin, 'you can't entertain Sir Giles now; you're not exactly looking your best!'

'I don't doubt it. Pass me my mirror, if you please.' Letty did as she was bid and Alyssa shuddered as she looked at her reflection. The face staring back bore little resemblance to the one she was used to. The ravages left by the fever were clear to see: her cheeks, which had burnt fiercely a short time ago, were now devoid of colour, dark shadows lurked under heavy eyes and her lips were cracked and dry.

'I look positively haggard, but that is to be expected after three days of fever,' declared Alyssa ruefully.

Retrieving the mirror from her loose grasp, Letty administered a comforting hug. 'How you look now is of no consequence and I was foolish to mention it, even in jest. You will soon be back to health but it will be a week, possibly longer, before you feel ready to venture out of your room.'

'I hardly have strength enough to talk or hold up my head. What a poor creature I am.' Alyssa yawned and added, 'I think I need to go back to sleep.'

'Then do so, and concentrate on getting well again.'

'I'll do as I'm bid, but tell me one thing first, Letty – does Charles know?'

'I wrote to him. I thought he *should* know, although I don't think Charles will be an influence for the good in your recovery.'

'Don't worry, Charles will not venture within fifty miles of Hawkscote – he is a chronic hypochondriac,' muttered Alyssa drily, before closing her eyes.

Ten days later, Alyssa felt much improved and she began to chafe at the confines of her room. She appealed to the doctor to allow her downstairs until he eventually relented, observing she must be well enough if she was prepared to argue.

'But only if you do not overtire yourself,' he added. Shaking his head, he smiled and said, 'You are very determined, Miss Paradise. Most ladies retreat to their rooms at first sign of indisposition, however slight, and remain there for as long as possible.'

'But they emerge wreathed in shawls and smelling salts to confide every detail gleefully, however hideous, to their friends and profess it far more uncomfortable than anything they could have endured.'

He laughed. 'True enough. I have several such patients.'

'I promise to take sensible precautions, Doctor,' she said, eyes twinkling, 'I'm aware I'm not fully recovered.'

Alyssa's spirits lifted in the pleasant surroundings of the drawing-room. Letty and Mrs Farnell rearranged the furniture, which made Alyssa laugh indulgently at their efforts to ensure her every comfort was provided for.

Mrs Farnell, finally satisfied, withdrew and Letty asked, 'Would you like another shawl?'

'No, it's is delightfully warm. I'll not behave like an insipid dowager, reclining full length and needing the blinds drawn against the light. The gardens look very fine at this time of year, don't they?' she said, leaning forward to improve her view.

'Yes, I explored them over the last week or so.'

Alyssa raised her brows quizzically. 'Did you ramble through them alone?'

'Not always.'

'Oh?' enquired Alyssa, with a smile. 'Has my cousin been making himself agreeable while I have been indisposed?'

Letty blushed but tilted her chin defiantly. 'Yes, and I enjoy his company. We walk in the garden and, since he brought over the mare he mentioned in Dorchester, we occasionally ride out over the estate. Piers has told me about his childhood, his house in Lincolnshire and life in London; he is extremely knowledgeable about the *ton* and shared amusing anecdotes. I can't deny I find him an entertaining companion. And, true to his word, he has continued to visit the workers. I understand Draper is still discontented, but no doubt Piers will tell you the details – he takes the trouble to keep my spirits up but does not confide everything to me.'

'Letty, I'm not admonishing you for spending time with Piers,' replied Alyssa gently. 'All I ask is that you take care. You're not a flighty or foolish girl, and your heart is a loving one – bestow it on someone worthy.'

'You believe Piers is unworthy?' replied Letty, with a trace of defiance.

'Oh, I don't know,' said she, with a sigh. 'He is charming, and has good qualities but I'm not sure about his morals: sometimes, I fear he has a venal streak. But, to his credit, he has treated you with the utmost respect since his arrival—'

'And continued to do so while you were ill.' interjected her companion.

'So he should. However, Piers has been fickle with his attentions in the past and that concerns me.'

'I won't throw myself at his feet,' Letty assured her. 'He is not at all certain how to deal with me and I enjoy keeping him on tenterhooks.'

'It will do Piers no harm to wonder what is in your mind' – Alyssa looked under her lashes – 'or your heart.'

Letty smiled but offered no reply. Instead she walked to the bureau, opened one of the drawers and removed a letter, saying, 'Speaking of which, I truly wonder what was in Charles's mind when he wrote this. I expected him at any time during this last week but instead, I received this letter today.' Letty passed the single sheet to Alyssa, and grimaced in disapproval. 'Pray, don't let it distress you.'

Alyssa smoothed out the sheet.

Dear Letty

I was astonished to hear of Alyssa's illness – scarlet fever is indeed a dangerous disease and it pains me greatly she is suffering its effects.

Unfortunately, it is impossible for me to travel at present. My business in London is at a peculiarly delicate stage and I cannot depart Town on a whim. Notwithstanding my business arrangements, the risk to my own health cannot be discounted, and it must be preferable for any danger to have passed before I return.

I have no doubt Alyssa is receiving the best care. Please convey my deepest regard and best wishes for her recovery, and advise I intend journeying back to Dorset following the successful outcome of my affairs in London.

Yours etc.,
Charles Brook

'*Dear* Charles!' she exclaimed, chuckling. 'I knew he would not venture near while there is the slightest danger.'

'How dare he refer to your illness as a whim!' observed Letty, with considerable feeling.

'Typical of Charles, and I find it amusing rather than upsetting.' Catching sight of Letty's indignant expression, she added, 'Don't be angry on my behalf, Letty. Oh, I would be devastated if I loved him – to receive such shabby treatment at the hands of a man I cared for would indeed be an odious thing – but this' – she indicated the letter – 'merely illustrates what I already suspected: Charles responds to a crisis by being completely self-centred. He loves himself more than he could ever love me, and I shall not feel the slightest pang of guilt at telling him definitively we would not suit. However long his business affairs engage his attentions, he will only visit when it is safe to do so because the idea of a sick-room fills him dread. And I rather think I am relieved: Charles's prosy lectures would set back my recovery by at least a month.'

'There we are in agreement,' said Letty, with a grin. 'Now, let me tell you about our gowns. Mrs Farnell has helped whenever she could so they are progressing. Do you think you will be well enough to attend – that is, if you still wish to?'

'Indeed I will – I would not miss that event for the world,' she replied, cheerfully.

They were deep in conversation, discussing alterations and the merits of various trimmings, when Sir Giles was announced.

'He asked to see Miss Ravenhill and enquired after your health, miss,' explained Rowberry. 'When I informed him you were feeling better and downstairs this morning, he insisted I convey his card. I ventured to suggest you might not be well enough to receive him but Sir Giles seems determined.'

Rowberry, who was normally disapproving of vulgar insistence in a visitor, was prepared to make an exception in Sir Giles's case. It was, he later confided to Mrs Farnell, impossible to forget his attentiveness when Miss Paradise was taken ill, and he was a blind old fool if he did not recognize the signs of a gentleman in the thrall of attraction, and make allowance for it.

'Show him in,' said Alyssa. Rowberry nodded in acknowledgement and after he had left, she asked urgently, 'Letty, do I look quite the thing? I-I mean – I know I am pale but tell me I am not completely hideous!' She smoothed her hair and tugged at the lace fichu of her gown.

'You look your delightful self apart from a lack of colour. And I am sure that is about to be rectified,' observed her companion, with a knowing smile. 'As I have much to do, I'll leave you and Sir Giles alone.'

'Letty—' Alyssa began to protest faintly, but it was too late: Letty departed and a moment later, Sir Giles came in.

He found Alyssa sitting on the sofa, dressed in blue and white muslin, her hair loosely confined and a fine silk shawl draped about her shoulders. On seeing her – pale and weak, but otherwise apparently well – a rush of emotion swept through him. Gil knew now she was essential to his soul, to him finding any joy in the world, and he yearned to tell her so when the moment was right.

Fighting the urge to rain kisses on those upturned wan features, he stood simply watching her before saying in voice which wavered slightly, 'Miss Paradise, you cannot know how glad I am to see you, and find you well enough to leave your room.' He reached her in quick strides and lifted her hand to his lips, kissing it and whispering with a crooked smile, 'I have been so worried.'

To Alyssa's astonishment, her eyes filled with sudden tears at his greeting and the manner of it, and she began to cry. 'Oh! Forgive me!' she said, a few moments later. Trying to dry her tears with a handkerchief, she gulped and continued haltingly, 'I-Indeed, I-I do not even know w-*why* I am crying.'

'My poor child, you must be exhausted,' said Gil, sitting down and taking her hands firmly between his. He ached to gather her into his arms but there were too many issues to be addressed first and he cursed inwardly that their situation was so complicated. He was also afraid of ruining everything with one clumsy inappropriate action now. But if he could not comfort her properly, perhaps he could divert her; Gil longed to see Alyssa smile again. Raising his brows, he said, eyes gleaming mischievously, 'Are you tearful because you have been deprived of our tête-à-tête discussions? There is no need – you will have further opportunity to marvel at my fascinating erudite conversation!'

'Wretch!' she replied, before rewarding him with a smile and an enchanting dimple. She sniffed, wiped away the last of her tears and said, 'I-I believe I have missed teasing you, Sir Giles, someone must keep you in check.'

'I rely on you to curb my worst excesses.'

Alyssa, feeling suddenly a little shy, gently removed her hand from his grasp. 'I hope I'll be well enough to recommence our dinners soon. Indeed, I am already much better, just more tired than usual.'

'I'll visit every day while you recuperate. Mr Bartley advises our dinners can begin again when you are well. Will you come to Eastcombe then? In addition to dinner and showing you a little of my estate, I can introduce my sister and her husband.'

'Yes, I'd like that. I must thank you for the fruit and roses, Sir Giles. The flowers were particularly beautiful, and Letty tells me they came from your rose garden. May I see it when I visit?'

'With pleasure,' he said.

The accompanying smile lit up his features and made Alyssa feel weaker than ever. 'But won't Miss Nash object?' she asked softly.

'Your visit is no concern of Caroline's.' Seeing her consternation, he sighed. 'Miss Paradise, there is much I want to say yet I hardly know how, or where, to begin. However, I do know now is not the right occasion, but could I extract a promise from you? It is wrong of me; indeed, most likely you will think it an extraordinary request, but even so, I must ask.'

'What is it?'

He smiled down into her questioning gaze and murmured, 'Simply that you make no plans about your future until you are fully recovered.'

There was silence. Alyssa eventually replied, 'Very well, making any decision at present would be foolish so it is not a difficult pledge to make.' She felt her cheeks growing warm under his mesmerizing scrutiny.

'Thank you for indulging me,' he said, relieved. 'When is Mr Brook expected?'

'Charles's business keeps him in London.'

'His business affairs are more important than your health?' he cried, incredulous.

She did not reply directly, but observed, 'He writes he will travel here when the danger has passed.'

'I'll renew my acquaintance with Mr Brook when he deems it safe to venture back,' he said, his lip curling in derision. 'Rest assured I am dealing with Ennis and you need have no concerns about the estate.'

'Have the workers been informed of the increase?'

'Yes, shortly after you were taken ill. The reaction has been generally positive I understand, although your cousin informs me Draper still complains the amount is insufficient. You know Mr Kilworth suggested he stay in contact with the labourers?'

She nodded. 'Letty told me. It is strange – Piers has never shown interest in such matters before.'

'I did wonder why he was so specific.' A frown creased his brow. 'I don't wish to criticize your relative – in fact, I approve of him in some ways – but Tom's opinions of his nephew were mixed and I cannot feel quite comfortable. Do you think he might have ulterior motives?'

'Knowing Piers, quite possibly, although I cannot conceive what they might be,' admitted Alyssa.

'Then would it be wise for me to keep a discreet watch?'

'I would feel happier if you did, Sir Giles. He is not experienced and Draper may be capable of more mischief than Piers can deal with easily.'

He nodded. 'Then I'll make the necessary arrangements. It would not be politic to make your cousin aware of my involvement though: if he has no other motive, he may take my interference as a slur on his ability. And while it may be unconnected, Ennis informed me of several recent incidents: a broken window in one of the cottages, sheep going missing, gates left open – nothing serious. A hayrick and a nearby abandoned outbuilding were also set on fire yesterday. Fortunately, the blaze was soon extinguished and there was no great damage done.'

'Set on fire!' echoed Alyssa faintly, looking up in surprise, 'But surely this is alarming news?'

'There is no evidence it was deliberate,' he replied soothingly. 'It could have been caused by a careless labourer or someone using the building for shelter. I only informed you now because you would be annoyed at hearing it later from another source.'

'How well you know me already,' she said, with a little laugh.

'And I want to know more,' he murmured. 'I hope you will be able to enjoy a few summer events. The Nashes' evening party approaches, of course – I understand you are invited?'

'Yes. We will go, even though Miss Nash and her mother are not the most emollient of people.'

'No,' he acknowledged, 'but I'll be there, and Squire Nash is a pleasant, easy-going man who looks forward to meeting you. Mrs Nash will be busy ensuring everything runs smoothly so she can bask for another year in having organized the highlight of the social calendar. Caroline' – he hesitated, before saying in a constrained voice – 'Caroline will have other matters on her mind then.'

'Miss Nash sent a note and enclosed some embroidery silks.' Alyssa gave a wry smile, and added, 'She made sure to mention it was her *second-best* thread.'

'As ever, Caroline is high-handed,' he muttered.

'I'm sorry, I shouldn't have mentioned it.'

'Not at all: I'm well aware of her flaws.'

Alyssa suddenly felt emotionally drained and, foolishly, close to tears again. Irritated at her weakness in body and spirit, she fervently hoped Miss Nash would not visit in the near future; Alyssa knew she was in no condition to stand up to her supercilious manner, and any reminder of her connection with Sir Giles seemed too much to bear at present. With her mind still sluggish from the fever, Alyssa could not think clearly. She wondered vaguely at the promise he had extracted from her but, afraid of reading too much into every look, gesture and word he offered, she gave up the unequal fight to make sense of it all and heaved an exasperated sigh.

Hearing this, Gil rose to his feet and said firmly, 'I've stayed too long. You need to rest and the doctor, I know, has asked you not to over exert yourself for a few days.' He pressed her hand once more to his lips. 'I'll return tomorrow,' he murmured and, with a brief bow, he was gone.

Alyssa leant her head back against the cushions. Notwithstanding the gamut of emotions in her breast, she felt relaxed, and minutes later, closed her eyes and drifted into a deep, untroubled sleep – the most refreshing she had enjoyed since her illness began.

It was almost a week before Alyssa managed to speak to her cousin alone. Now she felt stronger, she wanted to question Piers and the opportunity presented itself one morning when, having enjoyed an earlier visit from Sir Giles, Alyssa was humming happily over her needlework.

'Good morning, Coz,' said Piers breezily, coming in and taking the chair opposite, 'You look well. Where is Miss Ravenhill?'

'Letty has gone to change into her riding habit and will be down shortly.' She set aside her work and threw him a measuring glance. 'I'm glad you are early: I want to talk to you.'

'Oh? As a matter of fact, there's something I want to discuss with you.'

'Then I'll begin – how are the labourers, Piers?'

'I've explained why the wage rise cannot be more and have had some success. Of course, you can do no wrong in the Fletchers' eyes after sending the doctor to Samuel, but the consensus amongst the others is that it is a good start.'

'And Draper?'

'Still simmering with discontent. He says you could afford more if you chose.'

'I see. Then perhaps I should dismiss him; there are plenty willing to take his place.'

'It would be a pity,' said Piers, with a shrug. 'He has a wife and three children to support and he's a good worker.' During Alyssa's illness, he had continued to encourage Draper to do his bidding and Piers had paid for both his deeds, and his silence. He therefore saw no need to remove the fellow from Hawkscote. True, he disliked the man – Draper was a ruffian – but he had done was asked of him without query which was all that was of interest to Piers. 'Have you heard about the fire?' he prompted.

'Yes. Sir Giles told me of it, and the other incidents. He said it could be an accident.'

'It was no accident.' In fact, it had been carried out at Piers's behest.

'Oh?' said Alyssa, 'Why do you say that?'

'Because I dealt with the culprit first thing this morning.'

Startled, she asked urgently, 'But who was to blame?'

'An unemployed aggrieved labourer, intent on causing trouble for any landowner. He just happened to choose Hawkscote.'

'I never considered anyone would resort to such methods just to make a point,' she said, surprised. 'Did you catch them in the act?'

'Not exactly – Draper did.'

'Draper! Then he is to be congratulated, in spite of his discontent. We should inform the authorities.'

'I think not,' answered Piers, blithely. 'The man responsible is destitute as it is and, having received a severe reprimand from me, has gone on his way. There is nothing further to concern you; I handled the whole affair perfectly well. You see, Alyssa, you do need my assistance. I managed the situation better than you could have alone, and it was fortunate I was here to deal with it. I am firmly of the opinion Hawkscote needs a man in charge – people take advantage of a woman.'

'They will find I'm as fair and firm an employer as any man, and am no green girl to be duped in business!' she exclaimed, with asperity.

'But if you had someone to help you, they would not even attempt it.'

Puzzled, she queried, 'But I already have Ennis, and Sir Giles's advice.'

'No, I mean a true *partner*.' He rose to his feet, thrust one hand into his pocket and strode to the fireplace in the hope physical action might make the task ahead easier. Why was it proving so damned difficult? Deep in Piers's soul, something nagged that he was making a terrible mistake.

'You think I should sell part of Hawkscote?'

'No, not sell.'

'Piers, you are being deliberately obtuse. Come to the point.'

He cleared his throat and, choosing his words carefully, turned towards her. 'Very well. I've been thinking for some time and especially during your illness that you need assistance – running the estate is too onerous for you alone. I could help you, Coz! Haven't I proved by dealing with these incidents, I should be working alongside you? You need someone to share the burden *every day*, Alyssa – let me be your partner!'

She blinked in astonishment. It was a full minute before she said in an incredulous voice, 'Piers, I can hardly believe what I am hearing! Let me be quite certain – are you offering *marriage*?'

'Yes,' he said, fixing his eyes on her face as he waited for her answer.

CHAPTER TEN

Alyssa burst out laughing. 'You can't mean it, Piers! What an absurd suggestion – this must be some sort of joke!'

'I would not jest about a proposal of marriage!' he said coldly, raising his brows.

Undaunted, she gave another chuckle. 'But- but you surely don't profess to be in love with me?'

'Lord, no!' he admitted, 'Naturally I'm fond of you, Coz – you know that – but I don't *love* you! I thought we might rub along well together and no need for it to amount to more. A business arrangement is what I had in mind.' The idea had seemed plausible enough when Piers was planning it, but now he had voiced his proposition, he felt a little sheepish.

'You are offering a marriage of convenience?' she cried.

'Yes, that's it exactly – that's the term I was searching for.'

'And the reason, of course, is money.'

He shrugged. 'Damn it all, it *is* for money: you have something that is rightly mine; my crushing debts leave me no place to turn, and I see no other way out of my current difficulties. Are those reasons sufficient, Alyssa? I am desperate enough to suggest a marriage of convenience. I'd help you run the estate for a share in Hawkscote's wealth, but I'd place no other restrictions on you – you'll be free to go your own way, and I'll not interfere.'

'How very obliging,' she remarked, in a dry voice.

Piers ploughed on, 'Marriage to me would also relieve you of Charles's attentions, who is the dullest dog I know and not fit to kiss the hem of your gown. And he doesn't care for you one jot – by God, he can't even show his face because of a pathetic fear of catching scarlet fever, whereas I have proved my genuine concern for your well-being.'

Piers's indignation was manifest in every syllable, and he continued to argue his case. Alyssa listened in silence but eventually brought his discourse to a summary end by shaking her head and saying abruptly, 'Oh, cut line, Piers! You are mad to think of this, let alone speak of it.' She rose to her feet, and said, 'Thank you for the compliment but I will *not* marry you.'

'But you need help and I need money! If we married, we would both get what we want.'

'*No*,' said she, firmly. 'That is my final word and I beg you not to embarrass both of us by asking again. Indeed, I half expected you to – but no, I will not talk of that now. You must be blinded by your debts and a sense of injustice to suggest this. You might have known I'd never agree.'

'It was worth the attempt.'

'Worth the attempt?' she echoed, with a scornful glance. 'Were you so desperate for money you lost all sense of my character, and how I would react? Good God, if I were a man, I'd land you a facer for being a fool, and a mercenary one at that, and it would be well deserved!'

'I only wanted what is rightfully mine were it not for Uncle Tom's backhanded trick, but I should have accounted for your stubborn streak of independence,' he admitted, his tone increasingly defensive.

'I would not countenance marriage to express gratitude, or relieve me of Charles's attentions. I can achieve both perfectly well by other means.'

'I see that now,' he muttered, shrugging a petulant shoulder.

Piers fell silent and shuffled uncomfortably. Alyssa could see his anger ebbing away as quickly as it had appeared, to be replaced with disquiet and no small measure of embarrassment. Piers looked like a sulky schoolboy who had been caught red-handed on some escapade. She had responded to his proposal with laughter, but it was unconsciously done, and he thoroughly deserved to feel foolish. However, Alyssa had a tender place in her heart for her wayward cousin and could not help feeling sorry for him in his desperation.

Seeing his expression, she said in a softer tone, 'Come, Piers, I bear you no grudge for your proposal, or the flawed reasoning behind it. We need not speak of it again. You do not really wish to marry me, even for money. And haven't I promised to alleviate the worst of your debts when I can? You will not be rich but you will be comfortable; Uncle Tom would have wanted that much, I know. Besides, you have not yet fallen in love and when you do, you will not want a marriage of convenience. You will desire to be with the person you love every minute of every day, and find you cannot enjoy life without them at your side.'

Piers laughed ironically. 'Living in someone else's pocket sounds deuced uncomfortable. If that is being in love, I don't hold out hope of ever finding it. There are only two women I've met whose company don't irritate me: you are one, the other is Letty—' He stopped, looking up slowly as though a thought blinding in its novelty had occurred to him, and repeated in a whisper, 'Letty!'

Before Alyssa could reply, the door opened and Letty came in. She looked quite lovely, dressed in a dark-green riding habit trimmed with braiding à la hussarde. Her long skirt was swept up over one arm and she held her gloves and riding crop in the opposite hand; a single dark-green feather curled down over the brim of her dashing hat to caress one cheekbone. Piers stared at this charming picture as if he were seeing her for the first time, before muttering 'Damnation!' furiously under his breath and flushing to the roots of his hair. 'G-Good morning!' he stammered, 'I have been speaking to Alyssa.'

'I know.'

The guileless look accompanying this reply held no clue to whether Letty had overheard. Her colour was a little heightened and she was not smiling, but otherwise, her features were serene. She let the demi-train of her gown fall to the floor and, pulling on her gloves briskly, prompted, 'I am ready to leave now, Mr Kilworth – if you are?'

'Yes, yes of course!' he said, almost leaping forward in his eagerness not to keep her waiting.

Alyssa watched them leave with her brows drawn together. Letty would be extremely hurt and angry if she had overheard Piers's idiotic proposal. She was not a girl to show her feelings, but Alyssa thought she detected a dangerous gleam in Letty's eyes which did not bode well for her cousin. Piers, Alyssa was convinced, was more than halfway to being in love with Letty but had not yet realized it; whatever direction their relationship took now, his path would not be an easy one.

'It will do Piers no harm,' murmured Alyssa, to no one in particular, 'and might even be the making of him.'

After enduring Letty's frosty silence for over half an hour, Piers could bear her animosity no longer. As they skirted the wood riding side by side on the narrow path, he glanced at the figure beside him. Letty, sitting proudly erect in the saddle, stared straight ahead, every line of her body speaking eloquently of an uncertain temper and Piers wondered where to begin. Finally, he ventured, 'Miss Ravenhill, y-you may have heard me speaking to my cousin. If you did, I should like to explain—'

'There is no need!' she interjected furiously, roused at last from her self-imposed quiescence. 'I may as well confess to hearing most of what was said – unintentionally, as your voices were raised and carried into the hallway – but why you think it concerns me, I have no notion!'

'I was a buffle-headed simpleton to suggest a marriage of convenience,' he

said, urgently, 'and by God, I feel my idiocy more keenly now. I'm not proud of
my behaviour. Alyssa was right – like a regular Johnny Raw, I've been blinded by
a sense of injustice but that does not excuse my folly. Nor does it mitigate my
role in other events during recent weeks—'

'What events?'

'They no longer matter.' He coloured, and gave a short, humourless laugh.
'I've made a complete fool of myself. When Alyssa spurned me, I felt only relief.
She saw straight through my offer and laughed in my face, but her words afterwards' – he looked again at Letty and lowered his voice – 'well, her words made
me realize what was before me and I had not seen.'

She regarded him with kindling eyes. 'So, a few words from Alyssa and you
saw the error of your ways? How fortunate! Now you may extract yourself from
the moral turpitude you have fallen into and make amends for your infernal selfishness!'

'Yes . . . no! Letty, I understand you are very angry but—'

'Of course I am!' she exclaimed, her cheeks reddened with wrath.

'—you are furious at my cavalier treatment of Alyssa, and rightly so.'

'Yes! But also because . . . because I thought . . . oh, it cannot signify,' replied
Letty. She gave a sob, and waved one hand in a dismissive gesture. 'As I said, it is
your business entirely.'

'But I want to explain about seeing things clearly at last,' he protested.

'Then speak and be done. I wish to return home; I only accompanied you
because I was too proud to admit to hearing everything.'

'Damn it all, I *will* speak!' he declared, reaching forward to grasp the rein of
Letty's mare and bring both horses to a halt. 'Miss Ravenhill . . . *Letty!*' he
pleaded. 'I made a terrible mistake proposing to my cousin, but doing so allowed
me to see what I have been blind to all this time – it is *you* I love!'

Her eyes, wide with shock, flew to his.

'*I love you!*' repeated Piers.

Letty gasped and flung back in a low, throbbing voice, 'How *dare* you! Have
you no scruples? You propose marriage to one woman and declare passionate
love for another in the same morning. Astonishing! You are a consummate actor,
Mr Kilworth. From the desperate tone of your voice, I could almost believe you
mean it, but I know how charming you can appear. Your dramatic ability does
you credit and it might fool a more gullible lady. However, it is wasted on me.'

'But my love for you is no act! God knows I'm not worthy of you, but I beg
you will listen while I explain.'

Letty declared coldly, 'I cannot stop you when you have charge of my horse's
bridle.'

'I deserve and expect no succour, but hear me out!' He inhaled a steadying breath and tried to continue in a more composed fashion. 'I liked – was attracted – to you from the moment we met. When you appeared I thought I had summoned up a vision from my subconscious: you were the embodiment of my dreams. Even when you made me question my life and admonished me for scowling, I thought you beautiful. But it was not just your beauty which appealed, there was something else . . . you intrigued and beguiled me somehow.'

Letty gestured impatiently again with one hand. Piers grasped it, rubbing his thumb across her knuckles as he spoke again earnestly, 'I continued to enjoy your company, both before and during Alyssa's illness. I looked forward to our every meeting; I was conscious of bitter disappointment when you were busy and could not see me; I watched in admiration as you nursed Alyssa with little regard for your own health. Whenever I thought of you, I felt joyful and more content but, fool that I am, I was too busy making other plans to recognize what was in my heart. It was only when Alyssa said if I truly loved someone, I could not enjoy life without them that I suddenly realized I loved you! Darling, I've been a damned fool, but I'm placing my heart at your feet and asking your forgiveness.'

'Why should I?'

'Because you are what I have been searching for. I can't imagine life without you. Nothing else matters – Hawkscote, money, new carriages, fine clothes – all are worthless compared to having you. I can offer little else but my love but I'll do everything in my power to make you happy and give you the life you deserve.' He smiled ruefully, adding, 'I'm not flush in the pocket, but I'll try from now on to live within my means, if you will only give me hope. With you at my side, I'd willingly face the Devil and all his hounds of hell!'

'Fine words and a very touching speech,' replied she, removing her hand from his grasp, 'but you can hardly expect me to take you seriously when you offered marriage to Alyssa this very day. You might say anything to inveigle yourself back into favour.'

'Deuce take it, I wouldn't say I loved you!' he said, exasperated.

'But how many other women have heard those words from you?'

'None! There are depths to which I will not sink, and whispering false words of love is one. I love you, only you, and I have never spoken thus to any woman.' He edged his horse closer. 'Letty, believe me, I need you more than I can say,' he murmured. His gaze roamed her face and, seeing the curve of her cheek, the long dark lashes contrasting with the pale curls peeping out from beneath her hat and the stormy green-grey eyes that looked back with defiant candour, he said, 'Lord, how lovely you are! I cannot resist any longer. . . .' With that, he deftly transferred the reins into his other hand and slid his fingers along her jaw. Using his thumb to tilt her chin, he bent his head and tentatively pressed his lips to hers. For an infinitesimal moment, Piers felt her respond and emboldened, made a low sound in his throat and deepened his kiss. Desire shot through him, pounded through his veins and he reached for her, only to be brought sharply back from the edge of ecstasy by the crack of a riding crop across his forearm.

'Argh!' he cried out in pain, clutching where Letty had struck the blow. 'What was that for?'

'A reminder! I am not some light o' love to be treated with contempt then won over with a kiss.'

'Damn it, I do respect you: you have my *love* not my *lust!*' He rubbed his arm, winced and said indignantly, 'There was no need to place your crop about my arm!'

'On the contrary, there was every need and you were lucky not to feel it around your head,' she declared roundly. 'Don't take liberties with me, Piers, I'll not stand for it. Perhaps you should know an hour ago I would have given every-thing in this world to hear that you loved me—'

Hope flared in his eyes but Letty held him off with a shake of her head.

'—but after what has happened, it is no longer enough,' she continued. 'My feelings are not to be trifled with as you have done today.'

Piers's head dropped. 'Dear God, I'm sorry for causing you one moment of pain,' he said disconsolately. 'How can I convince you?'

'Show me.'

He studied the curve of her mouth, remembering their kiss, and muttered, 'I have tried.'

'Not in that way,' she said, sighing heavily. 'I don't doubt you could shower me with kisses but I need more; show me you intend to change, that you mean what you say – only then will I believe you truly love me.'

'But I can't be a paragon!'

'I don't want a paragon!' she cried emphatically. 'All I want is the man I have glimpsed beneath the selfish exterior – the engaging, kind, humorous man I know exists. I don't wish to change every aspect of your character, Piers, only remove the cynical veneer you insist on hiding behind, and ask you to become a man – a man aware of his responsibilities and his place in the world, and who is willing to embrace them.'

'I'll do anything you ask, but please say we can return to our easy relation-ship.'

She shook her head again, and blinked away a tear. 'If I can forgive, it will take time and there must be some distance between us.'

'Can't I see you?' he asked, eventually.

'Not alone. I cannot avoid you because we must occasionally meet in company, but I ask you not to importune me further until I choose to speak of it again.'

He uttered a deep groan and expostulated, 'How long must I wait?'

'I-I don't know. Truly, I don't . . . weeks; perhaps longer. I will be watching for the true Piers.'

'I won't fail you, my love, I swear it!' he asseverated, a little unsteadily.

Letty, her eyes moist with tears, gave a wistful half-smile and wheeled her horse around, urging the mare to lengthen her stride into a canter.

Sir Giles set the bell at the oak door of Frampton Manor pealing and waited impatiently for a servant to answer. He found even this slight delay irksome. Caroline's reaction to what he had to say would be unpleasant but she deserved no consideration other than politeness; her Machiavellian endeavours should have been stopped long ago. Towards his friend, however, he did feel compunction. Gil liked the easy-going squire and although he had never spoken to Henry about marrying his daughter, and was under no obligation to cry off formally, he thought it the honourable course. Henry, he hoped, would understand.

Every day he delayed declaring his love was purgatory and he gritted his teeth at the thought of Charles Brook touching a hair on Alyssa's head. When Brook returned, Gil intended to expose him for the uncaring portentous fraud he was.

The door was finally opened by Simmons the butler, who recoiled at the frown darkening Sir Giles's brow and his forbidding expression.

Momentarily flustered, he said, 'G-good morning, Sir Giles. May I help you?'

'I wish to see Squire Nash and then Miss Caroline, Simmons. Pray inform them I am here.'

The servant bowed, and said, 'I am sorry, but the Squire, Mrs Nash and Miss Caroline are away from home, sir.'

Gil stared in surprise. 'Away!' he thundered, 'But where? I received no word of their departure.'

'I believe their trip was hastily arranged. Mrs Nash's sister in Lyme has received a new carriage from London, and Mrs Nash was desirous of inspecting it,' he explained, with a speaking lift of one eyebrow. 'They left yesterday.'

Gil muttered an expletive under his breath. 'When will they return?'

'Thursday morning, sir.'

'That is the day before the evening party, is it not?'

'Yes, sir.'

'Very well – I shall call Thursday afternoon. Please advise the squire and Miss

Nash on their return.'

Gil strode back to his curricle angrily. He vented his annoyance by springing his horses and made the journey home in record time, but on entering the hallway at Eastcombe, he found his anger had abated, but not his frustration: Alyssa was coming to dine tomorrow evening.

'Gil!' cried a voice behind him. 'You have returned at last! Oliver and I arrived half an hour ago.' The dark-haired lady who had spoken these words robbed them of censure with an accompanying smile very much like Gil's own. She approached with hands outstretched and added mischievously, 'How like you not to be here to welcome your own sister.'

'My craven apologies, Marianne,' he said, laughing and kissing her cheek. 'I expected you this afternoon.' Holding her at arm's length, he looked down at his younger sibling. 'My dear, you look lovely – marriage and motherhood agree with you. How is my nephew?'

'James is well and troubled only by the appearance of two new teeth this week,' she replied, gaily. 'I know it is not fashionable to wax lyrical about one's own children, but he is a darling little boy; even at the tender age of eleven months, I declare he is the most intelligent child imaginable.'

'Oh? Then that attribute must be inherited from his father.'

She tapped him playfully on the arm. 'What an impossible tease you are! Come into the library – by now, Oliver has probably sampled most of your burgundy.'

Behind the desk situated between the library window embrasures sat a tall, powerfully built man, who was in the process of pouring burgundy into his glass.

'Gil! Good to see you,' said he, rising to shake hands firmly with his brother-in-law. Oliver waved towards the wine, and drawled, 'I hope you don't mind – your butler insisted I try this vintage while we waited.'

'Do you think it tolerable?' Gil asked, grinning. He heartily approved of this giant of a man.

'Very! I don't suppose you'd care to part with a bottle or two?'

'To you? Of course!'

'Oh! Do stop discussing wine,' protested Marianne, good-naturedly. 'We have more important things to speak of.' Slipping her arm through her husband's, she said, 'What time does Miss Paradise arrive tomorrow?'

'About six o'clock; I have organized an *al fresco* dinner.'

'Excellent!' replied his sister, clapping her hands. '*Al fresco* will be just the thing in this fine weather – and excessively romantic too, guaranteed to appeal to any lady.'

He chuckled, but, using the pet name by which he addressed her when they were children, said warningly, 'Manny, no one else is allowed to be present. It must be just Alyssa and me.'

'Oh, I would not *dream* of intruding,' she said primly. 'Don't worry – Oliver and I will look forward to meeting Miss Paradise before retiring to the dining-room for our own dinner *à deux*, won't we, my darling? What sort of a girl is she, Gil? Shall I like her? After what you have said in your letters, I am determined to, you know. Is she beautiful?'

Her husband sighed indulgently. 'Must you ask so many questions, my love? You will find out tomorrow.'

'Ah, but I need to know if *Gil* thinks she is beautiful.'

Gil hesitated, lost in thought for a moment. 'Yes,' he admitted finally, 'to my eyes, she is very lovely.'

Marianne, studying her brother's expression intently, said only, 'She sounds altogether delightful, but what of Caroline Nash? I hope she does not expect you to offer marriage – you know my feelings regarding *her*.'

Gil raised his brows and smiled wryly. 'As ever, you are astute. Caroline's spite and arrogance have been revealed during recent months and I have no intention of making her an offer. Indeed, I don't believe I ever had. I am honour bound to tell Caroline, but unfortunately the Nashes are in Lyme until Thursday.'

'A pity she is away, but at least you have made your decision,' said his sister, in a more sober voice. 'I'm glad – I've no wish to see my brother trapped in a love-less marriage. For God's sake, tell her immediately she returns, and don't lose your chance of happiness because of that woman!'

He laughed ruefully. 'Are my feelings so obvious?'

'Only to me,' she said.

'There are other difficulties, Manny: Alyssa already has a suitor.'

'Well, what is that to anything?' demanded Marianne, airily. 'If I recall correctly, I had three when I met Oliver, but he swept away all competition. Have you met him?'

'Yes, a pompous, prosy idiot if ever I saw one,' he replied, fiercely. 'Charles Brook refused to come near while she was ill. A poor kind of love he has for her!'

Marianne gave a trill of laughter and her eyes twinkled at this description of Alyssa's admirer. 'Oh, then she must be saved from him at all costs! Don't you agree, Oliver?'

'Undoubtedly,' said her husband, with feeling. 'Miss Paradise, who sounds very agreeable, cannot be allowed to suffer at his hands. If the man is an idiot, it follows naturally he will have the most appalling taste in wine which is an unpar-donable sin.' He took another sip, shook his head and grinned. 'Marry the lady quickly, Gil, and save her from the prosy ninny!'

'If you two have finished organizing my life, I'll go and change my boots before lunch,' declared Gil, laughing.

He left, and Marianne made a sound of delight before hurrying over to her husband. She placed her arms around his neck and breathed, 'Oliver! Is it not wonderfully romantic? Gil is in love – at last – and I cannot wait to meet Miss Paradise. Thank God he is not to marry Caroline, for I always dreaded he would do so! What say you? Am I right?'

'I think you are, love,' he said, as he enfolded her in a crushing embrace. 'I am also intrigued to see the woman who has finally captured his heart and rescued him from the odious Miss Nash.' He smiled slowly, and added, 'I wonder what other consequences this extraordinary will has in store?'

CHAPTER 11

The following evening, Alyssa's carriage came to a halt in front of Eastcombe House and she gazed up in admiration. The house, faced in white Portland stone, was built on classical lines and provided an imposing as well as an aesthetically pleasing welcome. Steps rose to the main entrance and above the portico, three rows of windows overlooked the gardens.

She climbed out and was ushered into a large entrance hall and, as she removed her cloak and handed it to the waiting servant, Alyssa looked around with interest, realizing this impressive grandeur even surpassed Hawkscote's. There was a high stuccoed ceiling, a marble fireplace and floor, and suspended above her head, two magnificent chandeliers sparkled in the candlelight. She blushed to recall she had once feared Sir Giles might use underhand methods to obtain Hawkscote; from this evidence alone, it was clear the value of his property far outweighed her own. The interior oozed elegance and distinction, and when Sir Giles appeared from a doorway to the right, dressed in an exquisitely cut coat, dark waistcoat and gleaming Hessians, she thought how well the house matched its owner.

He greeted her warmly and took her hand. 'I trust you are now fully recovered?'

'Yes, the doctor tells me my recuperation has been remarkably rapid.'

'That is wonderful news.' Gil's grasp on her fingers tightened and he raised them to his lips slowly, his gaze holding hers for a long moment.

Alyssa felt her skin tingle under his touch and she gave a shiver of sensual awareness. Flustered, she stammered, 'F-from what I have seen so far, Eastcombe is very elegant.'

'I'm glad you approve,' he said, smiling. 'I have made minor changes to the interior, but most of the improvements under my stewardship can be found in the gardens, and particularly the farmland. There is only one thing Eastcombe lacks now and the burden falls squarely on me to address that omission soon.'

'Oh?'

'The estate needs a mistress as well as a master – I hope my wife will share the task of improving it further.'

This reminder of Miss Nash quickly dampened the thrill running through Alyssa. Not knowing exactly how to respond, she simply murmured 'I see,' in a flat voice before adding, 'Is the clerk here?'

He nodded. 'Mr Forde arrived earlier and has promised to situate himself discreetly when we dine.'

As he spoke, his appreciative gaze ran over her and Alyssa's pulse quickened again. She knew her pale-green silk crepe dress showed her figure to advantage, the silk clinging to every curve and swishing sensuously with her every movement. Under his scrutiny, anticipation and desire spiralled through her and she blushed deeply.

'Please let me to show you to the drawing-room,' he said, 'my sister and her husband are waiting there, anxious to meet you.'

He led the way into another elegant room decorated in yellow, with pale-gold silk curtains and matching coverings on the chairs and sofas. Gil introduced his sister and brother-in-law and Alyssa returned their friendly appraising looks; she took an instant liking to the animated Marianne and her husband, whose languid manner was belied by his keen perceptive gaze.

Marianne, kissing Alyssa on the cheek, declared effusively, 'Gil mentioned you in his letters but I see he has been shockingly remiss and completely understated your charm.'

'No words of mine could do Miss Paradise justice,' said Gil, with a grin. 'Far better to rely on Shakespeare: " 'Tis beauty truly blent, whose red and white Nature's own sweet and cunning hand laid on." '

'Very apt,' agreed his sister, 'but why can't *men* ever be troubled with recounting the details *women* are interested in?' Alyssa laughed at this, and Marianne, eyes twinkling, continued, 'Ah, I see you understand, Miss Paradise! I would have observed you are of average height, with a Venus-like figure and hair of glorious chestnut. Add a pair of speaking blue eyes, delightful smile and friendly manner, and only then does an image form. Unfortunately, one can never trust a man, especially one's own brother, to report these matters assiduously. He does not understand I like to have every detail, however minor,' complained Marianne, her prim look contradicted by the merriment in her eyes.

'Do not let my wife put you to the blush, Miss Paradise,' said Oliver, indulgently. 'Although sadly talkative, she is harmless enough.'

'Indeed, you are generous in your praise, but a new gown and carefully arranged hair work wonders – I promise you, I looked positively haggard a few weeks ago,' observed Alyssa.

'Well, thank God you recovered, but knowing something of fashion, you must take my word that your looks are out of the common way and if you had enjoyed a London season, you would have taken the place by storm. However,' said Marianne, with a mischievous glance at her brother, 'the *bon ton's* loss is our gain. You do not mind if I call you Alyssa?'

'No, of course not.'

'Good, for we are to be firm friends, I'm certain of it.' Marianne sat down on the sofa and patted the empty seat beside her. 'Let us enjoy a comfortable talk before you are obliged to keep my brother company. I'm sure Gil and Oliver won't mind if we ignore them for a while.'

'We shall bear up under the strain,' replied Gil, amused. 'But you may only monopolize Miss Paradise's attentions until dinner, Manny—'

'When I intend to carry you off to the dining-room, my love,' concluded her husband.

Marianne smiled, blew her husband a saucy kiss and she was soon chatting amicably to Alyssa. Marianne's effervescence was as infectious as it was appealing, and it was impossible not to warm to her. Her curiosity resulted in a great number of questions about Alyssa's home in Oxfordshire, her parents and, most particularly, her uncle and his will. She answered them all without rancour and in return, Marianne unreservedly offered details about her own circumstances: her house near Bath, the many excellent qualities of her husband and her baby son, and ended with encomiums on her brother.

'I love Gil dearly – he is the most affectionate of brothers – but he finds it difficult to be open in his manner and, as a consequence, can sometimes appear blunt to those who don't know him.'

'I thought him so at our first meeting.'

'But he is not nearly as fierce as he appears,' explained Marianne in an urgent whisper, 'he is just used to being in control. You see, the obligations that came with our father's death were thrust on Gil at a relatively young age, and he takes his responsibilities *too* seriously at times. I think he has forgotten a little impetuosity is occasionally allowed. However, I detect recent changes to the good: he has smiled more today than I have seen for years! Under that natural reticence, he feels things deeply and apart from my husband, he is the most generous man I know. He also possesses an excellent sense of humour. Have you discovered it yet?'

Alyssa knew Marianne was only expressing sibling affection in her exuberant way, but the knowledge Gil was to marry Miss Nash was painful enough without the added torment of hearing his qualities extolled – it only reminded her he was unattainable.

Unable to voice these feelings, Alyssa glanced at Gil, who was talking to his brother-in-law on the other side of the room, and replied simply, 'Your brother's dry wit is amusing, and he has shown me kindness in many ways. During my illness, he often sent flowers or some other small token, and I appreciated his thoughtful gestures. He also found time to sit with me and run Hawkscote on my behalf.' Gil, who saw her looking towards him, raised his brows quizzically and smiled; Alyssa blushed and gave a shy smile in response.

This exchange was watched with furtive interest by Marianne. 'I am not surprised to hear of his kindness,' she replied. 'His generosity towards those he holds in affection is marked, but there must be a particular reason for his attentiveness to you. And it cannot be simply because of the will – that is a business matter.'

Alyssa sighed and murmured, 'Then I expect it is because I am his neighbour, and my uncle was his friend.'

Marianne looked at her companion in surprise: Alyssa obviously had no notion Gil loved her. Really, her brother should stop being honourable to Caroline Nash and kiss Alyssa passionately instead! She would not resist if she cared, whatever barriers eventually had to be overcome. And, in Marianne's opinion, other obstacles would melt away like snow on a spring day; the look Alyssa had just bestowed on Gil was certainly not that of a woman pining for an absent suitor. Marianne hid a smile. The signs Alyssa was in love with her brother were there so perhaps she could help matters along with a few well-chosen words.

'I hardly think Gil would show such considerate behaviour to every neighbour – old Mr Jarvis didn't receive flowers when he was ill,' ventured Marianne gaily. 'No, you are something quite special in my brother's eyes, Alyssa.'

Alyssa's gaze flew back to Marianne's and, in obvious bewilderment, she replied faintly, 'Oh! Do you think so? Something he said made me wonder, but I was ill and thought I had misheard. . . .' With a helpless gesture, she said, 'But you *cannot* be right, there is Miss Nash to consider.' Alyssa grimaced. 'Your brother's kindness earned an admonishment from her.'

'Pooh!' said Marianne, dismissively. 'Do not regard it. Miss Nash is a designing creature, and I do not like her!'

Alyssa, her eyes widening at Marianne expressing her opinion of her brother's *amour* so decidedly, replied, 'I confess, neither do I, but I understood Sir Giles . . . that he intends to. . . .' She stopped, confused as to how to continue.

'Make an offer of marriage?' suggested Marianne.

Alyssa nodded.

'Miss Nash would have everyone believe it, but I know my brother does not care for her,' replied Marianne, shrugging an elegant shoulder. 'Let me say this:

Gil has been sleepwalking into the web Caroline has woven but will do so no longer. He is an honourable man, but not a foolish one, and he will not propose marriage where there is no love or respect. Matters between them will soon be resolved, Alyssa, and afterwards' – she smiled – 'well, I wash my hands of my brother if he does not sort out his affairs urgently!'

Alyssa listened to Marianne in silence. She had tried to accept Gil's marriage to Caroline but in truth, she did not want to envisage her own future without him. She remembered her advice to Piers – *you will desire to be with the person you love every minute of every day* – and realized the words must have been unconsciously wrung from her own heart: she loved Gil.

He was the only man to excite her anticipation and longing each time he strode into a room. By virtue of a glance, Alyssa's heart beat more rapidly and she felt the warm glow of desire. Wherever she was, whatever she was doing, the mere thought of him sent quivers of need racing through her body. He could appear blunt and overbearing sometimes, but he had also demonstrated patience, generosity, humour, compassion, appreciation rather than disapproval of her spirit, and rare warmth of character and, notwithstanding their verbal sparring, she would be very happy in his love.

Her feelings could no longer be denied. She wanted him. Needed him. Desperately. And yet it had seemed that could never be . . . at least, not until this moment, when Marianne's words suggested he was not to marry Caroline after all. Alyssa, allowing herself a brief glimpse of a future where she luxuriated in Gil's love, ached with longing but was startled out of dreamy abstraction by his deep voice reverberating nearby.

He stood smiling down at her, and saying, 'Manny, I must take Alyssa away – dinner is ready.'

'Oh no!' protested Marianne, 'So soon?'

'Yes, if we are not to lose the light or the weather.'

He saw Alyssa's quizzical look. 'I took the liberty of arranging dinner to be served in the rose garden.' When she did not immediately reply, he added anxiously, 'You expressed a desire to see it.'

'Oh, that will be wonderful!' she cried.

'I knew you would appreciate Gil's plan,' laughed Marianne, rising to her feet. 'I see my husband is waiting to carry me off, just as he promised. Enjoy your *al fresco* dinner!'

Marianne and Oliver left and Gil drew Alyssa's arm through his to lead her out on to the terrace. It was the end of a warm summer's day, and the intense heat had begun to lose its oppressive edge. The sun dipped in a blue sky marred only by wispy clouds, and the drone of insects filled the air. Alyssa breathed deeply and sighed; it was a perfect setting with Gil at her side and whatever happened, she would always treasure these moments.

They walked across the lawn to the rose garden, where neat gravel paths interspersed with blooms of every colour. A table and two chairs were set in one of the secluded arbours and they sat down to dinner. Later, Alyssa was to marvel at the unobtrusive way the food was served and the covers removed after each course. It was an open yet intensely intimate setting, enhanced by the exquisitely prepared menu of soup jardinière, turbot, and roast quail. Conversation was light-hearted and humorous and, as she hesitated between apricot soufflé, pineapple jelly and elderflower ice cream for dessert, Alyssa was conscious of a childlike wish for the evening never to end.

So was Gil. He wanted to please Alyssa with a sublime evening and, judging by her smiles and demeanour, he had succeeded. Even the weather had been kind and silently, he damned Caroline's unexpected departure and wished he were free. Perhaps if he could show Alyssa even a whit of how he felt, it might allay his frustration until doing his duty by Squire Nash. Leaning back in his chair, he decided to wait for an opportunity, taking enjoyment from the expressions flitting across her features and the sparkle of pleasure in her eyes.

'Hmm . . . I think I *must* choose the apricot soufflé, but it is a difficult decision when every morsel has been superb,' said Alyssa. 'You employ an excellent chef, Sir Giles.'

'He is temperamental, as only French chefs can be, but I find him well worth his exorbitant wage,' he replied. 'And not only are his wages expensive – an ice house was built last year after François informed me pithily that he could no longer work at an establishment which did not possess one.'

'Ah, so that is how he concocted these wonderful desserts! Perhaps I should consider an ice house for Hawkscote.'

'If you decide to, I would happily help you draw up suitable plans.'

She smiled. 'I am indebted to you once again. "Thank you" seems an inadequate response for your help and advice, but it seems all I can offer in return.'

He shook his head, observing, 'The only thanks I ask are to see you happy and relieved of burdens, Alyssa.'

She blushed at the warmth in his voice and then, taking a sip of champagne, she regarded him from under her lashes as she said, 'Sir Giles, I must take you to task.'

Gil furrowed his brow. 'Oh? Have I offended you?'

'I asked Dr Plant for his account yesterday and he informed me it had been forwarded to Eastcombe – at your request.' Alyssa twisted the stem of her glass between her fingers, appearing to study it intently. 'Of course, I said there must have been a mistake, but he was adamant you gave instructions to that effect and indeed, went on to say he has already received payment.' She looked up and said accusingly, 'Have you paid the doctor's bill on my behalf?'

He nodded. 'Guilty – but it was not my intention to upset you. My object was to spare you further worry and for that I cannot be sorry.'

'He seemed astonished that you offered to pay.'

'I expect he was,' said Gil, unruffled. 'But, while I'm grateful for the excellent care he gave you, I don't give a damn for his opinion on why I chose to pay his bill: your feelings, and yours alone, interest me.'

Alyssa leaned forward and, cupping her chin in her one hand, declared frankly, 'Well, it *was* generous, but I really should not allow your impudence to go unpunished!' Her mouth quivered with suppressed laughter.

He stared at her rosy, trembling lips, a seductive gleam in his eyes. 'What have you in mind?' he said, huskily. 'I have not forgotten the *pleasant* punishments spoken of at our first dinner.'

Her cheeks grew warmer still. 'I-I was thinking of something else.'

'Then I am disappointed,' he said, looking crestfallen.

'You are *quite* abominable,' she whispered, her mouth curving into a smile. 'The recompense I had in mind was that you show me this delightful garden without delay.'

'Gladly!' He came to stand at her side and, offering his hand, he looked down into her eyes and said, 'Come with me, Alyssa. There is much I want to share with you.'

Alyssa allowed him to pull her to her feet, and draw her arm once more through his. She had touched very little wine or champagne, but felt intoxicated with exhilaration or happiness – or both. They strolled through the walkways, some covered with climbing roses whose heady scent filled the still, humid air. The sun had disappeared behind ominous grey clouds, but Alyssa did not notice as Gil pointed out the varieties of rose and explained that the original inspiration for the garden came from his mother.

'She loved roses. On my father's estate, she designed planting themes and nurtured a rose garden, even experimenting in new varieties. Apart from my father, roses were her greatest passion. I created this garden in her memory, although I am not as knowledgeable on the subject as she was and leave the main work to the gardeners.'

'Your mother would be proud of what you have achieved,' she said, 'I find it fascinating.'

He picked a pink damask bloom and gave it to her, saying softly, 'But not one of these roses is as beautiful as you are.'

'You flatter me,' she murmured. He was very close and she could see the faint shadow along his jaw.

'No, I could never do so.' Taking her hands in his, he said urgently, 'Alyssa, I wish I could make fine speeches! I don't find it easy to articulate my emotions but I think – I hope – my actions recently might have given you some clue as to how I feel.'

'You have been very kind—' she began.

'Being kind was not my only motive,' he interjected. 'Of course, I wanted to help in any way I could, but I want to be more than a friend. After years of searching, I have found what I didn't think existed—' He stopped and muttered fiercely, 'God, I'm making a mull of this! I must find the right words somehow!'

Taking a deep breath, he continued, 'After my boorish behaviour when we met, I was surprised you spoke to me again. I regretted what I said as soon as it was uttered.'

She glanced down at the strong hands which still grasped hers and then back to his face. His eyes were a vivid blue in the gathering gloom and her voice wavered as she whispered, 'My behaviour wasn't without fault – I enjoyed provoking you.'

Gil laughed softly and slid his hands to the top of her arms. 'So you did, my darling termagant, and you must never stop. How exquisite you look at this moment! With you in my arms, my feelings must find voice: I love you, Alyssa! I desired you from the moment we met but now I love you, not only for your beauty, your elegance, that entrancing dimple that appears when you smile' – his grasp on her tightened – 'but for your mind, and your soul. I love your spirit, your laughter, your forthright manner and, in spite of my reserve, the thought of you makes me want to shout from the rooftop with sheer joy. Without you, I have wealth, position and status but I'm only half alive.'

Alyssa gasped and could only gaze up in astonishment.

He pressed on, 'When you were first ill and I-I thought' – he raked his fingers through his hair and shuddered – 'I thought I might lose you, it was unbearable. I'll never know how I got through those dark hours. I love you with all my heart, and will try my utmost to win you. Damn it all,' he added fiercely, 'Brook's not worth your affection! I won't rest until I have made you mine. Alyssa, say something before I go mad, even if it is only to rebuke me!'

Thunder sounded in the distance, but Alyssa scarcely heard it over the pounding of her heart. Her silence came partly from shock at his fervent declaration – and for once his emotions were clearly written on his features – and partly from the heady feeling that her wildest dreams were coming true. His mention of Charles brought her back to earth a little: she had barely given him a thought since her illness.

'Charles?' she queried, faintly.

Gil made a sound of frustration. His arms stole around her and he muttered thickly, 'Tell me I have a chance . . . that you might learn to love *me!*'

She gave a little laugh which wobbled uncertainly. 'I might.'

'Thank God! At least you have not condemned me to a bleak and barren future. Brook is not worthy of you.'

'But Gil, I—'

He interjected gently, 'Let me continue – there is something else I need to explain. I would say more now, Alyssa . . . much more . . . but I have a matter of honour to settle first. It tears my heart out to be obliged to speak to Caroline, and the squire, but I want no further misunderstandings. Can you appreciate why I must do this?'

The movement of his mouth as he spoke held her fascinated, his lips hovering tantalizingly above her own. 'Yes,' she whispered, 'as an honourable man, you feel you must first extricate yourself from the arrangement with Miss Nash.'

He nodded and traced one finger down her cheek. 'It was never official; it was not even consciously done on my part, for, like a piece of flotsam upon the sea, I drifted into her plans while never really caring for her. I must have been mad, and should have put a stop to her manipulative arrogance long ago. I intend to do so at the earliest opportunity. Then, my love, you will have to choose between Brook and me – and I vow to fight hard.'

There was another dull rumble overhead, and a flash of lightning. Large rain-drops began to fall from the leaden sky.

His hands moved rhythmically over the smooth fabric of her dress. 'Never have I wished honour and integrity to the Devil as much as I do now! But, while I may not *speak* absolutely freely, nothing will prevent me *showing* you how I feel. Nothing,' he said, placing a soft kiss on her forehead, 'will' – he kissed her again, this time on her cheek – 'stop' – and again, nuzzling under her ear – 'me' – two more, at the base of her throat and another on the exposed skin of her shoulder – 'from' – he feathered his mouth along her jaw making Alyssa moan softly – 'doing' – a kiss at the corner of her mouth – '*this* . . .' he concluded, as his lips fastened fiercely against hers.

CHAPTER 12

The touch of his lips unleashed a molten longing which broke through any barriers of restraint and Alyssa returned his embrace instinctively; Charles had never attempted to kiss her in this way, and she had never desired him to.

But this was heaven. Alyssa felt the solid warmth of Gil's body, the pressure of his fingers through her dress as he gathered her closer. His lips – gentle at first, then more demanding – searched, teased, and tasted hers and she rejoiced in every sensation; her body had craved his touch for so long, it welcomed him with a visceral pleasure. Enthralled, she savoured this newly discovered sensual awareness and sank into his embrace, returning his kiss eagerly and sliding one hand up to revel in the feel of his hair against her fingertips. Slowly, enticingly, his lips moved over hers until his kiss left her quivering with desire and she lost any sense of time – was it seconds or minutes until she became dimly aware of the rain beating down steadily?

Gil, aware his fierce need was distilled from of weeks of longing, tried desperately to be tender and briefly succeeded until he felt Alyssa's eager response. Then, desire seared through him and he kissed her with unbridled passion, wanting to fill her senses until she could think and feel only him. Deepening the kiss, he drew her against him possessively.

Lightning again lit up the sky, followed by a deafening thunderclap, this time directly above. The rain fell faster and drummed out of the clouds with a growing insistence.

'We should go inside,' he murmured, against her lips.

'No, not yet,' she said softly.

A raindrop trickled down her cheek and Gil kissed it away before his mouth found hers once more, urgent and demanding.

Eventually, he whispered, 'I love you.'

Alyssa did not reply, not daring to trust her voice at that moment, but she did moan faintly in frustration when he pulled away. Without his enveloping warmth, she felt bereft and wrapped her arms around her body as she shivered: her dress was soaked from the rainstorm which had stripped the warmth from the air.

'You are cold,' said Gil, frowning. Placing his coat around her shoulders, he added, 'Put this on until we reach the house. Damn it, I should be taking better care of you, not keeping you out in a thunderstorm!'

'But you *have* been taking care of me . . . and I'd hardly noticed the rain,' she said, with a seductive smile.

'Don't tempt me further.' His grin was endearingly lop-sided as he raised his voice to be heard over the rain. 'I'd willingly stay as we are but it won't do – you mustn't risk a chill after your illness.'

Alyssa considered ironically there was no chance of succumbing to a chill while the inferno ignited by his kisses raged inside her. She feasted her eyes on him. The rain had soaked his shirt which now clung to his body like a second skin, revealing a muscled torso and the shadow of dark hair dusted across his chest, and she drew in a deep breath in a vain attempt to regain control over her emotions.

Holding hands, they half-walked, half-ran through the downpour, finally re-entering the house through the terrace doors. There, they looked at their muddy, bedraggled state and began to laugh.

After the passion of moments earlier, Alyssa realized this shared laughter was another release, different in expression but no less acute. She felt light-hearted, playful, even exultant, and said softly, 'If *that* is your notion of punishment, you can administer it as often as you like!'

With a throaty chuckle, Gil stepped towards her, but he stopped when Marianne hurried in.

'I wondered if I might find you here – oh, you are both soaked!' she observed in dismay. 'Gil, what are you thinking of to keep Alyssa out in this rain?'

'It was my fault too,' said Alyssa, smiling at Gil, 'we – we did not immediately notice it was raining.'

'Ah, I see,' Marianne cast a knowing glance from one to the other but said only, 'Well, you cannot stay in those clothes, Alyssa. Come to my room and I will find you another gown – we are of a similar size, I think.'

Alyssa submitted, pulling the coat closely around her as she followed Marianne. She threw another glance and a smile over her shoulder towards a grinning Gil, who stood with hands on hips as rainwater dripped from his clothes to collect in a pool on the carpet.

Only when the door had closed behind her did Alyssa realize she was still clutching the rose and she quickly concealed it. Alyssa liked Marianne, but was anxious not to promote searching questions, wanting to keep the discoveries she had made this evening to herself for a little longer.

Once upstairs, Alyssa barely attended to Marianne's gay chatter. Sitting by the fire and dressed in one of Marianne's elegant *robes de chambre*, she rubbed her hair dry and responded only when necessary, reflecting on what had happened, glad of these moments to become accustomed to the knowledge that Gil loved her. No other man had touched her heart in the way Gil did. He was what her soul craved and to find he felt the same left her beyond words. Marianne did not ask what had happened, and if she did suspect the cause of Alyssa's heightened colour, she chose not to pry – for which consideration Alyssa was grateful.

Dressed in one of Marianne's muslin gowns, it was almost an hour later when Alyssa descended again to the drawing-room. Gil had also changed and his hair, still dark as a raven's wing with moisture, glistened in the candlelight. He was speaking in muted tones to his brother-in-law but stopped and looked up when they came in.

He smiled at Alyssa, his eyes warm and caressing but holding a hint of concern. 'I apologize for not bringing you back to the house sooner. You are not cold as a result?'

'No, quite the reverse,' she replied, in an admirably even voice.

Satisfaction showed for fleeting moment on his face. 'You look charming in my sister's gown.'

'Yes, how vexing that it suits Alyssa more than me,' remarked Marianne merrily.

In response to their combined pleas, Alyssa then agreed to stay another hour. She looked at Gil, who had come to stand nearby, and blushed as she confessed, 'I am enjoying this evening very much.'

'So am I,' he murmured.

'Then it is settled,' said Marianne, pulling the bell to summon a servant, 'I'll ring for tea and the four of us will enjoy a cosy hour. Do you play cards, Alyssa?'

'Oh yes,' she replied, adding with a laugh, 'I believe I am – or perhaps I should say *Mr Esidarap* is – considered something of an expert!'

'Mr Esidarap? Who is he?' asked Marianne, intrigued.

'A disguise I adopted – and he is an excellent card player as well as a sad rake!'

Oliver raised one eyebrow and a look of quizzical surprise crossed Marianne's face.

'You'll enjoy the story,' said Gil, laughing, 'but, as it's a long and involved one, Alyssa had best enlighten you while we play.'

Oliver moved to the card table and held out a chair for his wife. Gil and Alyssa followed, but as Gil did the same and waited for Alyssa to take her seat, he placed a hand on her shoulder and murmured wickedly into her ear, 'Remember, my love, I promised to teach Mr Esidarap a lesson when I encountered him over a game of cards.'

She chuckled softly. 'Wretch! Do your worst then, and we shall see who succeeds.'

'I'll claim another kiss if I win.'

'And what if *I* win?'

Another grin dawned as he said, 'Name your prize!'

Her gaze met his. 'Hmm . . . I think I should claim two kisses – to be certain I enjoy the first.'

Instantly, his eyes darkened with passion, but Oliver and Marianne were ready to begin so he had no opportunity to reply. The next hour passed very pleasantly: Alyssa chatted with Marianne, and Oliver's ironic humour and succession of *bons mots* made for convivial company, but it was her exchanges with Gil which thrilled Alyssa most.

Under his smiles and caressing looks, her cheeks grew warm and, whenever he could do so unseen by his sister and her husband, he swept her fingers to his lips or simply sat back to run his gaze longingly over her. His love shone across the short distance separating them and while no words were spoken, a great deal was understood.

They played with counters for imaginary and ridiculously high stakes which resulted in much hilarity, enhanced by the lurid retelling of Mr Esidarap's adventures. Alyssa played well and won steadily but, in spite of using all her wits, she suspected Gil was only toying with her and could easily best her efforts when he chose. And so it proved. Gil gradually raised the stakes and won several games in succession. When it seemed that he must win outright, and Alyssa sighed and said she was quite done up and out of counters, he offered to bet his winnings on the outcome of a final deciding game.

Alyssa smiled, a dimple appearing as she said, 'Very well, I accept,' before adding in a low voice, 'but keep in mind what is at stake here, Gil.'

'I won't forget,' he murmured, a gleam in his eyes.

With Oliver and Marianne watching, the game commenced. It remained evenly balanced for some time but Gil slowly gained the upper hand; his skill was astonishing and yet, when winning seemed assured, he made a glaring error and handed Alyssa an easy victory.

Marianne clapped her hands. 'You've won!'

'You lowered your guard and Miss Paradise took advantage,' observed Oliver.

'Were it not for that error, you would have won again,' said Alyssa with a rueful laugh. 'I admire your skill – even Mr Esidarap could not triumph over you!' She pouted in mock disgust as she added, 'But, alas, I believe you let me win.'

Gil's gaze lingered on her mouth. 'My concentration wandered – I was thinking of something else.'

'A word of advice, Gil,' drawled Oliver, collecting the cards, 'never drop your guard with ladies present, not even for a second: before you know it you will have agreed to a new wardrobe of clothes, shoes, jewellery, a new carriage with pink upholstery, and be ready to decorate the London townhouse from top to bottom.' He shook his head and grinned wryly. 'A devilish easy thing to happen and I should know: Manny is an expert.'

'I could never persuade you to buy a carriage with pink upholstery – *blue* perhaps, but not pink!' protested his wife.

Alyssa smiled at this but after glancing at the clock she gave a little sigh, and rose to her feet. 'I should leave now, otherwise Letty will be growing concerned.'

Marianne moved to embrace her, saying warmly, 'Dearest Alyssa – you are everything I anticipated, and more. I had begun to despair of my brother but, having met you, I am *very* content. We leave tomorrow but I expect to see you again soon.' She looked at her brother. 'You will want to exchange a few words with Gil before you leave so I'll send my maid down with my warm cloak shortly.'

When Oliver had said his farewells too, Gil and Alyssa were alone once more.

'Don't you wish to claim your prize?' he asked.

'Gil,' she said accusingly, but with a laugh in her voice, 'you *deliberately* let me win!'

'Most certainly I did,' he said, moving closer.

'Oh, you are incorrigible!'

'I know it. However, we digress . . . you must collect your winnings,' he said, smiling wolfishly.

She whispered, 'I want to – very much.'

'Then don't keep me waiting. Ever since we came in from the garden, I have been desperate to kiss you again,' he said, his mouth tantalizingly near.

In reply, Alyssa's hands curled around his neck and he crushed her to him, his lips finding hers in a heated, sensual kiss.

When he had left her breathless, Gil murmured, 'Shall we repeat that?'

'Yes,' said Alyssa, closing her eyes briefly while she drew in a ragged breath.

He studied her for a long moment, looking into her eyes before framing her face with his hands and kissing her again, first with passion and then placing slow, lingering kisses against her lips.

'Have I told you I love you?' he asked, smiling.

She clung to him more tightly as she said, 'Yes, and I tried to tell you earlier –

there is no need to win me because my heart already belongs to you. Until this evening, I refused to acknowledge I cared for you, even to myself – it was too painful when I believed you promised to Miss Nash – but when Manny said I was something special in your eyes, I began to hope . . . and then, when you spoke of your feelings' – she gave a little shake of her head, and confessed – 'I could hardly believe it but now I can.'

He drew back to meet her gaze. 'Thank God! I didn't dare hope you might feel the same.' Another tender kiss followed before he muttered regretfully, 'If only we were married and you did not have to leave.'

'I wish that too,' she admitted, tucking her head under his chin. 'When will you see Caroline?'

'Not until Thursday – she is away in Lyme until then.'

'Oh. So long?'

'Yes, damn it! It is only five days but now it seems an age.'

Alyssa sighed. 'But you must talk to her and then afterwards—'

'Afterwards, my darling, I want you to write to Brook and tell him you will be marrying me.' Then, placing one finger under her chin, he smiled and said in a lighter tone, 'Now, kiss me again before Marianne's maid arrives with that cloak!'

That same afternoon, Piers's plans went decidedly awry. He set off for London in good time, anxious to have discussions with his man of business and return for the Nashes' party. He was determined to put his finances into some sort of order. They were precarious but not entirely hopeless; there was no mortgage on his property in Lincolnshire and some items could be sold to clear his most pressing debts.

Having seen Letty twice in recent days, he was more in love with her than ever. Alyssa had also been present, but, although there was awkwardness between them at first, he quickly came to realize that while Letty might be firm in her resolve for him to change, she would not be cruel. The sadness in her eyes was tempered by a gleam of hope when he had spoken of his visit to London and the reasons for it, and she had smiled in silent acknowledgement at the changes he was making for her sake.

For the first time in his life, Piers was thinking not only of himself, and he had no intention of wasting the opportunity Letty had given him. He did not relish going away but consoled himself with the memory of that smile and the note he received before leaving this morning, now safely stowed in his pocket. The letter was precious for its warm tone rather than the few words on the paper. Piers did not doubt she cared for him, in spite of his behaviour to date, and it was now up to him to nurture that affection and inchoate trust into love. As he had already done several times, he took the letter from his coat and read it.

Piers smiled, replaced the note carefully and urged his horses forward at a greater pace. He was travelling down a lane on the outskirts of the Hawkscote estate when he noticed a pall of smoke on the far edge of the field and, reining in his horses, he stared in concern.

The weather had been hot for several weeks and a fire could have started accidentally in the hay which had been cut and left to dry; on the other hand, it might be no accident. Piers's mouth hardened. Although he had paid Draper and told him his services were no longer required, he didn't trust the man. He now felt utter shame for what he had done and intended to make a clean breast of his involvement on his return, knowing there must be no secrets to mar his relationship with Letty, or his cousin, in the future. Narrowing his eyes to the horizon, he tried to see what was causing the smoke. This was impossible as the source was too far away, but he thought he could discern the vague outline of a figure and Piers could not leave without investigating further.

Jumping nimbly down from his carriage, he tethered the animals to a nearby tree and began to walk across the field, heading towards the thin line of smoke. Sweat trickled down his back as he strode out under the hot sun. As he reached the mid-point of his journey, he could see orange flames licking at the base of the smoke and concern turned to fear: fire would spread rapidly among the hay which made for perfect tinder. Then, he observed the figure near the flames and swore fluently and profusely under his breath – Draper! He broke into a run, managing to remain unobserved until his last few strides as Draper was busy adding fuel to the pyre and did not immediately notice his approach. He finally turned at the sound of footsteps.

'What in Hades are you doing?' cried Piers, panting.

An ugly expression descended on Draper's thin features. He looked Piers up and down and sneered, 'What does it look like?' before returning to his task.

Piers caught hold of his arm to swing him violently around. 'Don't turn your back on me, you chawbacon! Explain yourself!'

Draper shook off Piers's grasp. 'I'm payin' your cousin back for not givin' me a decent wage!' he said tersely.

'Damn it, man, that's done with! I told you it was finished, and paid you well for your part!'

The flames spat and licked higher, eating eagerly into the hay, while Draper jabbed his finger in Piers's direction and snapped, 'Oh, so I have to end it on your word, do I, Mr Kilworth? Well, let me tell you this – mebbe I don't want to stop, after all! Mebbe I'm angry and sick of living on nothin' but potatoes and a few rag ends of mutton while the likes of you and your cousin get rich off the backs of poor folk, and then bring in machinery to take what little work we 'ave. Mebbe I intend to make you and your kind pay, and pay well! This whole field and many more like it can go up in flames for all I care, and good riddance at that,' he finished with an unpleasant smirk.

'You bastard!' growled Piers, 'I'll teach you a lesson you won't forget!' He swung his fist and Draper, caught unawares, fell to the ground, spitting blood from his mouth and cursing.

Piers stood over him with a furious expression and clenched fists. 'Damn you for an impudent fool! There's more of the home-brewed if you've the stomach for it!'

When Draper made no move, Piers curled his lip derisively and added, 'You're a coward as well! Help me put this fire out and when that's done, you can slink back to your cottage and prepare to leave. Stay only until you find accommodation elsewhere – for the sake of your wife and children, I'll not see you homeless – but don't take too long about it: when I return in a few days, I don't want to see your miserable face again.'

'What if I don't choose to?' asked Draper defiantly, wiping his mouth with the back of his hand.

'I'll have you thrown into jail.'

He eyed Piers truculently. 'You're very clever, ain't you, Mr Kilworth? But what if I tell your cousin about you bein' involved afore?'

'You cur! I intend to tell her myself so it would make no difference. Besides, my cousin would believe me over a dog like you. Now be quick and put these flames out, before it's too late!'

Grudgingly, Draper rose to his feet and, after spitting out blood and saliva on to the ground, took off his coat and began to beat the flames. Piers did the same, using both his jacket and a nearby fallen branch to attack the fire, but even with both their efforts it was five minutes before the flames were extinguished.

Piers stood with heaving chest and eyes streaming from the smoke. Drawing his shirt sleeve across his brow to mop up the perspiration, he eyed Draper with distaste; like Piers, he was streaked with dirt, soot and sweat but the labourer's unprepossessing features bore no sign of remorse.

'Well, what the devil are you waiting for?' snapped Piers. 'You have your belongings to pack. Just be thankful I don't intend to put the law on you!'

Draper swore under his breath. 'You'll be sorry for this,' he mumbled, savagely. Throwing Piers a final militant look, he turned on his heel and headed in the direction of the labourers' cottages.

When he had gone, Piers sighed with relief; he knew serious damage would have been done had he not, by sheer chance, passed by. His eyes narrowed as he watched the speck denoting Draper's retreating figure. The man was dangerous, and Piers cursed himself for ever encouraging him. It was imperative he confessed and apologized to Alyssa and Letty on his return, but there was no time now.

Piers spent further minutes ensuring the fire was completely out, before looking down at his singed jacket. His clothes, face and hands were filthy and he would need to call at The Antelope before continuing on his way. His coat was from one of the finest tailors in London and he felt a pang of regret at its ruin, but that was nothing compared to his anxiety at the sudden realization he might have lost something far more precious while fighting the flames. Hurriedly, he felt in the pocket and pulled out Letty's note, to find the fire had charred it around the edges but it was still intact. Piers touched the paper to his lips in a gesture of relief and began to retrace his steps to his carriage.

During breakfast the next morning, Letty watched Alyssa carefully, noting her companion's complexion was tinged with colour and a smile played constantly around her lips.

'Did everything go well last evening, Lyssa?' she ventured finally.

'Yes, very well.'

'What did you think of Sir Giles's sister, and her husband?'

'Marianne and Oliver are delightful. They are returning home today but would like to meet you on their next visit.'

'I'll be happy to, if I have not left for London. Did Sir Giles keep his promise to show you the rose garden?'

Alyssa flushed even deeper pink. 'He did; he arranged for dinner to be served there.'

'Oh? I expect that was pleasant.'

'Very,' said Alyssa, on a faint sigh.

Letty hid a smile, and said insouciantly, 'You seem to find his company agreeable.'

Alyssa looked up then and exclaimed, 'Oh, I cannot hide my feelings! I don't know how much you suspect, Letty, but things have changed: Gil told me last night that he loves me, and has done for weeks. He has no intention of marrying Caroline Nash.'

Letty grinned. 'And you love him in return.'

It was a statement not a question. 'Yes, but how could you know?' said Alyssa. 'I have been subconsciously fighting against it because I thought he cared for Miss Nash.'

'You told me yourself when you were ill. You said many things in your delirium, some of which I could not understand, but your love for Gil was unmistakable. I did not think it right to mention it before now.'

'Did I?' Alyssa gave a little laugh and pressed her palms to her hot cheeks. 'It seems my heart knew even then.'

'I am truly happy for you, Lyssa.'

'Everything is not quite settled. Gil is obliged to break with Miss Nash and explain to her father first. He intends to do so on Thursday.'

'Oh, but in that case, do you think should we still attend their party?' said Letty, raising her brows. 'Caroline will be furious when she hears she is not to be Lady Maxton.'

'I have been wondering about that myself,' said Alyssa. 'I will ask Gil's advice, but I think we must go unless Miss Nash or her family retract the invitations.'

'Well, at least our gowns are finished and you are in such high beauty you will put everyone in the shade.'

'Not you!' she replied. 'Only wait until Piers sees how lovely you look!'

A shadow crossed Letty's face.

Alyssa sighed and said, 'It does not seem right you should be miserable when I am so happy, but Piers knows he made a fool of himself. I believe he loves you, Letty, and is trying to change. There is much that is good in Piers and you are the one to reveal it. Do not lose faith in him.'

'I won't, but I shall insist he keeps to his word.' She looked at Alyssa. 'What of Charles? You must tell him about you and Gil.'

'I'll write, and if he wishes to see me afterwards, I cannot, in fairness, prevent it, although I do not relish a meeting under the circumstances.'

Letty chuckled and said, 'I don't suppose Charles would relish meeting Gil either! Does Gil plan to call here today?'

'Yes, this afternoon,' she replied, adding happily, 'and it won't be a moment too soon!'

On Thursday, Squire Nash escaped to his study after a generous lunch. Feeling decidedly mellow, when a knock at the door interrupted his reverie, he muttered a curse and a comment about a man finding no peace, even in his own home. He said 'Enter' and tried to shuffle his newspaper into a drawer, until Simmons announced it was Sir Giles. Relieved, he exclaimed when he saw his visitor, 'Good to see you, m'boy.' Waving one hand towards the chair, he urged, 'Sit down! Simmons told me you would call.' Grimacing, he continued, 'Lord, now Eugenie wants a high-perch phaeton like her sister. Monstrous thing! Eugenie's a terrible whip and although Caroline's a fair one, she'd overturn it in a trice – it's a show vehicle and no use on Dorset roads. At least we can speak sensibly, and I'm glad you have come.'

'You may not think so when you learn the reason for my visit.'

'Oh? What's wrong?' He said urgently, 'Miss Paradise hasn't suffered a relapse, has she?'

Gil smiled fleetingly. 'No, thank God, but I need to speak to you, even though the timing, with your evening party tomorrow, could hardly be worse. However, what I have to say cannot wait, Henry.'

'Then you had best continue,' said the squire, leaning back again and making a steeple of his fingers.

'Although you and I have never spoken of it, you must be aware over the last year an understanding has been allowed to develop between Caroline and myself. In short, she is hopeful of receiving a proposal of marriage, but I have to tell you no such offer will be forthcoming – now, or in the future. Indeed, I have been sadly remiss, and foolish, for allowing this situation to go unchecked. I never misled Caroline with promises or words of love, but—'

'She expected an offer anyway?' interpolated Henry.

Gil nodded, his expression sombre. 'Partly because I did not quash it, expectation has grown until everyone within twenty miles believes we are to be married.'

'That is Caroline's doing,' said the squire firmly. 'She's very clever at it – laying hints and suggestions that are taken as fact.' He looked at Gil. 'I never thought it would happen though.'

'You didn't?' murmured Gil.

'No. I always believed you would realize eventually it wasn't right. I probably shouldn't say so but I'm glad you have – I'm only surprised it took you until now.'

Astonished, Gil cried, '*You are glad?*'

'Yes, m'boy. Oh, there's no one I'd rather have as a son-in-law, but the plain fact is you aren't suited. Caroline has her good qualities: she respects her parents, is a stickler for the proprieties – not always a bad thing in these increasingly licentious times – and doesn't cause us any worries. However, she's also too cold and proud for my liking – some would call it arrogance – and that I don't approve of. It reminds me of her maternal grandmother, my mother-in-law.'

He stared into mid-distance, deep in thought. 'She's dead now, God rest her soul, but Lady Blackstock was as proud and disagreeable a woman as you could hope to meet. Didn't think I was good enough for Eugenie and made her feelings plain, in spite of my having a reasonable estate and fortune to offer. Eugenie had to coax her father for months to get him to agree to us marrying, and still her ladyship fought to stop it, right up until the banns were read. Ah, but we were so much in love – not even Lady Blackstock's objections could have stopped us,' he said, smiling at the memory. 'I do believe Eugenie would have eloped if I had asked her to, but her father had the good sense to agree to the match and here we are, almost thirty years later, still happy enough.'

He regarded Gil directly once more and continued, 'Now, I know my Eugenie is a touch organizing. She also gossips too much and nurtures foolish ideas about status foisted on her by Caroline but, for all that, she has a good heart and I love her dearly. I've tried to say what I think of Caroline's arrogance, but Eugenie would never have a word said against her little pet and it's too late now.' The squire gave a wry grin. 'I'll always love my daughter, but I don't always like the way she behaves, Gil. Caroline is not for the one for you. She needs a quiet mouse of a man who'll not complain when she orders him about, or better still, a pompous prig who places as much store by social position as she does. She'll not be happily married unless she has one or the other – and you are neither.'

There was silence until Gil exhaled on a long sigh of relief. 'I appreciate your understanding, Henry. Although there was never an official betrothal, I felt it only right to set things straight with both you and Caroline at the earliest oppor- tunity. And, if possible, I don't want this to spoil our friendship.'

'It won't, my boy. Oh, Caroline won't like it – she has a fancy to be Lady Maxton just now – but she'll recover because she doesn't love you. Better this way than you both be unhappy for the rest of your lives. She's a handsome girl in many ways and if she'd smile more, she would be prettier still. There's a size- able portion of money settled on her when she marries and some fellow will come along who finds that appealing, and who's more suited to her character. You've acted very properly towards her throughout and I thank you for that.' He raised his brows quizzically and said, 'So – have you found a lady you *are* about to offer marriage to?'

'I have,' he said, smiling.

'Miss Paradise, I'll warrant?' ventured the squire, with another grin.

Gil laughed. 'How did you guess?'

'You had a certain glow in your eye whenever you spoke of her. I'm sure she's delightful and I look forward to meeting her tomorrow.'

'You can't still think it advisable Alyssa and I attend?' cried Gil, leaning forward. 'I intend to speak to Caroline shortly and she will not want either of us at Frampton Manor afterwards.'

'Lord, yes! You must,' said Henry, nodding vigorously. 'It would be disastrous if you *and* Miss Paradise did not come. Everyone would discover the reason behind your joint absence and it is best for all involved if this news leaks out slowly. My daughter has enough sense not to make a scene in front of half the county; she has her pride and will want to keep up appearances, and I can't blame her for that. No, it's my belief you must attend. Ask Caroline if she is of the same opinion, but I shall be surprised if she isn't. I only ask one thing of you – and Miss Paradise.'

'What is it?'

For the first time during their discussion, the squire looked uncomfortable. He cleared his throat and said, 'I know what it is to be young and in love, but would you both mind being circumspect, just for tomorrow evening? It will make things easier for Caroline while in full view of her friends.'

'I understand, Henry. The situation is an awkward one and naturally, Alyssa and I will do whatever we can to ensure the evening runs smoothly. We will appear friendly and nothing more. Afterwards, however, I'm afraid I have no intention of hiding my love for Alyssa – even if that proves difficult for Caroline living nearby,' he said, a trace of defiance in his voice.

'No! No! Wouldn't ask you to do that, by God!' acknowledged the squire, 'Caroline must learn to accept the situation with good grace – her heart will not be broken. And I will not tolerate any discourteous behaviour from her tomorrow.' He pursed his lips in consideration and mused, 'In fact, following this conversation, I've a mind to agree to something Caroline has wanted for some time. She always had a desire spend the season with her aunt in Bath, but wouldn't countenance it unless I funded her visit sufficiently. In turn, I refused to open my pocket book completely, thinking she could enjoy a visit just as well on a reasonable sum as on an exorbitant one. Then, as becoming Lady Maxton looked more likely in her eyes, she did not press the issue. I believe she secretly intended you and she to spend the winter ensconced in the Royal Crescent, entertaining on a grand scale.'

At Gil's grimace, the squire chuckled and added, 'I didn't think it would be to your taste but there is no end to Caroline's ambitions. However, in view of your forthcoming marriage, I think it would indeed be best if Caroline went to her aunt's house. I shall dig deep into my pockets to dress her in the latest style, just as she wishes. She will enjoy it, and she'll be put in the way of meeting other young men too.'

'Whatever you think it best – neither Alyssa nor I desires to drive Caroline from her home.'

'Nonsense, Gil! Take my word for it, Caroline will be eager to go.' He chuckled suddenly. 'I might even hire a yellow high-perch phaeton for her to cut a dash in around Bath.'

Some ten minutes later, Gil left the study. Having shared a glass of wine and a handshake with the squire, they had parted on the best of terms. However, as he was shown to the drawing-room, Gil considered his next interview was unlikely to be so amicable. He entered and saw Caroline seated on the sofa, bent over some embroidery, and, as he waited for her to speak, his face was a grim mask of determination.

CHAPTER 13

'Giles,' said Caroline, snipping off her silk thread before she looked up, 'I heard you had come to see my father.'

'Yes – now I must speak to you.'

'I see.' She eyed him with an assessing glance. 'Then will you sit down?'

'Thank you, no: I prefer to stand.'

'As you wish. I gather from your demeanour you have something of import to say.' Caroline smiled like a cat that had unearthed a dish of cream after a long search, and put aside her embroidery. 'Now the moment has arrived, you must feel apprehensive, but there is no need when our acquaintance is long-standing. Let me congratulate you on your timing; it could not be bettered, with everyone of consequence at our evening party tomorrow to hear any announcements.'

A muscle flickered in his jaw. 'As ever, you presume to read my thoughts,' he replied.

'I do not presume to guess your thoughts *at this moment* – indeed, I expect you are suffering an excess of sensibility – but it would be foolish for me to appear coy when I can guess the subject of your conversation with my father.' She rearranged the skirt of her gown as she added confidently, 'No doubt you were asking his permission to pay your addresses.'

'No, I was not.'

Her gaze flew back to his face, her smile dissipating. '*No?*'

'No.'

'Oh, don't be absurd, Giles,' she said, rising to her feet and giving a high-pitched titter. 'You *must* have – I have been waiting an age for you to declare yourself!'

'On the contrary, my conversation with your father was to explain I will not be declaring myself, and I have come to say any unspoken understanding between us is at an end. You will receive no offer of marriage from me – now, or in the future.'

Caroline's habitually haughty expression slipped and she turned a little pale, her brows snapping together in a frown. 'But – but you must offer for me: everyone expects you to.'

'If they did, they are mistaken, for it will never happen.'

Caroline stared in disbelief. 'This is outrageous!'

'It is eminently sensible, and I am at fault for not bringing this charade to an end sooner,' he replied, with quiet authority.

'*Charade*! How dare you!'

'Oh, I dare,' said Gil, grimly, striding towards her. 'It is high time we had a frank discussion, Caroline. Charade is an accurate description when you consider the facts: we are not formally engaged; I have never hinted or suggested I was about to offer marriage; nor have I ever spoken to your father on the subject—'

'But we discussed marriage in general terms,' she interjected.

'No, it was always *you* who talked so while I remained silent. Stupidly, I allowed myself to be manipulated instead of making it clear I did not love you.'

'Love?' snorted Caroline, regarding him as she might a particularly repellent insect. 'Love and passion are emotions indulged in by people with little breeding. I did not expect you to . . . to slaver over me, Giles, and would have found it distasteful if you had.'

He gave a sardonic half-smile. 'I always knew you did not care for me.'

'It is true I do not feel affection for you in a romantic sense, but I admire and respect you and believe those sentiments are a good enough basis for marriage.'

'Are they?' he said, with a hard look.

'For those in our social position, yes.'

His lip curled. 'Well, they are not enough for me. I want more than a cold-hearted, efficient wife who admires me only for my title and my money.'

'You are being insulting!'

'I am being honest.'

'Oh, it is insupportable to be jilted like this!'

'But how can I jilt you when we have never been engaged?' asked Gil reasonably. Caroline made a sound of disgust and turned away, but he continued, 'Even so, I still felt honour bound to explain to you in person, and to your father also.'

'I never imagined you would prove such a callous brute,' she said, facing him once more.

'Call me callous if you wish – there was no easy way to tell you – but I am determined there will be no further misunderstandings. I do not love you and you admit you do not care for me either. It was wrong of me not to confess my true feelings until now, but you have taken full advantage of my silence. Through gossip and whispers, you encouraged your acquaintances to think our marriage is inevitable, and now the consequences of your indiscretion must be dealt with, to which end I shall play my part and dissemble no longer.'

'Oh, how noble!' she sneered. Incensed, she began to pace to and fro across the room. 'Have you no consideration for the position you place me in?'

'I bitterly regret both of us are in this situation, but to be blunt, it is mostly of your making. If you had kept your counsel instead of spreading rumours, there would be no need to feel uncomfortable now when you go amongst your friends.'

'You have the audacity to blame me?' she said, coming to a halt to fix him with the glare of a patrician basilisk.

'Pray tell me who else should I blame for the general acceptance we were to marry?' asked Gil. 'As I have explained, I readily accept my shortcomings, but at least I have never spoken on the subject of marriage to anyone. You are shortly to become a victim of your own gossip and I hope the experience proves a salutary lesson for you not to let your tongue run so freely in future.'

She blinked and drew in an indignant breath. 'I cannot believe what I am hearing. Good God, I shall be a laughing stock! What has happened to cause this change—?' She stopped and cried, 'Wait – there is more to this than you have yet told me.' Her eyes narrowed as she continued, 'Ah! Perhaps I should have guessed immediately – that woman is in some way responsible for your decision.'

'Are you referring to Miss Paradise?'

'Yes!' she hissed.

'Then I would be obliged if you would do so in a civil tone,' he said, gritting his teeth. 'Miss Paradise *is* involved, but I should have ended this before she ever came into Dorset. However, you shall hear exactly how matters stand because I want no more misconceptions: I have fallen in love with Alyssa and intend to ask for her hand in marriage as soon as possible—'

Caroline gasped.

'—indeed, I only delayed doing so because I thought it honourable to speak with you, and your father, first.'

Trembling with outrage, she managed to utter, '*What*? You intend to offer for *her* instead of me?' Caroline came perilously near to stamping her foot. 'Insufferable!' She drew herself up to her full height and added tersely, 'Have you no thought for my feelings? How am I to bear the ignominy of being passed over for a woman of her ilk?'

'Since you have just admitted you do not love me, I think you will bear it well enough. Only your pride will suffer,' he said, drily.

Caroline offered no direct reply to this: it was indeed her pride and reputation that concerned her most. Instead, she declared, 'Oh, I *knew* the moment I met her she was the most conniving, unsuitable young woman—'

'Have a care, Caroline,' he warned ominously, throwing his driving gloves down on to a nearby table, 'I'll not tolerate vicious slurs against someone dear to me.'

'You have run mad! You have been thrown into her company by the demands of that preposterous will which you compounded with ill-advised further help, and now you imagine yourself in love with her.'

'I don't *imagine* myself in love: I *know* I am – more than I can show Alyssa in one lifetime.'

Caroline uttered a hollow laugh. 'Where is the brisk, unemotional man of business I once knew?' she jeered, 'She's turned you into a romantic fool!'

He only grinned in response to this, which infuriated her further. 'I believe she has and I adore her even more for doing so.'

'As your wife, I would complement your wealth and position, and you could achieve a seat in Parliament, or even a peerage with me at your side,' said Caroline in throbbing tones, 'whereas *she* – she is a common, scheming harridan who will bring you *nothing*.'

His grin died away and he muttered an oath. 'Enough!' he snapped peremptorily. 'God knows I have tried to be honourable! I have also tried to show you civility and respect this afternoon but it seems you are unwilling to do likewise. I care nothing for your opinion of me, but I will not allow you to speak of Alyssa in that way without reply. So be it. You force my hand and I will give my opinion plainly: you are an ambitious, arrogant woman, Caroline, but I am no Macbeth figure, to be manipulated by an ambitious wife to the exclusion of all other considerations. I am and will continue to be successful for the benefit of my future wife and any children we have, not to obtain a peerage—'

'But—'

'I have not yet finished and you *will* hear me out! While I enjoy the trappings of wealth, I will not be a slave to them, uncomfortable as that may be to someone with your ambition. And Alyssa has shown me something else, a matter of principle I should have addressed sooner, and that is that I have a moral duty where possible to pay those who work for me an adequate wage to live on. It would be repugnant to grow rich while the children of those I employ are half-starved.' His gaze, full of antipathy, ran over her. 'I love Alyssa – she will bring me *everything* I need – and I'll thank you not to insult her further in my hearing.'

She blinked at the icy disdain dripping from every syllable of this speech. From his expression and the tense set of his shoulders, Caroline realized it would be unwise to antagonize him further and she fell silent, walking to the window to look out at the gardens.

When she turned back, two spots of colour burned in her cheeks, but she had collected herself and temporarily regained her *sang-froid*. 'You have made your feelings perfectly plain, sir. It is beyond my comprehension why you wish to marry Miss Paradise – I hope you do not live to regret it, but that is your affair. Indeed,' she continued, 'having witnessed your unfortunate manner this afternoon, perhaps it is for the best that our understanding is over. No gentleman worthy of the name would behave in this boorish way. I see now I have been sadly mistaken in you, and I refuse to repine at length. After all, I have my reputation to consider, and have no wish to be associated with a man sadly overwhelmed with moral virtue towards the lower classes, and with no desire to make his mark in the world!'

'I am pleased the situation is clear,' he said, executing a brief bow. 'Let us hope our future contact can be polite, if not warm, as we are destined to be near neighbours and your father is my friend as well as business associate. There is only one issue that remains to be resolved, and I discussed it briefly with your father: it is his opinion that Miss Paradise and I should still attend your evening party. Is that your wish also? I will perfectly understand if you feel to the contrary.'

'Good God, do you seek to embarrass me completely in society's eyes?' she cried. 'My father is right; much as I might wish otherwise, you must attend – if you do not, everyone will wonder why which will lead to questions and speculation. Oh, have no fear your presence will invoke tearful displays from me! I will waste no further time considering you, or Miss Paradise – after what I have just heard, you are deserving of each other.'

'I believe we are,' he murmured, his lips curving in a smile. 'There is nothing more to be said. Good day to you, Caroline. Notwithstanding what has passed between us this afternoon, please accept my best wishes for your future health, and my earnest wish that you find the kind of happiness you seek.' He bowed again perfunctorily, collected his driving gloves and marched to the door. He halted and, looking back, added in a withering tone, 'I will make my mark in the world but with a loving wife at my side, not someone infatuated with social advancement and wealth.'

With this Parthian shot, he left. Moments later, Caroline's pent-up fury found expression, first through an unladylike shriek, and then by throwing her embroidery against the door which had closed in his wake.

It was not to be expected that Caroline's temper would improve on reflection. Indeed, during the hours that followed, her anger hardened into cold fury. She was female enough to resent the man she had marked down for her husband offering for another woman, but rather than suffering the effects of a broken heart as a result, Caroline felt only incandescent rage at being thwarted.

While she deplored Giles's trenchant treatment of her and did not seek to excuse his conduct, Caroline decided the greater blame lay with Alyssa. It was, she reasoned, the wretched creature's influence which had brought about his change of heart. She had cast out her lures like a siren and he had been unable to resist. These were the circumstances behind his vulgar protestations that he was in love, and Caroline itched to take revenge.

A discussion with her father later that afternoon did little to improve her state of mind. He tried, with tact and kindness, to point out the differences which would have made her marriage to Sir Giles ill-advised.

'A union where neither cares for the other at the start is doomed to unhappiness,' he declared roundly. 'I do not wish that fate to befall you. You are upset, but it will pass because your affections were not engaged.' He smiled encouragingly. 'Come, Caroline! What say you to an extended visit to your aunt and uncle in Bath, with all necessary expenses covered by me?'

'That would, of course, be welcome, Father,' said she, 'but I am still convinced Giles and I would have enjoyed a compliant if not ardently affectionate marriage, were it not for that woman's intervention.'

The squire was of the opinion that any compliance would have been on Gil's side as Caroline always knew best, but he thought it wiser not to mention this. 'Do you love him, Caroline, or even hold him in affection?' he asked.

'No – but I'm astonished he should act like a love-sick youth towards Miss Paradise rather than realize the tangible benefits of marriage to me.'

'Dash it all, it is hardly proper to dictate who Giles should fall in love with when you do not care a fig for him yourself!' declared the squire, impatiently.

'Men are fools, too easily won over by flattery and smiles,' observed his daughter tartly, and sailed out of the room.

'And that,' said the squire to his wife later, when she approached him in his study, 'is the final word I intend to say upon the subject. While I understand Caroline's pride is hurt, I am out of patience with her and cannot contemplate her view that marriage is simply a means to improve one's status. That is not the example we set for her.'

'But it is too bad, Henry!' declared his wife tearfully, wringing her handkerchief and taking refuge once again in the smelling salts which had been her constant companion since hearing the news. The shock she felt on learning Caroline was not to marry Sir Giles, and that he in turn was to marry Miss Paradise, was severe. Her reaction had been similar when she had learnt Mrs Franklin had married off her youngest daughter, who suffered sadly from a squint, to the wealthy Duke of Umberslake; the breath was driven from her lungs and she opened and closed her mouth to no avail – not a single sound emerged.

Now, she rallied valiantly and harangued her husband for several minutes on the injustice of it all. She received no response until the squire vouchsafed an unexpectedly sharp set down: he would brook no condemnation of either Sir Giles or Miss Paradise for falling in love and challenged his wife to name one occasion when Caroline had spoken of her affection for Giles. Mrs Nash stuttered and prevaricated but could not provide an answer and was eventually forced to concur that, while her daughter coveted the social advantages afforded by Sir Giles, she held little affection for him otherwise.

'Even so, Henry, I had hoped Caroline was to marry him and now. . . .' Her voice trailed off unhappily. Misty images of her daughter becomingly dressed in orange blossom and lace as the new Lady Maxton were diminishing.

'She admits she does not care for him, Eugenie. Can marriage be right or proper in those circumstances? I think not, and you know it too,' he said. 'There is little hope of attraction developing in the years that follow, especially bearing in mind Caroline's unyielding nature. Only recall how much we were in love: nothing would have kept us from marrying, even your mother's displeasure.'

She dabbed her handkerchief to her eyes and sniffed. 'Oh yes! To be sure, I did not wish to marry that awful Lord Beesbury whose addresses she wished me to accept – with his bulbous eyes and drooping thick-lipped mouth, he resembled a fish, and a miserable one at that. My sister and I could not decide whether he looked more like a trout or a carp! You know, I thought he favoured a trout but Selina always argued he looked exactly like the carp Father caught the previous summer. We could never agree upon it, and whenever Lord Beesbury came to call, I found myself tongue-tied and staring at him, which vexed Mama greatly. Poor man! He was extraordinarily ill-favoured whereas you were very handsome, my love, and I desperately wanted to be your bride,' said Mrs Nash, adding with a sigh, 'It was excessively romantic.'

The squire grinned. 'Beesbury! Lord, yes – I recall him. Rich as a nabob but an ugly countenance with a character to match. Thank God I saved you from a man like a despondent fish.'

'Only imagine if I had married Lord Beesbury and been forced to sit across the breakfast table from him every morning. It does not bear thinking of.' She could not repress a shudder at the idea. 'Oh, but Sir Giles does not resemble a miserable fish in the least.'

'Of course not! There is no comparison,' said Henry, in surprise. 'I may say though, Eugenie, I believe you were right and Selina was wrong: Beesbury did bear a startling resemblance to a trout and, being an angler myself, I have seen many—' He broke off, suddenly recollecting himself. 'Hmph! Yes. Well. That is as may be but we are moving away from the point. Surely you cannot wish to see your daughter trapped in an unhappy marriage, my dear?'

'If you put it in those terms, no, but—'

'Neither would I,' he interjected. 'I have seen far too many such marriages. Caroline is in the fortunate position of not having to marry for money; she may choose her partner in life, freely and without coercion. I believe a trip to your sister Daphne will be just the thing now. She is a pretty girl with a handsome portion, and she'll have no shortage of admirers. I hope she will find a man with whom she's more in tune and holds in a modicum of affection.'

'Such a pity she is not to be Lady Maxton. Of course, she should care for her future husband, but a title would have been agreeable.'

'All the more reason for Caroline to go to Bath. Dukes, earls, viscounts . . . the place is crawling with peers of the realm and their eligible sons, and our daughter will be mixing with them all. She'll be decked out in expensive style too, I give you my word. Daphne's a pinch-penny so I won't rely on her to bear the cost.'

His wife's expression brightened at last and she began to feel something might be salvaged from this setback. For Mrs Nash, the faint scent of orange blossom was once more in the air, its fragrance sweeter still when accompanied by the vision of Caroline walking down the aisle as a countess. 'You are very good, my dear. Caroline's disappointment will soon dissipate when she moves in such company. Dukes, you say? Well, we cannot be hopeful of attracting a duke – Caroline is only comfortably situated with her dowry – but there is no reason why she should not engage an earl or a viscount. Indeed, I begin to be sanguine she can make an even more advantageous match if she goes to Bath – Daphne is extremely well connected.'

'Your sister has more starch than I care for, but there's no denying she has the entrée to every exclusive event and Caroline should take advantage of that. Perhaps you would enjoy a visit there, my dear? That is, if Daphne and her husband can accommodate you in that huge mausoleum of a house?'

'Oh, I would like that above all things! Shops, the concerts, the plays – there is pleasure to be had at every turn, and if you will not mind me accompanying Caroline, I should be happy to go.'

'Not at all,' smiled the squire, envisaging uninterrupted afternoon naps, fishing or reading his newspaper in peace. 'It'll be a mite lonely here, but I'll bear up. Go and enjoy yourself!'

'But, Henry,' said Mrs Nash, a sudden thought occurring to her, 'if Sir Giles is to marry Miss Paradise, will it not be excessively awkward tomorrow? Caroline is furious.'

'Perhaps at first, but it will pass. Can you imagine the speculation that would arise if they did not come?'

'Goodness, yes! Mrs Bailey would think something was amiss at once, and ask me all manner of questions I would not know how to answer. And I could not be untruthful – the news will be all over the county soon.'

'Exactly so. I have spoken to Gil on this and there will be no hint of how things stand to give rise to comment from our other guests, or cause Caroline further upset.' He raised his brows quizzically, and murmured, 'I need not add it behoves you to be a gracious hostess to both Gil and Miss Paradise.'

'Naturally,' said Mrs Nash, indignant. 'Miss Paradise is unconventional, but I cannot fault her manners, and if Sir Giles has fallen in love with her, there is nothing to more to be done. I suppose he never offered marriage so he has acted honourably towards our daughter.'

'I knew I could rely on you, Eugenie,' he said, nodding with satisfaction. 'As long as Caroline does not let her anger outweigh her judgement, the evening will not go awry.'

'Oh, I hope it does not,' she said. 'This is the most important event of the year. It takes weeks of planning, you know, and I have even managed to obtain ostrich feathers, just as Mr Kilworth suggested! I want my appearance to be as much of a surprise for you as it will be for our other guests, my dear!'

The squire swallowed and a pained expression passed over his face; the thought of his wife in connection with ostrich feathers brought no rest to his soul.

'Good Lord!' he said. 'Well, well. Indeed. Yes, indeed. Ostrich feathers, eh?' Rendered temporarily bereft of speech, he cleared his throat as a method of breaching this awkward lull. He pottered over to his desk and picked up a sheet of paper. 'Perhaps we had best continue our discussion of the menu. . . ?'

When the guests began arriving at eight o'clock the following evening, the squire was heartily thankful the moment was here. He could not comprehend why there needed to be so much deliberation over where the card tables should be situated; where the food must be laid out; how much room needed to be set aside for dancing; the numbers of chairs provided for those unfortunate enough not to have partners or who merely wished to watch and criticize.

He should have known better because it was the same every year. In the hours leading up to this event, his house resembled all the calm of a chicken coop being attacked by a fox, but he had learnt that it was useless to complain and ambled from room to room, regarding the preparations with bemused vagueness.

He did not always avoid the servants rushing back and forth, or indeed his wife and daughter, who tut-tutted at his ability to be constantly in the way. To be a mere onlooker in this hive of activity made the squire's head spin and the one coherent thought that brought him succour was the sanctuary of his study and the tantalus of reserve port residing there. The annual ball called for the best and a restorative bracer of finest reserve, taken secretly during the early evening, meant he could greet his guests with equanimity at the appointed time.

Disaster having only narrowly been avoided when it was discovered that the incorrect coloured lanterns had been put out to light the gardens, Mrs Nash was late completing her toilette and, as a result, and had not yet come downstairs. It was therefore left to the squire and his daughter to welcome their first guests. Although he had heard her say little, Caroline's mood seemed reasonable. She looked attractive dressed in a jonquil gown, long evening gloves, and wearing her maternal grandmother's emerald necklace, and she had made an effort to bestow a smile and murmur a pleasant greeting to everyone who had arrived thus far. If his daughter could stifle her resentment, the squire was hopeful this gracious approach would be maintained towards Sir Giles and Miss Paradise.

He was to be disappointed. When the squire saw Giles and the lovely young woman he took to be Alyssa approaching, he glanced hopefully at Caroline standing next to him. But instead of feeling uplifted by an urbane courteous expression, he almost had to clutch the wall behind him for support; the glare Caroline directed first towards Gil, and then towards Miss Paradise, was one of metaphoric disembowelling.

Gil had been waiting for Alyssa to arrive, and his breath caught in his throat when he saw her alighting from the carriage. She was wearing a blue silk dress over a figured white lace slip, with darker blue ribbons at the hem and sleeves. Sapphire drops glistened in her ears, a gossamer gauze scarf was draped around her shoulders and her hair was gathered up, with blue flowers placed amongst the silken chestnut curls. She walked towards him and, eyes twinkling, held out one white-gloved hand in greeting.

'You look enchanting,' he murmured thickly, raising her fingers slowly to his lips. 'Every man here will want to be at your side.'

She smiled a little shyly. 'Do you think so? Well, that is flattering, but my thoughts will be with you.' Alyssa then added softly, 'I have written to Charles.'

'Do you think Brook will come here when he receives your letter?'

'Knowing Charles, he will want to repudiate me in person.'

'Good God, only let him try!'

Alyssa placed one hand on his sleeve. 'He can be dealt with another time and this evening will be difficult enough as it is. I received your note that we were still expected – have you spoken to Miss Nash and her father then?'

He nodded. 'Henry was very understanding. Caroline was' – he grimaced – 'less so. I think we should expect one or two spiteful comments this evening, my love, but I don't believe Caroline will cause a major scene.'

Alyssa saw Letty was walking towards them. 'Letty knows about us, Gil,' she murmured. 'I could not hide my delight from her.'

He chuckled. 'I'm surprised no one has asked me why I am sporting a permanent grin like a half-wit!'

Letty joined them; she was dressed in an ivory sarsnet gown with tiny pearl buttons down the bodice, a deceptively simple design which showed her trim figure to advantage. Ivory evening slippers and a matching reticule completed the ensemble and she wore a single string of pearls and artificial sprays of lily of the valley in her hair, threaded through with ribbon to match that on her gown.

They entered the hall a few moments later to find Squire Nash and his daughter greeting their guests.

Gil whispered, 'Remember I love you,' into Alyssa's ear, before stepping away to let the squire greet Alyssa effusively.

'Miss Paradise! I have been looking forward to meeting you. Caroline and Eugenie spoke of you, and of course Gil – that is to say, Gil told me of your illness. You have recovered, I hope?' Henry Nash was not a pusillanimous man but he could not help casting another nervous glance at his daughter, standing to his left.

'Why, yes, thank you!'

'Excellent! And I am not disappointed in what I see,' he said with a grin. 'Good Lord, I had no idea an old curmudgeon like Tom Paradise possessed such a lovely niece! Charming, absolutely charming.'

Alyssa blushed and laughed, then introduced Letty with whom the squire was equally enamoured and murmured, 'Good Lord', 'Charming' and 'Delightful' before he moved on to speak to Gil.

It was fortunate for the squire's temper and nerves that he did not hear the conversation that followed between his daughter and Alyssa; it would have been worthy of several restorative quaffs of reserve port.

CHAPTER 14

Alyssa, aware of Caroline's malevolent expression, expected some vitriol but felt obliged to attempt politeness and searched for a comment that would not be hypocritical. 'Good Evening, Miss Nash. May I compliment you on your gown?'

'You may but I shall not regard it,' said Caroline, bristling.

Alyssa raised her brows. 'I see.'

'Your views are of no interest and I refuse to return the compliment for the sake of courtesy.'

'Which is just as well since I would disregard it,' said Alyssa. 'Praise not sincerely meant is worthless.'

'I will not utter platitudes to you!'

'Pray do not feel obliged to; it is nonsensical for either of us to be mendacious. Miss Nash, you disapproved of me from the outset, so let me advise you the sentiment was mutual. Your discomfort this evening is understandable and I am sorry for it, but, since you and your father expressly requested Sir Giles and me to attend, the least we can do now is be civil.'

'Oh, I will be civil, gracious even, when there is a chance I may be overheard,' hissed Caroline, fixing Alyssa with another Medusa-like glare. 'No one here will guess how much I dislike you! But don't imagine because you see me behaving so, I have any kinder feelings hidden away, for you would be mistaken. I *will* have revenge for how I have been treated! I do not like you and never have. Your idiotic uncle's *outré* will started this, and now your wiles and romantic nonsense have turned Giles's head! At every turn, you have tried to make me look foolish!'

'Oh, it was not difficult,' quipped Alyssa, 'you are capable of that without my help.'

'You are impertinent,' Caroline replied, icily.

'And you, Miss Nash, are graceless and arrogant,' said Alyssa, smiling, her voice honey-sweet but her gaze hard. 'Don't ever malign my uncle's memory again by calling him idiotic because you will regret it.'

Caroline swallowed. It seemed she could not, after all, intimidate through a few well-chosen comments. She had expected a stammering retreat – her verbal arrows were usually effective – but instead discovered Alyssa to be more than her equal. Her indignation grew, and a deep tinge of colour crept into her cheeks.

Alyssa continued, 'I wish you a pleasant evening, Miss Nash – thank you for the delightful welcome.'

Gil, overhearing this comment, looked at Alyssa quizzically. She smiled and gave an infinitesimal nod before moving into the drawing-room.

Piers, having hurried back from London, stayed at The Antelope only long enough to change. When he arrived at the manor, he headed for the entrance with a jaunty step, eager to reach Letty and having missed her even more than he imagined. Only a few weeks earlier the delights of the capital would have given him no desire to rusticate again so promptly, but everything had changed. Wherever Letty was, Piers wanted to be also. So, he completed his business briskly and with more acumen than his shocked agent could comprehend. Gone was the languid, bored young buck who had no inclination to look at any documents and who threw bills one by one into the fire with a curse. In his place was a keen-eyed enquiring man, conscious of the delicacy of his financial position but willing to take uncomfortable decisions to find a way out of his maze of debt. After a two-hour meeting, an agreement was at last reached which met with Piers's satisfaction. Two paintings and a clock were to be sold from his property in Lincolnshire to address the most pressing bills. A partial mortgage would also be raised to fund repairs and future investment, and to leave some ready capital. Piers felt satisfied it was the best that could be contrived for now.

He would, at least, be left with a little money in hand; it was not much but he'd be damned if he would offer marriage to Letty with an empty purse. If she would have him as a husband one day, he wanted to buy her a trousseau of bride clothes and jewellery that befitted her beauty.

Relatively pleased with his achievements, he sauntered in, looking forward to telling Letty, but first he had to deal with the squire who threatened to keep him talking for half the evening when he discovered Piers was of a sporting turn of mind, and then Miss Nash, whose arrogance he deplored. It was, therefore, some time before he could search the crowded rooms for Letty.

He soon found her. She was in the large room at the back of the house where the musicians were playing and the furniture had been moved aside to allow for dancing. She was besieged by a group of young men, James Westwood, his host in Dorset, among them, all eagerly trying to secure a dance. Piers, instantly of the mind to ask James what the deuce he was about, soon realized he was not his only obstacle and watched with chagrin as a fellow with Byronic good looks led Letty out to take their place in the set. His heart sank as his eyes followed her; she was unaware of his presence and smiling up at her partner.

She looked exquisite – a fairie queen in a shimmering ivory gown – and for the first time he grasped how little he had to offer. No great estate, no fortune, no grand London townhouse – only a rather decrepit property saddled with a mortgage and a sheaf of unpaid bills. Poor fare indeed to place before this lovely creature. Letty did not possess a large dowry, or a title, but with her face, figure and disposition, Piers knew she could hope to make an excellent marriage to a man of means. Already she was the centre of attention for the young men here and jealousy writhed in his breast. A voice nearby woke him from his uncomfortable reverie.

'Piers! You have arrived back in time – good.'

'Hello, Alyssa,' he said, summoning up the ghost of a smile. 'I rushed back in the hope of engaging Letty for a dance, but' – his gaze drifted back to Letty and her Adonis-like partner – 'it seems my luck is out, and there's a crowd in line before me,' he concluded, with a gloomy nod towards her admiring swains.

Alyssa chuckled. 'Don't be so poor-spirited! Have you asked her yet?'

'No – she's not even aware I'm here.'

'I know she's been looking for you.'

'Has she?' he asked, longing in his voice as he watched his *amour*. He turned back to his cousin, his expression brighter. 'Then she missed me a little while I have been away?'

'That you must discover yourself, but I believe something has prevented her from completely enjoying this evening, despite what you see. How did your business in London go?'

'Well enough,' admitted Piers. 'I went a fair way to disentangling my affairs, but it's such a damnable mess, there is no hope of solving matters overnight. However, there is potential in my estate I had never bothered to look for until now and eventually, it could become profitable.' Glancing again at Letty, he murmured, 'I am determined to make it so.'

'I have confidence in you.'

'I only hope Letty does.' Turning to study her, Piers murmured, 'My compliments on *your* appearance, dear Coz – I've never seen you looking lovelier. The Dorset air and absence from Charles's cloying company obviously agrees with you. Little wonder you and Letty are the most sought-after ladies here, and' – he added, scrutinizing her attire with a critical and expert eye – 'the best dressed.'

'We have been urged to divulge the genius behind our gowns, which is diverting as we made them ourselves,' said Alyssa, laughing.

'Did you? Well, my compliments again – the most exclusive *modiste* could not have bettered your efforts.'

Piers saw Sir Giles moving towards them through the surrounding crush. He had caught sight of him earlier, both before and during his conversation with his cousin, and noted that Giles, while not obviously in Alyssa's company, hovered nearby, glancing often in her direction and never moving completely out of sight. Add to this Miss Nash making no attempt to speak to or acknowledge Sir Giles, and Piers began to think something was very odd.

Gil greeted Piers courteously and asked for the news from London, but it was the brief look he exchanged with Alyssa which made Piers start in surprise. The scales fell from his eyes; even to the most insensitive blockhead, there was no doubting the sentiments in that glance, or that they were reciprocated by his cousin.

So that's the way of things, Piers thought, controlling the urge to whistle softly in amazement. He did not refer to what he had witnessed – it was none of his business until they chose to tell him, after all – but when his initial surprise ebbed away, he felt pleased. Alyssa deserved better than that dull dog Charles, and Piers had liked the cut of Sir Giles's jib at their first meeting, his good opinion reinforced by Gil's actions during Alyssa's illness.

It said much for Piers's rapidly increasing maturity that he remained silent and felt only fleeting jealousy. If his cousin married Sir Giles Maxton, her wealth would increase, but his main regret was that Alyssa's future seemed shortly to be settled while his aspiration to share Letty's remained uncertain.

Guilt suddenly assailed him: he needed to make a clean breast of the business with Draper to Alyssa soon.

With this in mind, he said, 'By the way, Coz, I must speak to you on an important matter. Would tomorrow be convenient?'

'The following day would be preferable. I shan't reach my bed until three or four in the morning, and Gil and I have our usual dinner arranged. Can it wait until Sunday?'

He nodded. 'Shall I call then?'

Alyssa replied in the affirmative, adding, 'I may have some news for you, too.'

Gil's fleeting grin was not lost on Piers, but he only chuckled and said, 'Secrets eh, Coz? Lord, we're all guilty of harbouring secrets – good and bad!' Eager to change the subject, he saw Caroline and commented, 'This event must have cost her father a pretty penny yet Miss Nash looks as sour as a lemon. There's no pleasing that lady.'

'Miss Nash is ill-tempered this evening,' murmured Alyssa.

'Has she been discourteous?' said Gil, quickly.

'Nothing to concern me.'

Gil, who was not sanguine that Caroline intended to let the evening pass with-out incident, said, 'If her expression is any measure, she is anxious to vent her spleen before long.'

'I wonder what can have put her in an ugly mood?' mused Piers, with commendable nonchalance. 'Whatever it is, she'll frighten away prospective dance partners if she does not smile more. How strange Mrs Nash is nowhere to be seen yet, but I approve of the squire: he seems a congenial man, a touch vague perhaps, but that's only to be expected when you consider the distaff side of his household.'

Their conversation was interrupted by the flutter of applause when the music stopped. As Gil began to murmur the names of the formidable array of dowa-gers lined up against the far wall into Alyssa's ear, Piers watched Letty.

Having thanked her partner and laughingly declared to her other admirers that she needed to rest, her gaze scanned the room and met his. His heart leapt at the brief but unmistakable spark of pleasure he saw when she registered his presence and it took all his self-control not to push his way across the room, and take her into his arms.

She came to him, the fabric of her dress and her expressive eyes sparkling in the candlelight. 'Piers!' she cried, putting out both hands in greeting, 'It is good to see you—' She seemed to recollect herself, and added in a muted voice, 'That is, I hope your business was successful.'

He smiled, swept her fingers into his firm grasp and kissed them. 'No, don't change it – I much prefer your first response. You look beautiful, and I'm not surprised to see you have a crowd of admirers. Pray tell me,' he asked, through suddenly clenched teeth, 'who was that simpering Adonis dancing with you?'

'Simpering Adonis. . . ?' began Letty, puzzled. 'Oh, you mean Lord Wentworth. He is down from Hertfordshire.'

'He was paying you an excessive amount of attention, damn him!'

'Lord Wentworth has a pleasant manner.'

'Hmph! Well, I'd be happier if he took himself and his pleasant manner back to Hertfordshire, and stayed well away from you.'

Her eyes twinkled up at him, full of laughter. 'I was only dancing with him, Piers.'

'Well, I might forgive you if you promise to dance with me – at least twice – and while we do, I'll tell you about my trip to London.'

But before they could join the set for the next dance, the doorway from the hall opened and Mrs Nash entered.

Her appearance lulled the hum of conversation almost to silence. She was wearing a deep pink gown and a matching pink silk turban decorated with five enormous ostrich feathers, standing vertically to attention from a jewelled aigrette at the front of this confection. While Mrs Nash's entrance was spectacular, it was hardly graceful; she had given little thought to the practicalities of a headdress that would not have disgraced an Indian maharajah with a vast palace and huge doorways at his disposal. It was definitely not designed for the low doorways and the sad crush of guests at the manor.

The combined height of turban and feathers forced her to bend her knees and turn sideways to complete her crab-like manoeuvre into the room with no damage to the millinery disaster adorning her head. Her neck and shoulders were held in a curiously stiff way, as if she had spent all morning exposed to a howling nor'-westerly and was suffering the after effects. She did not look at all comfortable but a smile was pasted determinedly on her face.

Piers's jaw fell open on its hinge at this vision, but he quickly recovered as she headed towards him like a trireme. 'My dear Mrs Nash, you look' – he cleared his throat as he sought desperately for a suitable adjective – 'astonishing!'

'I thought you would say so – it is but a trifling effort,' she replied, modestly. His reaction pleased her; a woman of less restraint would have jumped for joy to receive praise from a man who knew that doyenne of the fashionable set, Lady Jersey. But since jumping for joy would also require some movement of the head, such a display was impossible. She therefore contented herself with a smug smile and carefully turned her head an inch to murmur a greeting to Letty, her movements resembling an owl suffering from rigor of the neck muscles.

'Truly astonishing, upon my word,' breathed Piers, in an awed whisper.

'I see you are almost lost for words, Mr Kilworth. *Bang up to the knocker*, was the expression you used, was it not?'

'Lord, yes! Complete to a shade, dear lady!'

'Thank you. However, keeping this upon one's head is difficult and I daresay I shall be unable to move tomorrow for the pain.'

'But think of the impression you have made! Your guests will talk of nothing but the sight of you wearing those ostrich feathers for months.'

'Did you know Mrs Bailey was also rendered speechless when she saw me? Of course,' she added in a prim voice, 'she was envious.'

'Most likely,' agreed Piers innocently. 'Not everyone can wear feathers with such aplomb.'

'No. Sadly, she does not possess the necessary poise.'

'Quite so, dear lady – or the necessary stamina,' he said, noting Letty struggling to stifle a giggle as Mrs Nash tried to incline her head in acknowledgement. 'At the first opportunity, I will describe your attire to Lady Jersey,' he added.

'You will?' gasped Mrs Nash, her headdress quivering with her excitement. 'Ah, you are too kind! I hope she will enjoy hearing of my efforts to follow the latest fashion – Caroline and I do our utmost not to appear provincial. Well, I must circulate, but I should congratulate you on your gown, Miss Ravenhill. Such delicate work! Such exquisite design! Send me the name of your dress-maker and I shall favour her with some commissions.'

She walked away, holding her head rigidly still, to speak to Alyssa and then Sir Giles; Mrs Nash was every inch the gracious, if uncomfortable, hostess.

It was after supper that Alyssa became aware that some guests, particularly ladies, were whispering. She thought she had imagined that their attention was directed solely at her, but eventually admitted that, for whatever reason, she had become the topic of conversation. Murmurings behind cupped hands and disap-proving looks became commonplace and, try as she might to ignore them, Alyssa felt like a newly discovered unpalatable species.

Had she committed any social *faux pas*? She could think of none: she had danced with those gentlemen she needed to according to etiquette, smiled at and made small talk with the dowagers, and had not confused her wine and water glasses at supper. It was unlikely to be connected with Gil as they had limited their time together.

Yet all eyes were now upon her. Overhearing a snigger as she walked by a group of ladies, Alyssa lifted her chin but began to feel hunted. In need of reas-surance, she looked for Gil but there was no sign of him. Only Piers and Letty were close by, and it was Letty who spoke first.

'Lyssa, I was coming to talk to you,' she said, looking concerned.

'And I you: I suddenly seem to be the subject of everyone's attention.'

Letty glanced at Piers, then back to Alyssa. 'Piers and I had noticed.'

'I don't understand why,' said Alyssa, with a shrug and a wry smile. 'I remem-bered my manners and even laughed at Mr Pendlebury's appalling jokes. It's disagreeable, try as I might to ignore it. I wonder if Gil is aware what sin I have committed.'

Piers murmured, 'I know, Coz. Mere tomfoolery, of course, but unpleasant all the same. I wanted to land a facer on the fellow who repeated it to me, damn him!'

'Tell me what I am accused of, Piers.' When he hesitated, Alyssa demanded urgently, 'What is it?'

Piers gave a sigh of resignation, 'Your supposed adventures as Mr Esidarap have become general knowledge and, as is usually the way, the story has not only spread quickly but grown more outrageous with each telling. To the ladies present, you are now renowned for masquerading as the most profligate rake ever to grace London and consequently, unsuitable for this genteel gathering. It has had a different effect on the gentlemen: most of them think you a regular out-and-outer, and up to every game, although some are—' He stopped and then added, 'Well, I will only say that the fellow who told me was lucky to escape a punch in the bone box. I didn't like his tone or the way he referred to you, Coz.'

The colour drained from her cheeks. 'Good God! B-but how can this be? I never intended – it was only said as a *joke*! Few people knew that Banbury tale; Letty and Gil would never speak of it in company and the only others were Mrs Nash and her daughter. . . .' Her voice trailed away and she raised her eyes to Piers in dismay.

'Think you've hit the nail on the head,' he said, in a sombre voice. 'Miss Nash has been letting her tongue run away with her, and to my mind, deliberately.'

'The spiteful miss knew exactly what she was doing,' declared Letty.

'She spoke of exacting revenge, but I did not imagine she would do this.' said Alyssa. 'My reputation will be ruined if that ridiculous tale becomes generally known – and she knows it.'

'Hmm . . . things do look a mite sticky, Coz.'

'I must confront her.'

'No, don't do that. Not wise,' said Piers, shaking his head vehemently.

'I am not afraid of Miss Nash!'

'No, dash it, of course not! Just not the thing to make a scene, that's all. Lord, you might look guilty if you march up to that hellcat and start accusing her in public. Most likely that's exactly what she wants you to do. She's been damned subtle and you need to think how to respond.'

'Perhaps you're right,' admitted Alyssa slowly. 'Oh, where is Gil? He will know what is best.'

'He's coming towards us, and he looks exceedingly angry,' observed Letty.

Gil did look forbidding: he was frowning, his lips compressed into a thin line. Having heard the whisperings about Alyssa, he had bit back the retort that sprang to his lips and instead had taken pains to tease out the original source. When his suspicions were confirmed, anger suffused him. He had expected Caroline's spite to manifest itself in some way but with this, she had gone beyond the pale. He, too, wanted to face her, but to do so would embarrass the squire and his wife and might be the reaction she had set out to provoke. But her mischief-making could not be left unchecked, for while Gil did not care for gossip, many others did and would believe the tale to be true. Alyssa's name could be irrevocably damaged if the story was not nipped in the bud.

'Gil! Have you heard?' said Alyssa, in urgent whisper when he reached them.

He nodded. 'It is at Caroline's instigation, her attempt to wreak revenge on us, and you in particular. It will not be allowed to serve,' he said, soothingly.

'Oh, I wish I had never invented that nonsensical story,' she cried.

'Don't say that. It was funny, and Miss Nash deserved it,' said Letty.

'Letty is right,' agreed Gil, warmly. 'None of this is your doing, my darling.'

Piers, who had been watching and listening, grinned. 'Lord, I *knew* there was something afoot,' he said, throwing Gil and Alyssa a mischievous glance. 'Should I wish you both happy now?'

'Pray lower your voice, Piers,' begged Alyssa. 'No one here knows, and Gil promised the squire we would be circumspect.'

'You may do so at a more appropriate time, Piers,' said Gil, with a clipped smile. 'For now, let us return to the matter at hand.'

'But how can we stop people thinking the story is true and preferably teach Miss Nash a lesson at the same time?' queried Alyssa.

'What if I ask her to dance?' said Piers, inspiration having descended on him with near-perfect timing.

'Ask her to dance?' echoed Letty, in amazement.

Gil cocked an eyebrow and drawled, 'I cannot see how doing so will afford Caroline a lesson.'

'Wait and see,' said Piers, with another enigmatic grin and a wink.

'Very well, you obviously have something in mind so I leave it to your discretion. In the meantime, the three of us will instigate a counterplot.'

'What shall we say?' asked Alyssa.

'Make a joke of the whole thing, my love. We must laugh nonchalantly and explain it was in fact your *distant relative* who masqueraded as Mr Esidarap. It will be the simplest way, rather than deny it completely, or give the truth that it was a nonsense story; people will readily accept that a fictional relative is to blame. I shall explain to the squire what has happened. He will not be too pleased, I think, with his daughter's behaviour.'

'Lord, yes – an excellent suggestion, Coz,' agreed Piers. 'Best say it was some cousin on your father's side who was responsible, twice or thrice removed – you know the sort of thing! Blame the escapade on a bad offshoot of the clan; every family has one.' Piers laughed. 'Right, while you three apply yourselves to counterplotting, I'm going to claim Miss Nash's hand for the next dance.'

Spying his quarry, Piers made his way purposefully towards her. Any guests idly observing the dancing thus far would have confirmed that Piers was the most elegant gentleman taking part. Sir Giles was skilled, too – in spite of his size and build, he was light on his feet – but Piers possessed that certain panache of young men who have graced the finest ballrooms in Europe and his sense of style combined with an entirely masculine flamboyance left ladies eager to be his partner. When he danced with Letty, even the sharpest critic amongst the dowagers declared they made a pretty couple.

Miss Nash had also noted his expertise and when Piers approached, smiled engagingly and asked if she would do him the honour, she was pleased of this opportunity to shine in front of her guests. She accepted Piers's invitation and smiled with satisfaction as he led her to join the set.

Mrs Nash, observing this gratifying little vignette with a sigh of pleasure, was also delighted. This evening was compensating somewhat for the shock of Sir Giles's matrimonial plans not including Caroline. The event was an acknowledged success: every person of consequence within thirty miles was present, the food deemed superb, the musicians declared praiseworthy, the coloured lanterns in the garden marvelled at and best of all, each lady stunned by her magnificent headdress. A stiff neck was the only blight marring her pleasure, but even painful muscle spasms could be forgotten when she espied Piers leading Caroline out for the next set. Her bosom swelling with pride, Mrs Nash prepared to enjoy the spectacle.

At first, Piers made amiable conversation. He was experienced in flattery and Miss Nash was susceptible to it – something Piers had been quick to realize. So he smiled, cooed, complimented and told one or two anecdotes, all the while carrying out his steps gracefully.

Caroline, for her part, soon relaxed, enjoying partnering this handsome consummate dancer. It was therefore astonishing to Caroline, Mrs Nash and everyone else watching, when Piers's elegance began to falter and he acquired all the grace of a length of wet muslin. Where his movements had been precise, now his co-ordination deserted him and he stumbled, murmuring an apology. His partner was not pleased, but she gave a gracious smile; after all, even the best dancer could err once. But his clumsiness continued and when Caroline turned, expecting to be facing him, she found herself in embarrassing isolation instead – Piers had gone the wrong way.

Momentary chaos ensued and Caroline blushed fiercely, not helped by interested spectators tittering loudly. Piers, who seemed totally unconcerned, uttered another smiling abject apology and blamed tiredness for his lack of expertise.

'Then I advise you to wake up – unless you wish to make me look ridiculous,' she muttered.

He bowed and whispered, 'My apologies, Miss Nash. I shall attempt to do better.'

His movements, however, did not improve, and became even more disjointed. Piers fell out of step and missed his cues, but smiled disarmingly throughout.

Caroline's rage mingled with acute embarrassment. A guffaw of laughter came from among the growing audience as Piers bowed towards the gentleman next to him instead of his partner. A deep crimson blush burnt in her cheeks as she clenched her teeth together in anguish. There could be no immediate escape; it was unthinkable to leave her partner in the middle of the dance and whether Piers's clumsiness was deliberate or accidental, she had no choice but to stay until the end. Something she anticipated would reflect well upon her had instead turned into a disaster which could not end a moment too soon.

Gil, who did not have the opportunity to appreciate Caroline's embarrassment in dancing with Piers when his limbs resembled those of a jellyfish, was encountering his own difficulties.

The campaign to convince everyone the *on dit* about Alyssa was a case of mistaken identity had been largely successful. Almost everyone he spoke to was initially only too eager to decry her, but Gil's calm, almost offhand manner combined with the weight of his authority, soon took effect. He laughed and blithely dismissed the story, declaring the tale an old one – infamous indeed but carried out by a distant cousin. Alyssa was not involved and it was, he observed drily, idiotic to assume she might have been. Could they not see Miss Paradise was a lady wholly incapable of this misdemeanour? His audience would then nod sagely and declare they had known all along she could not commit a scandalous masquerade. Gil continued in this way, gradually diminishing the notion of Alyssa's involvement. As Caroline's embarrassing moments with Piers were reaching full tilt, Gil, satisfied with his progress, found himself next to Mortimer Tilbury.

Mortimer Tilbury was a stout, middle-aged roué, an unpleasant man full of his own importance and one who was not generally liked. He also had a predilection for heavy drinking, and Gil could see at once he had partaken readily of the contents of the squire's cellar.

Gil eyed him with distaste. As a drunkard, Tilbury's opinion did not carry weight in most quarters and he therefore saw no need to discuss Alyssa with him. Instead, he gave a curt nod of acknowledgement before attempting to move on but Mortimer Tilbury detained him.

' 'vening, Maxton! 'S fine gathering, is it not?' said Tilbury, waving an arm to indicate the collected company. '*Damn* fine gathering, and Nash's not one to be close-fisted with his wine.' Mortimer held up his glass and owlishly studied the red liquid, trying to focus. 'Take this burgundy, for 'xample – 's wonderfully mell-mellow,' he said, slurring his words.

'I'm sure it is, but you're already as drunk as a wheelbarrow.'

'Me? Drunk?' He shook his head slowly and replied, ' 'S not true. Sober as a judge, Maxton. Sober as a judge. 'S nothing wrong in enjoying the free fare on offer though.' He chortled at this, and Gil grimaced as he caught the reek of liquor on his breath.

'If you will excuse me, Tilbury—'

'Wait a minute. Want to talk to you about something. See that lovely filly there,' he nodded in Alyssa's direction; she was talking to a group of people close by.

Gil tensed. 'I assume you mean Miss Paradise?'

'That's the one. A prime article, if ever I saw one,' observed Tilbury, running his eyes lasciviously over Alyssa. 'She's a neighbour of yours, ain't she?'

'What of it?'

'I want to ask you about her. Been hearing some tales about that lady this evening.'

Trying to remain calm, Gil shrugged. 'Scurrilous nonsense. Miss Paradise was not involved; it was a distant cousin of hers.'

'Oh? That's a pity, but cousin or no, she looks a lively piece to me and I'd be obliged if you'd introduce me, Maxton. I've a mind to know her better, as she looks the type to know 'xactly how to satisfy a man!' He finished with a knowing grin.

'I strongly advise you to stop now, Tilbury, before I do something you will regret.'

But Tilbury was too drunk to heed this advice. 'Now, now – 's no call to be prudish. We are both men of the world.' He leered at Gil, winked and whispered, 'No doubt, with her being a neighbour, you've already found opportunity to sample her delights—' He was forced to halt mid sentence. Unseen by other guests, Gil had grasped the lapel of his jacket and pushed him against the wall.

'You damnable louse!' he hissed, in a voice replete with menace. 'I'd like to rip your tongue out and ram it down your throat!'

'Eh?'

'Unfortunately, my respect for the squire prevents me besmirching his house with an unseemly brawl so another method of redress must suffice. Name your weapons, Tilbury.'

'Eh?' The two bottles of burgundy he had consumed had made Tilbury's brain decidedly sluggish, and he was dazed from being manhandled against an unforgiving wall.

'Is your hearing fogged as well as your sense, man?' retorted Gil. 'Name your weapons!'

'Weapons? D'you mean a duel?' asked Tilbury, still struggling to comprehend.

'What else could I be referring to? Of course I mean a duel – I demand satisfaction,' muttered Gil, still gripping his coat. 'You will answer for slurring Miss Paradise's character in that fashion.'

There was nothing as effective as shock for sobering the inebriated and Gil's challenge acted like a bucket of cold water over Mortimer Tilbury. He blinked again, and shuddered, then sought desperately for a way out. Mortimer had no intention of meeting this man in any form of physical or sporting contest; Sir Giles was a notable shot, an expert fencer and renowned amateur pugilist, so he retreated with alacrity.

'Good God! Y-you must have misunderstood me!' His slurred bluster went up a full octave to a high-pitched whimper. 'You have misunderstood me. Indeed, I meant no offence. She's a respectable young woman with no hint of scandal attached to her name, and you've totally misinterpreted my words. I do not explain myself clearly when in my cups.'

'I did not misinterpret you.'

'Damn it, Maxton, you misconstrued my meaning, I tell you!' he squeaked.

Gil, appearing to consider the matter, said, 'I'm not sure I should take the word of a jug-bitten fellow. However, unsurprisingly, I see valour has deserted you in the face of being called out – you are quaking like a frightened rabbit. I give you the benefit of doubt on this occasion, but make you this promise: one more word in denigration of Miss Paradise and I will seek you out!'

Tilbury swallowed the lump of fear which had risen painfully to his throat. Mightily relieved, he removed his coat from Gil's grasp and turned quickly away.

But, in his hurry to escape, Mortimer's head swam as did the room about him. He managed only five teetering steps before staggering from the effects of the squire's burgundy. Pitching sideways violently, he fell into the table situated at the edge of the area set aside for dancing, and which bore the enormous silver punch bowl.

This occurred at the same moment as Caroline, fresh from the ignominy of dancing with Piers, stormed away from the dance floor. Everything happened quickly; there was no chance of escape. The punchbowl and several silver goblets jumped into the air with a deafening clatter after being struck by the considerable mass of a flying Mortimer Tilbury and the entire contents of the punchbowl cascaded towards Caroline with unerring accuracy.

Silence ensued. Interested onlookers, who included Gil, Alyssa, Letty, Piers, Mrs Nash, every other guest present, Simmons the butler and two junior footmen, all held their breath. Caroline was drenched from head to foot in sweet smelling punch, and not an inch seemed to have escaped its attention. The liquid dripped from her hair and face, and her jonquil gown was soaked from bodice to flounce. To add to a vision that would not have disgraced Pomona, a slice of lemon was perched amongst her carefully arranged curls and shavings of orange peel decorated the lace at her bosom.

A frozen rigidity descended upon Caroline, like Lot's wife when turned to salt. Only her tightened lips hinted at inner fury and mortification despite the best efforts of the lemon slice and orange peel to soften the image. Eventually, she made a moue of disgust and threw fulminating looks at Piers, Gil, Alyssa and finally towards her nemesis, in the unlikely form of the prostrate, moaning Mortimer Tilbury who lay surrounded by punch cups and the splintered wreckage of the table. Then, with a clipped cry of outrage and as much dignity as a lady bedecked in a macédoine of lemon and orange peelings and soaked in punch can muster, Caroline walked to the door, not forgetting to grind the heel of her evening slipper into Tilbury's hand as she passed by.

Laughter rippled around the room – Caroline, like Mortimer Tilbury, was not generally liked.

In contrast to Caroline's paralysis after being dowsed in punch, Mrs Nash, watching these tragic events unfold, had developed a nervous tick which made her ostrich feathers twitch alarmingly. She stared at the tableau before her in disbelief and wilted visibly, her anguished gaze switching from Caroline's retreating figure to Mortimer Tilbury, pushing aside punch goblets and cursing profusely as he struggled to his knees.

Overcome, Mrs Nash closed her eyes and groaned. She sank into a nearby chair, moaning at the pain in her neck even this invoked and offering up a fervent prayer the ground would open up and swallow her if Mrs Bailey gloated even for an instant over this concatenation of embarrassments.

The unexpected denouement to the party was spoken of by many the next day, including Alyssa and Gil as they dined at Hawkscote. Only when the covers had been removed and the servants had retired were they able to speak freely.

'I cannot feel too sorry for Miss Nash,' admitted Alyssa, 'but I hope the squire was not annoyed by the fracas. When Letty and I left, Miss Nash, rather than Mr Esidarap, was the topic on everyone's lips.'

'Caroline was hoist by her own petard,' said Gil. 'She set out to ruin you without a qualm and, having chosen that path, it was fitting that she was responsible, albeit indirectly, for what befell her. Once I had a chance to explain to Henry how things came about, he was mortified, and furious with Caroline. Although no blame could be attached to her for Tilbury's drunkenness, he felt she was ultimately culpable.'

'I wonder what she will do now. She is very proud and will find it difficult to face everyone for some time.'

'Henry had already offered to despatch her to Bath, and Caroline is apparently anxious to leave as soon as possible – after the embarrassment she suffered, a spell away from Dorset is advisable.'

'And what of Mrs Nash? Was she angry?'

'She was naturally upset to see her daughter drenched by the contents of the punchbowl but seemed more concerned with her own discomfort, as far as Piers and I could ascertain. The combined weight and difficulties of perching silk turban and feathers upon her head had led to an acute stiffness of her neck. Even as her guests were leaving, she was calling for lavender water and hot compresses. Piers was sympathetic and suggested several remedies; I think he felt responsible for her predicament,' he explained.

Alyssa shook her head but could not repress a smile. 'Oh, I could box his ears for suggesting those feathers!'

'I suppose Mrs Nash was silly enough to take his word to the extreme. I did not witness the whole thing, and I should not condone his behaviour when danc-ing with Caroline either but' – his deep chuckle sounded – 'it was the funniest thing I have seen for some time.'

Alyssa laughed. 'He would not have done it if Caroline hadn't provoked the situation. Piers can be a devil, but he would not ridicule anyone for the sake of it.'

'I don't believe he would.'

Alyssa was quiet for a moment and then murmured, 'I want to thank you, Gil.'

He gave her a quizzical look. 'What for, my darling?'

'Oh, several things,' she mused. 'For making a difficult evening bearable . . . for watching over me . . . for being willing to defend my honour . . . would you really have fought a duel for my sake?'

'I would lay down my life for you if necessary.'

She smiled, but said with a tremor in her voice, 'I don't want you ever to have to.'

He lifted the hand he was holding to his lips. 'There was no need to be concerned. Tilbury would have struggled to be sober enough to crawl out of bed, let alone fight a duel, even if he possessed the necessary courage,' he said with a grin. 'Now, enough talk of everyone else—'

He pulled Alyssa gently to her feet. Holding both her hands between his, he whispered, 'Let us speak of our future. Finally, there are no obstacles in our way.' He kissed her passionately before his gaze searched hers and he said, 'My heart is yours, Alyssa. I love you more than I can ever put into words, and want you near me always. Will you do me the honour of becoming my wife?'

'Oh, my love,' she said, smiling tenderly up at him. 'Yes – there is nothing I want more!'

'Then you have made me the happiest man alive,' he said, in a husky voice, his arms stealing around her.

Lost in spiralling passion, neither was aware of voices emanating from the hall. They gradually grew louder and more insistent until the door was suddenly thrust open. Charles stood on the threshold in a long driving cape, his silhouette illuminated against the light from the hallway beyond. His gaze fell immediately on Gil and Alyssa, locked in their passionate embrace, and he uttered a violent expletive before demanding, 'What the *devil* is going on here?'

CHAPTER 15

'Charles!' exclaimed Alyssa.

'I'm sorry, miss,' explained Rowberry, casting a look of withering disapproval at the visitor, 'I asked Mr Brook to wait until I informed you of his arrival—'

'It seems just as well I was not announced,' interjected Charles unceremoniously.

'Thank you, Rowberry, you may leave.' Alyssa gently disengaged herself from Gil's embrace but he did not release her entirely, reaching out for her hand instead; she could feel latent tension pumping through his every sinew and muscle. 'How like you to arrive at an inopportune moment, Charles,' she added in a cool voice.

'Inopportune?' He snorted derisively as he strode forward. 'When I find you being mauled like a common serving wench? On the contrary, I arrived most propitiously. Sir – I presume you have something to say?' he added, raking Gil over from head to toe with a hard look.

Gil moved imperceptibly to stand in front of Alyssa, tense but perfectly in control. 'I have a great deal to say and am delighted to have this opportunity.'

'Bah!' Charles waved an impatient hand. 'My impression of you was fixed from the start: once a rake, always a rake!'

'Indeed?' replied Gil sardonically, raising his brows. 'Then perhaps we should discuss this further in private, away from Miss Paradise?'

Alyssa took a purposeful step forward. 'No! I want to stay.'

'It might be best if you left,' murmured Gil, eyeing Charles's rising choler.

'I would prefer to hear since it concerns me also.'

'And so you should, Alyssa. Your morals have gone a-begging and I am sadly disappointed in you.'

'Another lecture, Charles?' she queried. 'You must find them very tiring. You have no jurisdiction over me.'

'I claim that of a long-standing friend, and you would do better to listen to me than cavort in that infamous way with this fellow. As for you, sir, you are nothing but a disgrace!'

Gil's lips tightened and he said in a voice of icy politeness, 'Mr Brook, you should ascertain some facts before interceding further in this clumsy fashion. Neither I nor Miss Paradise has behaved improperly.'

'That is a matter of opinion; from what I witnessed, you were taking advantage of Alyssa.'

'Of course he was not!' she retorted.

But Charles was no mood to listen. The weeks spent in London had increased his self-importance to the point that he considered his opinion almost inviolate. No one thought more highly of Charles than Charles himself and, having set himself even further apart from his fellow men because of his recent change in circumstances, his superior attitude had increased. He had a right – a duty even – to correct and admonish when he saw fit and if ever a scene and its players warranted correction and admonition, this was it.

He had also spent the last hour in a draughty carriage, bumping over pot-holed country roads in the company of a whining pug dog, all of which had tried his patience sorely. His consolation had been the thought that his discussions with Alyssa could be despatched quickly and, notwithstanding her natural disappointment, followed by epicurean refreshment before returning to his warm bed at The Antelope.

Instead, he found Alyssa in an embrace that would not have disgraced a scullery maid, and indignation rushed through his veins. What he saw grated horribly upon his sense of propriety as well as his empty stomach, and fanned the vestiges of his temper into self-righteous anger.

Alyssa would receive a piece of his mind, but first he was eager to teach Sir Giles Maxton a lesson. A physical outlet for his disapprobation beckoned appealingly. He was not a man whose thoughts naturally turned towards violence, but the art of pugilism was a necessary accomplishment amongst the *ton* and a man who could acquit himself well in a mill for honour's sake was considered a Corinthian of note. Charles had a rare fancy to be considered a Corinthian and here was a chance to put those recent sparring sessions with Gentleman Jackson to good use. This damned fellow had rubbed him up the wrong way from the first time they met – he would enjoy drawing his cork.

Charles eyed Gil carefully, measuring his opponent's reach and weight while Gil returned the scrutiny with an equally purposeful flint-like gaze.

'It is my opinion,' began Charles a moment later, removing his cape and pulling off his gloves, 'that ruffians like you understand only one language, and you need a sharp reminder of how a gentleman behaves.'

Alyssa regarded him with puzzlement and some misgiving. 'What on earth are you doing, Charles?'

'Preparing to teach this fellow a lesson.'

She laughed incredulously. 'No, you cannot be so idiotic! I wrote a letter which explained everything – did you receive it?'

'Letter? I received no letter, but that is of no matter now.' Charles shook off his jacket. 'Stand away, Alyssa. There will be time enough for explanations afterwards.'

Alyssa was conscious of a strong desire to slap Charles's smug face. She repressed it with difficulty, saying, 'You *are* a pompous ninny! I think you have run mad while you have been away.'

'Hmph! It is your state of mind that is questionable, but we will address that when I have dealt with Maxton.' He looked at Gil. 'Now, sir, have you the stomach for this or are you a *coward* as well as a rake?'

'Are you certain what you are about here?' asked Gil, in a silky voice.

'Quite certain: you are a rag-mannered libertine! Is that sufficient challenge or must I offer still more?'

'Charles!' cried Alyssa, horrified at his rudeness and manifest desire for confrontation. She glanced across to see Gil strip off his coat and throw it on to a nearby chair. Hurrying over, she placed a detaining hand on his arm and whispered in a low desperate voice, 'No! No, Gil! I don't know what ails him, but you should not, you *must not* encourage him.'

'Would you have me insulted to my face with no right of reply?' he asked softly, a hint of a smile in his eyes.

'Well, no, but this – this is sheer folly! You cannot engage in fisticuffs in the dining-room!'

'It is as good a place as any other,' said Gil, flexing his shoulders. 'At least the china has been cleared away.'

'If I can extract a moment of sense from him, I will explain.'

Gil shrugged. 'Brook does not want explanations; he wishes to teach me a lesson and to settle our differences in quite another way. So be it – I am more than willing to oblige him. I did not start this, but by God I shall finish it.'

'But you might be hurt,' she pleaded.

'I doubt it. He may have more science and recent sparring practice, but I can give him height, reach and a stone in weight,' observed Gil. He rolled up his shirt sleeves and sat down to remove his boots, as Charles had already done.

Alyssa, studying him in disbelief, whispered, 'So, you still intend to respond?'

He nodded. 'I must.'

'You are *both* mad!' she cried, aghast.

'Quite possibly, but it will be satisfying nonetheless.' He stood up and gazed at Alyssa, tenderness mingled with understanding in his look. 'Try not to worry, my darling. This meeting was inevitable after all that has happened, and Brook is obviously determined to have the matter out between us, here and now. I'm only sorry you are here to witness this but there is still time to leave and I would prefer it if you did.'

'I have already told you I will not. Oh! I am out of patience with both of you for this piece of nonsense, and I could cheerfully strangle you, Gil, for your insistence on being honourable,' she cried, watching perturbed and, she was ashamed to admit, with no little degree of fascination as he deftly untied his cravat, placed it to one side and unfastened the buttons of his shirt to reveal the strong muscles of his neck and upper chest. Incredibly, even at this moment, she felt desire spiral outwards from the pit of her stomach as her eyes drank in his masculine beauty.

'I hope after we are married you will curb your desire – understandable for the most part – to punish my intransigence in such an unsophisticated way, my love,' he said laughing softly.

She gave a watery smile but said, 'Gil, do be serious for a moment. I do not want you to fight Charles.'

'Neither do I, but now he has insulted me and more importantly, questioned your honour, I have no choice but to respond in kind.'

She fell silent, seeing there was no possibility of dissuading him. In truth, she could hardly blame him after the insults Charles had unleashed, coupled with his swaggering manner – even she had been tempted to slap him. 'Then there is nothing I can say or do further to prevent this,' she said with a heavy sigh. A smile trembled upon her lips but there was deep apprehension in her eyes. 'Please take care.'

He lifted her hand to his lips and said, 'I promise I will; I have some ability and we are both gentlemen so once satisfaction is obtained, I hope that will be an end to it, once and for all.'

'Are you ready, Maxton?' said Charles curtly, casting him another look of dislike. The sight of Gil kissing Alyssa's hand had again offended his sensibilities and he was eager to get the matter over with. His boxing skills having improved during his time in London, he did not consider it would take long and the fellow could then be thrown out by his ear, suitably cowed. The physical exertion would add an edge to his appetite.

'I am at your disposal,' drawled Gil, thrusting the heavy table across the floor before bowing slightly. 'But before we begin, may I offer a few candid words?'

'Very well, but it is too late for an apology now, even one prompted by fear of a beating.'

'I do not intend to apologize, Brook,' said Gil curtly. 'I wish to tell you I find your manners priggish, your sanctimonious prattling tedious in the extreme and your refusal to venture into Dorset when Alyssa was ill, unforgivable. I'll not tolerate your behaviour towards her any more.'

This speech fanned Charles into a fury and his habitual punctiliousness fell away. 'Damn you, Maxton! I'll make you regret those words!' he cried.

The two protagonists began to circle each other slowly in front of the fire-place and Alyssa moved behind an oak chair. She gripped the carved back, feeling utterly helpless. Uncle Tom peered down from his portrait and Alyssa, attributing it to a trick of the light, could almost believe he was smiling again. How had events moved to this so quickly?

Alyssa wanted to cover her gaze, but she also needed to see what was happening. Could she have done more to prevent it? No, she thought not. Her entreaties had fallen on deaf ears and, short of offering physical restraint to both, there was no more she could have done. Arrogance on one side and a thirst for recompense on the other meant each man was hell-bent on a mill.

It began with harmless sparring. Charles demonstrated good technique but moved too slowly. To any experienced onlooker, it would have been clear he had been taught well – his recent practice with Gentleman Jackson was evident – but his ponderous stilted style was no match for Gil's agility, greater power and reach. Time and again, Gil parried Charles's blows and, quick as lightning, moved in over his guard.

Eager to land the first telling blow, Charles suddenly spied an opening and feigned a left then struck with a right jab. But again Gil was too quick and the blow glanced harmlessly off his jaw as he moved aside. His face was a study in concentration and determination as he lifted his guard and advanced towards his opponent, putting in a deft right then a blow to the body which made Charles stagger backwards. A vase of flowers, caught by Charles's flailing arm, smashed upon the floor. He grimaced but regained his balance and fought back, aiming a flurry of blows in quick succession, none of which did real damage to Gil whose fleetness of foot ensured he moved out of range for most of them.

Alyssa watched in mute anguish as they swayed towards each other, their feet padding back and forth across the floor. She could see that Gil had the better of the contest thus far, but she watched intently and with bated breath in case of injury. By now, she was sure all the servants had their ears pressed against the door. She was also certain Letty would have been made aware and was outside, waiting to enter.

They closed again and even to Alyssa's inexperienced eye, Charles seemed to be struggling for air. His breath was now coming in great gulps and beads of sweat rolled off his forehead as he ploughed on doggedly. Gil was still full of energy, easily avoiding the increasingly wild lunges that came his way. Several chairs and ornaments went crashing over in the mêlée.

'Stand and fight, damn you!' cried Charles, irritated by his opponent's ability to dance nimbly out of reach.

'With pleasure!' said Gil, through gritted teeth and landed a short, effective jab to his opponent's cheekbone as he charged with his guard down.

Gil had drawn first blood: Charles's left eye quickly began to swell and close and, with a growl of frustration, he lunged, managing a glancing blow to Gil's throat. Gil stumbled and fell to his knees, winded and gasping for breath.

'Oh! Have done, for God's sake!' cried Alyssa, stirred from her silent vigil. 'Surely you both have satisfaction now? Are you fighting for my sake, or for your own sense of honour?'

Her pleas went unanswered; the contest was too intense for either combatant to listen. As soon as he recovered, Gil rose quickly to move out of range of the advancing Charles who looked much worse than his opponent. His face was badly disfigured: his left eye was nearly closed, and blood oozed from a cut on his opposite cheek.

'Not finished, Maxton?' panted Charles, exhaustion receding momentarily as he sensed victory might be near. 'You're a game one, I'll grant you. That blow would have finished a lesser man.'

Gil smiled crookedly and gave a mocking salute in reply, all the while waiting for his opportunity to strike.

It soon came. Thinking he had the upper hand, Charles grew over-confident and rushed in, dropping his guard. Gil judged the distance and weight of his blows to perfection and threw in a short, quick jab to the body, followed by a devastating right uppercut which caught Charles on the point of his jaw. His head wobbled on his neck and he went crashing backwards like a felled tree, insensible.

Gil stood over him, prepared for more if needed, but Charles lay inert and slumped against the wall. The quiet was broken only by the sound of Gil's laboured breathing as he looked down on his prostrate erstwhile opponent.

Alyssa hurried out from behind the chair, hardly knowing if she was incandescent with anger or relief. The latter won and she threw her arms around him, saying hoarsely, 'Oh, I thought for a moment he had hurt you badly! Are you all right?'

He grinned as he folded her in his embrace. 'Apart from a few bruises, I think so. It must be difficult for you to believe after this but I am not usually a bloodthirsty fellow! Brook seems to bring out the worst in my temper.'

She whispered in some alarm, 'You have not killed him, have you?'

He smiled. 'No, he is still very much alive. We can continue our conversation when he regains his senses.'

'No, Gil. I think it would be best if you left now, before Charles awakes.'

He released her to look into her face quizzically. 'What?' he cried, grasping her shoulders, 'Slink away like some scared mongrel? I'll not give him the satisfaction!'

'But what is to be gained if you stay?'

'He will receive a pithy account of my opinion of him.'

'Now is not the time. You are rightfully angry and Charles will be furious, and more likely embarrassed when he realizes you have beaten him. Give me an opportunity to explain about us; he deserves that from me at least. Speak to him when you can both be calm. He must be stopping in Dorchester overnight so there may be a chance sooner than you think.'

'What if he tries to browbeat you when I have gone?' he asked, unconvinced.

'If he does, you know I'll not stand for it. Let me deal with him in my own way now. Please, Gil?'

He sighed. 'If you really think it best then I must agree even though I don't like it. Damn it, Brook will consider me a coward if I am gone when he wakes up.'

'After what I have just witnessed, I rather think Charles will be relieved you are not here.'

He smiled but said soberly, 'I will leave only because you ask it of me – not because of Brook. My actions have caused you hurt tonight, even though they were forced on me.' He shook his head and ran his fingers roughly though his hair. 'I wanted us to plan our wedding and our future this evening.'

'You could not have foreseen Charles's arrival any more than I could. Our plans will wait a little longer – we have a whole lifetime ahead.'

'Will you send word to me tomorrow? I'll not rest until I know Brook accepts that he has lost you.'

She reached up to caress his cheek lovingly and whispered, 'I promise. Now go, before I throw water over Charles and let him feel the edge of my tongue.'

'Very well.' He tilted up her chin and kissed her once and then again before putting on his boots and retrieving his jacket. 'Don't forget – I shall be waiting to hear from you, my love. And I promise to deal with Mr Brook in a more collected manner when next we meet.' He kissed her fiercely and, feeling her respond, groaned in frustration. 'Until tomorrow then?' he murmured.

'Tomorrow – now hurry.'

Gil opened the door to reveal a comical scene. Rowberry, Mrs Farnell and Letty were all waiting near the door, and almost fell over in surprise when it opened unexpectedly. Several other servants stood a little further back, their eyes wide with curiosity. Gil gave Alyssa a rueful lop-sided smile and, throwing Charles a final glance, crisply asked Rowberry to tell the groom to bring his horse.

Letty watched him leave and after ordering the other servants back to their duties, came in and queried hesitantly, 'Lyssa?'

'Charles arrived unannounced,' she said, indicating the figure on the floor. 'I'll tell you more in a moment. Mrs Farnell, set the furniture to rights and remove any broken china – I need to speak to Mr Brook privately.'

'Very good, miss,' said the housekeeper, no trace of the astonishment or curiosity she felt showing on her features as she set to her task.

When she had gone, Letty said, 'Charles must have received your letter but he has travelled here very quickly. I presume Gil is responsible for Charles's indisposition?'

Alyssa explained what had happened, adding, 'I can hardly blame Gil for retaliating. As you see, he came out of the contest far better than Charles.'

'But where has he gone?'

'Back to Eastcombe – I persuaded him to leave.'

'Then it must be just coincidence that Charles came back at this moment. Oh, why didn't he go and boil his head instead of coming back and upsetting your happiness?'

Charles moaned and moved his head slightly. Eyes still closed, a frown passed over his face.

'Sleeping beauty awakes!' said Letty with a chuckle. 'Lord, if he dares to prose on with that bruised eye, I shall not be able to stop myself from giggling.'

'Time to provide a little help for our visitor,' said Alyssa. She took a small jug from the sideboard, removed the cut flowers and emptied the liquid contents over Charles's head. 'I have wanted to do that for some time,' she muttered.

'What—' Charles coughed and spluttered, and his eyelids flickered open as there was a knock at the door.

Rowberry, his face a study of confusion, came in. 'I am sorry to disturb you again miss, but there is a young lady demanding to be admitted,' he said, raising his voice to be heard over a dog barking.

'A lady! Who is it?'

His eloquent sniff hinted at his disapproval of yet another strange chapter in the evening's events. 'She has not yet given me her name; she appears – er – agitated.'

'How strange,' said Letty, puzzled. 'Perhaps she is a traveller and an accident has befallen her carriage.'

More yapping and snarling emitted from the hallway, and Rowberry said in a faintly disparaging tone, 'The lady has a small dog with her, miss.'

'I see.' Alyssa glanced at Charles, who was groaning and gingerly touching his chin with his fingertips. 'Oh dear! Now is hardly the time for visitors.'

'Perhaps I should go and see—' began Letty.

But before she could do so, a dark-haired girl rushed in. She was very young, in her early twenties at the most and her figure, though neat, had a tendency towards plumpness. She was undoubtedly a lady of means, dressed in a green pelisse decorated in extravagant style and a green bonnet trimmed with rust-coloured ribbon. Huge brown eyes looked out from a pretty, heart-shaped face, accompanied by a *retroussé* nose and a prim little mouth. Expensive perfume filled the air and she held a fine lace handkerchief in one hand and carried a pug dog, still yapping loudly, under her arm.

Alyssa and Letty looked on in astonishment as this second visitor scanned the room and cried out in dismay at Charles's reclining figure. Pug made good his escape as she loosened her grasp and ran under the sideboard, where he clearly intended to repel all boarders if the subsequent snarling and baring of teeth were any indication. The girl paid no heed and instead flung herself at Charles's side, put her arms around his neck and began to weep, saying, 'Oh! Oh dear! My darling Bobo! You are hurt! What has happened? Dorset is indeed a wild, unciv-ilized place!'

While she talked, she dabbed his bloody face with her handkerchief until he winced and said firmly, and with a hint of impatience, 'There is no need to fuss over me, my dear. It is only a few cuts and bruises!'

'But Charles, who did this?' cried the girl. 'I have been waiting over half an hour in that cold, uncomfortable carriage, Rex made my head ache with his whining and I thought you would never come back.' Her large eyes were full of tears as she looked adoringly at Charles, who had struggled to his feet. She added with a trembling lip, 'I did not know what to do.'

'*Bobo?*' repeated Alyssa, lifting her brows questioningly. 'Charles, has this lady arrived with you? It appears you know her well since she refers to you by that affectionate term.'

'Of course I do.' He flushed crimson as he moved his lower jaw from side to side experimentally.

'Then would you be kind enough to introduce us? Letty and I are eager to become acquainted.'

Charles shifted his position to accommodate the girl, who had cast off her bonnet and was presently sobbing into his shirt front, already wet from the water tipped over his head. He patted her shoulder consolingly before looking at Alyssa.

Plainly disconcerted, he cleared his throat twice before speaking. 'I-I – er – meant to explain to you about Evanthe immediately, but when I encountered you and Maxton, well, all thought of it went from my mind.' He glanced around the room and asked, 'Where is Maxton?'

'Gone.'

'Damn it, I wanted to talk to him.' He pressed along his jawline and grimaced. 'Whatever I think of his morals, he has a fine right hook; it sticks in my throat to acknowledge it but he fair near broke my jaw! I fear the wretch has loosened one of my teeth.'

'Then it is your own fault. Sir Giles was the victor, morally and physically, and do not think he left from a want of courage: he did so at my request and most unwillingly on his part. I thought the next time you meet should be in less heated circumstances.'

Charles grunted, but his attention was claimed again by the sobs of the diminutive figure whose curls brushed his chin. With a few words from him, her tears disappeared as quickly as they had arrived and he encouraged her to face Alyssa and Letty.

'These are Miss Paradise and Miss Ravenhill, my dear.' He then addressed Alyssa and hesitated briefly, before continuing, 'May I introduce the former Miss Evanthe Crawford-Clarke, who recently became my wife.'

'Your *wife*!' Alyssa repeated, thunderstruck.

Evanthe bobbed a dainty curtsy and, her tears already forgotten, said with a smile, 'Yes indeed! We have been married for exactly one week. Excessively romantic, is it not? Our wedding was in St. George's in Hanover Square, just as soon as could be arranged, for I could not be parted again from dear Charles when he left town. I am pleased to meet you both – my husband has told me about you.'

'Has he? Then I'd like to know what—' began Alyssa, before she suddenly collected herself. 'Forgive my manners, Mrs Brook, I am astonished, but I offer my sincerest congratulations.'

'And please accept mine also,' said Letty.

Charles attempted a smile, winced at the pain this invoked, and bowed. 'Thank you. Evanthe knows about our previous friendship, Alyssa. I came to Dorset to tell you our marriage had taken place – I did not think it a proper subject matter for a letter, and besides, I had no time to contrive a suitably worded missive. I thought visiting would be a better way of mitigating your disappointment.'

'How thoughtful, Charles,' she said, with sarcasm. 'I can well understand why such a letter would have been difficult to write. I'm surprised but not in the least disappointed to hear you are married.'

'You're not?'

'No – on the contrary, I am delighted for your happiness. However, I wonder how you had the audacity to judge Sir Giles and me when your own behaviour' – her gaze rested for an instant on Evanthe – 'has been less than honest.'

Charles shuffled uncomfortably. 'He was treating you abominably yet you did not seem to be struggling to get away. You might have done so when he was forcing his unwelcome attentions on you—'

'But they were not unwelcome,' she interjected.

'—in that way. I beg your pardon?'

'They were not unwelcome,' she repeated. 'It is not yet common knowledge, but Sir Giles and I are betrothed.'

'*What?*'

Alyssa smiled wryly. 'Now I have shocked you. At least *I* thought it proper to write!'

'Good God!' said Charles. 'This changes matters completely.'

'Ah, another wedding,' cooed Evanthe, as she retrieved the growling Rex from under the sideboard and swept him under her arm. 'That is wonderful, isn't it, Bobo? I wish everyone to be as happy as we are.'

'Yes, yes, of course. If you say so, my dear, but Alyssa—'

'Oh, but I have just remembered,' interrupted his wife, unheeding, 'you have not yet explained how you came by your injuries.'

'I will tell you in a moment, Evanthe.'

She pouted and, demonstrating a tenacity of purpose belied by her demure exterior, said firmly, 'No, now if you please, or I will ask Miss Paradise. It seems she was present.'

He sighed resignedly. 'It was at the hands of Sir Giles Maxton who was here until a short while ago – we had a disagreement.'

'Sir Giles?' she mused. 'Is that the same gentleman Miss Paradise is betrothed to?'

'Yes.'

'Then why were you sparring with him?' asked Evanthe.

'Yes, why were you, Charles?' murmured Alyssa innocently.

'Because I did not know then they were betrothed!' he roared, goaded beyond endurance. 'I saw, that is I *thought* I saw, Alyssa being mauled by a man she previously held in distaste. I took issue with his ungentlemanly behaviour and intended to teach him a lesson.'

'Oh, I see! Well, I suppose that was heroic, my darling,' cried Evanthe, slipping her arm through Charles's and smiling. 'He is so punctilious about matters of propriety, Miss Paradise – but you must know that already. It is one of the things my mama particularly liked about him, you know.'

'I know your husband is punctilious Mrs Brook but—'

'Oh, please call me Evanthe.'

'Very well, but Charles should have checked before jumping to conclusions and insulting both of us, leaving Sir Giles little option but to respond.'

Evanthe giggled and nodded her agreement. 'Bobo, it was rather silly to fight with Sir Giles and leave me all alone. I declare even now I am chilled to the bone. If Miss Paradise is betrothed to Sir Giles, she was no doubt happy to be kissing him and he would not be pleased at being interrupted either. Really, you should have enquired first.'

'How the devil was I to know?' he declared.

'I tried to tell you but you would not listen,' said Alyssa.

Evanthe tutted. 'You should not have charged in like a bull off the rope – then Sir Giles would not have hit you, and you would not have that badly swollen eye which does not look well with your new jacket. I will ask your valet to prepare a cold compress and tend to it myself. Poor lamb! I expect you *meant* well.'

'Damn it!' he shouted, only for Rex to snarl at his raised voice. He sighed, knowing it was useless to argue further. 'Yes, my love,' he said, meekly. 'Perhaps I was hasty.'

'Our betrothal is not yet common knowledge here but I wrote to tell you of it, Charles. Obviously, there was no need; you have clearly been busy during your stay in London,' observed Alyssa drily.

Charles had the grace to blush. 'I spent a great deal of time in Evanthe's company. At first our relationship was one of sincere friendship but it grew into love. Perhaps I should have written to you – indeed, I intended to – but you were ill and then I was caught up in the whirl of wedding preparations. I never received your letter because we left London immediately after the ceremony. We are travelling to Devon to stay on one of Evanthe's father's estates and your note must have been delivered after we left.'

'Oh, I do not blame you for falling in love, Charles,' observed Alyssa, with a chuckle. 'I, too, have fallen in love in your absence, but then I never professed to care for you in that way in the past. We would not have made each other happy – quite the opposite in fact.'

'Did you know we fell in love at Almack's?' mused Evanthe conversationally. 'Baron Spencer had just danced with me and I was wearing my white spider gauze with the Russian bodice when Charles told me – in the most *masterful* way – that if he did not dance the next waltz with me, his heart would be broken forever. I knew there and then that I would accept if he should offer for me.'

'Goodness! Did Charles say *that?*' asked Letty, which earned her a quelling look from Charles; at least, the best quelling look a man with a rapidly swelling eye could manage.

'Of course – he is *very* romantic. I liked him when we met again in London but in his pursuit of me, he showed himself to be a passionate man who set my heart fluttering. As for his kisses when Mama and Papa were not present—'

'Pray do not say too much, my dear,' observed Charles, hurriedly.

'Oh! I am sorry; I am such a pea goose!' she sighed and added, 'Well, he was very attentive.'

'Indeed? This side of Charles's character is unknown to me,' said Alyssa.

'He asked my papa for permission to marry me. He and Mama have been very careful of my suitors, on account of my money,' declared Evanthe artlessly.

'Your money?' queried Alyssa.

'Oh, it is not a large fortune by London standards – only thirty thousand – but there are so many fortune hunters nowadays and they wanted me to marry someone who loved me, not my money. They have known Charles and his family for an age and could not have been happier when Charles asked for my hand, although Papa said that he had never known a man who talked so much and yet said so little to any purpose—'

Charles coughed.

'Of course, *I* do not think that,' she continued. 'Bobo is the sweetest, most charming man alive, and I dote upon his every word. Even Rex likes him, don't you, Rex?'

Rex replied by drawing back his mouth to reveal a row of sharp, white teeth. Evanthe tapped his nose. 'Silly dog! Rex is very jealous, Miss Paradise. He is not at all happy that Charles has replaced him in my affections.'

'So I see,' observed Alyssa wryly. 'No doubt Rex will become accustomed to your husband in due course.' She rubbed her forehead, struggling to marshal her thoughts. 'Well, this has been an evening for surprises and I admit to feeling tired. What are your plans, Charles? I presume you and your wife will stay in Dorchester overnight?'

'Yes. We will continue with our journey tomorrow as Evanthe is eager to reach Devon as soon as possible.' He again looked a little sheepish as he added, 'I was hoping that we might obtain dinner here before returning to The Antelope. The food provided there, although wholesome enough, is not what Evanthe is accustomed too.'

'I'm certain you will understand, Miss Paradise, when I tell you I was offered only mutton stew or a slice of pig's cheek for supper,' said Evanthe, shuddering at the memory. 'When I refused to eat either, or give any to poor Rex, the landlord looked at me in *such* a disparaging way that I was overcome. An awful man! He said his food was usually good enough for the Quality so I began to cry, and told him I would rather die than eat a slice of pig's cheek! Then Charles remonstrated with him for upsetting me, and said that he was sure we would be offered a more palatable supper here.'

'An intolerable menu for a lady of your obvious sensibilities, Mrs Brook,' observed Alyssa, raising her brows and biting her lip lest she indulged in the urge to laugh hysterically – an hour ago, she would not have believed she would be discussing the merits or otherwise of pig's cheek! 'I will send word to the kitchen but it might not be possible to provide several courses at this hour.'

'Oh, no! No, indeed! I would not ask that, or wish to inconvenience you in any way. Just some simple fare will do. A little soup, cold chicken, ham, and wine . . . some fish if you have it, since it is a favourite of Charles's – I have no doubt my poor darling is suffering terribly with his bruised eye, even though he will not admit it – and then perhaps a syllabub, a few pastries and sweetmeats. That would be sufficient,' said Evanthe, with another smile. 'Oh, and Rex is partial to a slice of cold beef although the naughty puss must make do with ham if you have none!'

It was two hours later when Alyssa finally retired to bed, physically and emotionally exhausted. It had been an astonishing evening, beginning with a romantic dinner *à deux* with Gil and ending with a subdued Charles leaving Hawkscote in the company of his new wife, sporting bruises that would not have disgraced a prize fighter.

Evanthe had chattered incessantly throughout the meal, and while she was telling Letty of the amusements to be had during a London Season, Alyssa managed some private conversation with Charles. He was in turn defiant and embarrassed for his earlier behaviour; he still avowed it was an understandable mistake for him to have made but did apologize for not listening to her explanations, and for instigating a mill in her dining-room. He would, he said, write a note in the morning to Sir Giles and ask him if he might call upon him in two weeks during their return journey. He owned he could not like the man yet but if he was Alyssa's choice, he respected her decision.

He even graciously offered for Sir Giles to accompany him to Jackson's saloon when next in Town, adding that the great pugilist would be pleased to receive any gentleman who could throw such an excellent right hook.

Alyssa sighed happily as she climbed into bed. Caroline was leaving for Bath; Charles was married; she and Gil had no need to conceal their love any longer. As she drifted into sleep, she smiled at the thought of setting their wedding date, blissfully unaware that the morrow held something quite different in store.

CHAPTER 16

When Piers arrived the following day, he was informed that his cousin was out but Letty was in the drawing-room. Ushered into her presence moments later, he stood transfixed by the image that met his eyes.

Letty sat on a mahogany chair, reading; she was dressed in a pale twilled silk dress and bathed in the sunlight streaming through the window. This vision of her, hair that shone like burnished gold, the delicate curve of her neck, and dark lashes sweeping down towards her cheek, made him catch his breath. He had met and dallied with pretty women in the past but none had affected him as Letty did. Now, she looked radiant, a tranquil Circe, and he shivered involuntarily at the thought of her serenity changing to fury. Piers knew the next few minutes held the key to his future happiness, or his future misery.

'Oh! Hello, Piers. I did not expect you.' She closed the leather-bound book and put it aside.

'I hope you are pleased, all the same,' he replied. 'But I have interrupted your reading – what held your attention so raptly a moment ago? Is it nonsensical to admit being jealous of a book?'

She smiled. 'Quite absurd. It is *Guy Mannering* by Sir Walter Scott, and' – a faint blush stole under her skin – 'you have no need to be jealous of a hero from a novel.'

'Thank God! I could never measure up to young Lochinvar from *Marmion*, although I'd happily try to carry you off on my charger. As to my visit, I promised my cousin I would call today so here I am.' He clasped her hand and raised it to press his lips against her skin.

'Yes, but Alyssa thought you—' she began, with a puzzled expression. Letty shrugged one slim shoulder. 'Oh well, we can discuss that in a moment. I have some surprising news too. Can I help since Alyssa isn't here?'

'You've already done so in many ways, Letty, but I called today for quite another reason.' Piers took an agitated turn about the room. Then, turning to face her, he said in a sombre tone, 'In fact, I am glad to find you alone: I have a confession to make to my cousin and I want you to hear what I have to say first.' He continued, murmuring, 'It . . . it is important you know everything or you will never trust me, and I very much want you to trust me in future.'

'This is very mysterious, Piers,' she said, noting his expression and giving a little laugh. 'What have you to confess which requires you to be so serious?' His demeanour did not alter at her attempt to lighten the mood and she added quietly, 'You haven't come to say you are leaving for London again?'

'No, nothing like that.'

'I'm glad.'

'Never mind London, you may wish me at Jericho when you have heard me out,' he said, with an odd, humourless smile.

'Oh? I find that hard to believe, but you had best continue.'

Piers nodded. Dear God, this was the most difficult task he had ever faced. He flinched inwardly at what lay before him yet he knew she deserved the truth. Without it, they had no future: Letty would never suffer a liar.

'Do you remember when we were out riding and I declared my feelings?' he began.

'How can I forget?' replied she, with a wry smile. 'It was the same morning you proposed marriage to Alyssa.'

He groaned. 'Do not remind me what an idiot I was. That day you questioned something I said about my role in recent events.'

Letty nodded. 'I asked what you meant, but you said it was of no matter.'

'I was wrong: it did matter – it *does* matter. My actions have been shameful and I have no defence to offer.' He drew in a breath. 'There were several incidents of arson on the estate when Alyssa was ill.'

'Yes, I know. Draper caught the person responsible. How fortunate you dealt with the workers and with Draper in particular.'

'If only I were more deserving of your faith,' he said with a grim laugh. 'It was not an out-of-work malcontent who was responsible: it was Draper.'

Her eyes flew to his. 'Gracious! He always seemed a sullen, rebellious man, but I would not have believed he would go to those lengths – and working alone too.'

'But he didn't. He carried out those acts under *my* instructions and received payment for doing so.'

There was long pause and an uneasy silence as Piers, whose features were now pale and shot through with anguish, waited for her response.

'*You!*' she finally exclaimed, eyes wide with shock. Rising to her feet, she cried, 'No! No! That cannot be possible! What reasons could you have?'

'None that sounds anything other than despicable now,' he admitted. The disappointment he saw in her face seared his soul and he momentarily closed his eyes, struggling to contain his torment. 'When I discovered my uncle had left Hawkscote to Alyssa, I was furious and determined to see if matters could be redressed in my favour. I had no clear notion of how this was to be achieved; indeed' – he raked his fingers roughly through his hair – 'I can only marvel at my arrogance now. When I found the workers were unsettled, some clamouring for higher wages, I saw I might use it to my advantage. I listened with an apparently sympathetic ear to Draper's complaints and began to encourage his discontent, putting the idea in his head that my cousin was a nip-cheese.'

'No!'

'Yes, I tell you!' he interpolated. 'And it did not stop there: I led Draper to believe that if I was in charge I would give the labourers what they asked for.'

Letty stared at him, shaking her head in dismay. 'How *could* you?'

'A shocking confession, is it not?' he observed, the muscles around his mouth flickering as he fought to control his sorrow and his embarrassment. 'Please let me finish; you must know the whole of it. So, the seeds of my plan were sown. Draper was – still is – an ugly customer, and while I own did not like the man, I was prepared to use him: once he believed me an ally, I could control the fellow for my own purposes. I arranged for him to start several small fires.'

She drew in a sharp breath.

'Oh, nothing serious – I did not want to harm anyone or cause real hardship to Hawkscote. I knew it was wrong, but justified it by thinking it need be only enough to be noted and, when the "culprit" was caught, I could claim to have resolved a difficult problem for my cousin.'

'You manufactured the situation to win favour with Alyssa?'

He flushed darkly, and nodded. 'In my conceit, I reasoned the incidents would prove that she was unable to manage alone and she would agree to a marriage of convenience. I would then have a share of the inheritance I had long coveted.' Striking his fist into his palm, he continued savagely, 'I was mad even to think of it! Alyssa laughed in my face when I proposed and deservedly so. I have done stupid things before but nothing to compare to this. Now, I have not only hurt my cousin, whom I hold in great affection, but *you*, Letty, whom I love.' He exhaled on a shuddering sigh. 'There, you have it all! At least I found the courage to confess, but I fear you will not forgive me. All my dreams are in your hands. I pray you will not reject me, but, if you do, I must accept that I have lost you through my own selfishness,' concluded Piers, looking at her with fierce intensity, his eyes moist with tears.

Letty sank slowly on to the chair. The only sound in the room was the ticking of the clock until she said faintly, 'W-what you have said is extremely shocking and if I had heard this story from anyone else, I would refuse to believe it. Not only have you grievously wronged Alyssa, and indirectly me, you have betrayed your own conscience.'

'There is no censure I have not already repeated to myself a thousand times,' he admitted. 'If your opinion of me is ruined forever, tell me so at once and I'll not trouble you again.' He slumped on to the seat opposite, dropping his head into his hands.

'Oh Piers, what am I to say?' she answered eventually, a catch in her voice. 'I *am* very angry.'

'You have every right to be; so has Alyssa.'

'But, at the same time, I give you credit for admitting your misdeeds.'

'That is something at least,' he replied dully. 'You both deserved the truth. Shall I return later to see my cousin? You must feel nothing but contempt for me now,' he murmured.

Letty watched as he sat with head bowed in contrition and shame, shoulders sagging with defeat. There was no artifice in his manner and, for the first time since she had met him, he looked devoid of his natural *joie de vivre*. His confession made several things clear: there had been times when he appeared distracted or lost in thought which had puzzled her. Now she understood why, just as she understood why he had offered Alyssa marriage. Piers had been a mendacious fool, but admitting to his misdeeds had assuaged much of the anger she might have harboured towards him.

And, in spite of everything, she still loved him. He was a decent, caring man at his core, she was sure of it, and hadn't she asked him to show what lay behind that cynical veneer? With his actions this morning, he had certainly done so. She studied his handsome profile, now deeply etched with remorse.

She could leave him in an agony of suspense, but that was not her way. While she might still wish to see evidence that his love would last, she could not tease him cruelly. However, neither would it do to fall into his arms and declare her love – yet. Unseen by Piers, a little smile played about her lips as she said, 'No, I don't – indeed, I would be sad if you did not trouble me with your presence again.'

He lifted his head, hope flaring in his eyes. 'Do you mean it?'

'You should know by now I never say anything I don't mean. I abhor what you have done, Piers – don't imagine otherwise – but I believe you have finally grown up,' she observed, rising to her feet. 'Perhaps it has taken this to make it happen. Only a brave man could admit his guilt; the selfish boy you were a short time ago would never have bothered and for that reason, I will not reject you.'

'*Letty!*' he cried, in a husky tremulous voice. 'I won't let you down again, I swear it!' He leapt from his seat, his gaze zealously skimming her face. 'God, I want to kiss you, but I won't abuse your trust.'

'Oh, I think one kiss to herald a new beginning for you – and for us – might be permitted,' she whispered.

He grinned slowly. 'Darling Letty! You are a constant source of delight!'

She touched his cheek affectionately in response and Piers found it a poignant gesture after what had gone before. He needed no further encouragement and his mouth swooped down to take hers. Even as he exulted in her sweetness, he cherished her lack of sophistication and the open way she gave herself to his embrace. When it ended, he moved to kiss her again, but Letty placed her finger-tips against his lips.

'Enough,' she whispered firmly, but not unkindly, as her eyes smiled at him, 'for now.'

'Don't tell me you didn't enjoy that, my love,' he murmured, his breath warm against her cheek. His hand slid along her arm to capture her wrist. Slowly, and with consummate skill, he sensually kissed the tip of her thumb and then each finger in turn, watching her face as he did so. 'You see what you do to me with one kiss, but I feel your pulse racing as fast as my own.'

She knew it; her heart was hammering against her chest and every nerve ending tingled with pleasure. Exhilarated, she shuddered, laughed softly and admitted, 'You devil, Piers! I enjoyed it very much but I'm not willing to play the coquette – I value our relationship more highly than that. I don't want an ephemeral love, one that burns brightly for the summer and fades with the first chill winds of autumn; I need more.'

'I want the same. Patience was never one of my virtues, but for you I'll try, and somehow bear the wait if I can steal the occasional kiss,' he declared, grinning. 'And, one day soon when I've proved my love *is* enduring, perhaps I'll convince you to marry me.'

Letty smiled. 'That reminds me of my news: Charles arrived unexpectedly last night and brought his new bride. We were introduced, but not before Sir Giles had drawn Charles's cork!'

'Charles – *married*! Who has succumbed to his charms?'

'Evanthe Crawford-Clarke, a lady he met in London.'

'I know her a little,' he replied, nodding. 'An engaging little piece at first sight, but with a deceptively tenacious nature; Charles will not do what he wants with her. Fortunate, too, for Charles that she is quite the heiress.' He winked roguishly and laughed. 'Well, thank God he has renounced his claim on Alyssa, and at least now she won't be subjected to his sanctimonious fustian. But why did Gil draw the blushing bridegroom's cork?'

Letty giggled, and explained, adding, 'By the time Charles opened his eyes, Gil had already left and it was only then his wife came in. It was the most astonishing hubbub.'

'Lord, how typical of Charles! I envy Gil giving him what he deserved, for I have long wished to do the same and I'll offer my congratulations when I see him. But where have you learned boxing cant, miss?' he asked, with a chuckle.

She said primly, 'I really can't remember.'

'Oh?' said Piers amused. 'Perhaps we should return to that subject when I've confessed to Alyssa—'

She started suddenly and grasped his arm, crying, 'Oh no! Alyssa! Now it is my turn to be foolish!'

He frowned. 'What's wrong?'

'Piers, I should have told you earlier: Alyssa received a note this morning from Draper!'

'*What!*' he cried. 'What did it say?'

'It asked Alyssa to meet him in the barn at the edge of Winterborn wood,' said Letty, racking her brain to recall the scant content. 'It was badly written, of course, and hardly legible but it said the matter was urgent.'

'Has she gone alone?' he demanded.

'Y-yes! The note said you would be there also so Alyssa felt there was no need for concern on that point. The fact that you were involved *did* make her believe something was amiss, and she should go. That was why I was surprised to see you here at first. . . . Oh God, I should have mentioned this sooner!' she said earnestly, her lips trembling.

'It is not your fault,' he assured her. 'I received no word from Draper.'

'Then you think she is in danger?'

'I fear she could be. Draper has lured Alyssa there, I don't know what for but I'll wager it's nothing to the good! God, if he harms her. . . .' His voice trailed away, and he looked at Letty, urging, 'How long she has been gone?'

'About forty minutes. She intended to go across country.'

'Winterborn barn takes an hour at a steady pace and it is a hot day, so she will travel more slowly.' He grasped her hands. 'I need to hurry! Letty, as I left for London, I caught Draper starting a fire. I told him there was to be no more – indeed, I had already made that clear – but he threatened to tell Alyssa of my involvement. I gave him a bloody nose for his trouble and said I wanted him gone by the time I returned, but it seems he has decided to take revenge on Alyssa instead. Damnation, I should have foreseen something like this! Can you get word to the workers and ask them to make their way to Winterborn? They may be needed.'

'Yes, yes of course! Oh, I pray nothing has happened to her!' said Letty, in great agitation, 'But-but what of Gil? He needs to know.'

'Don't worry – he will.' He kissed her hand and made to leave.

'What are you going to do?' she cried.

'Fetch Gil so we can then make for the barn together, and stop whatever that cur has planned!'

Gil sat in his study, a frown creasing his forehead as he stared out at the lawns and gardens beyond. He had spent a sleepless night, not because of his injuries, which amounted to nothing more than cuts and bruises, but because of his conscience. While he could not regret sparring with Brook, he had caused Alyssa disquiet and for that he was bitterly sorry. What must she think of him in the cold light of day?

He had risen with the dawn, washed, shaved and dressed, and shut himself in his study, only to find no respite among his papers. His mind strayed constantly to Hawkscote and he tortured himself with wondering what had happened after he had left, and what Alyssa was doing now. Even a visit from the squire failed to divert him; Henry had driven over to idle away an hour now his wife and daughter had departed for Bath.

'Are you feeling quite the thing, Gil?' he queried, peering with interest at his companion's face. 'I'll not be so indelicate to enquire how you came by those bruises – dare say you wouldn't tell me if I did – but I'll bet the other fellow had the worst of the match. You seem distracted – anything I can do, m'boy?'

'No, Henry. It is something I hope to resolve today but I am not in the mood for conversation. Forgive my taciturnity.'

'Nonsense! A man should be silent on occasion if he wishes, as I've tried to explain to Eugenie many times.' He smiled and said with satisfaction, 'The house was as quiet as a tomb last night; I enjoyed a delicious dinner, with three glasses of wine, read *The Times* and took myself off to bed without once being gabbled at. Didn't address a word to anyone but the servants. Sheer heaven to a man usually surrounded by chattering females, I can tell you, although I dare say after a few weeks of Eugenie and Caroline's absence, the quiet will wear thin.'

'Their departure was rapid, was it not?'

'Lord, yes! Apart from avoiding whispers about Caroline's behaviour the other night, Eugenie was eager to take the waters for her stiff neck. Not sure if she intends to drink them or bathe in them for that malady. I may be tempted to endure the rigours of Bath myself if things become too quiet at home, but I won't have a single cup of that disgusting brew,' he said, grimacing.

Gil smiled reluctantly in response and the squire, observing this, rose to his feet. 'I'll take my leave now, Gil. Send word if you need anything.'

'I will.'

'Good. And I expect to see the banns for your wedding announced shortly so do not disappoint me! *"We shall meet again at" '* – he hesitated and frowned – 'now where is it? I can never remember the place in that quotation, although I've most likely mangled it a little.'

'I believe you mean *Philippi*,' said Gil, unable to repress a laugh. 'The line is from *Julius Caesar*, uttered by Caesar's ghost to Brutus.'

'That's the one!' agreed Henry, pleased. 'Stuck in my mind every since I was a boy and my tutor made me write it fifty times for putting a frog in his boot!' He went out chuckling and Gil fell again into moody silence.

He usually welcomed Henry's visits but not today. It was almost noon and there was still no word from Alyssa. Anxiety gnawed at him. Why hadn't she contacted him? Had Brook managed to influence her in some way? He did not believe so and yet he could not quell his fears. Gil did not doubt Alyssa, but their love was new, unconsummated and so precious as to make him afraid something, or someone, could snatch it away before it reached fulfilment, and he could not shake off the presentiment of foreboding which haunted him. A man of reason, he cursed himself with admirable fluency for allowing preternatural ideas even to register in his mind but, try as he might, passion overcame logic and with every minute that passed he grew more concerned. Mulling over Henry's comment regarding the banns, he balked at a month's delay before marrying Alyssa. There was another way, and he resolved to obtain a special licence if she agreed.

He ate a meagre lunch and took a small glass of wine as an emollient to his ragged nerves. As he tossed back the final drop, he muttered, 'How much longer am I to remain in this purgatory?' It was then that he made the decision to go to Hawkscote; the foreboding that something was awry could no longer be denied.

Hurriedly, he shrugged on his coat.

Piers was swinging up into the saddle when Gil arrived, pulling his gelding to a halt outside Hawkscote amid a shower of dust and gravel and prompting,

'What are you doing here at this hour?'

'Thank God!' cried Piers, 'I was never more pleased to see anyone in my life! I was coming to fetch you.'

Gil cursed under his breath. 'Has Brook been making things difficult for Alyssa?'

Wheeling his horse around to face him, Piers said, 'Charles left last night with his new wife but—'

'*Wife!*' Gil interjected, going white around his mouth. 'What bag of moon-shine is this? Alyssa is betrothed to *me!*'

'Deuce take it, *let me speak!*' demanded Piers. 'You are not thinking clearly and as I am about to explain, there is no time to waste.'

'I'm sorry,' acknowledged Gil, shaking his head. 'Go on.'

Piers described in few words what had happened the previous evening as Gil listened in growing astonishment. 'I always knew he did not love her as I did, but why haven't I received word from Alyssa?'

'Because she is not here. She may be in danger but I'll tell you why as we ride.' Urging his horse into a canter, Piers shouted over his shoulder, 'Follow me!'

Gil did so, but, as he caught up with Piers and they rode side by side down the driveway, he expostulated loudly, 'What the devil is going on, Piers?'

By the time Piers finished explaining, his companion's face had drained of colour and Gil looked as if he had received a staggering physical blow.

'Your actions have put Alyssa at the mercy of a dangerous man,' he cried scathingly. 'If I didn't need your help, I would mill you down.'

'And I'd deserve it, but ring a peal over me later – we need to find Alyssa first.' Piers's words were almost drowned out by the drumming of hoofs.

'Dear God, I only hope we are not too late!' said Gil through clenched teeth, using his heels to induce his horse to a gallop.

When Alyssa reached the barn, she dismounted from her horse, led him to a patch of grass and tethered the reins to an adjacent bush. It was a glorious late summer's day: the sun shone persistently out of a cloudless sky, lapwings dipped and rose over the field and she could hear the ripple of the river as it chattered along its way at the end of the meadow. The barn was a short distance to her left but there was no one in sight. It seemed that neither Piers nor Draper had arrived yet and, despite the background sounds of nature, it was eerily quiet.

Alyssa walked towards the building, humming softly and swinging at the long grass with her riding crop as she went. She wanted this business, whatever it was, dealt with as soon as possible. Alyssa wondered if she should have sent Gil a note but there was little time and she intended to be back at Hawkscote in time for luncheon so they could spend the rest of the day together.

The stone walls of the barn were now directly in front of her and she ran her gloved hand over the rough bricks. It was a low rectangular building, in need of a little repair on the thatched roof but otherwise stout enough. An oak door in the centre of the longest side faced her and high up at one end was a smaller door which Alyssa assumed led to the hayloft.

The sun was at its zenith and Alyssa decided to wait for Piers out of the stifling heat. She walked in, allowing her eyes to adjust to the cool, gloomy interior. It was empty apart from a few horse bridles, some old tools propped against the wall and scattered bales of hay. The barn was obviously awaiting the fruits of the coming harvest and she was pleased to note there was no trace of damp.

There was a noise outside which startled Alyssa. 'Is that you, Piers?' she called out.

No response. Alyssa gave herself a mental shake for feeling suddenly and unaccountably nervous; the sound was probably caused by a rabbit or some other wild animal. However, she was beginning to wonder why Piers had suggested meeting here. It was certainly most unlike him. She raised her eyes towards the roof and studied the thatch. A rickety wooden ladder led to the hayloft and specks of dust danced in the sunlight which streamed though holes in the stonework, giving the barn an almost church-like appearance and sense of peace.

It was therefore all the more shocking when a loud bang, followed by another dull thud, sounded behind her. Alyssa jumped violently and turned to see that the door was shut. How could the heavy door have swung to? Perplexed, she walked back to the door, lifted the iron latch and pushed. Nothing happened: the door would not move. Alyssa tried again, this time pushing with all her might but to no avail – it was jammed shut.

Banging her palm hard against the wood several times, she shouted, 'Piers, if this is your idea of a joke, do not be so foolish! Open this door at once!'

No reply came back other than distant birdsong.

'Can you hear me?' She tried to laugh but the sound came out tremulously. 'I'm ashamed to admit I'm a little frightened now. Let me out!'

Still no response and Alyssa realized this was beyond a joke, even for her mischievous cousin. She discounted the door shutting accidentally; the faint breeze was not nearly strong enough and besides, if the heavy timber plank had swung down into the iron bracket, it was certainly no accident. Could it be Draper playing a stupid trick?

It *must* be Draper – he had sent the note after all – but why would he do such a thing? Surely he would not dare treat his employer this way? Piers had not arrived so it seemed that aspect of the message was a lie, calculated to bring her to the barn alone. She continued to mull over various possibilities but nothing made sense so she abandoned her thoughts in that direction, and set her mind to finding another way out.

There appeared to be no other but the smaller door at the top of the steps. Alyssa fought to stay calm; she was in no immediate danger and Letty knew where she had gone – she would send help when she did not return. She also knew Gil would not wait long before searching her out. To be trapped here for an hour or two was nothing more than an inconvenience, albeit a considerable one, and while she did not relish the prospect of being without water in this heat, or seeing a rat scurry across the floor, she could manage perfectly well for a while. Removing her hat and gloves, Alyssa placed them near the door and systematically inspected the nooks and crannies of the barn, looking for loose stonework which might herald another exit. There was nothing: the barn had been robustly built to withstand the rigours of winter.

Sighing, she moved towards the wooden ladder, intending to look in the hayloft, when her attention was claimed by muffled sounds coming from the roof. Her instant thought was that it might be rats, but the movements were too loud and deliberate to be made by any animal: there was someone on the roof.

'Draper!' she cried. 'I know you are responsible for this but if you let me out at once, I will be lenient!' But only the now familiar silence floated back and Alyssa made a sound of frustration.

But, slowly, her irritation began to turn to horror when she realized what was happening. The unmistakable smell of burning came from the roof where a moment ago she had heard noises. Already a small patch of flames was eating into the thatch, and smoke swirled and congregated under the eaves.

Fear gripped her: she had to get out before it was too late. Even if the fire or smoke did not kill her, the roof would eventually collapse and bring the heavy beams down on anyone inside. With a pounding heart, and fighting back rising panic and nausea, she rushed back to the door and pushed but it was still barred. The smaller access to the hayloft was her only option, even though it meant getting closer to the flames.

Gathering up her skirts, she climbed the rickety ladder. Already the heat was stifling and almost unbearable this close to the roof as the fire blazed ferociously. Alyssa, coughing and with eyes streaming from the thick black smoke, crawled over to the door on her hands and knees. It was a long way to the ground outside but anything was preferable to remaining at the mercy of the inexorable flames. She lifted the rusty iron latch and grimacing, pushed, carefully at first in case the door flew open, but then with increasing force until her whole weight was thrown against it. Still it would not open, and Alyssa cried out again in anger and frustration.

Time was rapidly running out. The roof was well ablaze and although the fire would soon be seen for miles around, any help would arrive too late for her. She wiped her streaming eyes on her sleeve and saw a rope hanging to her right, attached to an old block and tackle mechanism suspended from the roof. There was one more thing she could try. Working as quickly as she could, Alyssa dragged a heavy hay bale to the rope. Rats and mice, already disturbed by the fire, scattered as it moved, but Alyssa no longer cared; rodents were the least of her worries now.

Sweat and tears trickled down her face as she hauled her burden across the floor. Her hair had fallen from its confines and impatiently, she pushed the tresses back – her every movement now had a desperate edge. After feeding the rope under and around the bale before tying it in a secure knot, she hurried to the coiled end of the rope and pulled, her arms aching as she heaved to lift the bale inch by inch off the floor until it was level with the access door. Staggering a little from the smoke and heat, she secured the rope and began to swing the suspended bale to and fro until it struck the door repeatedly but her efforts were to no avail: the oak refused to yield and eventually Alyssa collapsed to her knees, exhausted.

Two-thirds of the roof was now on fire and the heat and smoke in the hayloft threatened to overwhelm her. Alyssa realized she must quickly get back to the lowest point to gain what relief she could from the black acrid smoke. She crawled to the ladder and climbed down with shaking legs before stumbling back to the entrance door, and frantically rattling the iron latch in a futile gesture of despair.

Above her head, the roar of the fire as it devoured the timbers and thatch was incredible. She put her handkerchief to her mouth; smoke was filling her nose and lungs making it difficult to breathe. A huge charred beam crashed to the floor and ignited the dry straw and hay there. Alyssa flinched but she was struggling to hold on to consciousness. Slowly, with her back against the door, she slid to the ground and hugged her knees to her chest. It was too late: she was going to die here and she would never see Gil again. She would never know the physical fulfilment of their love. Never have his children. Never grow old with him. It was over.

She began to cry; great, heart-wrenching sobs racked her body as she buried her head in her arms and waited to meet her fate.

CHAPTER 17

The rising smoke was clearly visible; a black curtain starkly delineated against an azure sky. The image branded itself on Gil's brain as the slow graceful ascent of that dark lodestar mocked his earthbound urgency to reach it. Knowing it came from the vicinity of Winterborn barn made him feel sick with fear: Alyssa was in danger, he was certain of it. In another cruel trick, his mind replayed every smile she had given him; every kiss they had shared; her laughter and the humorous sparkle lurking in her eyes; the faint scent of lavender and roses which clung to her and sent a frisson of desire through his body . . . Gil was haunted by a sweet collection of images juxtaposed against the barely acknowledged dread that there could be no more in the future. At the same time, his anger towards Piers was intense, but he could not allow his attention to be diverted – he would have to be dealt with later.

Piers, who was as anxious as his companion to reach the barn, muttered a few inarticulate curses under his breath and fell silent again. Conversation had been sparse because of the speed at which they were travelling but during the last mile no words had been exchanged at all. Their journey was unhindered by any delay but time – as whimsical and capricious as ever – seemed to slow down and only after an apparently interminable ride did they skirt along the river to reach the meadow where they dismounted.

'Dear God!' cried Piers.

Gil's blood froze at what he saw. The roof of the barn was well alight and flames leapt high into the air. Alyssa's horse, skittish and nervous from the conflagration, was tethered to a bush nearby but Alyssa was nowhere to be seen and he knew instinctively that she was inside the building.

'No!'

The single word, torn from the depths of his being, reverberated through the air and he ran the final yards, discarding his jacket as he went. He lifted the timber plank to wrench open the door and a sharp edge gashed his palm, but Gil barely noticed the pain, or the blood that began to trickle towards his wrist. A blast of hot air hit him in the chest and thick smoke swirled out, filling his eyes and nostrils. As he blinked to clear his streaming eyes, he peered frantically into the Stygian gloom and glimpsed Alyssa, lying fearfully still, on the stone floor.

The acrid smell of burning assailed him as soon as he entered. He could see little as he felt his way slowly through the smoke, but Gil knew it was imperative that he take some precautions because any rescue attempt would fail if he were injured now. He edged along the wall until he was parallel with Alyssa's barely discernible silhouette and then, crouching, reached her in quick strides and knelt down. There was no time to search for injuries or even a pulse; he had to get her outside, well away from the fire and falling debris.

Lifting her into his arms, he muttered in a voice which shook, 'You cannot die, Alyssa! *Do you hear me?* I won't let you go!'

Gil carried her limp body a safe distance away and laid her gently on the grass in the shade thrown by a horse chestnut tree. Trickles of perspiration ran down his back and chest and dimly he was aware of the salty taste of tears as he smoothed back the hair that clung to her dirt-streaked face.

'Is she . . .' Piers's hushed question trailed away; he could not bring himself to utter the word.

He had run to the barn in Gil's wake but now he stood back, watching, with his lips compressed as he fought a gamut of emotions. There was nothing more he could do. He was unwilling to intrude as Gil sought for signs of life and indeed, had he tried to, he believed Gil would have snarled like a wild animal to warn him away.

At the moment Gil found a pulse, Alyssa's eyes flickered open and she looked at him, her gaze wide and questioning but lucid. Immediately, she was racked by a bout of coughing and only when it had finished did she croak,

'Gil! You came to find me after all.'

Relief, so acute it was almost a physical pain, flooded through him and he gathered her into his arms. 'Did you doubt it, love?' he murmured, his voice, barely above a whisper, wavered on every syllable.

'No,' she admitted, huskily, 'but I was afraid you would not be in time.'

Piers, thankful his cousin was seemingly unhurt, felt elated until the realization of what he had done returned with a vengeance and he suddenly felt a traitorous and hateful interloper on this intimacy. He turned on his heel towards the river, unobserved by Gil or Alyssa.

Gil relaxed his embrace a little and said, 'I sensed something might be wrong and went to Hawkscote before following you here. Oh God, when I arrived and saw—!' He stopped and rubbed his hand across his eyes, adding in a choked voice, 'I-I thought I had lost you.'

'I'm sorry,' she whispered, through her tears. 'Please don't be vexed with me, even if I was a wet goose to come alone.'

He shook his head and threaded his fingers through hers. 'I'm not vexed with you – I love you! I need to say those words now and every day in the future.'

'Say them as often as you like,' she replied earnestly, wiping away tears with the back of her hand as her mouth wobbled into a smile. 'I shall not tire of hearing them, nor will I ever stop telling you I feel the same. In th-there, w-when I was trapped and thought I wouldn't see you again, the sense of loss was overwhelming.'

Gil placed a featherlight kiss on her lips. 'I know,' he said softly. 'It must have been far worse for you, alone and incarcerated inside that hellish place. But I am a bird-witted rattle, Alyssa, I should have asked immediately if you are hurt.'

'No, I don't think so. I still feel a little faint though.'

'Hardly surprising, given your ordeal. Thank goodness, you seem to have suffered nothing more serious than shock and the effects of inhaling smoke,' he said, relieved.

She nodded, and then coughed again. 'Can you help me to sit up?'

'Is that wise?'

She gave a shaky laugh, saying, 'Perhaps not, but I believe I will feel more the thing if I do.'

Alyssa struggled to raise herself and, with Gil's help, soon lay with her head against his shoulder. Slowly, after some minutes held thus, her breathing returned to normal and her body stopped trembling. She sighed deeply and placed her hand against his cheek: she had somehow regained this exquisite sanctuary when it had seemed forever lost to her. Tender understanding shone in his eyes and, as he turned his head to place a kiss in her palm, she whispered, 'I feel much better already. You know, my fate would have been sealed if you had not arrived when you did.'

Gil, who glanced at the fire still blazing with unbridled menace, felt another shudder run through her body as her gaze followed his. 'It is best not to dwell on what might have been, love. You are safe now and that is all that matters.'

'Yes, you are right, of course.' She cast another concerned look at the barn. 'But should we at least try and stem the flames – in case the fire spreads?'

'No,' he said, emphatically shaking his head. 'It is too dangerous to go near the building again. There is little chance of it spreading because the wood is some distance away but when the labourers arrive, they can dig a fire break as a precaution. The flames will most likely burn out in an hour or two once the roof has been consumed.'

'I hope so,' she replied, obliged to be satisfied. Alyssa chewed at her bottom lip as she mused on her escape and then, looking into his face, she smiled and added, 'What excellent timing you have, Gil! Thank God you did not wait to receive word from me before coming here.'

'So, I am forgiven then?' he asked, raising an eyebrow.

'Forgiven? For what?'

'Why, for deliberately riding roughshod over your instructions last night. I have been quaking in my boots as to your opinion of me for doing so, but now perhaps I shall be absolved.' Amazingly, considering the horror of only a short while ago, his lip quivered as he struggled to preserve his countenance.

Her eyes laughed back at him. 'Oh! Detestable creature! I should have guessed you were bamboozling me.' She feigned a grimace, saying, 'Well, I suppose I can forgive even an unprincipled, overbearing wretch like you under the circumstances.'

'Flatterer!' he asserted, with a rich chuckle. 'That deserves a fitting riposte.'

'Oh?' she replied teasingly, opening her eyes a little wider, 'And what do you suggest?'

'Only this, my beautiful termagant.' Tightening his embrace, he crushed her mouth under his in a fervent kiss. Long moments later, he whispered with a smile, 'Now, do you still think me detestable?'

'No, indeed,' she said, sighing in contentment. 'Mad perhaps, but not detestable. However, it is an axiom that lunatics must be humoured so I am prepared to let you kiss me again.'

'Gladly,' he said, laughing, and did so.

'But Gil, how *can* you think me beautiful?' she protested afterwards, a little breathlessly. 'To be sure, I must look *ravishing* with my face and clothes covered in soot and my hair in disarray.'

He grinned. 'Must you argue over every point? My good girl, you look a bewitching hoyden and I will brook no disagreement on the matter.'

Alyssa's smile quickly vanished when she noticed the deep red stain amongst the dirt and grime marking the front of his shirt and she started forward in alarm, crying, 'There is blood on your shirt!'

'From a veritable scratch, nothing more.' He shrugged and held up his palm to show the deep cut there, still oozing blood.

'Indeed, it is more than a scratch!' she exclaimed, sitting up. 'Give me your handkerchief so I may bind it.'

'Very well, if you have recovered sufficiently,' he said, relinquishing the item.

'I have and you don't need to fear I will be sent into another swoon by the sight of blood.'

'I didn't imagine you would be,' he replied, with another grin. Watching as she knelt beside him and began to wrap the cloth around his hand, he waited a moment before asking tentatively, 'Can you recall what happened?'

Alyssa nodded and described it in detail, from receiving the note, to her plight in the barn. 'It has to be Draper who is responsible,' she concluded, 'but I can't comprehend why. Surely he cannot be so angered by his situation that he wished to *kill* me? Perhaps Piers can shed some light on his motives.' She put her head on one side to examine her handiwork critically. 'There, I have done now.'

'Thank you – a definite improvement on what I could have achieved.' Gil's brows drew together in a frown as he considered her words. When she had already endured so much, was it was right to subject her to further disquiet now? On balance, he thought it was: she would want the truth and it was important she heard her cousin's confession as soon as possible. He watched her face as he ventured, 'My love, there is something else you must know but Piers will need to explain.'

'Oh dear, that sounds ominous,' she said, wrinkling her nose. 'He is here then?'

'Yes, we travelled together.' Gil looked up to see Piers walking back from the river. With shoulders slumped and head dipped low, his demeanour was one of self-loathing. Gil, pointing out the solitary figure, said, 'Piers must have wandered away while we talked – he is returning now.'

With his assistance, Alyssa rose to her feet and waited.

'Hello, Coz,' said Piers, in a subdued voice when he reached them. 'I-I'm damned glad to see you are all right. Gil had things in hand so I left the two of you alone once I realized that you weren't badly hurt. Thank God you are well, but it's no thanks to me you haven't been injured, or even killed.'

'What do you mean?' asked Alyssa, noting his hands trembled.

'Has Gil spoken to you yet . . . regarding me?' His glance flicked nervously from one to the other.

'No, he has only said you have something to explain.'

'I thought you would prefer it that way, Piers,' said Gil grimly.

He nodded. 'Yes, of course. Thank you.' He turned to his cousin. 'This is my fault, Alyssa,' he said, gesturing hopelessly towards the fire, 'the result of *my* wretched folly.'

'You take too much upon yourself,' she said soothingly, 'I believe Draper is to blame. You cannot be held accountable.'

'No, *I* am to blame,' he said, gloomily candid, 'and if it were not for Letty and her faith in me, I'd drown myself in the river.'

Alyssa stared. 'What on earth! It is not like you to say such a thing and I see from your face you mean it, too. You had better tell me the whole.'

He did so while she listened in stunned silence. 'I can only say I'm devilish sorry, Alyssa,' he concluded, reddening.

'Upon my word,' she cried explosively, her eyes sparkling with wrath, 'I can hardly credit what you have told me and yet I know it is true – it explains many things. You should be ashamed as well as sorry, Piers!'

'I am.'

'What a selfish irresponsible blockhead you have been!'

'I know.'

'Why?' she urged. 'Why didn't you speak to me on this subject when you came to Dorset? You should have told me how deeply you felt.'

'But if I had, it would have not have changed anything.'

'I wish you had confided in me all the same. At least we could have discussed the matter in a civilized way and it might have prevented you from behaving like an idiot. I knew, of course, that Uncle Tom's will had angered you – you made that plain enough in London – but I did not realize you would act in this underhand way,' she exclaimed, still incensed.

He shrugged disconsolately. 'I offer no excuses. You've always been fair, Coz; Tom's will was not your doing and you promised to help me financially when you could, but I was blinded by selfishness, wanting a share of Hawkscote. Please believe me when I say, however misguided my motivations and deeds were, I truly *never* intended things to go this far.'

'Am I supposed to take consolation from that?' she demanded.

'Yes – no!' Piers raked his fingers through his hair. 'Oh God! I admit to making a mull of everything. I have been racked with guilt for weeks and that was why I arranged to see you this morning – so I could confess – only to discover instead that Draper had decided to take revenge on you.' He flushed scarlet and said in a despairing voice, 'I wanted to cast up my accounts when I heard! Gil has every right to land me a facer for putting you in danger.'

'I'm sorely tempted to go further and wring your neck, you young fool!' retorted Gil through shut teeth, his eyes blazing.

'I sympathize with the idea, but don't think any useful purpose would be served by it, Gil,' she said. The storm of anger began to die out of her face as she gave Piers a long measured glance. 'It seems my cousin is already suffering torment because of his misdeeds. Piers, I've never seen you look so cowed. Your contrition is obviously no act and, quite apart from torturing yourself over your part in this, what fate might have befallen me, and being obliged to explain to Gil, no doubt confessing what you had done to Letty was a punishment akin to tearing out your heart with your bare hands,' she observed intuitively.

'It was,' he admitted, with a shrug and a rueful sigh.

'I thought so. How *did* Letty react?'

'She was bitterly disappointed but has not rejected me. In fact – oh, she is an angel! I'm not worthy of her, damn it!'

'At last you are talking sense,' observed Alyssa tartly. 'Of course you are not worthy of her regard now, but she obviously considers you might be in the future. You are a lucky man indeed to have gained her affection, and even more fortunate to retain it; don't jeopardize that good fortune.'

'I don't intend to.'

'Your behaviour I find hard to excuse but your remorse has the ring of truth,' remarked Gil, subjecting him keen scrutiny. 'And you acted promptly this morning.'

'Deuced handsome of you to say so, after everything,' said Piers, flushing again. 'If Letty had been inside that barn, I'd want to murder whoever was responsible.'

'Oh, I would still like to murder you – and Draper,' Gil observed, his tone scathing. 'I'm only prepared to show leniency because your cousin escaped unhurt. Had she been injured, or worse, I would have swiftly become your nemesis.'

'Lord, I believe you would,' replied Piers approvingly after a pause. He gave a reluctant laugh. 'Knew you were a great gun the moment we met.'

'Thank you for the compliment,' said Gil, with awful sarcasm.

A tinge rose again to Piers's cheeks. 'Well, it's true – and I'd far rather have you for a friend than an enemy, Gil.'

'Then oblige me in not causing Alyssa anxiety again and you will find me the most affable of men.'

'Piers, I don't want to hear you talk of throwing yourself in the river,' said Alyssa. 'You have been excessively stupid and it is fortunate that there is no lasting harm done. The signs which tell me you are mending your ways are there and with Letty's help, you can and will do well. For your sake – and hers – put your energies to that task and let it be recompense for what you have done. And we are family after all; Uncle Tom would not want us to be adversaries.'

He took both her hands between his and clasped them tightly. 'You're a capital girl, Coz! I owe you a debt of gratitude after cutting a sham like this. I had been thinking I might enlist to get away but that would have been deuced difficult because I'd have to buy a commission, and my scruples would not allow me to touch you for money after my curst folly.'

'You considered joining the army as penance?' said Alyssa, with a flicker of a smile.

'Yes, although I wouldn't have liked it above half,' he admitted ruefully. 'But I could not have stayed in England and would have sold my estate if necessary. There would have been nothing left for me here anyway if you and Letty had shunned me.'

'Then it is as well you confessed, for I agree life in the army would not suit you at all,' she said. 'There is, however, one more thing I want you to do.'

'Willingly, Coz – just ask.'

'I leave it to you to ensure Draper is caught—'

'But *I* had determined to deal with that scoundrel!' interjected Gil, his eyes kindling.

'Don't you trust me to apprehend him?' asked Piers in an aggrieved tone.

Gil's lip curled. 'No, by God, I don't!' he cried, savagely. 'Why should I? Alyssa almost died today because *you* encouraged a dangerous man. Your cousin is willing to forgive you and I must concur with her wishes, but how can I have any confidence you will find Draper and deal with him appropriately? I prefer to oversee his capture and punishment personally.'

Alyssa laid a hand on his sleeve. 'Well, I can see why you wish to Gil,' she said calmly, 'but as Piers has admitted to being the cause, I think he should be given the chance to bring the matter to a close, don't you?'

'Only if he can be relied on,' came the sardonic response.

'Damn it, I give you my word,' said Piers, a mulish look about his mouth.

Gil surveyed him in silence. 'You are prepared to swear it, as a gentleman?'

'Yes!' Piers snapped. 'Despite what you may think, I do have some morals! You can leave the rogue to me and I will see that he receives suitable retribution—'

'No: the law must decide his punishment,' Alyssa interpolated, firmly.

'But then I won't have the satisfaction of dealing with the cur,' argued Gil.

'Nor I!' cried Piers.

Alyssa, suddenly feeling very weary, gave an exasperated sigh. 'I understand how you both feel – indeed, I share your impatience to see justice done – but arguing will not help,' she said. 'This matter must be settled in the proper way and not with violence.' She raised her eyes to Gil's face, and, taking his hand in hers, she pressed it, saying, 'Please, let Piers find Draper.'

He looked down at her, and the fury in his eyes subsided as he caught her hands between his and kissed them. 'Forgive me, my love,' he said, instantly contrite. 'It is unpardonable that we are squabbling like recalcitrant children when you are exhausted.' With a shrug and a wry smile, he added, 'Very well: since you think Piers should seek out Draper, and he has given his word, I must agree, albeit reluctantly.'

'Then it is settled,' she said, smiling warmly. 'Piers, you will deliver Draper to the authorities.'

'Consider it done,' he said quietly, his glance at Gil a peculiar blend of remorse, indignation, and respect.

'And, in spite of providing fare for the scandalmongers, I think you must also declare your part,' said Alyssa.

'Naturally; that was always my intention.'

'You will have me to answer to if you do not,' declared Gil, grimly. 'However, leave Draper's wife and family out of it – Alyssa and I will secure their immediate future. I don't believe they knew of this, and he always treated them abominably; they do not deserve to find themselves in the poorhouse as a result of his exploits.'

'I agree, and—'

Wearily, Alyssa interjected, 'There is nothing more to be said at present, Piers. Go now – he cannot have travelled far – and come to Hawkscote later to tell us what success you have had.'

Piers nodded and extended his hand to Gil, who, after an infinitesimal pause, returned his grasp with a clipped smile even though his features were set in forbidding lines. Piers, grateful that this man whom he admired was still prepared to acknowledge him, then hurried away to collect his horse.

As she watched his retreating figure, Alyssa sighed and said, 'Did I do the right thing, Gil? Should I have forgiven him so soon, if at all? He acted appallingly, but oh, he is good at heart, I'm sure of it, and he has learned a valuable lesson. I don't believe he ever meant harm to befall me and he is still my cousin, indeed my only blood family now Uncle Tom is dead.' Frowning, she added meditatively, 'Yet perhaps I am allowing *who* he is to colour my judgement.'

Gil, who had been watching the expressions flit across her face rather than Piers's departure, kissed her cheek. 'You chose the right path, love,' he said, heavily. 'I am furious with him but, on measured consideration, it is better this way. He is eager to make amends and seems ultimately an honourable, if impulsive, young man. His conscience will prove more effective punishment than any we could administer. Let us hope it will also make him behave less like a peep-o-day boy from now on.'

'And do not forget Letty – he loves her.'

'If he truly cares, then he will strive for her good opinion, and love.'

There were shouts and cries from the far side of the field.

'More help appears to have arrived at last,' he said, eyeing the small crowd of farm workers hurrying towards them. His gaze wandered back to hers as he said softly, 'Come, it's time I took you home.'

Alyssa returned his smile and slipped her hand into his.

*

Gil still intended to obtain a special marriage licence and mentioned this to Alyssa after dinner on the evening following her rescue. Initially, she demurred over the extortionate cost of five pounds and suggested they could wait for the banns but he silenced her, first with a kiss, then by saying resolutely, 'My love, twice I have almost lost you: once through your illness, the second time to the fire and I am not prepared to wait another three weeks to make you my wife. Besides,' he continued, with a grin, 'when my desire for you grows hourly, would you be so cruel as to prolong my agony?'

'No, indeed!' she said, smiling. 'That would never do.'

'Of course, if, after all my protestations, you still wish for the banns then so be it; I will perfectly understand if you want more time to make arrangements. The details are more important to a woman than a man, I believe.'

She shook her head. 'I prefer a quiet ceremony and as it is not yet a year since Uncle Tom died, it would also be more appropriate.' Alyssa, blushing rosily, then whispered, 'It is shockingly forward to admit it but I-I desire you very much, Gil. A special licence will be just the thing.'

He made a low sound of approval before kissing her again.

Moments later, he asked, 'My love, you understand Henry, as a local magistrate, is now aware of Draper's crimes and your cousin's role in the affair?' When she nodded, he added, 'Henry thinks Draper's probable sentence will be transportation. With regard to Piers's involvement, I believe we can trust Henry to be discreet.'

'But what if Draper speaks of it?'

'He may do so to try to save his own skin. He may even claim Piers was involved in the arson, but he was well known as a malcontent before this and no one will give his story credence. Besides, Piers committed no actual crime: he is only guilty of selfishness, and stupidity,' he observed. 'At least arrangements have been made for Draper's wife and children; your idea to employ her as a dairymaid is an excellent one and means they will not be disadvantaged. Piers told me she was crying when he reached their cottage yesterday. Her brute of a spouse had only stayed long enough to collect a few clothes and then, without a word of explanation, tossed three shillings towards her and the children and left.'

'Piers did well to find him so soon. I believe he was on the Salisbury road, making for London?'

'Yes. He admitted his guilt almost immediately and did not resist, probably realizing to do so would be pointless when every farmhand and landowner for miles would be looking for him.'

'Transportation to the colonies is not a pleasant thought,' she observed, with a shiver.

'No, but he will be considered lucky not to hang.'

She nodded, and gave a little sigh. 'The children can attend school in Dorchester when everything is settled.'

'You know I will help with setting up the school, but we have more important things to attend to first, love,' he murmured, before his lips captured hers once more.

Alyssa sat in the large bedchamber on the west front of Eastcombe, sipping wine with Gil. Their marriage day had passed in a happy blur; now, dinner was over, the servants had retired and finally, they were alone. The glow of a spectacular sunset shimmered outside the open window and the warm evening air carried the scent of honeysuckle and stocks from the gardens below. They relaxed on the sofa, ostensibly to watch the sunset but more often to observe each other in the fading light.

The day had heightened Alyssa's anticipation for the night to come. Gil's eyes burnt with a fierce unadulterated passion which sent shudders of desire rippling through her body. The touch of his hand engendered the same effect, and as for his kisses . . . the sensations that pooled in her stomach when he kissed her were both delicious and shocking in their intensity. She sipped her wine and watched her new husband over the edge of her glass, her mouth curving with amusement.

'Why do you smile,' he murmured.

'Because I am happy.'

Gil grinned. 'And I, profoundly so, but something particular made you smile then,' he said. 'I know your smiles, my love, and adore them all, but I am particularly fond of that one.'

'Which one?' she teased.

'You know exactly what I am referring to, *Wife*.' His quiet purr made the final word a caress. 'The smile which tells me an amusing thought crossed your mind.'

She pulled her face into an expression of dismay and fluttered her eyelashes. 'Fie on you, sir! We have been married less than a day and already you can read my thoughts. Is a lady to have no secrets?'

'None she need keep from her husband,' he replied, a roguish gleam in his eye.

She laughed softly. 'I was thinking I am glad you obtained a licence, otherwise we would still not be married.'

'And you would be at Hawkscote, while I—' He leaned closer and continued, 'I would be lying alone in my bed dreaming of you as I have done every night since we met. But tonight' – he nuzzled tiny kisses along her jaw – 'you are here and I don't have to dream any longer.'

'Neither do I,' she whispered, contentedly. After a pause, she said, 'You know Gil, he did not say it but I could tell Piers was pleased I asked him to give me away.'

Gil leaned his head against the cushions, glass of wine in one hand, Alyssa's fingers clasped in the other. 'He did seem pleased,' he admitted. 'And despite being somewhat preoccupied myself during the ceremony, I noticed he could not take his eyes from Letty.'

'She looked as charming as I've ever seen her. Poor Piers! He only remembered at the last moment to give my hand to the clergyman.'

'Did he?' he said, raising his brows a little. 'I confess I did not register his omission because I was too busy staring at my bride.' He grinned. 'What a pair of moonlings we must have looked! But Henry fared no better: even he was lost for words at the lovely picture you presented.'

'Oh yes, the squire,' she said, taking a sip of wine. 'I'm pleased he could attend, although I was not sorry Mrs Nash and Caroline were unable to leave Bath at short notice.'

Gil chuckled. 'Henry tells me Caroline is exceedingly busy there and has secured the attentions of a gentleman, who, much to Henry's chagrin, is quite as high in the instep as his daughter. I understand he is only the *second* son of the Marquis of Fairfax, which will be a slight blow to Caroline's plans,' he said sardonically. 'Nevertheless, Lord Storey is an excellent catch. Moreover, his conceit and the consequence he feels he is owed because of his family name and wealth are apparently insufferable.'

'Oh dear, he sounds odious,' said Alyssa, amused.

'Perhaps notice of their betrothal will have been posted when we return,' he said, regarding her from under half-closed lids, a lazy smile curving his mouth. 'We shall be out of the county for some weeks.'

'Oh?' she queried, with a look of surprise. 'Where are we going?'

'Once our affairs are in order here, I intend to take you on a short tour of the Continent.' Lifting her hand to kiss the soft skin on the inside of her wrist, he asked, 'Should you like to see Rome, Vienna, and Paris?'

'I would love it above all things!' she exclaimed.

'Then we shall go, but *en route*, we will travel to London; as you know, we have something we must do before journeying to Europe.'

'Of course! We have to see Mr Bartley. It is only three weeks until the end of the period I was required to live at Hawkscote.'

'Just so, my love; I received a similar letter from him, if you recall,' he said serenely but with a faint tremor at the corner of his mouth.

The ready laughter sprang to her eyes. 'Gil, have you sent Mr Bartley word of our marriage yet? I confess I have had no time to do so.'

He shook his head and acknowledged with another chuckle, 'No. I considered advising him, but thought it is news best kept until we meet him in person. Mr Forde agreed to keep our secret a little longer and assured me there is no issue in relation to the terms: officially, you are still resident at Hawkscote even though our time is currently divided between there and Eastcombe. Naturally, now we are married,' he added, grinning at her, 'we are dining together *more* than once a week.'

Alyssa smiled. His dry humour was one of the many things she adored and for some moments, she studied the face she loved. His features were capable of appearing hard, almost ruthless, at times, but they were also mobile and expressive, with laughter lines that creased the skin around his eyes when those blue-grey irises glowed with warmth. She held her breath at the love and desire she saw there now, and whispered, 'I will never willingly move far from your side.'

Gil's gaze held hers for a long moment, and then drifted slowly to her lips; soft and pink, they quivered invitingly under his scrutiny. The pale skin of her throat swept down to the enticing curves just visible above the bodice of her gown, the silk fabric clinging provocatively to her figure. Sliding one hand to her waist, he moved the other to brush against her breast; she sighed and shuddered, and he felt the crest immediately peak and harden against his palm. Gil swallowed. Dear God, she was bewitching and already he wanted her with an all-consuming aching desperation.

'Alyssa, take your hair down for me,' he said, drawing in a steadying breath.

She reached up to pull out the pins until it lay about her shoulders.

'Beautiful,' he breathed, and ran his fingers through its silken chestnut mass. 'I have dreamed of doing this so many times.'

With her hair down and curling around her face, she looked wildly sensual and yet her eyes held a note of artless candour alongside the desire lurking in their depths. Why had he never noticed how thick her eyelashes were, or realized that flecks of green nestled among the brilliant blue of her eyes?

'Wait here,' he muttered thickly, before he took both wine glasses and placed them on the table.

Alyssa, watching as he returned to sit beside her, saw that his tender smile did not disguise the longing in his eyes. She eagerly returned the light teasing kisses that followed but, pleasant as these were, she needed more and when at last he tightened his embrace and crushed his mouth fiercely against hers, she welcomed it and instantly reciprocated, surrendering to the desire sweeping her along.

She arched her neck as he kissed the sensitive skin beneath her ear, and began to nibble softly on her earlobe. Slowly, seductively, his mouth reached the exposed flesh of one shoulder and Alyssa gasped as he nuzzled along the lace edging her bodice, the faint stubble along his jaw gently brushing against her skin as he did so. She shuddered with delight when his hand cupped her breast, his thumb grazing back and forth over its crest until it peaked and strained against her gown. Her breathing quickened and with a soft moan, she uttered in a ragged voice, 'That feels wonderful!'

'Good,' he said, with a tiny smile of satisfaction.

He kissed the base of her throat and along her collarbone, cupping her other breast as he did so, caressing the soft flesh with his fingertips until he bent his head and, with exquisite yet agonizing slowness, teased at its peak through the sheer fabric with his lips. Another moan of desire escaped her.

He murmured approvingly, 'Your skin tastes of honey and roses, and I need to sample more of it.' Pulling her closer and continuing the tantalizing, seductive exploration of her breasts, he unfastened three buttons of her gown and eased it off her shoulders to reveal the smooth skin beneath. 'You are so beautiful,' he breathed. Then, he kissed her again and, eyes burning with indigo fire, asked softly, 'Will you come to the bed with me now, love?'

CHAPTER 18

She nodded and unfastened his shirt with fingers that trembled slightly. The garment fell open and, finally, she could touch the warm skin beneath.

'So many times I have dreamed of doing this,' she echoed with a little sigh, as she let her fingers glide over his chest. Another searching kiss, full of sensual promise, followed and she arched closer, desire rippling through her as her breasts craved his touch without the distraction of barriers.

'Slowly, my love,' he said, smiling into her eyes, already dark with passion, 'we have the whole night before us.'

A flush stole over her cheeks. 'But Gil, I want. . . .' Her whispered request died away. It was impossible to articulate what she was feeling; her body ached for something intangible, an instinct her body understood perfectly even if her mind did not.

'All in good time,' he said gently. 'I want to pleasure you first.'

She shivered again and then murmured, 'How shall I bear more pleasure than this?'

'This is only the beginning,' he replied, trailing yet more kisses over her skin.

Entwined, they moved to the bed, and Gil dealt with the delicate pearl buttons of Alyssa's silk chemise one by one. He let it slide to the floor before staring in frank admiration at her body.

'Dear God, you are delectable,' he said, in a husky voice. Her breasts, now fully revealed, were ripe and full with beckoning rosy tips, her skin luminescent in the fading light.

Alyssa looked away, suddenly self-conscious, but he placed a finger under her chin to draw her gaze back to his. 'My love, you are perfect – from the top of your head to the tips of your toes. I could look on you forever and not be sated.'

Captivated, Alyssa watched as he removed his remaining clothing with lithe efficient movements. He too was beautiful: naked, his body was as lean and well-defined as a marble statue. Fine dark hair covered his chest and arrowed down his stomach but it was the expression in his eyes which quickened her heartbeat still faster.

He slid into the bed and gathered her close, and in the midst of so many new sensations, Alyssa discovered simply lying next to him – skin touching skin, the hard ridges of his body against her soft curves – was incredibly erotic.

Gil kissed her slowly while his hand caressed her body, skimming her leg from ankle to thigh, over the curve of her hip until he reached her breasts. He teased and honoured each in turn by cupping them gently and brushing their sensitized taut crests with his fingertips before lowering his head to lingeringly caress each pink tip with his mouth.

Alyssa gasped and murmured on a rapturous sigh, 'Don't stop. . . .'

'I won't,' he promised, huskily, 'I want this to be as perfect as it can be.'

Her body shivered again with pleasure in response; she was lost to his relentless sensual exploration.

He ran his tongue tantalizingly along her lips, deepening his kiss before moving to capture the erect peaks of her breasts again as he made lazy circles on her stomach with his fingertips. Gradually, he drifted lower, and she drew in a breath and opened her eyes.

'I love you,' he whispered, against her lips. 'Trust me, and relax.'

A smile curved her mouth and, as he continued to weave his beguiling aura, she surrendered to bliss on a long shuddering sigh, luxuriating in the feelings he was creating. Her hands strayed with increasing assuredness and Alyssa discovered by exploring his body she could give pleasure as well as receive it. Adrift in a sea of sensation, she barely recognized her own voice as it murmured rapturously on some distant shore.

'*Please*, Gil,' she implored eventually.

Her murmurs of pleasure and the movement of her body against his made it increasingly difficult for Gil to control his own arousal. His breathing came fast and ragged but he fought to hold on a little longer.

Moving above her, he whispered, 'Look at me.'

Her gaze found his. 'I'll try not to hurt you,' he murmured. Her reply was a desperate whimper of longing and he entered her moist heat, every muscle and sinew straining as he fought against the desire to bury himself completely. He waited, allowing her body time to adjust and gritting his teeth against the exquisite feeling of it tightening around him.

Alyssa's mouth sought his as she lifted her hips in eager welcome and her hands roamed over his shoulders urging him closer. Wave after wave of sensation began to radiate outwards from her core until she suddenly tensed.

'Alyssa?' His breathing was rasping and uneven as he searched the flushed face inches from his own.

Through a haze of passion, she whispered, 'It's all right . . . I. . . .' Another deep quiver ran through her body and she wrapped her arms around him tightly, saying, 'Please, I need you so much.'

Gil whispered her name again, this time as a benediction, and immersed himself in her warmth with a guttural moan. It felt unbelievably, astonishingly good but not nearly enough to sate his desperate need – or hers: she clung to him, breathless with yearning. Love overwhelmed and consumed him. He wanted to pleasure her, possess her, and never let her go. With another fevered groan, his mouth captured hers as he moved in the age old rhythm, slowly at first and then with relentless urgent passion as her movements and gasps of pleasure matched his. Bound together, their desire soared to impossible heights and to that dizzying explosion of ecstasy. Her cry of joy was followed a second or two later by his, as he relinquished the last shreds of restraint to reach his own shuddering release.

The quiet that followed was broken only by their unsteady breathing.

Slowly, by degrees, Alyssa floated back to reality, still entwined with Gil, still with his warm weight above her. Lying in dreamy contentment, she realized this was how it felt to be truly loved. He had been the gentle and considerate lover she knew he would be, arousing feelings she was unaware she even possessed until tonight.

Stroking a strand of hair back from his forehead, she sighed with pleasure and said simply, 'I love you.'

He moved his weight on to his elbows to gaze down at her. In the aftermath of their lovemaking, her pupils were dilated, the wild silken mane of her hair was spread over the pillow and a flush tinted her cheeks; she glowed with sensual satisfaction. Arms around her, he rolled on to his side, taking her with him. 'You are breathtaking,' he said, a look of wonder on his face. Then, kissing the tip of her nose, he whispered, 'I hurt you, didn't I?'

'A little but I wanted you so much the pain was fleeting.'

'Next time will be even better,' he said, brushing his lips against hers.

'Then I shall think I have died and gone to heaven,' she murmured incredulously. 'I can scarcely believe the pleasure we have just shared exists, let alone imagine it could be transcended.' Alyssa felt him chuckle at her words.

'So how do you feel now, my darling?'

'Wonderful,' she mused, smiling. Then, trailing one fingertip down his chest, she added softly, 'And *very* glad you obtained that licence.'

'An infinitely preferable arrangement to waiting three weeks until you could share my bed!' he said, kissing her again with consummate thoroughness. 'Your description reflects my own feelings; there is no happier man than I now we are truly man and wife.'

They lay in each other's embrace and enjoyed long wordless minutes of communication as lassitude engulfed them. Through the window, Alyssa could see that the sun had almost disappeared below the horizon and above the spectacular red and gold streaked sunset sky a few stars were already visible. It was the perfect end to a perfect day.

Sated with love and contentment, she felt her eyelids growing heavy. 'Gil?'

'Hmm?' he replied, his eyes closed and his voice already mellow with sleep.

Seeing he too was drifting off into slumber, she snuggled closer, saying, 'Never mind.'

He tightened his hold, and asked, 'What were you going to say?'

'Oh,' she muttered into his chest. 'Well, I was going to ask – that is, I was just wondering when we can . . . when can you—' She broke off, leaving the sentence unfinished.

He opened first one eye and then the other and, seeing her expression was one of blushing confusion, he grinned. 'Love you again?' he whispered.

'Yes,' came her husky reply.

His gaze ran over her possessively before lowering his head to bestow a passionate kiss. 'I will be more than ready whenever you wish, my love.'

With a contented sigh, Alyssa tucked her head into the hollow of his shoulder and replied, 'That is all I wanted to know.'

Two weeks later, Letty and Piers were scouring the hedgerows near Hawkscote. They had dismounted from their horses during their afternoon ride to search out early blackberries and cobnuts. This activity provoked a great deal of laughter from both, along with the occasional scold from Letty, who pointedly accused her grinning companion of eating more berries than he placed in her handkerchief which served as an improvised container.

'Piers, you *are* eating them!' she protested, laughing, 'If you continue, we will only have a few to eat when we reach the top of the hill. Wretch! You will be well served if you suffer stomach pains.'

'But I haven't eaten any,' he said, giving a guileless look as he placed his hand behind his back.

'Truly?' she asked, lifting one brow quizzically.

'I would never lie to you, Letty.'

'Then where have the berries you have just picked disappeared to?'

He grinned. 'I assure you I haven't eaten them.'

'Oh? Then perhaps you are hiding some to eat later,' she said, with a gurgle of mirth. 'Let me see!'

Letty tried to peek behind his back where he now held both hands, rolled into loose fists.

'For the price of a kiss, you may,' he announced, moving out of reach.

She shook her head and cast him a prim look. 'You must think me shockingly *volage* to agree to that! Will you show me, Piers? Please?' she begged, with laughing eyes.

Unable to remain impervious to this plea, he declared, 'Only if you take pity and grant me one small kiss – before I go out of my mind.'

She nibbled on one fingertip, giving the matter some thought. 'Very well, but a kiss on the cheek will have to suffice.'

'Is that all?' he said, crestfallen.

'No more until I see what you are hiding.'

He sighed, and said in an anguished tone, 'You force a hard bargain.'

Piers kissed her cheek and opened his hand to reveal five large blackberries, announcing with a grin, 'I was saving these as a surprise, my love.' His face fell in ludicrous dismay when he realized two of the fruit were squashed and his hand was liberally smeared in blackberry juice. 'Deuce take it, how did that happen?' he exclaimed, staring at his palm in disbelief.

'You held them too tightly, you goose!' said Letty, laughing. 'Never mind, it was a sweet thought. Here, put the remaining berries into my handkerchief and we'll eat them together when we reach the top.'

He did so, joining in her laughter as he wiped away the sticky residue from his hand. They tethered their horses and climbed the remaining distance to stand in silence admiring the vista before them. The hill overlooked the slight valley where Hawkscote was situated and in the late afternoon September sun, the mullioned windows and fine architecture of the house displayed to advantage against the tapestry of the countryside.

'Come and sit down,' said Letty. Rearranging the skirt of her riding habit, she patted the grass invitingly, a flush rising to her cheeks as she smiled up at him.

Piers's heart turned over at that dazzling smile. He needed no second invitation and, tossing his whip aside, sat down beside her.

They studied the landscape while they shared the blackberries and cobnuts.

'A wonderful view,' exclaimed Letty. 'It was well worth the effort to get here. I'm sure I can just see Eastcombe in the distance. Do you see it?'

Piers, narrowing his eyes against the sun, looked in the direction she was pointing. 'Yes.' Then, he indicated another landmark and said, 'That collection of buildings to the south must be Frampton Manor.'

'Of course.' She turned to study his profile, and enquired, 'Did Squire Nash speak to you about what happened with Draper?'

'Lord, yes!' he admitted, 'and I was mightily relieved when he had finished.'

'Oh dear!' An anxious furrow clouded her forehead as she covered his hand with her own. 'Was he very angry and unpleasant?'

He glanced down at her. 'No, quite the contrary – he gave me a glass of port and spent a full hour dispensing the most convivial tongue-lashing I've ever endured,' he said, grinning ruefully as his fingers stole around hers. 'Plenty of jovial tut-tutting, shaking his head, and saying "very foolish of you, m'boy" and "what were you thinking of?" and "don't want to hear of you being involved in any tomfoolery like this again" until I felt five years old again, and utterly chastened.'

She began to laugh. 'There's a clever man lurking beneath that easy-going exterior.'

'The squire is a good sort. I can see why Gil and Alyssa like him so much; he's nowhere near as much starch as his daughter, or his wife.'

Letty agreed and they sat in companionable quiet until she ventured, 'Dorset is beautiful. I shall be sad to leave.'

Piers's expression changed instantly. A crease appeared between his brows and his eyes were troubled as they scanned her features. 'So you still intend to go to London for the winter and stay until the end of the Season?'

'Yes – I leave in two days.'

'Two days,' he uttered, faintly. 'Must it be so soon?'

'I'm afraid so. Alyssa and Gil travel to the Continent shortly and I could not stay here. It was good of Melly, my old governess, to keep me company at Hawkscote since Alyssa's marriage – she is naturally spending a great deal of time at Eastcombe while she and Gil sort out their affairs – but I want to visit my aunt, and have at least one London Season.'

'But surely you don't plan to travel alone?'

'Oh no! Melly will accompany me until I reach London.' She regarded him from under her lashes. 'Will you be returning?'

'I was planning to do so within the month, dependent on your plans. I could not impose on the Westwoods' hospitality any longer so I'm putting up at The Antelope, but if you are leaving soon, I will too! I'll escort you on the journey if you'll have me, but, damn it all, Letty, how am I to bear it when those town bucks start chasing you?' protested Piers unhappily, with an entreating look. 'I'll be mad with jealousy! They'll flock to your side while I'll struggle to exchange two words with you during the whole Season. Unlike Melly, your aunt is most likely a Gorgon who won't allow me anywhere near.'

She asked insouciantly, 'Do you think I'll have plenty of admirers then?'

'Undoubtedly,' he replied, through gritted teeth.

'Oh. I will enjoy that,' said she, in a blithe tone. 'It would be dreadfully morti-fying if I did not *take*.' Letty was silent for a moment before prompting, 'Piers?'

'Hmm?' He was abstracted, a frown of misery marring his brow.

'My aunt is not a Gorgon; she is a young matron with an array of children ranging from six years to six months, and her chaperoning of me will be careful but not stifling. She will encourage me to sample many of the entertainments on offer.'

'Well, perhaps it may not be as bad as I thought, but it will still be deuced hard after the time we have spent together this summer,' he grumbled, idly plucking daises out of the grass. 'When shall I see you?'

'Well, I *have* always wanted to go to the opera. Would you take me while we are in London, please?' said Letty.

At the warm husky note suddenly present in her voice, he looked up sharply. 'I'll reserve a box,' he murmured, meeting her gaze.

'And the theatre?'

'I'll book a box there too.'

'I would like to see the Tower of London.'

'Been meaning to go myself for years,' he said, grasping her gently by the shoulders.

'Vauxhall Gardens?' she suggested, with twinkling eyes.

'Full of rakes – so I'll escort you to the fireworks.'

'And the Pantheon Bazaar. . . .'

He swallowed hard but recovered quickly and said with admirable fortitude, 'Very well, the Pantheon Bazaar it is. I've heard it is excellent for shopping and I'd be glad to take you.'

Her lip quivered with amusement. 'One more thing, Piers.'

'Lord, *please* don't ask me to accompany you to Bullock's Museum!' he begged, rolling his eyes in anguish. 'I'm besotted with you, but a man must draw the line somewhere.'

'I wasn't going to ask that.'

'Oh? What then?'

'Only that I'd like you to take me to a wedding, perhaps in May,' she said, softly.

There was silence until his face lit up with a slow grin. '*Letty! Darling!* Does that mean—?'

'Yes,' she interposed, and added with a ripple of laughter, 'but you had better ask for my hand *after* taking me shopping – you might change your mind in view of that experience.'

'Never! You *know* I love you!' replied Piers, pulling her into his arms and muttering thickly before he kissed her, 'Deuce take it, I'm not letting those London bucks near you!'

Letty, who considered Piers had been transformed to a man fully aware of his responsibilities if he was willing to accompany her on a shopping expedition without complaint, welcomed his embrace eagerly.

Later that month in London, shortly before three o'clock on a Wednesday afternoon, there was a knock at the door of Mr Bartley's office.

'Enter,' said he, absently, not raising his eyes from the paper he was perusing.

His new clerk scurried in and announced, 'Sir Giles and Lady Maxton are here to see you, sir.'

'I don't believe I heard you correctly, Smith,' said Mr Bartley, looking over his spectacles at the young man. 'Surely you did not say Sir Giles *and* Lady Maxton?'

'Indeed I did, sir; he and his wife are waiting in the outer office.'

Mr Bartley stared in blank astonishment. 'Bless my soul, I had no idea Sir Giles had married!' he exclaimed. Thrown into confusion, he shuffled through the paperwork on his desk, rapidly scanning several documents before shaking his head and saying, 'It is as I thought: Mr Forde made no mention of this in his letters.' He paused a moment to reflect on the significance of this information and then asked, 'Has Miss Paradise arrived?'

'No, sir,' said his clerk, 'only Sir Giles and his wife.'

Mr Bartley sighed. 'What a pity she is not here yet. This may prove even more difficult than I anticipated.' Leaning back in his chair, he removed his spectacles and placed them on the desk. Closing his eyes, he pinched the bridge of his nose as he paused in thought. He had not forgotten his last interview with Sir Giles and Miss Paradise. In view of the tense, strained atmosphere he witnessed then, it was probable Miss Paradise would object to Lady Maxton's presence since she was not directly involved. However, Sir Giles would also be displeased if he was kept waiting, and it would certainly not be politic to suggest excluding his wife. Mr Bartley opened his eyes to glance at the clock; the appointed time had arrived and it seemed he had no option other than to continue.

'Well, Smith,' he said, 'this is most irregular. I suppose you must show Sir Giles and Lady Maxton in since we cannot keep them waiting in the outer office. However, you must advise me the instant Miss Paradise arrives.' He shook his finger at the clerk, adding, 'On the instant, mind! I do not want Miss Paradise to feel slighted in any way.'

'Very good, sir.' The clerk left, closing the door behind him.

Mr Bartley stood up and walked around his desk. He paused to straighten his jacket and cravat using the small mirror on the wall and, pursing his lips, prepared to discharge his duty as General Paradise's executor in as efficient a manner as possible, well aware he might need to negotiate a path through this potentially volatile meeting.

A moment later, the door opened again to admit his visitors.

'Good afternoon, Sir Giles,' said Mr Bartley, extending his hand in greeting. 'I'm afraid Miss Paradise has not arrived yet.'

Gil returned his handshake. 'I see. Do you expect her soon?'

'Yes, imminently. You are well, I trust?'

'Exceedingly, thank you,' replied Gil, smiling.

The lawyer looked at him in surprise. Sir Giles's smile was genuine; indeed it was more than a smile, he was positively grinning. Obviously he was in a propitious mood and Mr Bartley wondered hopefully if he need not be so concerned after all.

'Do sit down,' he said, waving to the chairs in front of his desk.

'Thank you, but first I wish to introduce my wife, Mr Bartley,' said Gil, the corner of his mouth twitching as he stepped aside.

Despite years of schooling his features into an expression of detachment, whatever his inner emotions, Mr Bartley failed markedly on this occasion. His jaw dropped and his eyes almost started from their sockets when he saw Lady Maxton was in fact the young woman he knew as Miss Alyssa Paradise.

'Good Lord!' he cried, involuntarily. Then, looking from one to the other, he stammered, 'I-I did not know – that is, I did not realize Miss Paradise and Lady Maxton were one and the same person!'

'Oh dear, you must forgive us for not sending you word of our marriage, Mr Bartley,' said Alyssa. Her eyes danced with amusement but they also held a hint of compassion for his astonishment. 'You see, we asked Mr Forde not to give our secret away because we could not resist the temptation to tell you in person.'

'Now I understand why he made no mention of Sir Giles's marriage,' said Mr Bartley, still staring. 'I am shocked, not least because the last time you were here, relations were slightly – er – awkward between you.'

'They were, weren't they?' said Gil, laughing. 'But, as you see, things have changed dramatically.'

Mr Bartley watched as Sir Giles reached out, took his wife's hand and bestowed on her a look of such passionate regard that the lawyer blinked in amazement; Lady Maxton, a flush rising to her cheeks, responded with a delightful smile. From the evidence of this swift but revealing exchange, they were very much in love.

'Good Lord!' he murmured again, his eyebrows almost reaching his receding hairline. 'I hardly know what to say, or where to begin.' He cleared his throat as he struggled to regain his composure. 'Please – I must beg your pardon for not offering my heartiest congratulations at once.'

'Thank you,' said Alyssa, warmly, 'but there is no need to apologize; your astonishment is perfectly understandable.'

'Yes, perfectly,' repeated her husband, with a disarming twinkle, 'when you consider the atmosphere that surrounded our previous visit.'

Mr Bartley smiled in agreement and with great relief, sank on to his chair, his poise and gravitas slowly returning. 'So, meeting the terms of your uncle's will was not as difficult a task as you originally envisaged, Miss Par— I mean Lady Maxton?' he asked, with interest.

Alyssa, who had already taken her seat beside Gil, admitted, 'No, indeed. Uncle Tom's will has led to happiness I could never have foreseen.'

'I see,' said the lawyer. 'An unexpected turn of events on the face of it, and yet perhaps the general had something of this nature in mind. The will was obviously designed to ensure you spent time in each other's company.'

'You might be able to help on that point, Mr Bartley. You said Uncle Tom had left two letters for me, and I have been intrigued from the very start as to their content.'

'Yes. Yes, of course, my dear Lady Maxton,' he said, replacing his spectacles. 'I have them amongst my papers, and will give them to you directly. Would you both be so kind as to complete a few legal formalities first?'

After several minutes, when all the necessary documents had been signed and dated to his satisfaction, he found the two sealed letters.

'Your marriage has no effect on the will,' he explained. 'You have met the terms laid down and are therefore beneficiaries as per the general's stipulations. Lady Maxton, I should also tell you that I have asked Mr Kilworth to call later this afternoon. Your uncle arranged for investments in Mr Kilworth's name to be made available to him at the end of the six-month period but instructed me not to disclose any details until then.'

'So Tom did leave Piers something after all,' mused Gil.

He nodded. 'In addition to his annuity, Lady Maxton's cousin will possess property and investment bonds in his own right which amount to a very respectable value.'

'That is good news!' said Alyssa, 'I'm glad Uncle Tom chose to do so, and he was perceptive to realize Piers would ultimately benefit from waiting.'

'Quite. Now, these are the two letters your uncle left in my care. This one' – he lifted the envelope in his right hand a little higher – 'was to be opened if you failed to meet the terms.'

'Have you any objection to me reading it now?' she asked.

'None whatsoever; I have no instructions to say you may not,' he replied, passing the letter across the desk.

Alyssa opened the envelope and smoothed out the single sheet.

'It was written two weeks before his death, Gil,' she said, indicating the date as she held the letter between them. 'Would you read it with me?'

'Of course, if that is what you wish,' he replied.

3rd December 1817
Hawkscote Hall, Dorset

My dearest Alyssa

If you are reading this because you chose not to accept the terms, then I must admit to an error of judgement and send you and Sir Giles my sincere apologies from beyond the grave. I hope you will still think fondly of an old man who loved you as a daughter. Gil, I hope, will also remember me with affection.

You will not have received the full market price, but it will be more than enough for you to enjoy a comfortable life. Piers will be furious that I have left the bulk of my estate to you. However, I had my reasons – he shows little inclination yet to behave like the man I know he could be. Even so, I am fond of the boy and hope he will eventually see sense. Guide him whenever you can; I leave it to your judgement to decide what monies to bestow on your cousin, and when. This letter is intentionally brief as I believe you will never read it in circumstances where you refused to meet the terms.

Your loving uncle,

Tom

Postscript – I realize I do not want Piers to remember me with bitterness, whatever our past differences, and have decided to make extra provision to encourage his sense of personal responsibility. I have therefore purchased further investments, and also land and property near his Lincolnshire estate. These are in Piers's name and amount to a meaningful but not excessive sum. I hope he will use them wisely but I have instructed Mr Bartley not to divulge their existence until the end of the six-month period – it will do my nephew no harm to remain ignorant of them until then.

'Dear Uncle Tom,' said Alyssa, in a constricted voice, looking up from the letter into her husband's face, 'He knew us better than we knew ourselves.'

'Yes, and it seems he knew his nephew's character well too,' observed Gil.

She nodded. 'He realized it might ruin him for good if he inherited wealth overnight. I am pleased he decided to make separate provision for Piers after all.

That, along with the monies I shall bestow on him, will ensure he has the means to make a success of his affairs from now on.'

'The general was an astute man,' agreed Mr Bartley, his curiosity piqued as to the content of the letter. 'Would you like to read the second missive now, Lady Maxton? If you will excuse me a moment, I will step into the outer office to collect the documents pertaining to Mr Kilworth.'

'Yes, of course, Mr Bartley. Thank you.'

He passed over second sealed envelope and Alyssa opened it, removing several sheets which she and Gil began to read as the lawyer went out.

3rd December 1817
Hawkscote Hall, Dorset

My dearest Alyssa
I fear I have little time left and am therefore writing this while I can still commit words to paper.

First, I ask you do not shed tears for me. I have lived a long and varied life, and my only regrets have been for those events sadly out of my control – the early demise of my beloved wife and that we were not blessed with children.

I am certain there will have been times when you wondered if Uncle Tom was drunk or not of sound mind when he wrote his Last Will and Testament. I assure you I was neither, to which Ezekiel Bartley will testify. The idea came to me quite suddenly one day when I was musing over how much pleasure I took from my conversations with Sir Giles.

Due to circumstances, you never had the opportunity to meet him hitherto, but I have come to know him well. He is a man I respect for his business acumen but I also admire his sense of humour and his honourable principles. It struck me forcibly that you and he might be well suited. Extremely presumptuous of me, I know, but I began to wonder what would happen if I were to take the role of matchmaker? I could set in motion events that would at least oblige you to meet regularly and thereafter, the outcome would be whatever the fates decided.

This mischievous idea took firm hold and I devised my extraordinary will. Its purpose was to secure your financial future and that of Hawkscote, and to act as a means of putting you and Gil into each other's company. I did not believe either of you would refuse the challenge, however in extremis you considered my actions.

Unless I am granted an opportunity to view events from the afterlife, I have no way of knowing the result. If I am proved wrong and you feel ambivalence, or even dislike, then accept my sincere apologies for meddling outrageously in your affairs; I hope you both bear me no lasting ill will. However, I have the unshakeable notion that you will grow fond of each other, and might even fall in love. I pray my instincts have served me well and hope nothing will stand in your way if you discover that you care for each other. In that event, I rely on your mutual ingenuity and good sense to deal with other, ultimately insignificant, matters.

I wish both of you happiness. Remember me with a smile and cherish, as I always have, the delightful times we shared.

Your loving uncle,

Tom

'The postscript regarding Piers is the same,' said Alyssa, a tremor in her voice. She turned towards Gil, her eyes bright with tears. 'Oh, Gil! *Gil!* Tom *did* think we might fall in love!' she cried. 'He arranged it all, hoping everything else would follow, and I'm so glad he did for I might never have known you otherwise.'

Gil folded her in a comprehensive embrace. 'I feel as you do,' he whispered. 'We have much to thank him for.'

She nodded, but then hiccupped on another sob so he tilted up her chin and kissed her.

'Don't cry, my love,' he said softly. 'Tom would be pleased to know his will was indeed the spark that led to so much happiness – just as he intended.'

She smiled as she replied, 'Yes, he would, wouldn't he?'